Return of the Darkness

Book Three in the Lost Kingdom Saga

Laura Carter

Return of the Darkness – 1st Edition

Paperback ISBN: 978-1-0683144-1-4

Ebook ISBN: 978-1-0683144-0-7

Edited by Eden Northover

Cover Design by Aly Scasares, Owner of Sincerely Theirs Ltd

Map by Cartographybird Maps

Chapter Heading Emblems by Aly Scasares, Owner of Sincerely Theirs Ltd

Formatted by Laura Carter via Atticus

Additional Information

<u>**Trigger Warnings:**</u>

Your mental health and experience whilst reading this book matters to me. This book contains death, violence, explicit sexual content, references to child abuse, self harm, references to the deaths of characters you may have liked in book one and two. If these are topics you find difficult to read, please approach with caution and at your own discretion. If you read Return of the Darkness and feel there are other trigger warnings missing, please notify me via my social channels so I can amend this page.

Due to the presence of sexually explicit scenes, this book is classified as 18+

<u>**Glossary and Pronunciation Guide:**</u>

If you wish to check the pronunciation of character and place names as you read them, you can find a pronunciation glossary at the end of the book.

<u>**Playlist:**</u>

I do some of my best writing after listening to music and as a result have created a very large overall series playlist. I have taken the songs relevant to certain chapters and placed them in a Return of Darkness Playlist. You can find the playlist linked in my socials or by searching 'Return of the Darkness' on spotify and clicking 'playlists'. At the rear of the book, you will also find a guide for which songs relate to which chapters in the book. I recommend only listening after you have finished the book or finished the relevant chapter, otherwise the lyrics of some songs may act as a spoiler.

For anyone that has felt the pain of loss in its many forms, do not let it blind you from seeing you are just as strong as the characters in this book.

ISLE
THE KINGDOM OF
NOVISIA
ELVERA
AZURIA
THE FROZEN FOREST
TISOVA
ZIVOI MOUNTAINS
MARNOVO
VOJTA
VALA
THE VELLIUS SEA
THE NEUTRAL CITY
AMORO
NERIDA
THE BAY
MERA
TROSSO
TO NOVISIAN SEA BORDER

NOTABLE SETTLEMENTS
CAPITAL CITIES
CITY STATES
MYARA
KERES
ABIS FORGE
TABHERI
THE ASHUN DESERT
NEFERE VALLEY
KHAMI
HYBROOKE FOREST
SELEY
STEDON
HYSTONE FOREST
ANTOR
DOLTAS ISLAND
GARRIDON
ALBYN
ASDALE

Contents

Prologue

Elisara

Elisara immediately felt a chill when she draped the talisman over her neck—not the chill of the air during Vala's snowfall as it raised the hairs on her arms, or the bitter cold that burrowed into her bones when she plunged into the Vellius Sea, nor was it the aching cold of loss settling over the broken remnants of her heart. Amid the starfall, the cold cocooning Elisara felt like a warning. Something primordial was nearby.

The night sky was awash with light as thousands of stars fell across the atmosphere. Some collided with the crimson trees on her left in the distance, brightening the leaves like garnets and casting a kaleidoscope of red across the forest's edge.

Elisara resisted wrapping her arms around herself; her military instincts forced her to be alert and prepared for anything, despite how easy it would be to allow someone to take her, like Caligh had taken Kazaar. The fabric of Kazaar's shirt between her fingers was as comforting as it was agonizing as she clenched her fists around it, mirroring the way she had clung to his dying body before it dissolved into ash and floated away on the Keres breeze. Elisara blinked, uncertain if there were any tears left to stream down her numb cheeks. One moment, she stared at her reflection, her incandescent, glacier blue eyes haunting her as she placed Kazaar's talisman around her neck. The next, she found herself here, in a place that would always remind her of him.

The carved throne room on the Unsanctioned Isle was as she remembered, save for one important detail. The walls had crumbled, like they had once in her dreams, leaving only the chequered floor with a deep crack through its centre, and the onyx and marble thrones naked to the blanket of darkness and cascading starfall.

The bitter air stilled as Elisara took a cautious step forward in her blood-stained boots. The ground felt unusually uneven. Sand shifted around her feet, but it was no longer the burnt orange of the Ashun Desert. Elisara bent to scoop the fine granules into her hand. The glittering dust fell through her fingers like sand in an hourglass, though counting down to what she did not know.

"Stardust." An ethereal voice echoed from behind the onyx throne, a stone's throw away. Elisara's head whipped up, but she felt no need to form a defensive stance. Instead, she slowly brushed her hands together until her palms tingled, and the remaining dust fell to her feet. "Such a magnificent consequence of a star's death." Elisara tilted her head at the tired lilt in the owner's voice, who stepped from behind the throne. "There is beauty in death, my child."

"From where I stand, there is only ever torment in death." Elisara responded flatly. The two women watched one another, assessment deep in their gazes. Elisara trailed her eyes up the woman's body from where her bare feet stood buried in the stardust, piling up around the throne's base. She rested a delicate hand on the arm of the throne to the right of where she stood. Her inky dress shimmered, as if it had stood beneath the star fall for so long its dust had made the folds of her skirts their home. If the dust was the remnants of a dead star, she was simply a walking graveyard. The woman felt like death, emanating the bitter cold, yet a luminous sheen on her dark skin reminded Elisara of the sun's glow—the glow of life.

"Ah, but from pain, the greatest beauty of them all can bloom. Strength. Resilience. Power. All will make you even more beautiful." The woman smiled with full lips and Elisara wanted to believe that good could follow the heartache shattering her chest, but that was difficult knowing she was at her strongest and most powerful by Kazaar's side. His absence only highlighted her weakness and damaged heart. "You cannot see it now. I understand why, trust me." *Trust*—a word so foreign to the queen, who felt so accustomed to betrayal. With a regal posture, the woman waded through the stardust and sat on the onyx throne, glancing longingly at the marble throne at her side. Elisara's eyes flickered to the symbols: the sun engraved on the marble's base, and the moon she knew was hidden behind the woman's skirts. Elisara, with the power flooding through her veins, had an innate awareness of the air, which was still and undisturbed around the marble throne. The stardust around its base sparkled less, as though it was still and waiting, too. It was almost like the fabric of the universe recognised the absence of the being who should sit alongside this grieving woman and was mourning the loss as well. Elisara finally met the woman's eyes, knowing who she faced. Her irises held the birth and death of stars. Crushed sparkles glistened in her dark eyes—darkness she had only seen once in Kazaar's eyes, interspersed with threads of light.

"Sitara, I presume." Elisara lifted her chin, allowing the goddess to assess her. Elisara's first encounter with her own goddess, Vala, had been unsuccessful, leaving her cautious of the rest. But Elisara felt no fear when challenging Vala. She thought perhaps that had been because of the goddess's translucent state when she had appeared in the Neutral City, unable to inflict harm upon her descendent. But watching Sitara now, she realised it was because Vala did not exude the same level of power. The goddess of her realm was not the same primordial being as Sitara. Around the goddess, the surrounding air rippled with darkness, and the universe hummed in response. Elisara tasted the power in the air and only needed to glance at Sitara and the way she commanded attention from the world to know she was *the* Goddess, the first after Chaos and Order. Beside the pain in her chest, Elisara felt awareness too. The being before her could release chaos on the world, not just Elisara.

Resting her head on her hand, the goddess smiled and tilted

her head, like they were merely two old friends reconnecting. Her twisted crown of twinkling stars tilted with her, disorienting Elisara. Though she had never pictured meeting Sitara, the Goddess who birthed the kingdom's gods and goddesses from not only love but the essence of her power, Elisara would have expected someone far more stoic and rigid. Instead, Sitara gazed upon her as though she had known Elisara her entire life.

"You presume correctly." Sitara shifted and patted the marble throne beside her. "Come. Sit." Elisara glanced at the marble but did not move. "Nobody will take his place anytime soon," Sitara added, quieter this time. She briefly closed her eyes. She was grieving, and the shared feeling prompted Elisara to move towards the throne.

The coldness sharpened the closer Elisara approached, as though it were slowing her movements and seizing control. Shaking the feeling, she sat upon the uncomfortable marble, trying to angle herself towards Sitara, whose dark braids hung over her shoulders as she smiled, waiting for Vala's queen to speak. Elisara kept her mouth shut. She had not come here willingly and thus had nothing to ask of the goddess who transported her here.

"Ah, I did not transport you." Sitara flicked a braid over her shoulder.

"You can read my thoughts?" Elisara asked, and Sitara hummed.

"It is more like an innate knowing. I am the first god, created by Chaos himself. I know everything." Elisara frowned, wondering about the limitations, if any.

"There are some," Sitara confirmed. "I sense events unfolding, but I cannot predict the future. All I know are the many threads of possibilities and different destinies." Elisara nodded. "In answer to your original thought, I did not transport you. We are not physically on the…" Sitara trailed off as though remembering the names of lands was too mundane a task for a being of her importance. "*Unsanctioned Isle*. Your body is still in the Ashun Desert. This is simply in our minds."

Elisara could hardly process her thoughts, let alone Sitara's rapidly changing topics.

"I apologise. Sonos always said I spoke too swiftly and acted too rashly." Sitara's smile vanished as she glanced at the other throne. Elisara shifted beneath the goddess's gaze; the throne was rather uncomfortable. It was not just its coldness that brought such discomfort, or the hard, solid marble; something inside Elisara urged her to stand and move from the throne, as though it was reserved for another. But why? Caligh had named Kazaar the essence of Sitara, and thus the rulers had deduced Elisara held Sonos' essence. Should she not feel at ease upon his throne? Perhaps the unease was caused by the god's absence, as though the essence within her knew it was still alone, its owner missing.

"Where is Sonos?" Elisara asked, despite sensing it was a risky question. Sitara's smile dropped. Shadows swept the stardust along the floor and stars blinked out of existence, consuming everything in its wake and creeping towards Elisara and the goddess. The beautiful, falling light was drained, leaving only threatening and all-consuming darkness. Sitara straightened and waved her hand. The shadows dissipated before reappearing and winding up her arms. "Gone." Sitara tapped her fingernails on the arms of her onyx throne. "Taken."

"By Caligh?"

"Please do not speak that traitor's name," Sitara murmured, turning her hand over, where shadows wrapped around her arm and squeezed. Elisara frowned. The goddess knew Caligh well then.

"Can you find him?" Elisara asked. While she had little left to live for, perhaps she could learn to defeat Caligh and enact her revenge, seeing as she was created from Sonos' essence.

"That is why I am counting on you—all of you." Sitara crossed her legs and planted her clasped hands on her knee. Her warm smile vanished as she pursed her lips. "It will be harder with Kazaar dead, but not impossible." Elisara flinched at the bluntness in which she said his name. Sitara peered sideways at her. "You do not have time to mourn, child." Anger bubbled up within Elisara, who shifted against the pain in her limbs. "You feel it, don't you? The power I planted within you."

"You?" Elisara asked, confused. She never realised the goddess could control Sonos' essence. Sitara scoffed.

"Have you not worked it out yet?" Sitara pointed at Elisara, beckoning the shadows closer. Elisara did not flinch, although the darkness felt different without Kazaar nearby. "It was never him, child. He is a part of it all. You all are. But he is not the one with my power. Caligh lied to you to release your pain, and with it, your power. Or so he thought." Sitara clenched her fist, and the shadows creeping around Elisara's wrists tightened, holding her hands captive against the white marble. Elisara tried to pull her arms free, but the shadows only tightened with her attempts, ropes that burned into her flesh with every twist of Sitara's command.

"What are you doing?" Elisara asked, shoving back against the throne as Sitara rose and leaned in until she towered above her, consuming the space. At Elisara's feet, stardust stirred and merged with Sitara's shadows, creating a furious blaze of darkness and light in chaotic plumes.

"I have waited too long to reach this point for you to ruin it with your grief." Sitara's mood shifted, and her smile darkened with her eyes. "I want him back. We need him back to restore everything. There is far more you don't know, but you will begin to. And if you think I—or my *children*—will sit by while you squander our only chance of fixing things over a MAN!" Elisara flinched. "You are sorely mistaken." Sitara's delicate hand was far bonier up close as she reached for the talisman around Elisara's neck. The large black onyx stone appeared to stir with shadows beneath the goddess's touch, calling to its power. The talismans enhanced power, so what would become of Elisara if Kazaar's talisman did the same?

"Says the goddess telling me I must find a man for her," Elisara spat, and Sitara narrowed her eyes. The shadows tightened further around Elisara's arms, like claws finding purchase in her skin; they could tear her arms right off if Sitara willed it.

"Sonos is far more than a man. He is a god, he is my partner in life, and the father of my children. I created Kazaar's strength from the last of Sonos' essence, and now I do not even have that, because Caligh thought killing him would release your power." Sitara trailed her long nail along Elisara's neck and hooked it under the leather cord of the talisman. "I cannot continue to exist without him by my side and neither can any of you. This world crumbles because Caligh took him, and soon, you will see that. Minds will awaken. Memories will return. Soon, you will discover you are nothing but a piece in the game of power, and I will not lose, Elisara. Not to *him*." Sitara held the talisman in her palm while the shadows continued restraining Elisara. "Now, I want to try something I've seen elsewhere. This may hurt a little."

Elisara had no time to ask questions as Sitara turned the talisman with a determined glint in her eye and forced it into the centre of Elisara's chest, splintering bone. The once cool stone burned as Sitara held it in place. Elisara screamed. With watering eyes, she glanced downwards at the blood bubbling around the stone in her chest. The goddess's hands were cold and unyielding as one held the back of Elisara's head and the other forced the stone deeper.

"The quicker you accept your power, the quicker we can defeat Caligh." Sitara gritted her teeth as Elisara struggled against the pain searing in her chest, rushing through her shoulders and down her arms, all-consuming. "This should amplify your powers and overcome the barriers you've unknowingly had against you." Elisara bit her lip to refrain from crying out. A flurry of images flickered past her: people she did not recognise, places she did not know. "Let it in, child." Sitara pushed harder, and Elisara was certain her chest would crack in half. Clenching her eyes shut, Elisara's head pounded at the flickering images and colours in her mind until one finally slowed, and her focus sharpened, settling on a vaulted stone hall with no windows. Eerie statues of winged creatures lined the hall on pillars. She did not recognise them.

"This one," Sitara said. "Pay attention."

Elisara grunted, trying to control her breathing beneath all the agony. There were two men: a man who resembled Keres, and another man with flowing black hair, who dipped a sword into a steaming, bubbling iron pot swinging above ravenous flames. The sword hissed and fizzed as he withdrew it. The Keres-like man squinted and flinched when the sword spat at him.

"This is it. The poison is imbedded in the metal," said the man with flowing black hair.

"Perfect. Now we know it works. Do this one next, Orphian." Turning to the wielder of the weapon, he handed over a golden sword Elisara knew to be the Sword of Sonos.

"The poison will kill anything, no matter the weapon it laces. Are you sure you want to use this one, Sulien?" Orphian asked, bowing his head under the man's glare.

"It has to be this one. This sword will do far more than kill."

Elisara screamed and opened her eyes; darkness crept into the edges of her vision as scenes continued flying past her, flashing images of vast turquoise oceans, dark and towering stone cities, and purple banners in a city of white.

"Do you understand?" Sitara asked. Elisara's eyes rolled back, but Sitara steadied her chin with one hand, tightening her grip. "Do you understand?" she shouted. Elisara tried to focus on the goddess, but everything was a blur. Murmuring under her breath, Sitara's shadows began twisting up Elisara's arms and neck, wrapping around her throat and caressing her temples. Elisara tried to move her arm and push herself up, but her body was numb. With each passing moment, her eyelids grew heavier and her breathing shallower. Her eyes drooped and the many visions slowed. "Focus, child," Sitara hummed.

Elisara's awareness sharpened as she heard voices she would never forget. She tried to cry out for them, but her voice failed as the vision slowed to highlight her parents, younger than she had ever seen them. Her father's smile lines hadn't yet settled as he gazed into the blanket in her mother's arms, cooing and wiggling his finger. Her mother moved with the blanket, entering a room Elisara recognised as her own in Azuria, but with a crib instead of her fourposter bed. A display of dangling silver snowflakes circled slowly in the breeze above the crib. When Vespera lowered the blanket into the cot, Elisara recognized the infant as a younger version of herself.

"She is beautiful, Vespera," Arion murmured, wrapping an arm around his wife's waist. Vespera kept silent but nodded, smiling.

"Elisara. How did you choose the name?" she asked, and he shrugged.

"It came to me in a dream." Arion stooped to plant a kiss on his daughter's temple before leaving the room. Despite her clouded state, Elisara choked at the tenderness she so desperately missed from her father. Vespera hummed a familiar lullaby, watching her baby sleep; Elisara had heard the melody most nights as a child. The humming abruptly stopped when a shiver passed through Vespera, who glanced around the room, pulling her shawl tighter around herself. The air appeared to thin, as if something was capturing the space and drawing everything towards it.

"She is indeed beautiful." An ethereal voice floated through the room. Elisara instantly recognised it. Vespera whirled, looking for the source. Backing up against the cot, she instinctively reached towards her baby to protect her from the intruder. A flame flickered to life on her free palm. "I am not here to harm her, Vespera." Slowly, Sitara stepped from the shadows cast by the stone archways in Azuria castle.

"Who are you?" Vespera demanded. Flames erupted in a circle around the mother and child, trickling from Vespera's hands. Sitara stepped into the moonlight. Like the four gods in the Neutral City, her body was a glowing apparition. The goddess blinked, and the flames dampened. Vespera twisted her hand in a desperate attempt to summon more fire, but nothing ignited.

"I am Sitara, Goddess of Dusk." Her voice softly echoed through the room as shadows twisted up her arms. Immediately, Vespera bowed her head, prompting a smile from Sitara. "Your daughter is destined for greatness, Queen Vespera," Sitara whispered, silently padding bare foot over the stone to the opposite side of the cot. The goddess reached in, gently removing the blanket from Vespera's sleeping daughter. The queen shifted forward, gripping the edge of the cot as the goddess stroked Elisara's forehead.

"She will likely marry a prince." Vespera flashed a tight smile at the goddess, who scoffed.

"She will do far greater than a prince in this kingdom. She will achieve far more than marriage and children." Sitara touched the onyx talisman at her neck—the same one now burrowing into Elisara's bones—but something was different. It was not solid onyx. A shimmering substance glistened within. Sitara turned it over, summoning shadows in one palm until it faded and left a small dagger behind. "She will bring war, change, and peace. Eventually, she will restore everything. This time, it will work." Sitara thrust the dagger into the back of the talisman, and a small fragment flew free, freezing mid-air amongst the shadows. "We have all the timings correct this time, all the right players, all the pieces in place."

"I do not understand—" As Sitara waved her hand, Vespera stopped talking. Sitara handed her dagger to the shadows, where they held it midair. She glanced at the small black fragment floating above Elisara.

"Eventually, you will understand your role in triggering the prophecy," Sitara murmured to the queen, fixing her eyes on the black fragment. Furrowing her brow, she closed her eyes and splayed her palm across her chest, murmuring words in another language until she tilted her head back. Slowly, she withdrew her hand, and a thin trail of light followed with it, pulsing like a living heartbeat. Her essence. Sitara flourished her fingers, and the thread of her essence wrapped around the black fragment, cradling it. Sitara reached down and picked up the sleeping baby, yet the movement stirred Elisara from sleep. Vespera frowned as she tried to move but found she could not. Her chest rapidly rose and fell, and her eyes widened, looking manically between the goddess and her daughter.

"Shhh," Sitara hummed, reaching for the dagger held by the shadows. "You will be my greatest child, Elisara." Sitara poised the dagger against the baby's arm. "With you, I get him back." The baby shrieked as the dagger pierced her skin, drawing one short line down her forearm. Vespera's eyes widened with panic, unable to move while watching her child bleed. With a wave of her hand, the floating, essence-encased fragment drifted towards Sitara and the baby, hovering above the blood. "This won't mean anything until we meet again, child. But make the most of life until we do," Sitara whispered, pushing both her essence and the fragment into the open wound. Infant Elisara stopped crying, and her eyes flickered to black momentarily before closing. As Sitara wiped her thumb over the wound, it slowly knitted itself together.

Padding across the moonlit floor, Sitara approached Vespera and handed Elisara back. Hugging her daughter close, Vespera hurried to the far side of the room, away from Sitara. She raised her hand to create a barrier of fire against the goddess, but Sitara was before her in seconds, clutching the queen's wrist.

"You won't remember any of this." Sitara's voice softened, like she genuinely regretted the pain yet to come. "I am sorry this will end your life, Vespera, but Elisara is the best chance we have." Sitara glanced back at the baby and gently traced her forehead. "You are his star, Elisara, and together, you will rule the skies."

The vision washed away, tearing Elisara's mind apart as she opened her eyes to meet Sitara's glistening ones.

"Please understand," Sitara murmured. Elisara tried to shift her focus elsewhere in the throne room, fighting against the final vision forced upon her. She blinked as someone struck a hammer against a black sword, similar to the material of the talisman and fragment within Elisara, before they encased it in a muted silver. Women in dark-hooded cloaks circled the blade, chanting under their breaths as diadems on their foreheads glinted under the moonlight. They positioned their blood-coated palms skyward as wisps of black shadows circled the space, bodies, things, and creatures—Elisara could not discern it all. One moment they were there, and the next, the chanting stopped. The shadows clinging to the sword faded. Looking at the figures, Elisara noted a pendant around each of their necks, the symbols matching the front of Sadira's Wiccan book. There was something different about it, though, with the lines curving in different directions. A man handed a black stone to another man, whose expression was grim as he held out his palm and furrowed his dark eyebrows above even darker eyes.

"That was all that was left of the material," he grunted, pocketing the onyx stone now embedded in Elisara's chest. The vision flickered, and Elisara's head drooped forward.

"No!" Sitara shouted. "No, we aren't finished." The many images had vanished until Elisara could only focus on the black onyx stone in her chest. Blood still bubbled around it. Sitara grunted, yanking it free. Elisara had no strength left to scream as it clattered against her chest. Instead, a final image of Sitara remained, planting the dull grey sword, hiding its true material on the Unsanctioned Isle. The piercing cold of the stone sent Elisara crashing into reality, and she blinked the water from her eyes and raised her head to face Sitara. She met fury.

"That wasn't nearly enough! You must know more to understand everything fully!" Sitara screamed, backing away from Elisara to pace the stardust-covered floor. Elisara collapsed against the marble throne, inhaling deeply as she processed what had happened. She tugged the talisman aside to rub her chest. Only a small circular scar remained, yet it was perfectly concealed by the large onyx stone—the only trace of the lives and visions that had bombarded her mind. Elisara's skin crawled, and something moved within her as a wave of anger overcame her. She glared up at Sitara through her lashes.

"I'm really sick of gods withholding information from us."

Sitara whirled to face her. "If I could simply tell you, do you not think I would?" Sitara spat. "It would be far easier, but instead, we must use riddles to show you what we can in any way we can." Elisara frowned. *What could possibly stop a goddess—the first goddess—from acting freely?* Sitara scoffed. "Please tell me you understood enough from that." Sitara's eyes pierced Elisara as she impatiently tapped her crossed arms. Sighing, Elisara leaned forward to rub her temples.

"The Sword of Sonos is laced in poison, which kills the creatures." Sitara simply nodded. "It is not imbued with power by the Wiccans?" Elisara asked, and Sitara shook her head. Frowning, she added, "Then what did Sadira imbue?" Sitara opened her mouth to answer but closed it with a frustrated sigh. Instead, Sitara tapped her chest, prompting Elisara to reach for the talisman around her neck. She recalled the onyx stone encased by the dull sword left on the Unsanctioned Isle, and the piece planted in her as an infant. "But what does it do? What does it mean?" Elisara asked. Sitara looked up at the sky, clenching her hands. *She truly cannot tell me.*

"The Sword of Souls." The goddess's voice rang through her mind before she crippled over with a groan. Elisara took a cautious step forward, but Sitara raised her hand before straightening.

"Remember, I cannot predict the future." Sitara stepped towards Elisara until they stood toe to toe. "I can only see different threads." Sitara clutched Elisara's head until their foreheads touched. Different images of the Ashun Desert flicked through her mind, but one stood out. Elisara stood before Caligh, wielding all four elements, while the rulers stood behind her. She widened her eyes as she watched herself pull the sword from her back and pierce the ground. Darkness exploded from her.

Elisara stumbled but Sitara caught her, resting a hand on Elisara's chest.

"Do you understand?" Sitara asked, and slowly, Elisara nodded.

"Will it defeat him? Is the power enough?"

"It is one of the threads."

"How do I access it?" Elisara asked, and Sitara smiled gently.

"It has always been within you. Caligh will believe he unlocked it when he killed Kazaar, that your pain would bring it to the surface. But that is not true, child. I may have awoken it, but you control it, not your emotions. *You*." Sitara cupped Elisara's cheek. "I will be with you, though only briefly."

"I..."

"You can do this without him, Elisara. Kazaar would believe in you," Sitara murmured. "Avenge them for us."

Chapter One
Sadira

While Sadira hoped the security of Caellum's hand would uproot her fears, her questions were overgrowing. She was unprepared for another battle and needed to keep away from the action. The sand shifted below her feet as she swayed, gripping tighter to Caellum's arms to hold herself steady. Sadira understood her skills, and hand-to-hand combat was not one of them. But one did not need to be physically strong to be a warrior, which was much easier to believe when she was stationed far from the battle atop the dunes, wielding her power to block the copper soldiers and protect her own from the swing of blades. Now, she was trapped between three armies.

Caligh's army was still larger than Novisia's and stretched across nearly half of the desert. Yet it was nowhere near as large now and no longer stretched as far back as Myara. The Novisian archers had successfully eliminated nearly all the creatures, bar the few that could transform. The remainder stood in grey leathers, scattered amongst the copper soldiers. But while the army was smaller than before, the soldiers were nowhere near as exhausted as Novisia's. While Sadira was unsure of the army of shadows ready to shield them at Elisara's command, she was grateful they had further protection. The addition of Elisara's shadows balanced the playing field.

Caligh, the Historian, grinned, taking in the sight behind the rulers. The shadows differed little from his own, except from their adopted corporeal forms and a shimmer of light drifting through them at times as the shadows whirled. Sadira cringed at his expression. His eyes were greedy rather than intimidated as he assessed Elisara in the centre of those commanding the battle. The rulers, Farid, Alvan, Soren, and Sadira, stood at the top of a slight dune. From there, they peered down at Caligh, who stood several paces ahead of his army, with Osiris and Arik by his side, and Tajana in tow. Sadira shifted closer beside Caellum as she, too, turned to look at Vala's Queen, who had successfully trapped the copper army in a moat rapidly filling with rain. Elisara's dark eyes burned, reflecting the flames she had wielded down below, encasing twisting vines encircling around the copper army. Sadira was too numb to even shiver against her wet, green satin shirt. Leaning into Caellum's embrace, the pair exchanged an uncertain look. Elisara had struggled to unlock any presumed power with Kazaar, and yet now, something had given her far more than any of them imagined. What could a mourning queen do with such a tool for destruction? Elisara stepped forward into the rain, her wet hair plastered to her face. The sword hummed as cracks of dull silver metal fell to the ground, revealing an onyx sword beneath. Sadira squinted. The inkiness shimmered. Swirling smoke and twists of silver within the stone matched Kazaar's talisman hanging around Elisara's neck. The two sung to one another, finally united. The origins of Kazaar's talisman should have been questioned sooner. Unlike the others, the stone was larger and whole. Perhaps Sitara had somehow altered it. Elisara, channelling the power from the Goddess of Dusk, had delivered a message in Sitara's voice. Sadira feared the weight of their connection, foreseeing a number of chaotic and destructive outcomes.

Nyzaia stole a glance at Elisara; still, the Keres Queen gripped the Sword of Sonos, as though it had the power to do anything. How could they have been so wrong? Had the Wiccan purposefully given Sadira the wrong imbuement, knowing her attempts would fail? Elisara had not yet explained any further why the Sword of Sonos did not work, she only shared it was made of a special metal laced in poison. It could kill anything. So, what had Sadira's imbuement done to the other weapons? And whose side were the Wiccans on? Larelle reached for Elisara's shoulder, as though someone may halt her from acting rashly, from throwing them all into chaos. When the queen moved her head in her direction, Alvan tugged her back.

"Kill them all." Elisara had said with unwavering, deadly confidence before she stepped forward. Sadira stilled as Elisara took another step forward now, planting her feet apart and dragging her sword along the sands. When she finally raised it, it was like all sounds were pulled from the universe. Elisara's arm rose slowly, lifting the sword over her head, like an extension of herself. Lightning struck the tip of the blade, and electricity sizzled around the sword and its wielder. Sadira glanced at the copper army, rigid and ready. They waited for Caligh's command, unfazed by the display of power.

"This is for you, Kazaar," Elisara murmured, lowering her sword to point directly at Caligh. Lightning struck before where he stood, and Soren flinched beside Sadira. Caligh simply grinned while backing away towards his army. A humming came from the shadow forms, like constant chatter behind the rulers before they lunged across the sands. While the flickering shadows revealed no facial features, Sadira imagined the soldiers' stern and readied expressions. Sadira felt Caellum's arms encase her, and she tucked her head into him, flinching as cold blurs rushed past them towards the copper warriors. Yet the eerie silence pulled her back when the metal swords hit nothing but darkness. Silently, the copper soldiers methodically swung at the approaching shadows. The former creatures, now dark-winged shadows, plucked the soldiers from the ground and dropped them from the sky, one by one, littering the moat with broken bodies. And still, they did not scream.

"They truly are servants," Larelle said, further down the line. Standing side by side, the rulers watched Elisara's army tear into the soldiers. All the while, Caligh did nothing but watch, too, tracking the moving shadows, and then Elisara, as if seeing whether she would act on her own accord, rather than use the army for her bidding. He cast his arm to the side, batting away the shadowed soldiers creeping too close. He stood in the centre of the chaos, with Osiris and Arik behind him. Still, he held a chained Tajana, whose head peered around the soldiers, looking for something—or a certain someone.

"What do you mean?" Sadira asked Larelle, approaching the queen with Caellum. Soren remained still, watching the battle with a furrowed brow.

"He controls them all. All his soldiers do exactly as he wills. They lack any emotion or personality; they all move and act the same," Larelle explained, watching the methodical movements of the soldiers.

"Osiris and Arik act differently," Alvan commented, and Sadira's gaze turned to the man and younger boy in the centre of the battle. Arik still wore dark grey fighting leathers while Osiris donned a velvet jacket embroidered with amber swirls and an unrecognisable flower. Their heads were close as they whispered together, glancing at Caligh's back. They seemed unconcerned by the surrounding war. Osiris stopped talking and turned his head, locking eyes on Larelle.

"They are enslaved differently," Larelle murmured, glancing at the sword in Elisara's hand. Elisara ignored them all and watched her army. "The eyes always give it away. That's what Caligh said when he spoke of Tajana and Talia."

Soren finally turned from the battle to listen yet averted her eyes, but not before Sadira noticed the sad glint within them, a look she recognised from when they were children. Sadira frowned. "If Talia was a failed attempt, she would have no eyes, but Tajana's transformation was successful. She can change at will. I assume if we get close enough, her eyes will be black." Larelle became rushed as she spoke. Tajana remained slumped between Osiris and Arik, hanging her head. The tips of her leathery wings scraped the floor.

"What colour are Osiris's eyes?" asked Caellum.

"Black," Larelle said. "But with a golden ring around his irises, the same as Arik's. When I was taken, Osiris said they owed a debt, and Arik said he did not want to be trapped again. The ring around their irises is a mark of the debt they owe Caligh for freeing them." Sadira tried to follow Larelle's train of thought.

"Freeing them from where, though?" Nyzaia finally asked, her eyes remained fixed on Tajana. Beyond, the shadows moved in body-like forms. Sadira's imbued weapons trapped the souls of slain soldiers, and it was Elisara's sword, the Sword of Souls, that brought them back in their shadowed forms. At the same moment Sadira pieced it together, Elisara turned to face them with black eyes. Sadira refrained from flinching at the emotionless look haunting Elisara's expression.

"They were freed from this sword," she said, turning the black stone in her hands. It hummed at her touch as she stroked it with tenderness. The smoky wisps inside the blade followed the warmth of her fingertips. Sadira frowned. Did that mean Osiris and Arik were once dead and trapped within the sword? And was Caligh powerful enough to free them from it, returning them to their bodies? "I can feel them, a connection. It is like the sword wants me to take them both back," Elisara murmured, frowning. "They escaped long ago." Elisara whispered, her ear tilted towards the sword, as though it was feeding her secrets and instructions.

"But how did Caligh free them? If we know, then perhaps we can free the souls inside of it now," said Sadira. Pain bloomed in her heart for those who had their lives taken in this battle for doing only as Caligh controlled. Elisara's head whipped to Sadira.

"Why would we free them?" The darkness in Elisara's eyes pinned Sadira in place. While her voice was softer, there was still an echo in it from when Sitara had spoken through her. "They cannot be killed; they are an unstoppable army. We stand here having a discussion while they fight on our behalf. If we did not have them, our armies would be slaughtered."

Sadira jolted back at the ease with which Elisara spoke of the souls, used for her own bidding. How would she feel if Kazaar was used in such a manner? Or members of her own family? Sadira thought of her own parents and grandparents being manipulated to kill, and her stomach turned.

"We need to give them back their lives at some point," Caellum said, lifting his chin. Sadira wondered if he thought of his family, too. Elisara narrowed her eyes.

"We need to focus on avenging Kazaar and finding Sonos," Elisara said, raising her voice.

"I'm not even going to ask what this has to do with Sonos right now." Nyzaia reached for Elisara, but the Queen of Vala stepped away from her friend's hand. Nyzaia did not cower under her stare. "But I will avenge Kazaar with you. Together." She gripped Elisara's forearm. For a moment, it appeared as though colour returned to Elisara's eyes, but it was gone in a blink. She nodded at Nyzaia.

"This one seems rather intent on reaching you, Elisara," Alvan said. He gently pulled Larelle's hand, forcing her to take a step back. Safe beside Caellum, Sadira watched, intrigued, as the single shadow figure walked up the low dune towards Elisara. It was odd. The silhouette moved like a man, and the shape of its legs and broad shoulders could be easily distinguished in the shadows. He moved the same as all the other shadowed soldiers, but with more intent, like he had a purpose related to the queen. His shape and movements appeared almost real. From so close, Sadira could not tell if he was made of shadows or simply coated in them. But despite the reality flitting back and forth in the dark wisps, he left no footprints in the sand and shifted no grains as he approached. Soundlessly, he knelt before Elisara and bowed his head. What remained of his life before the Sword of Souls took him? Was he one of the copper soldiers killed by an imbued weapon only recently? Was he trapped in the sword while Osiris was freed? Or had this man of darkness been encased in this sword for far longer? None of the questions would answer why he appeared so loyal to

Elisara. Caligh said he had waited centuries for this moment. Was the man who appeared to pledge his allegiance to Elisara when shadows flickered towards her hand, just as old?

With a nod from Elisara, the man of darkness rose. He towered above the queen, prompting her to look up at him. She stared, like she was trying to discern his eyes within the wisps. She tilted her head and nodded again. Standing to attention, the man moved to Elisara's side, guarding her.

"Caligh is almost done with letting us think we have won," Elisara said.

"He can speak?" Nyzaia asked, scanning the shadow with apprehension. Elisara shook her head, turning the onyx sword over in her hand.

"It is more like a sense, an innate knowing." Nyzaia and Farid shared a look. Was it similar to their tie to one another? "We will need the armies momentarily," Elisara said to Larelle. Nerida's queen chewed her lip, glancing back at the Novisian army and then the flurry of battle ahead. Elisara tapped her foot, waiting. Finally, Larelle sighed.

"Do we have a plan I should relay to the commanders?" she asked. Elisara flinched at the word. *Commander.*

"Soon, Caligh will try to control my army. He won't be able to force them to do his bidding, but he will create distance between them and him. We need the armies focused on reaching him, a distraction, so Nyzaia and I can approach from a different angle."

Larelle nodded at Elisara's plan.

"Caligh seems unconcerned about the army and your power. What if this is simply a trap?" asked Caellum.

"I do not care," Elisara said bluntly.

"*We* care," said Caellum, glancing at the other rulers. "Vala can't afford to lose a queen right now, even if it is in the name of avenging someone we all respected." Elisara's determined expression wavered for a moment. "You are asking your people to follow an army that closely resembles Caligh's abilities. How can they trust them?"

"They can be trusted," Elisara snapped. "I can feel them. They do only as I ask."

"But—"

"Follow us or not, but I am going ahead with this plan," Elisara snapped at Caellum before looking at Larelle. The Queen of Nerida paused, glancing between Elisara and Caellum. She sighed and offered Caellum an apologetic smile.

"Alvan and I will discuss with the commanders." Larelle turned with Alvan, but before she could step forward, Elisara called to her again.

"Hurry, Larelle. This is merely a game to him. He will not delay his executions for much longer," Elisara said.

"What can I do?" Farid asked, spanning his wings. The flames on the feathers cast a glow across the group beneath the darkened clouds, flaring under the falling rain. The shadow beside Elisara stepped back from Farid, as though wary of the flames. Elisara frowned at the shadow before addressing Farid.

"Can you patrol the skies? Take out soldiers as and when you can but primarily focus on covering Nyzaia and I." Elisara glanced at her friend, whose face was stoic. Nyzaia stood with her shoulders pushed back, twirling her daggers absent-mindedly. She scanned the army, ready for her mission. "If it looks like the plan is failing, get Nyzaia out of there."

"Excuse me?" Nyzaia snapped her head to Elisara, crossing her arms. "I'll decide what kind of threats I can and cannot face."

Elisara stared at her and whispered, "I won't lose someone else" before turning back to face the battle. Sadira's heart splintered at Elisara's pain. Nyzaia opened her mouth to speak but closed it before looking at her feet.

"We need to get you somewhere else," Caellum said, his voice hushed in Sadira's ear. She turned to look up at him, her hands gravitating to his waist. His hair had darkened from the now slowing rainfall, sticking it to his forehead. He cupped Sadira's face, his eyes brimming with concern.

"You heard Elisara. We do not have time," Sadira said, her hands cold against the metal of his breastplate.

"Do not be foolish, sister. You cannot wield a sword," said Soren, standing nearby with her arms crossed. Her wolves had returned to her from wherever they had lingered, with all six gathered around her feet. She watched Tajana and Caligh.

"What would you suggest, then?" Sadira snapped. "I cannot escape the battlefield quickly, and while I can use my power to block and deter, I cannot physically impact the soldiers for long. Any vines I manage to entrap them snap with far more ease than normal." Sadira wondered if Caligh's control was why their powers proved less effective against the soldiers. Perhaps his power was interlinked with the soldiers' bodies, and this stopped the rulers from directly affecting them with the usual strength of their power. Larelle had used a wave of water to repel the soldiers but had failed to make the soldiers choke on any she attempted to conjure internally. Could that be because of Caligh's presence in their veins—his control in their minds? Even Soren had explained her vines barely held a soldier down, but since they were children, Soren had only ever used her power to decay Sadira's own, so she had no measure as to whether her sister's vines were strong enough to begin with.

"Create somewhere safe." Soren shrugged. "You're strong enough. You grew a tree through the stone floor at your engagement ball." Caellum tensed. They all knew Soren referred to the moment she had stepped back, letting the creature kill Caellum, which it would have had Sadira not intervened. Sadira frowned when Soren glanced away, kicking her foot in the sand. Baelyn, one of the sable-coloured twin wolves, pawed at Soren's leg until she stopped kicking.

"Can you do it again?" Caellum asked. "Can you create a tree-line? It would be somewhere to shield the archers." Sadira looked down at the battle again; the moat had already created a small barrier. If she grew trees outside of it, it would be far enough from Elisara's flaming vines and awkward enough to keep the copper soldiers from reaching it.

"I can attempt it, but it requires a sturdier foundation. It could be weakly rooted compared to the vines I used during the battle." Caellum gripped her hands, smiling with encouragement.

"I believe in you. They just need to keep you safe. That's all I care about." Sadira rested her forehead against his. The beating of their hearts thrummed in her ears, intertwined with the matching rise and fall of their chests. "How can I live a fairytale without my queen by my side?" he murmured. "This is just our first chapter. I intend for us to reach our happily ever after." Eyes watering, Sadira stood on her tiptoes to plant a promise-filled kiss on Caellum's lips, relishing the warmth and security they offered.

"I will give you hundreds of happily ever afters."

"I'll hold you to that promise," Caellum said, kissing her back. Sadira turned to focus on her power but caught Soren staring before hurriedly looked away. Sadira frowned. Something had been different about Soren since the first battle. Sadira opted to push the thought aside until everyone was safe and Caligh was defeated. Raising her hands, she curled her toes, trying to imagine the feel of the sand against her feet, despite the laced boots protecting them from the heat. She always felt more connected to her power when barefoot. Inhaling deeply, Sadira closed her eyes and focused. She thought of the power twisting like vines in her blood, calling to be planted. When she opened her eyes, she flipped her palms, and trees shot through the ground and grew around the moat. They appeared slower than the oak tree she had summoned in Garridon, but it did not take long for the leaves to bloom. Their trunks were not as thick, nor the leaves as big, but their curving branches and foliage provided enough coverage for Sadira and the archers. One day she would spend her time travelling the rest of Novisia to catalogue every plant in her mind.

At the same moment Sadira felt her power cease, Elisara's army shifted, rattled by uncertainty as Caligh finally moved. He flourished his hands, and his own shadows seeped from his fingertips. While they did not form corporeal bodies like Elisara's shadows, they moved with clarity and speed as he directed them to weave amongst the army.

It was time for the rulers to face darkness yet again.

Chapter Two
Soren

Uncertainty gnawed at the heavy weight on Soren's chest, uncertainty of how she should feel and act. To her left stood Sadira and Caellum, a pair bound only because Soren had saved him on the battlefield. Yet Soren was confused by her actions. Why had she saved him? Something about the memories of Sadira with Caellum had triggered Soren to act—to rescue him. Yet she eventually did as Caligh asked, separating Elisara and Kazaar, and freeing the path for Caligh to kill Vala's commander.

Before her, Tajana was trapped between Osiris and Arik on the battlefield—one of her oldest friends, bound by chains. *Friend.* Soren frowned. Tajana *had* been a friend, and yet Soren unknowingly sent her away to become a monstrosity. The slumped, defeated woman was not the fighter Soren knew. A stabbing pain pierced Soren's heart as she questioned what else Caligh had done—or could do—to her. Why would he hurt someone he knew was Soren's friend? It was not only Tajana. Another old friend, Talia, was dead too. Grief swam amongst her other feelings, but the weight of the unknown overpowered everything else as she watched Caligh.

While her headache had stopped, Soren still recalled odd flashes of memories. There was something detached about them, like she was watching them unfold behind iron bars. She remembered none of them. It was like her mind was trying to tell her something, but what? All she could focus on was her next steps. The battle had two possible outcomes, and she was uncertain about her place in either. Should Caligh win, would he grant Soren her kingdom?

Or would he cast her aside, disappointed in her efforts? If the rulers won and defeated Caligh, what did she have then? Caligh promised Soren the Garridon throne. She was entitled to it, but if Caligh died, who would praise her efforts or stand by her side? Would Sadira ever forgive her? Why did Soren care?

Scanning the sands, Soren's mind whirred as she decided what to do. A flash of white fur crossed the edge of Sadira's treeline. Varna was ready and waiting should Soren need her, which meant the rest of the pack was scattered amongst the trees. Baelyn and Tapesh flanked Soren, tucking their sable bodies close to her side. Though Soren had commanded them to join the others, they were unusually reluctant, and Soren lacked the energy to make them leave. At the very least, they would be there for her, no matter what happened next.

A different tree tarnished her vision—the large oak tree on Doltas Island. Two young blonde girls ran circles around it. Soren closed her eyes and shook her head. The same memory kept returning, but she could not decipher its meaning or focus.

A flurry of movement began to her left. The rulers were moving. Farid launched into the sky as the Novisian army began their march, their collective footfall echoing on the hard-packed sand. Soren was momentarily mesmerised by his uniqueness as sparks fell from his wings, raining in his wake. He soared towards the clash of copper soldiers and shadows. Nyzaia and Elisara strode forward, allowing Novisia's army to consume and hide them as they made for the moat. The shadow attached to Elisara's side appeared to be scouting ahead on her behalf. They were going after Caligh. A ringing filled Soren's ears as she searched for the man who had guided her from childhood. Her heart thundered in her chest as she whirled in all directions. Still, she had little understanding of what she was doing or fate's path. All she knew for certain was she needed answers. She needed his reassurance that no matter what happened, she would be okay.

Soren followed the path forged by Caellum and his army towards the eastern treeline, ensuring it appeared like she was on Novisia's side. She made a show of focusing on the safety of Garridon's soldiers and people. *Caellum's people*, reminded her mind. Soren glared at Caellum's back as he led the moving army with Sir Cain at his side. He glanced at the treeline, where Sadira was perched in the canopy. Caligh's victory or defeat hardly mattered when Soren had still failed. Caellum lived. Killing Garridon's king was Caligh's first request, and she had not even managed that. *Should that be my priority?* Caellum appeared distracted by his army and betrothed. Perhaps he would not see Soren coming. She needed to know what Caligh wished for her to do.

Focused on seeking his guidance and approval, she scanned the battlefield until finding him, her Lord of Night. Grinning, Caligh stood amid the warring copper and shadow armies. His black cloak fluttered around him, blending with the shadows he wielded, making it difficult to ascertain where the shadows began, and he ended. His shadows differed from Elisara's. Caligh's darkness was unceasing, promising nightmares and torture, a stain on your soul, as it wrapped around you and pulled your bones so tight they broke in seconds. They called to Soren, as if recognising her allegiance and dedication.

Yet Elisara's army was also dark—there was no denying it. Her eyes, as vengeful as the shadows themselves, shifted with the sword in her hand. A light smokiness appeared, like there was some good within, clinging to the possibility of redemption rather than death. Although they took the lives of copper soldiers, they did so swiftly and quietly, as if placing them in an eternal slumber.

Caligh's shadows twisted around the members of Elisara's army, attempting to halt them. Frowning, he planted his feet firmer in the sand. His shadows sharpened into threads and began stabbing at the army, trying to dissipate them. He pierced through one, obliterating the shadow into pieces and watching it fade. The shadow acting as Elisara's scout halted, peering back at his queen, who remained hidden among the soldiers. Soren could just make out her stumble as Nyzaia reached forward, gripping her arm. Caligh's smirk showed he had seen it too. A moment later, shadows drifted from Elisara again, until pieces of the fallen soldier reformed and ran back into battle. *He cannot kill them. Can anything?*

Caligh had only defeated one, and not permanently, yet hundreds swarmed the copper army, forming a protective ring around him, Osiris, Arik, and Tajana. Tajana. She locked eyes with Soren, a silent plea for help as she stumbled under the weight of her new wings. Soren looked back at Caellum. His death could wait. Soren would rather protect the Lord of Night. She threw herself into the centre of battle, trying to reach him and Tajana, her only loyal friend.

Whistling lowly, Soren summoned the rest of her pack. The wolves stalked from the trees as Garridon's arrows flew overhead. They halted and lowered their heads, raising their hackles as they searched for an entry point into the battle. Baelyn and Tapesh still flanked Soren, while Octavia, Serene, and Varna formed a triangular formation with the pack leader up front. Soren looked for Seiko and found his deep grey fur behind her, protecting their pack from the rear. Together, they continued through the clearing path.

Larelle stood on a raised dune beside Alvan and a handful of soldiers, creating the path ahead. As Novisia's soldiers approached the moat, Larelle pulled at the lapping water, allowing Sadira to create a bridge of vines between both sides. The soldiers filtered over in pairs, no more than ten at a time, but enough to tackle the copper soldiers circling the shadows in their attempts to reach the Novisian army. A woman screamed, and Soren whipped her head towards the sound. Elisara doubled over in pain while Nyzaia held her upright. At least fifty shadows fled from her at once to rejoin the fight. Soren looked at Caligh. The first soldier he took down had simply been a test. Practice. His shadows now skilfully and confidently threaded through multiple of Elisara's soldiers at once, taking them down in one fell swoop. In doing so, more copper soldiers were free to make for the moat where Novisia's army resided.

A flash of light captured Soren's attention as Farid flew towards Nyzaia and Elisara. The surrounding army retreated to give Farid the space he needed to land. Though it was not long before he was air bound again, this time carrying Elisara into the thick of the battle towards Caligh. Elisara's shadowed guard was by her side in seconds as they landed, readying to battle any approaching copper soldiers. He backed away when Farid returned with Nyzaia. Soren looked at Caligh. They were close. They might succeed.

Soren took off at a run towards the vine bridge expertly crafted on the eastern side. To her left, Seiko howled as the rest of the pack pulled into formation on either side of her, protecting Soren from all angles. She shoved past the soldiers waiting to step foot on Sadira's bridge and moved with unwavering certainty, rushing across to the island, where the battle was in full swing. As soon as they touched sand again, Baelyn and Tapesh ripped into the exposed legs of two copper soldiers, sinking their teeth behind their knees and tearing through the flesh. When the soldiers fell, the shadows descended, blanketing them momentarily before they rose once again.

Up close to the action, Soren struggled to see. Flashes of copper and darkness swarmed her vision in amongst blood as her wolves continued their path of destruction. She considered swiping a breastplate from a fallen soldier, like she had before, to allow quicker entry through the battle. She remembered the black veins creeping from the wounds of the fallen in the first skirmish, slayed by Sadira's imbued weapons. Was that a sign the sword had claimed them? She had little time to check the wounds of the fallen, to determine precisely how Elisara's shadow soldiers took the lives of Caligh's men. Could he really control this many people at once?

Soren stumbled at another memory—she and Caligh stood in a clearing, shadows still hiding his identity whilst her youthful face hid the atrocities she was capable of. Varna nuzzled her side, keeping her upright as Soren pushed her braids from her face and rested her hand on the wolf's back for balance. She drew her hand back at the wetness on Varna's snow-white fur, now streaked with blood. Any thoughts of her plan vanished. Soren stooped and ran her hands through Varna's fur, searching for the wound. Only when she found none did Soren's breathing even. The blood was simply a marking of her victories. Seiko nudged her from the side before she heard the whines of Baelyn, Tapesh, Octavia, and Serene. The pack circled her amid the sound of clashing metal. The copper soldiers fought not only Elisara's shadows but now Novisia's soldiers, who had breached the island.

"Get up!" A gruff voice shouted from her right. Soren glanced around, remembering herself. She looked up at Sir Cain. "I may not like you, but you're one of our best fighters." He drove his sword through the gap in a soldier's armour and shoved the fallen body off his weapon. "Get the fuck up!" he yelled, spinning in the opposite direction. The wolves stalked forward, forging a path for Soren towards the centre. Elisara's army blocked her path. Would they know Soren's intention if she tried to break through? She had no time to think as a rope of shadow she knew all too well pierced through the line of defence. Soren did not hear Elisara scream this time; she no longer knew where she was. How close were they to reaching Caligh? As the soldiers dissipated, Soren saw her opening. A small gap between the last line of copper soldiers offered a view of Caligh, controlling the darkness. Elisara and Nyzaia were not there.

But Tajana was. Her old friend knelt and draped her leather wings around her like a weight, cocooning her until only the crown of her head was visible. Osiris frowned and rolled back his shoulders, glancing between Caligh and Tajana to check if he was watching. Quickly, Osiris loosened his grip on the chain around Tajana's neck and rested a hand on her shoulders to pull them back until the wings no longer consumed her, the tips resting behind her on the sand as Tajana hung back her head with relief. A moment later, Osiris resumed his rigid stance, like he had not moved or helped at all.

With the wings no longer obscuring Tajana's face, the tears streaming down her dirt-ridden cheeks were clear to see. Soren rushed into the opening and opened her mouth to scream Tajana's name. Even with her blackened heart, Soren wished to reassure her friend she had come to save her. The chain in Osiris's hand was suddenly in Arik's as he rushed forward in a blur of black, blocking Soren's advance. Finely tailored black covered him from head to toe, except for his visible face and hands, revealing skin much paler than Soren's. His hair was just as dark and tied back low. Everything about him was pristine, except for the scar starting midway down his cheek and ending beneath the high neck of his collar. He stared Soren down, the amber rings around his irises a splash of colour amid the darkness. Judging by his appearance, he likely aligned with Caligh, blending into the shadows.

"I wouldn't if I were you." His tone was hushed, his meaning unclear. "Not if you truly want to end up dead." Osiris angled his head in Caligh's direction, who turned to survey his surroundings. He had not yet seen Soren's arrival or watched her rush to Tajana's aid. Foolish. She was foolish to have placed someone above him. When Caligh's shadows cleared, he finally noticed Soren, who glanced around cautiously for prying eyes. She was ready to kneel and apologise for her failures, begging for his forgiveness, when she spotted the flaming wings circling above. If Farid was near, so were Nyzaia and Elisara. Her steps faltered, and she stilled, watching the shadowed guard tower above the army. To his left, a determined Elisara moved, her face etched with fury. She was three lines of soldiers away from reaching the centre, where Soren faced Caligh. Nyzaia swung and brought down a soldier. When he fell, their eyes met, and she furrowed her brow, glancing between Soren and Caligh.

This was it. This was the moment Soren either won her place by

Caligh's side or was named a traitor to the Garridon crown—to Novisia. *Stay calm*, her mind whispered. She reached for the pommel of her sword, angling it low in Caligh's direction. He laughed.

"You are wiser than I thought, making it appear as though you are here to kill me while we talk." Soren glanced around, but Nyzaia and Elisara were no longer there, swallowed by the shadowed army now blurring with Novisia's. The occasional copper soldier broke through the lines. Caligh's voice skated over Soren's spine; what was once a gentle caress felt different now she knew his face. Soren had never questioned the life lived by the Lord of Night; she had only ever wondered about their future. But now, as she truly acknowledged his existence, she questioned his intentions. What had led him down this path? He was old—centuries old, in fact—but his true face, not that of the Historian's, was more youthful. The dark stubble on his jaw had not greyed like his hair, and his scar-coated hands were not yet wrinkled. Who had inflicted such scars?

"Tell me, little bird. What do you desire from this conversation?" Slowly, Caligh circled Soren, constantly scanning the surrounding battle. If he continued this path, Elisara and Nyzaia had no chance of making it here. He was assessing every entry point. "From where I stand, you have failed at nearly everything I asked of you." Soren winced. "But you have always been so loyal, so unwavering in what I ask. Loyalty is hard to come by these days." Osiris scoffed behind Soren, and Caligh narrowed his eyes and continued circling. He paused behind her and stepped closer, slowly moving her braids aside until his breath tickled her ear. "We could have been so successful, Soren."

Could have. Soren opened her mouth to plead, but he shushed her, bringing a finger to her lips.

"You could have been Queen of Garridon or the queen of this entire kingdom. You could have taken Osiris's place as the commander of my armies. Perhaps I would have even made you my queen, if you had so desired." Soren froze, listening to all the power she craved. A memory flashed through her mind of a young girl running carefree through the fields. Had she always wanted this?

"I did not fail you," Soren whispered as Caligh trailed his hand over her braids and gripped the back of her neck. "I separated them, as you asked. I separated Elisara and Kazaar during the battle. Had I not, you never would have reached or killed him." She raised her voice, trying to plead her case in the hope he would change his mind.

Chuckling, Caligh stepped back.

"I suppose you're right, little bird. You are the reason Kazaar Elharar is dead." Grinning, Caligh peered at something over Soren's shoulder, his shadows grazing her cheek one last time. When he stepped away, Soren turned to find Nyzaia across the sand, with Farid hovering above her. Flames coated Nyzaia's arms, her eyes ablaze.

"I'll make you wish you were dead." Nyzaia spat. Then, she lunged.

Chapter Three

Nyzaia

The Queen of Keres propelled herself forward. She heard it all, every sickening word of Soren's true betrayal: the dreams Caligh fed her about the throne, the things she willingly did at his request. Soren Mordane was the reason Nyzaia's brother was dead. Nyzaia was conflicted between ending her life right there or making the death slow and painful, torturing her for information. All Nyzaia knew for certain was Soren deserved to feel pain, and she alone would inflict it.

All aspects of the plan left Nyzaia's mind after hearing Caligh's declaration. *You are the reason Kazaar Elharar is dead.* Without checking to see if Elisara had made it to the other side of the clearing, Nyzaia ran at Soren. Flames burned in her eyes and sparks flew from her skin. Soren ducked at Nyzaia's first swing, narrowly avoiding a blow to the face. Soren stumbled back with wide eyes, confused, looking from Nyzaia to where Caligh had been. She reached for the head of the sable wolf beside her, steadying herself before dodging Nyzaia's next swing. She could set her alight in seconds, but what was the fun in that?

Nyzaia had watched Soren fight before but was surprised by her speed. She ducked every punch, rolled from every kick, and dodged every one of Nyzaia's fury-fuelled moves.

"Fight back, you coward," Nyzaia spat as the pair circled one another. Soren's face remained neutral, her eyes devoid of emotion. She mirrored Nyzaia's movements before glancing at Caligh. Despite the sweat dripping down Nyzaia's forehead, she felt a chill run over her as he wielded his shadows. She followed Soren's eyeline briefly, watching him. He was uninterested in the pair. Instead, he wielded his darkness amongst Elisara's army. Nyzaia winced at the pain still to come for her friend. Every felled soldier reemerged from Elisara, and now multiple streamed from her at once. Although she had cried out before, Nyzaia knew Elisara was holding back just how much it was affecting her.

Soren's blonde braids spun in front of Nyzaia as she ran, flanked by two sable-coloured wolves. Nyzaia cursed. She should know better than to let such a small movement distract her. Springing into action, Nyzaia followed Soren across the opening, where Osiris, Arik, and Tajana waited metres away, close enough to watch the fight unfold. The younger boy, Arik, widened his dark eyes. Nyzaia imagined she looked like a predator hunting prey, teeth and all. Unlike the others, Osiris seemed amused. He stood with a smirk, his arms crossed and legs wide, gripping the chain connected to Tajana's bindings. Nyzaia clenched her hands, digging her nails into her palms for focus. If her eyes lingered on Tajana too long, she feared she would run to her.

"Are you that much of a coward, Soren?" Nyzaia sneered as Soren hid on the other side of Tajana, who frantically turned her head between the women as they strategically danced around the chained female. Nyzaia would chase Soren forever if she had to. For Kazaar, she would follow Soren to the edge of the universe. When Nyzaia's eyes met her lover's, she wavered at the deep black within them. Gone were the pools of evergreen Nyzaia had so often lost herself in over the years. Her golden-brown skin lacked its former glow, and it was like she hadn't seen sunlight since the day she left Novisia.

Tajana's arms were bare beneath her torn leather sleeves, exposing a littering of scars on her skin, some still fresh. Tears stained her dirt-ridden cheeks. Tajana never cried. In the years they had known one another, Nyzaia had never glimpsed a trace of sadness in her eyes. What had she endured to develop the wings weighing on her back? Was the pain enough to mirror how Nyzaia felt at the stab of her betrayal? Nyzaia narrowed her eyes, her pity quickly replaced with the reminder of what she had done. How long could Tajana have pretended to love her?

"You think hiding behind your friend will protect you?" Nyzaia called to Soren, who moved again. Nyzaia tore her eyes from Tajana to face the blond braids appearing between Tajana's wings. "I'll happily gut her to get to you." Nyzaia ignored the voice inside her head, calling her a liar. She also overlooked the pain in Tajana's eyes.

"No, you won't," Soren goaded with a smirk. "No matter how much you hate her loyalty to me, a part of you will always wonder if her feelings were ever real." *She's trying to distract you. Do not fall for it.* "I can tell you, if you want." Nyzaia lunged around Tajana to snatch Soren's braids, but Soren was too quick, kicking sand into Nyzaia's eyes before turning to run. Tajana was no longer between them when low growls entered the clearing. Blinking the grit from her eyes, Nyzaia saw the four wolves approach, watching her intently. Soren retreated, moving towards a line of copper soldiers engaged with Garridon's forces. With a wave of her hand, the two sable wolves prowled to different sides, ensuring there was a wolf evenly placed in every corner of the clearing. Sir Cain towered over the other men, confusion etched on his brow as he looked between Nyzaia and Soren.

"Whilst we're talking of truths," Nyzaia called, loud enough for those fighting to hear. "If you were working for Caligh this entire time, why did he place you in Garridon? Was it to kill the king?" Behind Soren, the Garridon soldiers stalled, and their movements lost urgency. They were listening.

"I would not be stupid enough to tell you anything," Soren sneered, raising her sword. Nyzaia dived to keep Soren's eyes from Sir Cain, breaking through the final line of defence. Their swords met in a hurried match, with both women frantically aiming for the upper hand. Nyzaia grunted when their swords crossed. The shadows of Farid's wings darkened the clearing, raining sparks from above that burned Soren's hands, forcing her to either fall back or push towards Nyzaia. She must have known Farid would not risk harming his queen, for she chose the latter. Their swords clashed again, pressed closer this time, their faces inches apart.

"Come on, Soren. Don't lose your cockiness now." Out of the corner of her eye, a ring of Nerida soldiers broke into the opening. Caligh was now blocked on the other side. Nyzaia hoped Elisara had reached him. "You collected spies over the years. I know of the ones in Keres through the Red Stones, but I assume you had them everywhere, even Nerida." Nyzaia purposefully named the realm to garner the attention of the guards on her right. "What were his instructions? Convince Sadira to fall in love with Caellum in case you could not immediately take the throne? Do you plan for her to rip his heart out?" Nyzaia narrowed her eyes at Soren's changing expression, softening at the mention of her sister. She shook her head.

"No." Soren shook her head again, as if trying to free something from her mind, her determined expression replaced by a furrowed brow. "Sadira had nothing to do with it. It was all me." Soren stumbled, and growls rang louder around the space as the wolves inched closer.

"Don't lie. You were in it together." Nyzaia stepped forward, but Soren did not back away. Instead, her green eyes looked frantically around as she continued shaking her head. "You both colluded with Caligh to kill the King of Garridon, to separate Kazaar and Elisara, and have my brother killed!" Nyzaia screamed. Soren stumbled, with only her sword keeping her upright. "You and Sadira are traitors to the kingdom." Only a few paces behind Soren, Sir Cain stepped through the line of soldiers.

"No!" Soren screamed, meeting Nyzaia's eyes. "None of it was my sister. It was all me. I planted spies in all the realms and created doubt about Caellum's claim. *I* was supposed to kill him. Sadira didn't know about Caligh or the plan to separate Kazaar and Elisara. It was me. I failed," Soren panted, speaking quickly. "None of it was Sadira."

A grin spread across Nyzaia's face, but it soon vanished when Sir Cain lunged. He was about to steal her one shot at revenge. The Commander of Garridon lifted his sword as he ran towards the fallen queen. Nyzaia set his blade alight. If Soren could not die at Nyzaia's hand, she should at least feel Keres's flame when the weapon struck her flesh. Soren tilted her head when Nyzaia paused her advance, and as Sir Cain brought down his flaming sword, Nyzaia uttered two words.

"For Kazaar."

A strangled yelp pierced the air, followed by a wave of growls and whines. Soren spun as the wolf's head separated from its body, and its sable fur caught alight. The damned wolf saved her. Nyzaia cursed, but her words were swallowed by Soren's earth-shattering scream. Stumbling onto her knees, Soren reached through the flames decimating her wolf's dead body.

"Baelyn!" Soren screamed. "No, no, no!"

Nyzaia paused; she had never seen such emotion from her before, only fury. With a wave of her hand, Nyzaia extinguished the flames before Soren burned alive. She wanted to be the last person Soren saw before death. The growls grew louder now, prompting Nyzaia to reach for her dagger. Yet the rest of the pack paid Nyzaia no attention as they prowled towards Sir Cain. A second sable wolf howled, lying flat on the ground beside the charred body. Soren's screams turned to roars as her body rose and fell with rapid breaths. She reached for the approaching white wolf and buried her face into her fur before rising.

Slowly, the fallen queen stalked towards Sir Cain. While Nyzaia could not see her face, she imagined the pained fury twisting her features. Now she knew the weight of loss, but it was not enough. It was not revenge. Nyzaia followed her footprints to where Garridon's soldiers formed a line before Sir Cain with their swords raised.

"You killed her!" Soren screamed.

"And you're next," he said, his words thick with promise.

"You killed her," she whispered. "She's dead." Soren clutched her head. "She's dead, she's dead." Nyzaia was only a step away now. "She's dead; how can she be de—" Soren stumbled, backing up into Nyzaia's chest.

The scent of pine needles struck the air when Soren whirled, whipping Nyzaia's face with her braids. She was stuck between two people who wanted her dead. Nyzaia ignored Soren's widened doe eyes; it was as though the pain of death finally made her realise the consequences of her actions. Nyzaia dropped her sword, the blade clanging against the discarded weapon at Soren's feet. Nyzaia thought of Kazaar's bloodied body on the sands, the life seeping from him while Elisara held him, sobbing. She thought of his laughter when they ran together as children, and the safety she felt whenever he was near. Nyzaia thought of every moment Kazaar would miss in her and Elisara's future. Fuelled by these thoughts, Nyzaia swung. Her fist collided with Soren's jaw, sending her stumbling into a Garridon soldier. Sir Cain shoved her towards the queen again when Caellum pushed through into the clearing, pausing at his commander's side. His eyes were wide, taking in the sight.

"What's going on?" he commanded, but Nyzaia ignored him. When Nyzaia swung again, Soren did not bother defending herself. A resounding crack followed as blood spurted from Soren's nose, spraying both women.

"It's your fault!" Nyzaia screamed, kicking Soren in the shin. Her wolves approached then, snapping their teeth. Nyzaia could not fight them all off.

"Down," Soren commanded, spitting out blood. With their swords raised, the soldiers cautiously circled the wolves, preventing them from reaching Soren. She did not fight when Nyzaia straddled her, pinning her arms beneath her legs.

"He's dead because of you!" Nyzaia shrieked in sync with her next punch. Scream. Punch. Scream. Punch. Nyzaia maintained a steady rhythm of hatred while Soren's blood sprayed her face. Blood filled Soren's mouth as she gurgled and angled her head, reaching for her dead wolf. Why wasn't she fighting? Why was she letting this happen?

"Nyzaia!" a voice she knew all too well screamed. Glancing up through her lashes and the hair falling free from her braid, Nyzaia's chest rose and fell heavily as she glared at Tajana kneeling on the floor. Tears spilled from her blackened eyes. "She's had enough," Tajana sobbed. "Please."

As the tears fell down Tajana's cheeks, she recalled the absence of her tears during the moments she hurt Nyzaia, the woman said to be the love of her life.

"She's had nowhere near enough," Nyzaia spat. Soren was silent and unmoving as Nyzaia rose to stand, wiping the sweat from her brow. With her head lulled to one side, Soren's swollen eyes focused only on the wolf's corpse. Nyzaia's eyes met Caellum's.

"She was working for Caligh. She was meant to assassinate you, and she's the reason Kazaar is dead," Nyzaia spoke plainly, watching the King of Garridon, whose jaw tensed as he peered down at Soren. "Technically, she is your prisoner, but I want her." Nyzaia kicked Soren's arm to check she was still alive, eliciting a groan from the traitor. Nyzaia watched Caellum with steely eyes, waiting. Caellum assessed Soren on the desert sand and then glanced sideways at a distant treetop. Nodding, he turned back to Nyzaia.

"I'll have my soldiers hold her until this is done," Caellum said, gesturing to a handful of soldiers and Sir Cain.

"I want the wolves too," Nyzaia requested. Growls erupted from where the soldiers had entrapped them.

"It won't be long now," Caellum said. Nyzaia frowned until her focus returned to the battle. Overcome with fury, she had blocked out the surrounding battle. Garridon and Nerida's soldiers had secured their side of the island; the sands had returned, and the moat was gone. On the other side, over the sea of deep blue uniforms, shadow soldiers battled those in copper. Caligh's army had nearly halved. They could win, Nyzaia realised. They could take Caligh down and save their kingdom. "Nyzaia!" Caellum shouted. Behind him, men dragged Soren away. He pointed behind Nyzaia to where Osiris stood, flourishing his hand. Weak shadows appeared, pushing Nerida's soldiers aside. He began moving, holding Tajana's chain and leading her to the other side of the battle, where Caligh stood.

"Not him as well," Nyzaia muttered at yet another man with the power to wield darkness, though his strength appeared hindered by Caligh's control. Nyzaia made to step forward and follow, but darkness exploded like it had in the first battle, forming a wall that kept the surviving army from reaching Caligh. Nyzaia rushed forward, parting the lines of Nerida's soldiers until she reached the wall. A suffocating sense of déjà vu overcame her when she pressed her hand against the wall of shadows, watching Caligh and Elisara face one another again.

Chapter Four

Elisara

The darkness felt comforting as it wrapped around Elisara like Kazaar's arms once had—a moment to forget the pain in her chest, rattling with every step she took. She did not know how she had conjured the wall of darkness encircling her and Caligh. It towered so high, Elisara could not see its end. Perhaps it reached the clouds. While the dark walls appeared daunting, the threads of light interspersed within the whirling smoke reminded her of the starfall on the Unsanctioned Isle. Did it differ from Caligh's shadows and the black of her soldiers because of Sitara's essence within her? Did the Goddess of Dusk's affinity for the night sky and the beauty of the stars reside in Elisara's power? Perhaps this wall would protect everyone outside of it, while Caligh, Osiris, Arik, and Tajana, having dived forward when the wall appeared, remained within. The darkness sang to her in a way that promised peace of mind. She wished it would speak to her in literal words. While she sensed the souls in her army, she longed to hear their voices to alleviate her mind's solitude. Had Caligh understood that feeling once? When he first wielded his dark power? She assumed not, yet every villain had an origin story. Perhaps Kazaar's death was hers.

Elisara was done with others telling her what to do or how to behave, what her life was, and how it should be. They told her she would be a good wife, then a queen. That her celestial tie with Kazaar could win them a war. And when Caligh finally took his life, Caligh promised she was next. Sitara told her to wield the power of four alongside her darkness to defeat Caligh and find

Sonos. Elisara wanted to tell them all to fuck off. With her power, she could kill Caligh and prevent him from using her in his warped plan, whatever that might be. *Think of what you and I could create.* Had he truly intended to use Elisara to turn Novisia's citizens into something horrifying? Given the little Sitara revealed, Elisara was unsure of Caligh's intentions. All she trusted was her gut, which told her there was something far bigger at play.

Elisara had no patience or empathy, no desire to do anything for anyone except herself. All she wanted was to exact her need for vengeance. But what remained for her after that? Only an empty heart and an army of darkness, none of which mattered right now. All that mattered was figuring out how to kill the man before her, assessing Elisara like a proud father. With a glint in his eye, he admired the shadow wall.

"I knew it would work." He smirked, tucking his hands behind his velvet cloak. "I knew killing him would release your power." Remembering Sitara's warning he would assume as much, Elisara refrained from rolling her eyes. She controlled every part of her power. Elisara could have ignored that first flicker of a flame beneath her skin, but Kazaar's memory was all it took to release the powers Sitara had planted. For twenty-six years, the goddess's essence squirmed around the fragment of onyx under her skin, trying to break free. Now, it was awake and hungry.

"What did you hope to achieve?" Elisara asked. She itched to move her fingers and make the shadows do something—anything. Caligh chuckled again.

"You are a goddess. You understand that, don't you?" Caligh tilted his head, waiting for an answer.

"I was not birthed by Sitara," Elisara said. Caligh shook his head.

"No, but her essence lives within you. Anybody created from the essence of a god—or holds the essence of a god within them—becomes of the same affinity."

"Are you a god?"

"Would it make a difference if I was?" he asked, and Elisara shrugged.

"It will help me to determine how easy it will be to kill you." With a flourish of her hand, the shadow wall squirmed with snakes of smoke and light.

"Interesting," Caligh said, monitoring the shadowed wall again. "How our powers differ."

"I'm not particularly concerned. I would rather be as different from you as possible." Elisara sensed her army growing restless—the man beneath the shadows, who had taken to being by her side throughout the battle, wished to push through the wall. She did not know why she listened to his feelings, but silently, she granted him permission.

"For the love of Makaria," Arik cursed under his breath behind Elisara. She glanced over her shoulder to find him backing away from her newfound protector, who materialised through the wall and stood directly at his side. Two heads taller than Arik, he was closer to Osiris in height. Elisara imagined her protector looking the boy up and down, assessing. She sensed he was extremely critical at some point in his life. Tajana's chains clinked as Osiris shifted, eyeing the protector with a wary look.

The shadow was quiet as he strode to Elisara, positioning himself on her right, just a single step behind her. Caligh raised an eyebrow.

"Are you a soul I took?" Caligh asked. Her protector did not move. "You should know, Queen Elisara, not every soul in that sword was killed unjustly. Some are trapped for a reason." A soft shadow caressed her mind, keeping her from looking at Osiris. She wondered if he, too, was once trapped in the sword for a reason. Perhaps he would be more dangerous were he not indebted to Caligh.

"It does not matter why they were in the sword. All that matters is they now answer to me." Lifting her chin, Elisara surrendered her hold on the army. Hundreds of shadows drifted through the falling wall, shoulder to shoulder. Endless rows encircled the space—an impenetrable barrier against the copper and Novisian soldiers. Shadowed creatures circled overhead, and Elisara spared a thought for Talia, wondering if she was among them.

"So, you have no intention of freeing them?" Caligh asked curiously. Elisara did not answer. Even if she wished to free them, she did not know how. "It doesn't matter either way, I suppose," he hummed. "Even when you free them, they remain bound to you, indebted until you choose to release them."

"Or someone else frees them," Osiris chimed in solemnly.

"You have become far too confident in recent days, boy," snapped Caligh, glaring at him. Elisara looked at Osiris, who stared intently at her. "Come closer." Caligh bent his finger towards Osiris, who dragged his feet against the sand. The chain in his hand continued to clink as it pulled Tajana forward, with Arik following. Elisara willed her shadows to take a silent step—just one, quiet enough to go unnoticed. "It is not only you who owes me a debt, because of the sword or otherwise." Elisara lost interest in the pair, prompting the shadows to take another step forward. From her peripheral vision, she sensed people trying to push through.

It was like she felt the well of their powers—the rush of the ocean, a fire's blaze, overwhelming strength. The rulers were trying to reach her. With a silent command, her shadows parted to allow them entry. Larelle and Alvan stepped behind Caligh; a spiral of water snaked around the pair, hovering where commanded and aimed at the enemy. Caligh's shadows moved around him instinctively. On Elisara's left, Caellum and Sadira appeared, hand in hand, while spiked vines wove in and out of the sand towards their shared enemy. Nyzaia and Farid joined Elisara's right-hand side; fire blazed up the queen's arms, matching the brightness of the flames on Farid's wings. The rulers watched Elisara, their pity leaving a bitter taste in her mouth as she avoided their eyes.

"Ah, everyone is here." Caligh threw his arms in the air and turned in a circle. "Have you all come to witness the great essence of Sitara bow to me? The return of old lore, the one who will help your Kingdom fall." Elisara ground her teeth, frustrated with the showmanship. Silently, her army took another step closer. They were still too far. The circular space they had formed was no smaller than three throne rooms. "Enough!" Caligh shouted, spinning to face Elisara. "Do you think I cannot sense the shadows moving in or detect their slightest movements, even if they are not my own?" His arrogance vanished, replaced with distaste as he scowled at Vala's queen and began pacing. "You can come willingly, or I will make you, like I have done with so many others." Caligh glanced at Caellum and smirked. "It was so easy to get in the minds of those in Novisia, so easy to convince them they were protected on this land. I always hated Garridon. He was an arrogant man, who always looked down on me." Elisara glanced at Caellum, unclear as to the shift in conversation. Caellum's jaw clenched, but his eyes did not falter from their enemy.

If she took the risk and sent the army now, they might smother him. Her protector shifted beside her, as though telling her to wait—listen. "It was so easy to get into your grandfather's head. Jorah was already such a proud man. Compelling him to kill Errard was easy, though I did not anticipate Lyra's escape." Elisara frowned. All the heirs watched Caligh intently. "And then there was your father. Wren."

"What did you do to him?" Caellum asked. He spoke with clarity and strength, but it held a note of uncertainty; Elisara knew his feelings about his family far too well.

"Could you call him that? Father? After the way I had him treat you." Caligh smirked when Caellum moved, held back by Sadira's grip on his arm. Laughing, Caligh added, "He was such a happy man once. The happiest are the easiest to break. It took me barely a day to work my shadows into his mind and tell him his children were worthless, that they would never be a good ruler like him." Caellum's face paled. Elisara wanted to run to him. "You see, if even the king deemed his children unworthy of the throne, it would be so easy to place a new heir under his nose—a fallen queen, perhaps." Elisara's heart broke all over again as she watched Caellum tense in a bid to control his emotions, refusing to break before Caligh's taunts as the truth dawned on them all. His father had never intentionally abused his children; Caligh had controlled him the entire time. "He managed to break through on occasion. Would you like to know when?" Elisara hung her head, recalling the memory shown by the gods. "Once when he tried to decide which of his children to sacrifice, and then again before he died. Realising what was about to happen to his family, he tried to stop it. His last thought before his death was the morbid realisation of everything he had unwillingly put his children through."

Ripping free from Sadira's hold, Caellum surged forward, unsheathing his sword. Elisara blinked, and a wall of shadow appeared before him, just as Caligh's collided with it. Caellum's chest rose and fell with rapid breaths as he glanced at Elisara, who shook her head in silent warning. Behind the wall, Caligh laughed, but his eyes narrowed, as if noting the failure of his shadows to break hers.

"Caligh!" Elisara's shout drew his attention from Caellum, who returned to Sadira's side. Elisara dropped the wall. No one else would die today.

"What did you say?" Osiris demanded, stepping towards Elisara.

"Step back, Osiris," Caligh's tone changed, his eyes flitting between Osiris and Elisara manically. Osiris looked at Arik, wide-eyed, and moved to scan the surrounding army, searching for someone. "Stand still, Osiris. I command it!" Caligh roared. Elisara looked at her protector, who took a menacing step forward, watching the scene unfold alongside her. Doing as Caligh commanded, Osiris stopped directly before Larelle, gripping her hands.

"Remember," Osiris pleaded. "Remember what I told you when I asked about Zarya's name."

"I've had enough of this," Caligh snapped, summoning his

shadows. A swirling twist of threads gathered to pounce on Elisara, but her protector lunged, sending a flurry of darkness to slow Caligh.

"Remember, Larelle!" Osiris called as a strand of darkness wrapped around his throat, tugging him back. Elisara beckoned her army forward while her protector distracted Caligh. Larelle looked at Sadira.

"There is power in a name," the future Queen of Garridon called. Osiris nodded, spinning to face Elisara. She frowned, still not understanding. Caligh finally pierced a shadow through her protector, and she hunched as he retreated into her. For a split second, before he re-emerged, she caught a glimpse of a memory. A short woman was dressed in robes, her blonde hair slicked back, highlighting the metal diadem resting on her forehead. She stood before the man Elisara had watched coat the Sword of Souls. A pendant hung around her neck, not too dissimilar from that of the Wiccan. She gazed up at the man, nodding.

"There must always be balance. We need a way to reverse things to avoid living in a constant state of chaos." The man sighed but nodded. "There is power in a name, depending on how it is used. In this instance, a slave that knows a captor's name holds the key to their escape." Elisara did not have time to wonder if her protector had also witnessed the memory or its many implications. Elisara looked at Osiris again, who nodded eagerly. She straightened just as Caligh approached, his shadows swarming and ready to pounce. The flush on his face spoke of his fury as his mouth twisted into a snarl.

"Caligh Servusian," she announced loudly. Caligh halted, paling. It was his first emotion, other than arrogance or anger, she had seen.

"Caligh Servusian," Arik murmured before doubling over. He knelt on his hands and knees, dropping one of Tajana's chains. Slowly, Caligh turned from Elisara as a wisp of shadow climbed up and out of Arik's throat, who coughed and spluttered. Yet when he looked up, Osiris grinned. The amber rings around the boy's irises had faded, freeing him from his debt to Caligh.

"Caligh Servusian!" Osiris bellowed across the desert, carrying the name on the wind. Osiris cracked his neck as a shadow escaped his mouth and dropped Tajana's chain. He flexed his arms and cracked his knuckles while chants of "Caligh Servusian" bellowed around Elisara, with copper soldiers taking up the cry. Osiris stepped towards Caligh, who retreated, summoning his darkness once again.

"Two hundred and seventy *long* years." Osiris grinned, stalking towards Caligh. "It was so smart of you to take a different body, a different name when you sliced me with that sword." Osiris smacked his fist against the palm of his hand, and shadows twisted out from it, interlaced with sparkling amber. It cast a slight glow upon him, highlighting the scar running down his cheek and neck. "It is so good to be back, grandfather." Elisara looked between the two—their matching height, angled jaw, and dark eyes. The only difference in their dark hair was the speckled grey in Caligh's.

"You know damn well this is not the end, boy," Caligh spat, slowly stepping to one side. He glanced at his approaching copper soldiers, seeming to realise he had lost all control. Elisara frowned. The sword and fragment within her had not whispered about reclaiming the copper soldiers, only Osiris and Arik. So why had they needed Caligh's name to break his control? Regardless, Caligh could not stay and win this battle alone. Everybody had heard his name. "You cannot tell them everything. You know what will happen."

"I am fully aware, but I can do everything in my power to give them what I can." Osiris stepped forward. "Now, I think we're overdue a little family torture."

"No!" Elisara snarled, stepping forward. Osiris turned his head to Elisara, a gentle smile on his face. "He is *mine*," she growled, but before Osiris could turn back, Caligh lunged for the chain on the floor. In one quick pull, he yanked Tajana across the sand towards him, and shadows swarmed them both. Elisara ran forward, but it was too late. The ball of darkness faded into nothing, just like Kazaar had. Elisara was left with nothing but the emptiness of her heart and the knowledge she had failed to avenge her love.

Chapter Five
Larelle

The echoing scream across the desert took Larelle back to Riyas's death, where she, too, had endlessly screamed. Larelle's eyes watered as Elisara mirrored a pain she remembered too well. Nobody moved. Stood to attention, Elisara's army of souls remained in a barrier around the rulers. Murmurs began among the copper soldiers behind them, who glanced at one another as if awakening from a haze. Some of Elisara's soldiers fidgeted too, shifting from one shadowed foot to the other. Nobody quite knew what was expected of them now. Osiris and Arik pulled back from their embrace. Osiris moved to approach Elisara, who paced the sands. Her shadowed protector stepped forward, stopping him.

Tendrils of darkness bled from her skin and floated in the air, with her hair soon following suit, static and alive. Silver volts flickered within the strands, a sign of the lightning in her lineage. When she gripped the sides of her head and screamed again, the lightning trickled down her arms, blending with her shadows. "I was supposed to avenge him!" she shouted, glancing at Osiris. She continued pacing, her eyes flickering between unending black and Vala's bright blue. The darkness twisted in all directions, unclear and indecisive, unsure what their master wanted of them. "I was supposed to kill him and be done. I want nothing to do with Sitara's cause. I wanted to kill him and be DONE!" Elisara screamed again as tears flooded her cheeks. Osiris stepped forward again and pursed his lips, his jaw clenching. He glanced down for a moment and took a deep breath.

"Elisara, I understand how difficult it is when your power emerges. Allow me to help you." When he stepped forward, Elisara retreated. Her protector crossed his arms and widened his stance. The shadow and Osiris were nearly identical in height, but Osiris held more command as he rolled back his shoulders. Larelle tilted her head. Why had this soul attached itself to Elisara so quickly? "If you stand any chance at all at saving us, we need to help you control it." Elisara ignored him. Dark tendrils drifted from her skin and floated around her face. Her wide eyes shifted to deep black. "Shit," he mumbled.

"What do you mean 'shit'?" Nyzaia strode across the sand, with Farid following, his wings still splayed. Osiris flinched at his approach.

"The darkness has consumed her eyes. She's slipping from her consciousness. If she doesn't get a hold of her power soon, it will begin to control her actions until she comes round again." Nyzaia stepped towards Elisara, and her protector allowed it.

"Elisara, listen. Listen to me," Nyzaia murmured, but Elisara did not turn. She frantically watched her shadow army. "You need to come back to us so we can figure out what to do next." When Nyzaia stepped forward again, a tendril of darkness reached for her at speed.

"Nyzaia!" Farid shouted. He drew everyone's attention, including the soldiers. One day, he would be capable of commanding armies, Larelle thought. Before the shadow reached his queen, Farid intervened with a flourish of his hand. A blue flame sliced through the tendril, forcing Elisara to recoil. Her army grew restless, and those behind Farid and Nyzaia stepped closer. Larelle glanced at Alvan, whose concerned expression matched her own. Behind him, some of Elisara's soldiers began to retreat and melt into the background. Larelle knew grief. Nothing would help Elisara right now. She was consumed by her emotions, not her power.

"Star!" Caellum called. Elisara turned her head this time, intently watching the king with the black orbs of her eyes. Dark tendrils reached for Caellum, who tensed but did not move position. He allowed the shadows to climb his arms and caress his cheek. With a slow but seemingly steady hand, the king intertwined his fingers with the darkness, as if it were an extension of Elisara's own hand. Silence fell across the desert. Larelle could almost hear Sadira's intake of breath as the shadows continued inspecting him. Elisara's powers, or some part of her consciousness, seemed to recognise his past importance in her life. "Let me help you," he called.

"Let us all help you," said another voice from behind the dark army. Vlad pushed his way through the shadows, that willingly parted for him. Vala's new commander was covered in bruises, and blood splattered his armour. A faint sway hindered his steps, showing how much he had expended throughout the battle. "Let us take you back to Azuria. Back home."

"I have no home without him." Elisara's voice was raspy, and a jolt of pain and understanding shot through Larelle.

"I know, Eli, but we need you to focus. We need to understand everything that has happened, so we can protect the kingdom if Caligh returns," Caellum said. Elisara's power pulled away from him then and returned to her before another scream escaped her lips. She resumed her pacing. The others began muttering amongst themselves, discussing what to do with Vala's broken queen, and how to move forward without knowing the full truth. They focused on themselves—the kingdom.

Releasing Alvan's hand, Larelle strode across the sands, kicking up dust in her relentless path towards Elisara. Alvan called Larelle's name when the tendrils of darkness paused, detecting her approach.

"Larelle," Osiris growled when she passed him. He attempted to reach for her wrist, but she dodged it and barged past the shadowed protector with a glare. He made no move to stop her and instead stepped aside. Ignoring the encroaching darkness, Larelle stepped in front of Elisara and gripped her face, forcing their eyes to meet. Larelle did not balk at the darkness reflected in her gaze; she focused only on Elisara's streaming tears and rattled breaths.

"I understand," Larelle murmured, and Elisara squirmed, her power growing restless as it swarmed around the two queens. Larelle's skin prickled at the dropping temperature; the darkness was like cold silk as it swept over the two queens. "Elisara," Larelle said more firmly, maintaining her grip on her face. "I *understand*," she said again, stressing the words. "It's not okay. None of this is." Elisara stilled. Shadows fell around the pair, cocooning them in a smoky sphere of darkness. Larelle heard Alvan's shouts from outside, and Osiris and Nyzaia's cursing when they could not see or reach the two queens. She tuned it all out, focusing only on Elisara.

"You do not need to do anything." Elisara's breathing slowed while she listened to Larelle. "You do not need to focus or help us with a plan. You do not need to come back to us—not yet." Larelle's hands drifted from Elisara's face to her shoulders with a light squeeze. "It hurts, I know. It will hurt for a long time. You will never forget him, and nor should you. We do *not* need you right now, do you understand me?" Elisara's eyes shifted to a faint blue before fading to their usual brown.

"I cannot do anything. I cannot be anything for anyone," Elisara sobbed, and Larelle pulled her closer, holding her as she did. Tears soaked the shoulder of Larelle's blouse, but she did not dry them or attempt to draw her tears. Larelle tried not to wince at the sharp wail in her ear as she stroked Elisara's hair. "I cannot do this, Larelle." Pulling back, Larelle met Elisara's eyes with a soft knowing smile.

"Go," Larelle whispered, cupping her cheek. "You need only yourself right now. Go Elisara." Larelle scanned Elisara's face before squeezing her shoulder. Nodding slowly, Elisara's eyes switched to black, and the shadows cocooning the pair retreated from Larelle and gathered around their queen until she and the shadows faded into nothing. On the sand, Larelle remained silent, staring at the place Elisara had just been. She prepared for the fallout of her command. The Ashun Desert was brighter now; the army of shadows departed with her, leaving only a scatter of copper soldiers on the sands. As a sign of surrender, they raised their hands while Novisia's soldiers detained them.

"Where did she go?" Nyzaia demanded. Larelle took a deep breath and looked at the sky before sighing. "She's fragile; she needs to be around people," Nyzaia continued.

Larelle spun to face a line of the rulers and their confidants. Osiris narrowed his eyes on Larelle from where he stood beside Arik, his arms crossed. When Alvan stepped towards her, Larelle shook her head. She saw the look in his eye, the silent understanding of why she had been the one to reach Elisara. They had not spoken of Riyas since they had kissed, but she felt it now, an unspoken weight between them.

"None of you understand," Larelle said, lifting her chin.

"None of us understand?" Nyzaia sneered, stepping forward. "We have all lost people." She paused to swallow. "I lost Kazaar too."

Larelle's eye softened as she said, "But he was not the love of your life." Alvan flinched, and Larelle mentally chastised herself for how that could be interpreted, that Riyas still held that title—the love of her life. Larelle avoided Alvan's eye and cleared her throat. "You all expected something of her. She needed time."

"Where did she go?" Caellum asked, holding Sadira's hand. He appeared more relaxed than the others, his shoulders and jaw not as tight. He understood.

"I don't know," Larelle replied. "I imagine somewhere that reminds her of him."

"So, what are we supposed to do now?" Nyzaia asked, impatiently shifting from foot to foot. "How can we do anything when the one person with all the answers is gone?"

A deep chuckle sounded from Osiris, and Larelle finally turned to face him. He did not look as though he had been involved in two battles. His neatly pulled back hair showed no sign of dishevelment, and no blood marred his pale hands. His dark velvet jacket, impeccably tailored, was still as dark as the night sky, without a speck of sand. The only colour was the intricately woven amber thread weaving swirls throughout, adorned with a sunlit floral pin.

"I can help," he said.

"Be grateful you haven't yet been detained," snapped Larelle.

"Why haven't I?" He tucked his hands in his pockets and offered a lopsided grin.

"I'll happily detain him," Nyzaia chimed in, flexing her knuckles.

"Like you need any more physical outlet," muttered Sadira.

"Maybe we should take you in for questioning too, princess," Nyzaia said, redirecting her aggression. Larelle frowned. She was missing something. Nyzaia was riled up more than normal.

Sadira lifted her chin. "I have nothing to hide." Caellum released her hand and braced it around her waist.

"Do you mean to tell me you were clueless about Soren working for Caligh this entire time?" Nyzaia challenged. Larelle glanced between the women with wide eyes, while Osiris's eyebrows rose, mirroring her surprise. While Soren's wish for the Garridon throne had always been clear, Larelle had suspected nothing more sinister. Bile rose in her throat as she realised a close confidant of Caligh's, who wished to conquer not only Garridon but the entire kingdom, had been in her home, close to her daughter.

"Where is Soren now?" Larelle asked.

"Sir Cain has her detained by one of Sadira's trees," Caellum said. His voice was quieter than usual, his eyes distant. Sadira looked at her feet while they discussed her sister's vile betrayal.

"I've requested she be a prisoner of Keres." Nyzaia's voice rose. "She is the reason Kazaar is dead and was detained on Keres's soil. Not to mention, I am the most skilled at retrieving information." There was no need to question the particular skills Nyzaia referred to. Larelle looked at Caellum for confirmation, who simply nodded alongside Sadira.

"Nyzaia can have her," Sadira said, looking up at Caellum, whose focus remained on his feet. She rested her head on his shoulder. "I wish to have nothing to do with her." Caligh's words returned then, taunting Caellum about his control of Wren, his father. The king's quiet aura now made sense. How could one begin to process such emotions?

"It appears you've had more than just Caligh working against you from the inside," Osiris finally spoke again after hearing of Soren's betrayal.

"Vlad," Larelle called, and the blonde captain stepped forward. Drying blood and orange sand splattered his pale blue uniform. "Have the commanders guide the armies back to the tents." Larelle did not want anyone else to listen to their upcoming conversation.

"And the enemy soldiers, Queen Larelle?" Vlad asked, glancing nervously from Osiris to the copper soldiers. With smiles on their faces, the men behind Osiris muttered to one another and clasped each other's forearms.

"They will cause no harm," Osiris said. "They swore a binding oath when they joined my army. It is because of that oath that my debt to Caligh extended to them, putting them under his control, too."

"How am I to trust that?" Larelle asked, narrowing her eyes. "The moment our soldiers are gone, you could have us all taken." Osiris smiled.

"Who gave you the talisman?" he asked plainly. Larelle was taken back to the cave, how certain Osiris had been as he peered among the rocks, how open he had been in revealing the other rulers searched for the missing halves of their talismans. He had been slow to snatch the talisman from Larelle when she had taken it. In fact, he was the one who dropped the stone to begin with. Osiris smirked as she looked him up and down. "I also steered the creatures away from you during the battle."

Larelle glanced at the other rulers for their thoughts, but Caellum still stared at the floor while Sadira looked only at him. Nyzaia shrugged. Alvan, though, the only other person she trusted, appeared sceptical. His face was neutral, but he scanned Osiris, as though trying to get a measure of him.

"I can take him if they try anything," Nyzaia said.

"So can I," Farid said cooly from her side as blue flames licked his arms. Osiris stepped from the pale glow cast from Farid's wings and moved towards Larelle. There was something about Farid's flames Osiris did not like, and it offered Larelle more confidence in her decision.

"The soldiers can stay," Larelle said, meeting Osiris's eye. Vlad began shouting commands, and the Novisian soldiers retreated up the dune, rejoicing. They clapped one another's backs with grins, oblivious to the shared feeling among the rulers that this war was far from over.

"*Athenios!*" Osiris shouted. Larelle jumped at the sound of clanking metal as the copper soldiers stamped and drew their legs together. "*Rethea ai wyeth sylen!*" he bellowed again. The copper soldiers marched into a formation before turning back towards Myara. When they reached three quarters distance from the ocean-side settlement, they stopped, though their joyous chatter carried on the wind.

"You speak another language," Nyzaia said, eyeing Osiris closely.

"Observant one, aren't you?" he smirked. "It is the language of my homeland."

"And where is that?" A crash of thunder echoed across the sky as Larelle asked the question. Dark clouds rolled in. Osiris pressed his mouth into a thin line.

"I cannot say."

"You are related to Caligh. Is it the same place he is from?"

Osiris nodded. "Once. But my grandfather has called many lands home under different names and different bodies, like the Historian on Ithyion and Novisia. There is a chance he will take a new name and body now we know the one he uses."

"How is it possible for him to change body and name?" asked Nyzaia, tossing a dagger from hand to hand.

"It is part of his power," Osiris answered. He raised his hand before him, allowing his shadows to form a playful ball that danced above his palm. "He can control minds and use them for his bidding, like he did with my soldiers, despite their allegiance to me. In some cases, he can take someone's entire body." The ball of power on his palm twisted with glowing amber threads.

"Your power is different." Larelle gestured to his hand, prompting a smile from him before he locked eyes with the queen.

"It is a variant, yes. I cannot control people to the extent he can. I only alter minds." Osiris allowed his shadows to fade.

"And can you do anything else?"

"Perhaps."

Larelle rolled her eyes. He was an infuriating man to pry information from.

"Caligh called himself a general; is that his true station?" Farid asked, a tactical question.

"Yes. He was once a general, though he has not technically been so for two hundred and seventy years."

"Just how old are you?" Larelle asked.

"Too old for you," Osiris winked, and she scoffed. Alvan fidgeted from his place beside Caellum and Sadira.

"If your grandfather was a general, what are you?" Nyzaia asked. Osiris took the pin off his jacket and passed it between his fingers, watching them all as though debating what to reveal.

"A prince."

"Bullshit," she scoffed, and Larelle shot her a warning look. If he truly was royalty, they should not risk offending other lands whose assistance they may require.

"Last I recalled, my mother was a queen, which makes me a prince."

"And your father?" Caellum finally spoke, and Osiris looked at him. Larelle could sense pity in his dark eyes, now void of gold rings.

"He is currently an unwanted custodian of sorts."

"What does that mean?" Larelle asked. Osiris shrugged, examining the pin in his hand.

"My mother is dead, and I have not taken the throne, so my father still rules the land." Osiris cleared his throat before meeting Larelle's gaze. Her face softened at the grief he so desperately tried to hide in his expression. "A genealogy lesson on my family and land will not help you move forward. In some way, Caligh will return, whether that's here or somewhere else. He may no longer have my army, but others are still indebted to him, and he can easily call them into favour. Make no mistake; he will call them in to get to Elisara."

"Now we are finally getting somewhere," Nyzaia exhaled. "What does he want with her?" Osiris and Arik shared a glance before Osiris straightened.

"I am... *limited* in what I can say." He glanced up at the unusually dark clouds, almost black like Osiris's shadows. For a moment, Larelle glimpsed lightening skitter within it. "She holds Sitara's essence, although that much she has already shared. That power, combined with all of yours, is enough to look for—" Lighting crashed onto the desert sand, and everybody jumped. Osiris muttered under his breath. "Your lands are not the only lands under threat. We did not know he was already here in disguise. You were all meant to have more time before he attacked, more time to—" Lightning crashed again. "Okay! I understand!" He bellowed at the sky.

The rulers all looked at one another. Nobody understood what was happening. Something prevented Osiris from revealing too much, though Larelle could not think who or what. She recalled the way the gods' speech had been jilted and filled with riddles. Was the same force stopping Osiris? Perhaps someone far more powerful from Osiris's lands controlled what he could share. *What do you know of Thassena?* That was what he asked Larelle during her capture. It had to be one of the other lands he referenced now. *Eresydon and Asynthos,* Arik had mentioned too.

"What is stopping you?" Larelle asked. Osiris let out a heavy sigh.

"My lands are cursed. There is only so much I can say before my words have consequences." Osiris was interrupted whenever he discussed the rulers, Novisia, and Elisara. What did those from his land, and potentially others, know of Novisia? Why would they be cursed not to speak of them?

"This curse... is there a way to break it?" Larelle asked, and he nodded. "*We* can break it?" Osiris nodded again, glancing upward. "It is linked to why Caligh wants Elisara and why he has invaded other lands in the past." Both Osiris and Arik nodded this time, with Osiris smiling like a proud teacher. Larelle tried to recall more and gain more information.

"People are waking up, their memories resurfacing. They will not be prohibited from speaking to you," Osiris said cautiously. "When you were crowned, the prophecy began and undid powerful magic keeping thoughts and history at bay." Thunder rumbled overhead, and a light spit of rain begin to fall and dot the sands. Larelle clenched her hand to pause it, but the water disobeyed. She kept her face calm, unwilling to reveal any weakness to Osiris, despite his help. She flicked her finger and was relieved when a drop of her own water coated her thumb, but only when she saw a droplet run down Osiris's cheek did she see it for what it was. Blood. Blood fell from the clouds, an omen of warning for Osiris.

"The fate and survival of your kingdom determines not just your destiny, but that of all lands." The blood fell heavier now, urging Osiris to leave. He beckoned Arik to follow before they strode away from the rulers. With one last glance at the sky, Osiris halted and spoke quickly, as though reciting something he had known for years. The veins on his neck became more prominent as he clenched his hands and spoke in hurried breaths. "What once was hidden can again be found. Listen to the land and understand you are bound. A reverse, a reflection, a sister, a mirror, find the truth beneath you and all will be clearer—" He reached for his throat, coughing and spluttering as bloodied water poured from his mouth. Staring at Larelle, he pressed his hand to his mouth to catch the falling water. This was not her doing. She peered up at the skies, and thunder rumbled overhead. Perhaps their gods were the cause.

"I have received a final warning. I must leave," he said, wiping his mouth with the back of his sleeve. He clenched one fist around the pin on his jacket. "When you need me, I will come, Larelle Sevia Zerpane." Larelle opened her mouth to correct him as he added Riyas's surname to her own but stopped when he strode towards her. Feet shifted behind, and she knew it was Alvan.

"How will I find you?" She tilted her head up to look at him. His hands were cold as they reached for hers. Turning her palms, he dropped the amber flower pin onto her skin, and she closed her fists around it.

"Zarya will know how," he said, smiling. He turned again and walked to his armies. Larelle clenched the pin tightly, fighting back the rising fear for her daughter.

"*Dehparh!*" Osiris called. In the distance, his soldiers straightened into formation, and with a flourish of his hand, Osiris blanketed them, himself, and Arik in a fog of quickly dissipating shadows, leaving only the wet sands of Keres behind, and a cloud of uncertainty hanging over the rulers yet again.

Chapter Six
Sadira

Letting out a sigh of frustration, Sadira combed through her wet, tangled hair. She should have asked Nyzaia to dry it before they retreated to Tabheri Palace. With so much information to unpick, Larelle had suggested refreshing themselves back at the palace before reconvening. Sadira wished they were meeting tomorrow instead. After two battles, no sleep, and many uncertain discoveries, exhaustion was creeping in. Her emotions could not keep up with her body. With aching arms, she attempted to braid her hair again before slapping her lap and bowing her head.

"Allow me," Caellum said. He rose from the bench on the balcony, where he had sat silently since their return, and gently squeezed Sadira's bare shoulders. She did not even feel comfortable back in one of her off-the-shoulder gowns. Sadira sighed when Caellum gently combed his fingers through her golden hair, untangling the wet strands and stroking her scalp. As she watched in the mirror, Caellum expertly crossed strands of her hair into a thick braid that would eventually fall over her shoulder. After the revelation about his father and grandfather, he had been quiet. Restraining his emotions and thoughts seemed to be a natural result of his upbringing, though it pained Sadira to see his barriers were still up, especially with her. But he needed time to process.

"Where did you learn to braid hair so well?" asked Sadira. A small smile crept on Caellum's lips as he met Sadira's eyes in the mirror.

"I had three sisters and a distant mother. Elisara taught me so I could help them in the mornings or before balls." Caellum's smile faltered as they recalled Caligh's admission. Sadira's heart tightened, grieving the loss of his father and childhood.

"Do you think your mother knew?" Sadira whispered. Caellum shrugged.

"She was always distant. She ignored the abuse and stayed in her rooms. Maybe she didn't want to accept who he had become. She would have noticed a sudden change, though." Caellum reached for the sage green ribbon on the dressing table and secured the end of Sadira's braid. "Aurelia once said he hadn't always been the way he was. She remembered him being happy when she was a child."

"Did she say much else?"

Caellum shook his head, and Sadira's mind wondered to her own sister. Was she capable of calling her that after such betrayal? Her sister? Sadira wanted to forget Soren. It would be easier that way. Though it was not in Sadira's nature to be cruel, which made the idea of what Nyzaia might do to Soren all the more difficult. *It is the right thing to do*, she tried to convince herself. If someone else had betrayed the realm, Sadira would have accepted the need for punishment, whether it was uncomfortable or not. It could not be different simply because she was raised with the traitor in question.

A knock sounded at the door, and Caellum called for them to enter. Jabir, one of Nyzaia's guards, strode inside, lanky arms carrying rolls of parchment.

"I am to escort you to the war room," he said solemnly. Most of his eyeline was hidden beneath sweeping dark hair, but Sadira made out the darkening skin below his eyes.

"Thank you. We will meet you in the hallway shortly," Caellum returned, sighing and meeting Sadira's eyes in the mirror. He wrapped his arms around her and lowered his chin onto her head. Warmth filled Sadira's eyes as she blinked back tears, overwhelmed by the events from the last few days. Silent for a moment, they watched one another.

"I'm sorry. It doesn't look like the coming months will be much of a fairytale," he murmured before kissing her head. Sadira smiled.

"Having you by my side makes it a fairytale for me." He returned her smile, though it did not meet his eyes this time.

"They may want to discuss Soren," he finally broke the silence again. Sadira glanced down, smoothing the thin green silk with her hands.

"If we can avoid it, I would like to," she murmured. The reminder that she, too, had been oblivious to her own blood's deceit. It sickened her. Soren had wanted the throne, and Sadira had warned Caellum as much, but never did she believe her darkness ran so deep. The only way Sadira could move forward was if she tried to forget her sister ever existed. Caellum lifted his chin and nodded.

"She is Nyzaia's responsibility now," he said, offering his palm to help her rise. Despite Soren not being her responsibility, Sadira could not help but wonder if she could have prevented her from taking this path.

***

Sadira heard the echoes of disagreement through the archway before Jabir pushed the wooden doors open for Garridon's king and future queen. Despite the level of noise flitting back and forth, the room felt emptier without Elisara and Kazaar. Sadira glanced at the empty chairs on the right-hand side of the hexagonal turret room. While she had never been one to attend weekly worships on Doltas Island, she still placed a palm to her heart and sent a silent prayer for Elisara.

Caellum's hand was a steady comfort as he guided her to the chair opposite. They were silent, trying to discern what had caused the disagreement between Nyzaia and Larelle, while Alvan and Farid occasionally chimed in. Nyzaia's bangles clinked as she slammed her hand on a map of Novisia splayed across the table and readjusted the fabric of her dark lehenga that had fallen with the movement. If it had not been for the flames burning in the sconces or the slight glow of the setting sun through the open windows, Sadira would have assumed Nyzaia donned black attire. Mourning, Sadira realised, before glancing around the room. No one else wore colours of mourning; the deepest shades of their realms. Larelle was in a purple gown, Alvan donned a vibrant blue jacket, Sadira's wore a pale green dress. She hung her head, overcome with shame. She had not thought to show respect for Kazaar's death. Even Jabir and Farid wore shades matching Nyzaia's.

"I understand your frustration, Nyzaia. I do." Larelle clasped her hands atop her stomach. "But try to see reason. She would be in no fit state to help."

The flames in the sconces burned higher, raining sparks on the tiled floor. "Do not patronise me! I am as much a queen as you are, which means I can make the decisions that best suit *my* realm," Nyzaia snapped.

"I am not talking down to you. But right now, we need to prioritise the kingdom as a whole—not our realms."

Nyzaia spun to face Sadira and Caellum.

"She is acting as though she rules all four realms, not simply Nerida. She acted the exact same way on the sands—MY sands—deciding for all of us about the armies, Elisara, and Osiris." Sadira and Caellum glanced at one another, unsure how to respond. While Larelle had been the most vocal on the sands, Sadira did not think badly of her for it. Out of everyone, it came to Larelle most naturally. Nyzaia scoffed.

"Of course, neither of you would side with me. We've never got along." Nyzaia pointed at Caellum and then turned her flame-filled eyes on Sadira. "And you latched onto Larelle as soon as you arrived. Maybe you're hiding something like your sister. Perhaps you'll be responsible for Alvan's death or Farid's. Am I to lose someone else at the hands of a Mordane?"

"Enough!" Caellum slammed his fists on the table and rose from his chair. A thin crack splintered from where his hands met the wood, knocking over the goblets used as paperweights. Nyzaia straightened at his display of strength, and Sadira hoped she would take him more seriously. Silence fell, except for the table, which creaked from the impact. "You are not the only person in this room who has lost people, Nyzaia. Perhaps now you understand how I felt when I lost my siblings and you barely shed a tear, focusing only on the life you lost and not that of your family. Now, you understand grief can rear its head in many a form, and in you, it is your anger. You do not get to turn your grief on all of us or Larelle, who is easily the most intelligent of us all when it comes to untangling the web of lies we've been fed. You do not get to accuse me of clashing with you when you spent your adult life in the Red Stones, shielding yourself from friendships—how was I ever meant to *know* you enough to like you?" Nyzaia straightened at the table, glancing sideways at Farid, perhaps sensing something between their ties. "And you definitely will NOT speak to my future queen like she is nothing but dirt on your now, very well polished, sandals. You are so focused on the impact of Soren's betrayals on yourself that you have not for one second stopped to consider how her sister may feel in all of this. If anyone has the right to feel angry about Soren's allegiances, it is Sadira. Yet here she is, ready to plan to protect our kingdom, all while keeping her emotions in check. Perhaps you could learn something from her rather than berating her." Sadira looked up at Caellum with watery eyes, pride blooming in her chest. He had come so far in the time she had known him. Not only did he speak as her future husband and fierce protector, he spoke as a king.

"Damn," Nyzaia muttered. "Somebody grew a pair." When she slumped back in her seat, Farid grazed her shoulder with his hand, prompting her to glance up at him with a nod. Larelle cleared her throat and sat beside Alvan, reaching for his hand. His smile did not meet his eyes.

"I understand why you want to find Elisara, I do," Larelle said calmly. "But even if we found her right now, she would be in no state to help us. We need to allow her time to heal."

"My concern is we do not have any of the information she received from Sitara. All we know is that Elisara is the essence of Sitara; Kazaar was the essence of Sonos, and..." Nyzaia crossed her arms and sighed before continuing. "The Sword of Sonos is poisoned, and our weapons were all imbued to link to the Sword of Souls instead. We need to know what else Sitara said."

"We also have the information Osiris gave us," Larelle countered. Alvan shifted in his seat at the mention of his name.

"He said our destinies were not just aiding the survival of Novisia, but *all* lands. How many more could there be?" Sadira asked, having only ever learned about Novisia and Ithyion.

"He speaks another language, so we know there is at least one other land. I suppose we could assume Caligh will have fled somewhere else, meaning there is a second. Novisia has been hidden since our ancestors settled here. We have no way of knowing for certain how many lands there are." Larelle frowned and asked Jabir for the rolled parchments.

"These are all of Keres's records of any journeys to the outer border or beyond. I found them in King Razik's rooms. I would be happy to look over them with Farid to find any anomalies," Jabir said. Farid narrowed his eyes at Jabir for volunteering him.

"I can return to the church in Mera and continue studying the texts and find any maps they may have," Larelle added. "But we cannot save any new lands without knowing how to." She scanned the eyes of those in the room, waiting to see if anyone had any suggestions. Sadira waited a moment before opening her mouth.

"I had a thought," she said, glancing at Nyzaia to see if she would interrupt. She did not. Instead, she looked away. "Osiris mentioned two things that caught my attention. First, your coronations triggered the prophecy and the waking of people's memories. Second, his lands are cursed." Larelle smiled, encouraging Sadira to continue. "I found it odd that the two Wiccans who found

Caellum and I in Asdale knew so much about the sword, even if some of their information was wrong. They spoke like it was a common story among their people and said there is power in a name, as if knowing that knowledge would be vital for us. What if they are an example of people whose memories were locked away but are now resurfacing?"

Larelle nodded. "It is definitely a possibility."

"They would also perhaps know more about the curses and how to break them. I could seek them out again." Sadira's voice betrayed her doubt. She was uncertain she had the authority to make such plans.

"I can assist you," Caellum said. Sadira squeezed his hand under the table.

"You mentioned resurfacing memories," Nyzaia said, glancing at Jabir and Farid. "Something odd has begun happening in Tabheri with the Red Stones—well, it's more sadistic than it is odd." Larelle and Sadira's horror-stricken expressions matched, waiting for Nyzaia's explanation. "Someone has been sacrificing members of the pillars: slitting their throats, pinning them to the walls by their hands, and using their blood to paint symbols around their bodies." Sadira drew her hand to her mouth, fighting the nausea filling her stomach. "I cannot think of a reason why anyone would do such a thing, unless it is all linked to these memories—things that have been hidden."

"I think you're right." Larelle nodded. "If Caligh could control an entire army, even with the existence of a debt, he likely has the power to hide the memories of people in Novisia."

"If it definitely was him, wouldn't Osiris have slipped that into his admissions?" Alvan voiced from Larelle's side. "What if someone completely different cursed the other lands and hid Novisia's memories?"

Caligh made the most sense. His plans would have been foiled if memories about him resurfaced earlier. But Alvan had a point. It felt incomplete; there was more to it, but Sadira could not place what.

"If Nyzaia investigates the sacrifices, Sadira and Caellum the Wiccan, and me the lands, that still leaves us with Osiris's final message." Larelle unrolled a thin scroll and read from it.

"What once was hidden can again be found,
Listen to the land and understand you are bound.
A reverse, a reflection, a sister, a mirror,
Find the truth beneath you and all will be clearer–"

"It sounds like he recited it from somewhere," Caellum said. Sadira nodded in agreement.

"I believe it is something related to Novisia," Larelle said, scanning the map before them. "The focus on the land beneath us but I do not know what is hidden or what is a reverse." She rested her elbows on the table and clasped her hands under her chin.

"Maybe we should concentrate on what we currently have planned and then look for Elisara to see if she knows more that could help us link the rest," Nyzaia proposed. "It would give her more time." Nyzaia's eyes were hopeful as she looked at Larelle, who nodded.

"We keep in touch via letter. If in ten days we have no answers to communicate, we meet in the Neutral City. That gives us all a week once we have travelled home." They all nodded their agreement.

"What do we tell the people?" Sadira asked.

"For now, we tell them the threat has left the lands. But we must all remain alert, impose curfews, and increase patrols on the shores," Caellum said. "We do not know when we will be under attack again."

Chapter Seven
Caellum

The morning dew scattering the grass felt cold on Caellum's skin as he collapsed onto a patch. The meadow had become overgrown, and the reeds dampened his knees and elbows. With his arms propped on his knees, he twiddled the ring around his finger. He knew not to complain about the damp, which was much more preferable than Keres's dry heat. After spending one more night at Tabheri Palace, Caellum, Sadira, and Sir Cain led Garridon's army home, stopping only briefly in Khami upon Nyzaia's recommendation.

Word soon spread of their return, aided by the scouts who had travelled earlier in the day. As Caellum and Sadira rode through their realm on horseback, side by side, their crowns glinting in the welcoming morning sun, the people cheered them on. The army moved slowly behind them, despite having washed and changed since the battle. Clearly, it had taken its toll. Yet their faces lit up when they crossed into Garridon, seeing the people there to greet them. It was far too early for all citizens to be awake, yet many were. Residents hurried from their homes once word was received of the king and future queen's return. Caellum had ensured enough guards and soldiers had stayed in Garridon while the rest headed to war in Keres, and while no one knew yet about the extent of Caligh's power, the soldiers would likely relay what they had seen.

Upon reaching Antor, Caellum's heart warmed as children threw flowers in their path and smiled as Sir Cain dismissed soldiers when they spotted their family in the crowds. Relief overcame their loved ones, and Caellum committed such moments to memory. It was all he could think about as he sat in the grass with no family to return to.

At the edge of the castle estate, the early morning sun streamed through the trees and bathed his face in shadowed rays as he peered up at the treetops. He had left Sadira to rest at the castle and said he needed some time alone. She had understood, though that was no surprise. She was an extension of him at times. He had sought out Sir Cain and had guards move his parents' bodies, taking them out of the darkness of the crypts and reuniting them with his siblings. He sat in the grass for nearly an hour, never straying his gaze from the treetops. With a deep breath, he finally averted his eyes before the sun rose too high. He needed to continue with his day and kingly duties.

A single tear rolled down his cheek. He smiled, realising the remaining rays of sun dancing through the trees shone perfectly on two headstones. Of course they would. The sun always shone on Edlen and Eve. The sisters' graves were in the centre of the other six headstones. He smiled at their names and chuckled at the engravings; they would have ridiculed his poor handwriting. He laughed again, unable to control it. His body felt it, then, and slowly but surely his laughter dissolved into sobs. Bowing his head, Caellum cried into his velvet sleeves, permitting himself to cry. He had held it in after finding their lifeless bodies crushed under the table at the temple. He shed no tears at the funeral, either, too shocked by the realisation he would never hear Edlen and Eve's laughter again or listen to Aurelia talk of the servant boy she liked while Caellum braided her hair or jest with his brothers as he outmatched them in sword training.

Caellum sat in silence with his dead siblings, knowing the pain that had forged their bonds had never been intentional. His father's actions—slapping them, pushing Dalton down countless stairs and breaking his leg, sneering instead of smiling—were all involuntary. Controlled. Caellum flinched. Had a voice in the back of his father's head tried to reason with him when he strangled

Aurelia for flirting with the servant boy? Did he fight the shadows in his mind when Edlen and Eve sobbed in their rooms after he starved them for three days for interrupting a meeting? Caellum sniffed and finally looked up, wiping the tears with his sleeve. His father's headstone stood at the end of the row of eight, the mound of dirt in front of it devoid of grass from the recent reburial. Was he truly fighting Caligh's power when he said Caellum should be his last surviving heir? Was his father proud and believing of him, despite never having voiced it aloud?

"You said he used to be happy," Caellum murmured, looking at Aurelia's headstone. Ivy shadowed her name, but he brushed most of it away, allowing a few strands to linger, hoping the God of Earth would acknowledge her place in Garridon, despite their contradicting origins to the throne. "When did Caligh take over his mind? I would not be here as king or live in this castle if he had not taken my grandfather's mind too." Caellum did not know his grandfather and hated the bitterness brewing in his stomach, as though he was to blame for allowing Caligh's control. Had he been unsuccessful in warping Jorah's mind, it would be Sadira here now, alone, overlooking her family's gravestones. At least Caellum had Sadira.

"You would have liked her." Caellum reached to brush the ivy from the twins' headstones and trace their names with his fingertips. "She would have played hide and seek with you every Sunday; she would have grown any flower you wanted to place in your hair." Caellum smiled at the flowers growing at the stone's base, swaying in the wind; it was like his sisters acknowledged his presence. He looked to the left at his brothers' headstones. "She would have kept you all in line, too. She can be commanding when she wants to be. I miss you all," he whispered, wiping the tears from his cheeks. He imagined a gentle breeze against his cheek was instead a delicate kiss from his sister.

"They would be proud of you," said a gruff voice from behind. Caellum sniffed but kept his eyes on their graves. He would recognise Sir Cain's voice anywhere. The crunch of gravel sounded behind him as Sir Cain made the final steps on the path before collapsing on the grass with a thud. He mirrored Caellum's stance and rested his forearms on his knees, looking at Wren and Hestia's gravestones. A bandage was wrapped around Sir Cain's shoulder, who also refrained from putting weight on his left leg. Dark circles ringed his eyes and suddenly Caellum was struck by how much older he appeared while exhausted.

"You served him long before Aurelia was born," Caellum said, turning to look at the man who had raised him when his father could not.

"I did," Sir Cain said, scratching at the ginger scruff on his neck.

"Was he always…"

Sir Cain shook his head. "Before you were all born, we were friends," he said. "Did I ever tell you how we met?" His eyes remained on Wren's headstone as he continued, not waiting for an answer. "We were sixteen. I was riding through the fields between Stedon and Antor. My pa' had pissed me off, and I needed to get out of the house. There I was, galloping free as a bird, when a white mare burst from the forest and sped across the field with a girl atop it, screaming her head off. I steered my stallion to follow, and when I caught up, I brought her to a halt and expected her to be grateful. Instead, she turned to me, red in the face, and said, 'You've ruined the game!'" Looking down, Sir Cain shook his head with a chuckle. "Your father appeared then. Guiding his horse in a leisurely stroll, he called, 'What a shame, Hestia! I didn't catch you, so I suppose I cannot marry you.' Back then, he acted as though he wasn't madly in love with her, but he was. He turned to me and said, 'You've done me a great favour. I owe you one.' But I didn't see him again for a year." Caellum released a deep sigh, trying to picture a younger and happier version of his parents. The image did not come forth; his childhood was too dark to imagine it. "Then, I turned seventeen and wanted to enrol in the military. I needed a recommendation, so when his father paraded him around the city,

I told him he owed me. He was the son of the king's adviser; he would be a great recommendation." Sir Cain cleared his throat, smiling with crinkled eyes. "He grinned and signed the paper there and then. He said he'd make sure we were in the same training unit. We were inseparable from day one."

Caellum wanted to smile at the fond memory but could not reconcile this version of his father.

"I was by his side at the wedding. By then, I'd been promoted enough times to be granted a seat at the wedding table. Was with him the day his father locked us in the manor while he usurped the throne. Your father tried to condemn the usurpation, then. I healed his wounds the day after Jorah's coronation. I carried his parents' caskets alongside him when they died. I was outside the chambers the morning Aurelia was born. I was the fourth person to hold her, you know, after the physician, your mother, and him. Then..." Sir Cain choked on his words, glancing away.

"Something happened, something changed in him," Caellum said. Sir Cain nodded, frowning and rubbing his hands together, as though trying to decipher what happened.

"I never knew why. He said he'd found a journal in his father's belongings and there was something odd about it. He wanted to visit the Neutral City but wouldn't let me accompany him. He needed to do it alone. When he came back, he was a different person. I tried to ask him what happened and what was wrong, but he said if I ever questioned him again, he would have me exiled. He commanded me to move from my chambers in the castle to the guard's barracks and spoke to me only about military matters." Sir Cain shook his head. "I should have fought back, especially when he started hurting you all, but if I did, I would be gone, and who would have been there to care for you and your siblings?" Sir Cain turned his head, his chin wobbling. Caellum patted him on the back.

"I would never blame you for any of it, you know that." Sir Cain sighed and furrowed his brow, facing Caellum.

"It never made sense. He started to lose it, and I just thought he was sick."

"What do you mean 'lose' it?" Caellum asked.

"He just didn't seem right in the lead up to the explosion. I'd catch him talking to himself as he left meetings, pacing the gardens alone, and shaking his head. I just wish there was something I could have done." Sir Cain sighed and picked at the grass by his feet. "I saw that behaviour again in Soren, right before we headed to the desert for battle."

Caellum pulled back.

"What do you mean?"

"She was erratic like your father, talking to herself. It was like watching someone lose their sense of the real world." Caellum tucked the information away, wondering if there was perhaps something more to Soren and Caligh's relationship.

"There is nothing you could have done for my father. It wasn't him," Caellum said softly, and Sir Cain scoffed. "No, listen to me—it *wasn't* him," Caellum stressed. Sir Cain finally met Caellum's eyes. The sun shining through the treetops highlighted his faded ginger hair. "It was Caligh. He controlled my father. It must have been when he went to the Neutral City. He must have taken over my father's mind. It was not him, Cain. None of his actions, words, or plans from that point onward stemmed from his free will."

Slowly, Sir Cain nodded, his shoulders relaxing. A sense of understanding brightened his eyes. "It wasn't him," Sir Cain whispered, looking back at the headstone. "I wish there was peace in that knowledge, lad, but instead all I am left wondering is 'what if?'"

Chapter Eight
Nyzaia

Nyzaia was grateful Larelle and Vlad had remained longer in Tabheri. Sadira and Caellum had stayed for only one night, while Larelle and Vlad stayed two. Nerida's queen wished for Zarya to have a full day's rest before travelling back to Mera. Vlad had stayed to give the soldiers a break before trekking through the Zivoi mountains, but as she looked at his glistening eyes now, she knew he wanted to be here to say goodbye.

While the rowdy calls and celebrations of the combined armies were a welcome distraction from the ruckus of her thoughts, Nyzaia had wanted this to be a quiet moment. Peaceful. Kazaar would not have wanted a big celebration in his honour while people with their tainted opinions feigned their commiserations. His wish was granted. There was no body to burn or ashes to place in the palace while people danced and drank in his memory. Instead, there was merely the oasis at the edge of Nefere Valley. She wished Elisara was here, so they could remember him together. Nyzaia had endless stories to share with her to help her through her grief.

She had thought of several places to say farewell to Kazaar: the canyons surrounding the Red Stones' den, the middle of the Ashun Desert, or drinking over the edge of the docks in Myara. But one small memory lingered in the back of her mind while she had tried to decide.

It was the day after Elisara and the recruits in her unit had completed their two years of mandatory training. Vala's princess at the time had returned to her kingdom, and Kazaar had three weeks off before the next set of recruits. After her fourth year with the Red Stones, Nyzaia wanted to celebrate after completing her final trial with the Dealers. Whenever she completed a year with a pillar, they had the same tradition: meet at the edge of the capital and travel to Myara for a weekend of eating, drinking, cards, and, above all, laughter. There was once a time when Nyzaia was the only person Kazaar laughed with. When she sought him out in his chambers that day, the guard by his door said he had left for Nefere Valley. Unable to comprehend why, Nyzaia left on horseback to find him.

It took little time before the palm trees appeared in her vision, where a black stallion drank from the oasis. When Nyzaia dismounted, she found Kazaar sat at the water's edge, with his boots and socks off and his feet submerged in the water. With his sleeves rolled up and forearms resting on his knees, he stared silently at the high canyon walls, casting a shadow over the calm surroundings.

"Fancy seeing you here," Nyzaia called, removing her boots. She walked barefoot across the sand, wriggling her toes as she went. He did not turn his head as she sat beside him and bumped his shoulder. Nyzaia frowned at the prominent circles under his eyes. "I was all packed ready to head to Myara, but was missing a vital person," she jested, smiling.

"Sorry," he mumbled. "I had to get out of the city and didn't want to stare at Vala's god-awful mountains in the distance. Ashun Desert was too hot; Myara was too far. This was easiest and quickest."

"Why did you want to get out of the city?" Nyzaia asked, filtering the sand through her fingertips. Kazaar shrugged. Together, they sat in silence for a while, watching the sun shift around the canyons, moving the shadows over the oasis with it.

"Do you think I'll ever have what you and Tajana have?" Kazaar asked. Normally, Nyzaia would have made a joke, like siblings did, but she sensed his forlornness as he stared into the distance. "Someone who understands every part of you, like an extension of yourself. When they look at you, it's like they're looking at their whole world." Nyzaia raised her eyebrows. It was an unusual question. Kazaar so rarely spoke about his feelings. He had opened up on a few occasions, usually when their father had done something to anger or upset him, but this felt different. He shook his head. "Ignore me. That was stupid. Just a thought."

"Your thoughts aren't stupid, Kazaar—your card playing abilities perhaps, but never your thoughts." The corner of his lips quirked; they both knew his card skills were far from stupid. "One day, you will meet someone who lights your soul on fire and sees you for everything you are. They will love you so much, they will give over every part of themselves just for you."

"That was an extreme answer, but I appreciate it." Kazaar scoffed, and Nyzaia bumped his shoulder.

"I mean it, Kazaar. You'll be happy. I know it."

There was something about that moment, knowing how deeply Kazaar yearned for love, and for a brief time had it, that prompted Nyzaia to choose the oasis to commemorate him. Elisara would have liked the memory too if she had been here to hear it. Kazaar got everything he hoped he would: a woman who gave every part of herself to him and believed she was nothing without him by her side. Nyzaia wished he could have experienced Elisara's love for a lifetime.

Beneath the setting sun, Nyzaia swigged from the bottle of amber liquid and hoped Kazaar was watching. She had never subscribed to the idea of an afterlife; many in Keres believed you either burned for eternity or were delivered to an oasis. For the Red Stones, death meant death. It's an easier notion to live in certainty than spend the rest of your life wondering if your lost loved ones are happy somewhere where you're not. Because knowing they were gone but happy made you feel selfish for a part of you would rather them be alive and miserable, as long as they were still with you. There was no room in the mind or heart of a Red Stone for dreams, desires, or 'what ifs'. Still, Nyzaia found herself wondering.

"What was his favourite card game, Nyzaia?" Jabir called from the horses, fishing in his satchel for a pack of cards so worn you could barely see their drawings.

"Snap," Nyzaia muttered. Farid choked on his drink beside her, and she clapped him on the back. "He didn't have a favourite; he could beat me in any."

"I have never played, so I shall sit this out," Larelle said from where she sat with her feet in the water. She rested her head on her knees, twisting spirals of the oasis in her hands. Smiling, Alvan watched her with flushed cheeks.

"I'll play for the both of us," he said. Larelle followed him with her eyes as he rose and sat beside Farid, Vlad, Issam, and Rafik, in a half-moon formation. Nyzaia wanted to smile at their joy but thought of Tajana instead. First Kazaar, and now Tajana. While she betrayed Nyzaia, seeing her chained up and in pain made her sick. Currently, the only remedy was swigging the amber liquid and feigning laughter. She would be fine eventually, particularly after a visit to the dungeons to unleash her frustrations on a certain blonde enemy.

Nyzaia swigged from the bottle again, her mood having soured with thoughts of Soren. "I'll sit this round out." Nyzaia glanced at her split knuckles, where the wound was slowly scabbing over. A very appropriate look for a queen. Nyzaia found it rather odd how Soren had not fought back. She had never backed down from Nyzaia before. Nyzaia hoped she would fight back during their next encounter. Torture was no fun when people accepted it.

A flicker of warmth skated over her heart when Nyzaia stole a glance at Farid, watching her intently. The sunlit glow on his skin reminded her of his wings. He tilted his head to the side, and Nyzaia nodded to reassure him. Their silent awareness of one another had become second nature. The bond between them had never felt odd—it felt right. Farid turned back towards the rest of the men and glanced quickly at a laughing Jabir. The comfort Farid provided twisted into fear. She had lost Kazaar; she could not lose

Farid too, no matter how new their friendship was. She hoped their destiny together lasted long into the future.

Behind her, Rafik and Issam spoke in hushed tones about the Pillars. Nyzaia sighed, knowing after today there would be no time for grieving. She was to return to her duties and investigate the sacrifices. But for now, she had a moment to mourn.

Despite being wrapped up in her thoughts and worries, Nyzaia sensed when Larelle rose from her spot and padded over to sit closer. The oasis seemed to ripple quietly as she did, as though mourning the loss of the water queen's attention. Nyzaia focused on the water and the reflection of the palm trees. An uncomfortable feeling crawled in her stomach, reaching for her chest.

"I apologise if I said something that upset you earlier," Larelle said in a voice that screamed she was a natural born queen. Awkwardness consumed Nyzaia, who was never one for apologies. Hell, what did she—the queen of the assassins, and then the realm—have to apologise for? Nyzaia did not reply. Instead, she took another swig, hoping the alcohol would numb this conversation, too. "Everyone handles grief differently," Larelle said. Nyzaia tried not to roll her eyes at what she expected was another pep talk. "Olden once told me there were stages of grief: denial, anger, bargaining, depression, acceptance." Nyzaia did not think she would ever experience the latter. "But what people do not acknowledge is the lack of order to feel such things. You might circle back to the beginning again or flit between all the others." When Larelle paused, Nyzaia finally looked her in the eye. Cross-legged, Larelle rested her palms on her knees and straightened her back, staring into the water. "Anger appeared to fuel Elisara initially, but when I was with her, depression was at the forefront. It's okay for her to feel both emotions, even if we do not always understand it." Nyzaia put down the bottle of liquor and clasped her hands, running her fingers over the wounds. "The same way it's perfectly okay if you feel anger, too, Nyzaia, but—" Larelle paused, and their eyes met, grey meeting brown, water meeting fire, calm meeting fury. "Do not let your anger consume you to the point of pushing those you love away. They will be the ones to support you when the depression takes hold."

Nyzaia turned and hung her head. Larelle was right, as she so often was. Nevertheless, that feeling still sat in her stomach—the unease at not being able to admit her feelings.

"Larelle, we need a judge! There's cheating happening!" Alvan called, earning many complaints of the men.

"She's biased!" Jabir cried.

"She will obviously side with you!" Issam hung his head back, already admitting defeat. Larelle chuckled and rose, lifting her dress to guide her feet over the sand to the others. Nyzaia assessed how Alvan's gaze tracked her every step; he had the same look in his eye that Kazaar had when he thought nobody was watching him watch Elisara. Pain flitted through Nyzaia's heart, the pain she shielded with anger. She sighed.

"Larelle," Nyzaia called. The queen paused and turned back, the sun bathing her in serene light. "I'm sorry. You know that, right?" She could not meet Larelle's eye.

"I know," Larelle said.

Chapter Nine

Larelle

"Shh!" Alvan hissed, grasping Larelle's waist to silence their laughter.

"I stubbed my toe! I'd like to see you attempt being quiet through that!" Larelle whispered, sliding her hand into Alvan's arm. As the dusky sky quickened to the deep blue of oceans, Larelle straightened on the steps of Tabheri Palace.

"You wouldn't have hurt yourself had you kept your shoes on," he chuckled.

"I couldn't walk straight in the sand," Larelle accepted his hand as Alvan led her up the stairs one step at a time.

"I think that's the wine."

"It was dark too!" Larelle exclaimed, tripping on the skirts of her dress.

"Maybe we should take a minute," Alvan suggested before reaching their chambers. Larelle hummed in agreement as he turned her back to face the palace walls. The palace steps were much higher than those in her own castle, mainly because this one was built into the red canyon rock, offering a glimpse of the city rooftops over the boundary walls. Alvan sat on the top step and tugged gently on Larelle's waist, guiding her to sit on the step below, between his legs.

Larelle felt the coolness of the mosaic tiles through her thin silk gown, but the warmth of Alvan's arms soon distracted her when he embraced her from behind. With a content sigh, Alvan rested his chin on her head and she melted into his grasp. His embrace felt natural now, and her heart-rate spiked with excitement rather than anxiety. She no longer had to wonder what it meant. Reaching up, she stroked the veins and fine hairs on his arms, paying particular attention to his biceps. How had she never paid attention to how muscular he was before?

"What are you thinking about?" Alvan murmured into her hair. Larelle cleared her throat, fidgeting.

"Nothing," she said quickly. Alvan pulled back slightly and freed one arm, keeping the other around Larelle, who continued tracing his skin. With his free hand, he reached up to tuck her curls behind her ear.

"Are you certain?" he asked, his voice hushed but close enough to tickle her neck with his breath. "It definitely sounds like your mind is preoccupied, or is it simply the wine again?" Alvan chuckled, threading his hands through her hair, twirling pieces around his finger as he did.

"Definitely the wine," Larelle mumbled.

"You seem relaxed for the first time since the battle."

"I spend every day worrying about someone or something. After Caligh left, it felt like I could breathe again, even for a moment. Instead of being a queen, I could just be myself before I must return to thinking of everyone else's needs again."

"You know you can always relax around me," Alvan whispered, leaning to plant a gentle kiss on her shoulder. "Allow me to remind you to breathe when you are doing too much." His hand moved her hair aside, freeing her neck and back. "Let me take away the world's stresses when you are by my side each night." Larelle's heart fluttered, her skin suddenly sensitive beneath his touch. He moved his other arm from her grasp and trailed the back of his hand along hers before placing another kiss on her neck. "Let me be your sanctuary." Another distracting kiss followed. Larelle tried to concentrate on the emerging stars in the sky rather than the twisting feeling of need within her—something she hadn't felt in what seemed like forever. But she needed this distraction. She needed a moment to not think of all the responsibilities her crown now bore. Alvan's hand was gentle but commanding as he grazed her chest and cradled her neck, tilting her chin up, forcing her eyes to his. "I will always worship you as a queen, but to me, you are just Larelle." Alvan stroked her cheek, his expression serious. "My Larelle." He lowered his head and pressed his lips to hers.

Larelle soaked up Alvan's words, believing every syllable. She surrendered to the gentle caress of his kiss as he silently waited for permission to deepen it. Larelle kissed him back with desperation, and finally, she let herself breathe. His hand moved to the back of her neck, his firm grip making her squirm in anticipation.

"Let me worship you," Alvan murmured. Twisting from his grip, Larelle faced him and knelt on the step below his, so his knees rested on either side of her hips. "You're so beautiful," Alvan whispered, devouring her body with his eyes as his hands came up to grasp her hips and pull her closer. "Where should I worship first?" Larelle opened her mouth, but no words escaped. "Should I start with your curves, which cast a silhouette every night as you walk onto the terrace at sunset?" He tightened his hold on her hips before trailing them up her side. Searching her eyes for permission, he brushed the side of her breast and gently grazed the thin silk clinging to her peaked nipples, betraying the calm she was trying to portray. Larelle swallowed loudly. "Or maybe this is where I should worship you first?" Larelle clung to his shoulders as his hands travelled over her body. She tilted her head back to grant greater access to her neck.

"Everywhere," she finally whispered. Finally, Larelle surrendered to her wants as she moved to kiss him again, feeling everything she had wanted to since they reunited on the ocean floor. Larelle had faced loss, war, and too many deaths to count. Larelle would drown in Alvan every night until her last night on this earth. Life was too short to not experience such happiness.

Someone cleared their throat at the palace entryway. Larelle immediately withdrew from Alvan, who rose and stood beside his queen, keeping a respectable distance. Larelle smoothed down her dress and straightened, a queen yet again.

"I apologise for the interruption, your Majesty," said one guard she knew from outside her chambers, not quite meeting her eyes.

"There is no need to apologise. What can I do for you?" she asked in her regal tone.

"The princess is asking for you," he said before turning to escort the pair. Larelle frowned. Zarya never needed her in the middle of the night.

***

"I apologise, Larelle. I tried to calm her so you could have your evening to pay your respects, but she asked for only you. I didn't want to wake Olden; he's been so tired lately," Lillian stammered, tightening the robe around herself as Larelle entered the chamber. Her friend's blonde hair was dishevelled, having clearly been roused from sleep.

"It is perfectly fine, Lillian. Please, go back to sleep." Larelle reassured her, approaching Zarya's bed. Her daughter hid beneath the silk sheets, prompting a shiver from Larelle as she moved closer. The open balcony doors welcomed in the cool night breeze. Alvan strode to the adjoining doors to their chamber while Larelle perched on Zarya's bed. A moment later, he wrapped a shawl around Larelle's shoulders.

"I'll be in our rooms," he whispered, kissing Larelle's forehead.

"No!" Zarya shouted from under the covers, having pulled the sheets all the way over her head. "Mr Alvan can stay." Alvan said nothing else, but he pulled up a stool beside Larelle.

"What's wrong, sweetheart?" Larelle asked, reaching to pull the sheet from her daughter's face.

"No!" Zarya shouted again before Larelle's' fingers grazed it. Zarya pulled it tighter around herself, and Larelle frowned. She removed her hand, abiding by her daughter's request.

"Did you have a nightmare?"

"They don't feel like nightmares," Zarya mumbled. "They feel real."

Larelle and Alvan exchanged a glance, frowning. "That's why nightmares are so scary, because we cannot tell if they are real or not," Larelle said gently.

"He said it was real," Zarya mumbled. Larelle was still, and Alvan straightened, glancing around the room. The thought of a man speaking with her daughter at night made her heart sink and her hands clam up.

Larelle spoke seriously now as she asked, "Who said it was real, Zarya?"

"The man in my dream." Larelle's mind instantly went to Caligh, remembering the ease in which he controlled the minds of Caellum's father and grandfather—an entire army. Larelle swallowed the bile in her throat.

"Was he a scary man?" Alvan asked. Zarya shook her head under the sheets, though it did little to ease her mother's worry, especially as Caligh could appear in a different body, like that of a kind, frail old man.

"He knew my name. He said mumma knew him and that I could trust him," Zarya said. Larelle narrowed her eyes, recalling Osiris's assurances Zarya would find him.

"Did he have a name?" Alvan asked; his voice strained.

"I don't know how to say it," Zarya mumbled. "He was only there at the end. He told me not to be frightened."

"If he wasn't the scary part of the dream, what was?" asked Larelle, who no longer attempted to pry away the sheets. Instead, she gently rested her hand on Zarya's trembling knee.

"Everything felt dead." Larelle and Alvan frowned, waiting for Zarya to reveal more. "I was in our old house, and I stepped outside to find you and Mr Alvan, but everything had lost its colour." Zarya sniffed, and Larelle squeezed her knee. "It was like there was no more happiness."

"Can you try to describe what it looked like, like we do when we're telling bedtime stories?" Alvan asked. Zarya's small head nodded beneath the sheets.

"There were no pink and blue buildings at The Bay. Everything was pale, like the colour of the sand when it's dry."

"Like the colour of the buildings when we stopped for bread in the Neutral City?" probed Alvan.

"Yes!" Zarya exclaimed. "The stone was really pale. I couldn't tell which flowers were pink and which were purple. They were all an ugly brown."

"What did the sky look like? Was it night-time?" Alvan's question made Zarya pause.

"I don't know if it was morning or night. The sky was brown."

"Can you remember anything else?" asked Larelle.

"Everything was back to front. I kept getting lost trying to find you." Zarya sniffed again.

"Were you scared because you couldn't find us?" Alvan asked. "Was that the only reason?"

Zarya shook her head. "I was sitting on the wall where we used to get bread. I hoped you might find me there, but then two big black shadows shaped like people came from the sea and tried to walk to me. It looked like they were going to steal me." Larelle frowned. She hoped this was simply a nightmare, but the shadows sounded all too similar to Elisara's, and potentially Osiris's, though she was uncertain. "That's when that man Ossie came and got rid of the shadow people." Larelle stifled her laughter, envisioning Osiris's face at Zarya's nickname. Alvan did not share her smile. His jaw clenched.

"It was nice of Ossie to save you." Alvan tilted his head at Larelle, confused.

"He said mumma would need to get a message to him soon, and I had to find him there when she was ready." Larelle was furious at Osiris for entering Zarya's mind without her mother's consent, especially after the effect Caligh had on Caellum's father. Surely, he must know any parent would worry about someone entering their child's mind. But she was also curious about how he had done so and grateful they could reach him if needed. What was so significant about the location and how it appeared? Had Zarya created it in her mind? Had Osiris? She liked to hope Osiris would have made the setting more comfortable for a six-year-old, but why would Zarya picture The Bay so changed?

"Did he say anything else?" Larelle probed. When Zarya lifted her hands under the sheet, Larelle knew she was wiping her eyes.

"He said I should trust my intu...inshuish..."

"Intuition?" Larelle asked, and her daughter nodded. Alvan leaned forward.

"Do you remember what she said before the battle?" he whispered. "She asked who was going to die, and then Kazaar..." Alvan trailed off as they realised Zarya had been right. Larelle shifted closer to her daughter.

"Zarya, sweetheart. Can you show mumma your eyes?" Larelle asked gently. Zarya was slow as she reached up to push the sheet over her curls. She kept her head down and eyes closed. "Zarya, please." Larelle leaned forward, stroking Zarya's hair. Finally, her daughter looked up and her eyes were all too familiar, the midnight blue now glowing brightly with power.

"He said you're running out of time."

Chapter Ten

Elisara

"*Levanna!*" *a voice she knew all too well screamed from the other ship, prompting Levanna to tighten her grip around the rope. Hanging off the side of the mast, she summoned all the power within her. The turquoise waves were rough as the river drake thrashed below, eager to be assigned a task.*

"I know, sweet creature. All in good time," Levanna murmured, reaching for the rope. She pulled it taut around her wrist and tied an unbreakable knot, securing herself to the mast. A flash of fire blazed overhead, and the ship rocked when it hit the quarterdeck. Her white hair flew into her face, and she hurried to brush it aside, eager to keep sight of his ship and the waiting river drake below.

"It doesn't have to be like this, Levanna!" he shouted again. He was too far away to discern his expression, but she knew Kai well enough to know the urgency in his voice would be paired with a furrowed brow. Levanna scoffed. He had a funny way of proving his words as his soldiers flourished their hands, aiming fire at her ship. His chestnut brown hair, which Levanna once loved combing her fingers through, blew in the wind.

"Yes, it does, Kai! You know damn well I'm not returning to the mainland with you. I won't let you do this; I won't let you start this war!" Levanna screamed back. This was all a game to him; he could easily make the leap between the boats or have his soldiers burn the ship into ashes. He was toying with her. Either that, or a part of him truly still loved her before his heart had blackened, corrupted by greed.

"And what does sacrificing yourself have to do with ending my

attempts?" Kai shouted over the ship's edge. He crossed his arms, the deep red of his cloak billowing in the wind behind him. Levanna paused to look at him. She wished she could save him. She wanted to reveal everything she knew—everything they could have shared if he had never left Thassena.

"Goodbye, Kai," Levanna called. She did not look back at his ship to see if he heard. Instead, she stared down into the ocean, spotting the iridescent wings of the river drake spanning wide from its blue-scaled body. Levanna loosened the grip on the water and sent a silent command, twisting her power until the drake glanced up at her with purple irises and catapulted through the ship. As the deck splintered into pieces, taking Levanna with it, she could have sworn she heard the pain in Kai's voice as he screamed for her, like he was himself a gain.

Elisara woke with a start, clasping her neck and sputtering salty water from her lips. She was reminded of when Kazaar saved her from the Vellius Sea. *River Drake.* The creature in the dream looked so similar to the one she had encountered when searching for the other half of her talisman. Elisara's shadows crept up to stroke her skin like a gentle caress. Her flinch turned into a shiver when she realised how cold she was. She placed her palms on the stone floor and pushed herself up from where she lay, taking in her surroundings. Glimpses of the checkerboard floor appeared in her vision, though her shadows slithered along it, filling the majority of the throne room on the Unsanctioned Isle. She glanced up at where she knew the opening to be, but found only twinkling stars watching her. No wonder it was so dark. When she flourished her hand, the sconces instantly lit along the wall. Elisara jumped when the flames illuminated the shadow army lined along the walls and up the staircase. They extended so far that they were likely in the tunnel and fields as well.

Elisara had no time to process how effortlessly she conjured a flame; instead, she watched the swaying bodies, silently waiting. She wrapped her power around herself and shivered under the soldiers' stares. Imagining their eyes on her was unsettling. Elisara did not know what they wanted. As of now, she had no further use for them. She had already failed.

"You can leave. I don't want you here," Elisara called. She tried to draw the dark threads lingering over the floor back into her, but they disobeyed. They continued floating across the floor, forming a barrier between her and the army. She squeezed her fists, willing them to retreat again, but still, they did not obey. Though it appeared at least some of her soldiers had listened to her command, a handful of dark bodies filtered back and through the walls. Above, she sensed a creature shift on the rock face it clung to and fly towards her. She scrambled back, but as it neared, she saw its wispy form and recognised it as another soul from her sword. *There are no more creatures here. Caligh is gone*, she assured herself. The darkness shot up and wrapped around the creature's throat before flinging it against the wall. Elisara's eyes widened; she had not commanded them to do that.

"Take that as a warning!" she shouted, feigning confidence. "Leave!"

Still, the army remained, watching. It was as if they taunted her lack of control. A handful more shifted on their feet before drifting through the wall. Elisara frowned and tried to focus on them. Where she once felt their emotions, now only darkness remained in those leaving. Perhaps she had been too slow to try to understand them before they departed. None of those remaining in the room taunted Elisara. If anything, they pitied her—pitied the queen who had lost her everything, the queen who could not even control her powers enough to be alone. Despite the army's suffocating presence, Elisara was still lonely. Her body was cold without Kazaar's warmth while she slept. When Elisara willed her shadows to whisk her away, she had no destination in mind. Kazaar was simply the only image in her mind. But the Isle made sense, having been the only place that was theirs. As soon as her cheek touched the floor upon arriving, she had immediately fallen asleep.

Her body was exhausted, it made sense that her mind had run away with itself and dreamt of people she did not know. Elisara snapped her head up. Or did she know them? Peering around the throne room, Elisara tried to recall the snippet of a memory that surfaced when her shadowed protector had re-entered the sword. Had her dream been the memory of a shadow here? Was Levanna in the room with her? Or Kai? Scoffing, Elisara glanced at the shadows wrapping around her again. Perhaps she was just going crazy with the new power squirming under her veins.

The shadows around Elisara's body pulled away to circle her instead, revealing the clothes from battle still on her back. Elisara frowned at the crook of her arm and brought it closer, inspecting the skin in the bend of her elbow. Her fingers traced a raised scar, paler than her skin; it assumed the shape of a ship's sail that had never been there before. Like Kazaar's. Was this because Elisara had now conquered the elements during her grief-stricken display of power? She considered checking the rest of her body but halted when movement caught her eye. Her power seemed to subconsciously emerge when flames rose from the floor and formed a ring, protecting Elisara like Kazaar would have. Her newfound protector patrolled the room.

Elisara tugged her shirt sleeve over the scar. Kazaar's shirt. She brought it to her nose and breathed. Still, it smelled of him; smoke and ember intertwining with pine and snow. On her wrist was his leather band, which she had used to tie her hair into a braid. On her legs were leathers he had made just for her. On her feet were the knee-high boots he had gently unlaced. Everything reminded her of him. Everything. Elisara closed her eyes, refusing to look at the room, knowing they had once fought here, battling each other and then the creature. Kazaar had run to her with so much concern. Tears filled Elisara's eyes, and the threads of shadows tried to embrace her again.

"No!" she screamed. "I don't want you near!" Her joints were stiff as she tucked her knees up to her chest and hid her face, crying.

What was she to do now? She was alone with her grief and a lingering presence who would not leave her be. As Elisara sobbed into Kazaar's shirt, she sensed her protector's presence drawing near. She did not know why she appointed him such a title, but it felt wrong not to, especially after his silent declaration of allegiance. The shadows that were quick to throw the creature against a wall now drifted apart for him. Through blurry eyes, Elisara peeked over her knees and watched his shadowed boots come into view. His head blocked her view of the stars when she looked up. Deep down, a voice cautioned against trusting this being. She did not know his name, where he was from, or why he had been trapped in the Sword of Souls to begin with. She could differentiate between the killed copper soldiers and those who had been there before. The older ones felt cold in her soul, dead for far too long.

The protector tilted his head and offered his hand, keeping his movements slow, as though careful not to frighten her. Gentle. He had a gentle nature. She imagined his hands were gloved. The link imbued on the weapons tugged at her, willing her to accept. Carefully, she placed her hand in his, surprised at how *real* he felt. Despite the age sitting in his shadows, a flicker of warmth burned beneath. The protector pulled her up with ease and supported her waist when she wobbled on her feet. Elisara pulled back at the foreign touch. Kazaar was the only person who could touch her.

The protector bowed his head in understanding and gestured with his hand to cross the onyx and marble floor. None of the army made to follow them. He did not spare a glance at the two thrones as they walked between them, approaching the black waterfall. He pointed at it, and she understood his request. With a wave of her hand, the waterfall parted, revealing the hidden corridor. The army moved again when Elisara glanced back, mingling and pausing before each other, as though having silent discussions. She tilted her head, wondering if they could communicate and did so now, acknowledging there was no current duty. A gentle touch of shadow captured her attention, and she turned back around as only a wisp from his arm reached out to her. He hadn't touched her; he understood not to. Elisara nodded and followed him into the hidden room.

It was the same as when Elisara and Kazaar were last there. The thick white blankets remained strewn across the bed from where neither of them had thought to make it, assuming nobody would ever use it again. Paper no longer littered the writing desk after the pair had taken them all. Cushions remained scattered before the unlit fireplace, which she set alight with a single glance, promptly warming the smaller space. Elisara looked at the tapestry hiding the entryway to where a room of statues would greet her. She ground her teeth at the reminder of the gods and Sitara's statue. She did not wish to see them again. What had they done for her? She inspected the tapestry. Last time, she had been too focused on following Kazaar to pay it any attention. It was almost as dark as the onyx clashing against marble on the floor, but on closer inspection, it was the deepest dusk blue—a scattering of stars woven into the night sky. Below it were two thrones: a sun engraving on one, and a moon on the other. Something was scattered across the thrones, drifting into the night, but she could not discern what. It reminded her of the stardust on the throne room floor with Sitara. It was rather ominous for a bedroom piece.

Threads of shadows trailed Elisara, who twisted to face the room. The protector stood by the entryway, watching. He was taller and broader than the other shadows, moving with purpose and command. Perhaps he once had held a higher station in life than the others trapped in the Sword of Souls. When he gestured to the bed, Elisara narrowed her eyes. He simply bowed his head and turned, watching the entry to the room that was now apparently hers. Elisara assessed him as she slowly slid under the covers, pulling the thick blankets to her chin. Curling herself into a ball, Elisara tried to fall asleep while watching the fire, imagining she could see herself and Kazaar dancing amongst the flames.

***

Slowly, Elisara opened her eyes. She blinked several times at the embers in the fireplace. Footsteps sounded over the floor, and she instantly shifted, backing up against the headboard and pulling the dagger from the inside of her boot. Elisara waved it at the man approaching from the doorway.

"I cannot hurt you here, nor can you hurt me." His voice was smooth, and she detected no ill manner in his tone. "You are still sleeping. This is one of the few places I can talk with you as... myself." His voice trailed off, and he winced. Elisara narrowed her eyes, keeping her dagger high. "You are wise to be cautious, especially as you cannot normally see our faces." He attempted a reassuring smile, but Elisara was not swayed by it. "I have protected you in the real world and will continue to do so here." As he bowed his head, Elisara's hold on the dagger wavered. Slowly, she lowered her hand. It was him, the shadowed man who had immediately fought by her side in the second battle and kept Caligh away. But why was he so intent on protecting her? She was nothing to this man.

Elisara had not even considered how he might look beneath his shadows. He wore loose black trousers tucked into dark brown leather boots with mud-caked soles. A loose tan jacket partly concealed his white linen shirt. He wore no set colours—no clear indication of his allegiance to a realm. There was nothing significant about his clothing at all, but his features told another story. He looked as though he had lived through a thousand epic adventures. His skin was tanned, except for the pale skin beneath his collar. Scars littered his arms, and his hands were calloused. A light black stubble, seemingly well-maintained, concealed his firm jaw, and amber ringed his dark eyes, just like those on Osiris and Arik, a mark he was bound to the Sword of Souls. Despite their shade, there was no darkness in them. Crinkles formed around his eyes, and Elisara could read the jokes he likely told in amongst the lines. His black hair looked like it had once been short but was growing out, flopping to the side as he combed his fingers through it and scratched the back of his neck, glancing at her through his lashes. He was nervous. He was not the person Elisara had expected—the man who so selflessly defended her and stood by her side. She had expected a soldier, or royalty, but this man seemed... normal. Laughter erupted from behind him in the throne room, disrupting her analysis and making her jump.

"I apologise, your Majesty. They have not had the opportunity to socialise in so long. I can ask them to lower their voices?" said the protector.

"They?" Elisara swallowed, realising she had commanded real people into war for revenge. The laughter filtered through again. Human—they were all humans once, with lives and families, and now they were stuck in a sword to do whatever she instructed. Perhaps Sadira had been right about finding a way to free them. Her protector nodded with a smile.

"They are your army. You granted them some life when you released them from the sword, though it is certainly a saddened existence. When you are awake, they must watch silently as shadows, but when you slumber, you give them the greatest gift." He gestured to the chair by the desk in a silent request to sit. Elisara nodded.

"They awaken in their real bodies when I sleep?" she asked, and his smile faltered.

"Unfortunately, we do not have access to our corporeal bodies in the waking world. Still, we are but walking shadows, but here—" He gestured around himself. "Here, our minds come alive again."

Elisara nodded slowly. "And you are?"

"Sallos, your Majesty. I am yours to command." He smiled, watching her through his lashes. "I have been waiting an eternity to speak with you."

Chapter Eleven
Nyzaia

Nyzaia was in a room that was nothing like the torture chamber she preferred. She wanted the empty room with only a desk, a mirror, and a chair. She wanted her usual blades of differing lengths splayed on the table, not the different array of tools before her now: iron clamps to keep a mouth open, sharpened pliers for plucking teeth, and curved blades for flaying skin. Nyzaia preferred simple things, like a blade and fire. The last person she had tortured was Isha and gained nothing except for the simple warning to trust only the other heirs. If Nyzaia had listened, she would not be here now, about to slice into Soren's skin for her role in Kazaar's death.

Issam and Jabir had offered the usual room at the Red Stones, but she decided it would be best to return when she could focus on the sacrifices. She would certainly offend one of the pillar heads were she to arrive only to use their torture chambers. The sacrifices remained at the forefront of her mind—and next on her list of objectives—while the other rulers attended to their assigned tasks. But first, justice.

Nyzaia surveyed the room, ignoring the dull throb in the back of her head from guzzling two bottles of liquor the night before. She had allowed one day to celebrate Kazaar, and the next to avenge him. Larelle's words rang in her mind, reminding Nyzaia that her anger served only herself. Nyzaia pushed the warning aside. She did not care if she was selfish; she wanted to be—*deserved* to be.

A completely separate location would have been preferable, like a deceptive room, misleading Soren to believe she was being freed. Instead, the room was a modified prison cell. At least the dark bricked walls would remind Soren of her worth. It was nothing but a tool for Nyzaia, just as Soren had been to Caligh. The room would serve as a fresh location for Soren's nightmares, and every time Soren fell asleep, she would see Nyzaia's face standing over her.

With each step, Nyzaia splashed through the puddles on the cell floor. A large iron door, installed in place of the old, rusty bars, provided privacy and focus. The cobbled ground was dark enough to hide the extent of blood Soren would lose, with only two sconces illuminating the room. Nyzaia liked to control her flames to alternate the captive's cycle of pain: blades that sliced and flames that cauterised, keeping her victim awake. Far below the palace, the cool temperature meant Nyzaia would barely break a sweat and could continue for as long as necessary. Crossing her arms, she assessed the devices hanging from the wall: chains, branding tools, a contraption that stretched the body. Nyzaia would touch none of them, except perhaps the whip, tempting her with new forms of torture.

Three knocks sounded on the iron door and echoed throughout the chamber. Nyzaia took one last look around the room, ensuring the single chair was perfectly centred, and the five varying sized daggers were displayed on the stool. Usually, she would have completed her deep breathing before such tortuous activities, but she cared little about being calm or composed. Instead of her usual leathers to commit such acts, Nyzaia wore one of her everyday lehengas, her crown still atop her head. Soren would sit and face two queens: the one whose realm she betrayed, and the one who would cut and expose all her secrets.

"Enter," Nyzaia called. The iron door creaked on its hinges as Farid appeared, offering a simple nod. Jabir stepped into the dim light with Soren in tow. Nyzaia stilled, silencing her breathing, refusing to allow Soren a moment to confirm who she was meeting. The fallen queen appeared frail, her head lowered. Jabir said she'd refused to eat, perhaps still grieving the wolf. When Jabir shoved her inside, Soren's bare feet stumbled on the damp, uneven cobbles until her knees thudded against the ground. Fallen queen, indeed. Nyzaia watched, assessing. She still wore the clothing from the battle, but the blood-spattered breastplate was gone. Only her dark green tunic remained, now awash with blood and sand. Her blonde braids, flattened by a blindfold, were matting in places, and the sand, sweat, and dirt accrued over the last three days was clear in her appearance. Soren turned her head from side to side as she slowly pushed herself up, struggling against the iron chains clamped to her wrists and ankles.

"I can hear you, you know," Soren mumbled. Nyzaia tilted her head. Nobody usually could when she was in this state of mind, intent on vengeance and the task at hand. Nyzaia stepped aside, leaving a path clear to the chair. Soren's head followed the sound.

"Walk forward," Nyzaia commanded. Soren scoffed and lifted her chin defiantly.

"Am I here for round two?"

"Walk. Forward." Nyzaia enunciated each word clearly, and Soren gave no witty retort this time. She scraped her feet against the uneven floor until her shins hit the front of the chair and instinctively put her chained hands forward, grasping the top of the chair before falling.

"Turn," Nyzaia said. Soren did as she was asked and then sat—or rather, *collapsed*—into the seat. Nyzaia tossed her thinnest dagger, which grazed Soren's cheek before piercing the wall. "Did I say you could sit?" Nyzaia sneered, abandoning her tone of indifference. Soren did not clutch her cheek in pain. Instead, she let the blood trickle over the scar already tainting her cheek. Soren rose from the chair again, facing the door.

Nyzaia stalked behind Soren to where her blade met the wall and tugged it swiftly from the brick. When she turned back around, Soren still faced the door, slouching. The urge to approach her from behind, tilt her head back, and slit her neck open in one clear swipe was overwhelming. Nyzaia's face would be the last thing she saw while she choked on her blood. That seemed far too forgiving, given what Soren had done to Nyzaia, Elisara, Kazaar, Tajana—the list of her collateral damage was endless. Squashing the internal voice telling her to kill Soren, Nyzaia tugged off the blindfold, allowing the dirty rag to fall into Soren's lap. Soren blinked rapidly while Nyzaia circled back to face her. Her green eyes were dull when she met Nyzaia's gaze. Grief burned in them, mirroring Nyzaia's every time she stared at her reflection. Ignoring it, Nyzaia reached for her dagger, impressed when Soren didn't flinch as she smeared the blade across her wound, painting Soren's cheek in blood.

"Well?" Soren asked, lowering her head to avoid Nyzaia's stare. Nyzaia would not have that. She moved the blade under Soren's chin, forcing her head up.

"You will watch me the entire time you are in here," she said, her eyes ablaze.

"Why?" Soren asked.

"So, when you look into my eyes, you will see the rage residing there and know I will never extinguish it. I will hate you until the day one of us dies."

"And will I be dying first? Here?" Soren tilted her head, prompting a smile from Nyzaia.

"That would be far too easy. Would you like that? To be done with this life? To escape your guilt after everything you've done?"

"What did I do?" Her voice was high-pitched and sickly sweet as she frowned. Nyzaia clenched her jaw, trying to maintain her deadly calm composure. "Ah, *Kazaar*! That was it." Soren's head whipped around when Nyzaia punched her cheek. She laughed, spitting blood onto the floor. "Sore subject then."

"Whilst my anger is fuelled by your part in Kazaar's death, you are here to answer questions." Nyzaia strode back to the stool to pick up a new, longer blade, the length of her forearm. She returned to the chair, twirling it between her fingers in the dim light. Soren kept her eyes locked on Nyzaia the entire time. "You're good at following instructions," Nyzaia hummed, assessing the fallen queen. "Was it truly that easy for Caligh to make you do his bidding?" When Soren said nothing, Nyzaia yanked her arm up, forcing their eyes to meet, while angling the blade at the crook of Soren's elbow. "How did he sway you to his cause?" Still, Soren said nothing. Nyzaia applied light pressure to pierce Soren's pale skin, but she did not flinch. "How?"

Soren shook her head. "I don't know," she mumbled. Not good enough. Slowly,

Nyzaia dragged the blade down Soren's arm and watched the blood pool from the incision, before trickling down her pale skin and dripping onto the floor. Soren tossed her head back and grunted, clenching her teeth.

"Pathetic answer," Nyzaia sneered. "When did you first meet him?" Soren brought her head back up to meet Nyzaia's eyes.

"Young," Soren said, clenching her jaw.

"Where?"

"Doltas."

"Specifically," Nyzaia probed. Soren frowned, thinking, as Nyzaia began a new line of blood along her arm.

"I can't think," Soren grunted.

"Did he appear as Caligh or the Historian?"

"Neither."

"Clarify," Nyzaia spat, stilling her blade. Soren's face faltered, and she stuttered for a moment, frowning.

"H-He always appeared in shadows; he never showed his true self." Nyzaia studied Soren's pupils. She was telling the truth.

Narrowing her eyes, Nyzaia snarled, "You're answering very easily."

"Better to answer truthfully and take away your fun of cutting into me," Soren countered. Nyzaia smirked and seized Soren's other arm, drawing a new line with her blade.

"Oh, look! It's still fun, even when you're silent." Soren glared at the Queen of Keres without reacting.

"I have nothing left, regardless. If I give you answers, I have nothing. If I stay silent, I still have nothing. Either way, I am a prisoner nobody will ever want. I have lost the throne I was promised, the life I worked towards. Do whatever you want to me. I'm happy to rot away here in a cell, away from all the people who want me dead."

"All of this was for a throne?" Nyzaia sneered. Soren tilted her head.

"What else would it be for?"

"Caligh did not care about the Garridon throne; he cared about reaching Elisara through Kazaar. You must know more." Nyzaia removed her blade and crossed her arms.

"I-"

"You what?" Nyzaia slammed her blade between Soren's fingers, where her hand rested on the arm of the chair. "What did he plan to do if he got Elisara? What is his plan now he hasn't? Will he return?"

"I don't know anything else. He never told me." Soren frowned, drawing her eyes from Nyzaia to scan the room.

"So, you based your entire betrayal on the false promise of a throne? You knew of nothing else?" Nyzaia found it hard to believe and was certain Soren held more secrets. "Perhaps I ought to summon Sadira. Maybe seeing her in harm's way might stir up some answers." While Nyzaia had no intention of hurting Sadira, Soren did not know that. Soren's head snapped up as she recoiled in her chair.

"No," she muttered, shaking her head. "No, no, no." Her eyes widened, becoming frantic as she searched the room. "Sadira did nothing! She knows nothing!" Nyzaia recalled Soren's similar reaction after bringing up Sadira in the desert. Something about her sister triggered a reaction. Nyzaia bit her lip, suppressing a smile. She could use it to her advantage.

"She could be a better liar than you." Nyzaia crouched before Soren, resting the tip of her blade beneath her chin to force their eyes to meet.

"No, Sadira did nothing," Soren muttered. "Nothing. Don't take Sadira." Soren gripped the arms of the chair and leaned forward. "Don't take Sadira, take me," she repeated. "Don't take Sadira!" She screamed so loudly Nyzaia took a small step back. "Don't take Sadira, take me. Don't take Sadira, take me." Soren shook her head, her eyes clenched shut. "Don't take Sadira, take me. Don't take Sadira, take me." Nyzaia frowned and removed her blade, watching the fallen queen repeat the same five words while shaking her head back and forth.

"Soren." Nyzaia lowered her blade and reached for Soren's chin, prompting Soren to scream again, rocking back and forth until the chair legs creaked, accompanying the sound of dripping blood and Soren's frantic words. Nyzaia rose as the iron door creaked behind her, and Farid and Jabir stepped in.

"What's wrong with her?" Farid asked, touching the pommel of his sword. Nyzaia shrugged.

"I won't get anything else out of her right now. Take her back to her cell." Farid and Jabir approached Soren, forcing her to her feet. Nyzaia waited until the sound of Soren's repeated murmurings faded.

"Don't take Sadira, take me."

Chapter Twelve
Soren

"Don't take Sadira, take me," Soren mumbled as Jabir, a man she knew was one of Nyzaia's guards, shoved her back into the cell. She had only been outside of it for thirty minutes or so, although time felt uncertain, and she was quickly losing all sense of it within the cell. The damp stone walls indicated she was below ground, and the lack of light made it near impossible to track the days. "Don't take Sadira, take me," Soren mumbled again as the keys clinked, securing the lock to her cage. They won't take her; she wouldn't let them take her. Soren would always protect Sadira. Curling up on the floor of the cell, Soren clutched her head and scrunched her eyes shut.

"Soren!" Help!" a girlish voice cried. Soren whirled in the open expanse of grass surrounded by trees. Her braids lashed at her face as she continued spinning, realising she had returned to Doltas Island. "Soren!" Her eyes finally found the small blonde figure atop the tree branch in the centre of the field.

"Sadira!" Soren called; her voice was much younger and smoother, devoid of its usual huskiness. "What are you doing up there?" Soren ran towards the tree, where she herself had broken her wrist when falling from it as a child. "Be careful!" she shouted at Sadira. Her young sister wriggled along the branch, searching for a way down. "You'll tear your dress, and you know that will make you sad! Stop wriggling. I'm coming to save you." Soren finally reached the base of the tree and clambered up onto the highest root.

"I found a baby bird on the floor. It couldn't fly." Sadira sniffed, pointing up at the nest on the branch above; three small birds chirped inside. "I just wanted to return it to its nest."

"You did a great job, Sadira! But you should have asked for help."

"Last time you helped, mother blamed you for dirtying my dresses! I didn't want you to get in trouble again." Soren sighed and focused on her hand movements, spreading her hands wide in front of her, aimed at the ground. Sadira gasped. "What are you doing?"

"Saving you," Soren mumbled, focusing on her power. A warmth spread in her chest—small and delicate, but there.

"But we haven't been learning long enough for you to do anything big!"

"Do you want to get down?" Soren retorted. Sadira fell silent and watched closely as the vines twisted at her sister's feet. Soren furrowed her brow to focus before guiding the lush green vines up the tree in a twisting ladder for Sadira, whose eyes widened, her mouth dropping open.

"Be careful. I don't know how strong it is, but I'll catch you if you fall," Soren said. Sadira bit her lip at the makeshift ladder; her eyes shone with tears. "Hey, look at me," Soren whispered, and Sadira did, her curls tumbling around her face. "You are brave, you are strong, you can do anything." Sadira nodded slowly before beginning her climb down the vines, reinforced by Soren's power. White flowers grew from the buds, opening with a delicate scent as Sadira took a last step onto the tree roots and flung her arms around Soren's neck.

"Thank you, Soren," she whispered into her sister's braids.

Soren held her sister tight. "I'll always save you."

The bright sky of Doltas Island faded from Soren's mind until she was left with only a slither of light filtering in from a crack on the side of the wall. Her back was damp when she sat up from the wall and lifted her head. Jabir slid a tray under the bars and narrowed his eyes, watching. Some of the contents spilled from the bowl onto the tray, but Soren ignored the food. Instead, she reached for the bandages on the other side. She watched Jabir as she wrapped her arms, allowing the fabric to soak up the blood from the lines that would soon form scars, matching the one already on her cheek. When she tucked the final piece under the end of her wrist, Jabir finally left.

With a sigh, Soren kicked the tray away. She lost her appetite once they threw her in the cell. The thought of food sickened her, especially when her mind wandered to her wolves—to Baelyn. Her eyes watered as she stared at the bowl of meat and rice tipped on its side. She would give anything to have her wolves here. She dreaded to think about how Tapesh had been after his sister's murder.

Her shock at the sudden loss stopped her from fighting Nyzaia. One moment, she was screaming for her dead wolf; the next, she was blacking out on the sands. When Soren finally awoke, she was chained to a tree, with Sir Cain watching over her. She had immediately thought of her wolves again before her mind drifted to Caligh, wondering where he was. Based on the joyful soldiers walking past, and the lack of dark shadows, she quickly deduced Caligh had lost. Where did that leave her? A traitor and a prisoner, with no hope of ever returning to the man who had once guided her.

Glancing between Sir Cain and Myara in the distance, she had contemplated if she was fast enough to flee.

"Don't even think about it," he'd said. After that, Soren stayed where she was, allowing her mind to conjure more escape plans. But how would she flee Novisia? She had no boat, no loyal followers, no crew, unless she went to Doltas first. But she knew little about where Caligh would go from there, and that's when it hit her—she knew so little about him. Even if she wanted to flee, she couldn't. Not without her wolves. She would not abandon the others after losing one member of their pack already.

A sudden ringing crippled Soren. Doubling over in pain, she clutched her head as the same high-pitched frequency from the past few days pierced her mind, forcing her to remember a moment from the past.

"Stop, please stop," she mumbled, exhausted by the constant visions. She failed to grasp their significance, and it all proved rather tiring.

"It is a big responsibility for Sadira." The voice of Soren's grandmother was haunting. Authority dripped from her tone, despite not having sat on the throne in years. "And you must be the one to protect her. Can you do that?" Soren stood in the turret room of the castle on Doltas Island. Her grandmother Lyra did not face her; she remained where she always did, staring out of the window, overlooking the ocean and Garridon, her homeland.

"It would be an honour to protect Sadira and her new husband." Soren placed her hand on her flat chest. She was barely thirteen, still growing into her young teenage body. "When will this happen?" Lyra flicked through an old book with the Wiccan symbol on the front, pausing on an illustration of a dark sword. Her grandmother slammed the cover closed when she sensed Soren's prying eyes. Neither Soren nor Sadira were allowed near that book.

"I cannot be certain, but it won't be long after you see smoke rising from the mainland. A new king will come looking for a bride, and Sadira will be perfect. Their marriage will unite the realm and, one day, their child will bring peace."

"I will protect them with my life, I swear it," Soren said, running from the room to look for her sister. She halted at the sound of crying from their shared rooms and pushed the door open, peeking inside to find Sadira on the velvet seat by the window overlooking the gardens. Tears streamed down her face.

"Sadira." Soren kept her voice quiet and stepped inside, wiping her sister's cheeks with the sleeve of her gown. Sadira gave Soren a sad smile as she perched on the arm of her sister's chair. "What's wrong?"

"I have to marry someone else." Sadira sniffed, looking out of the window. Soren followed her eyeline and softened at the sight of Rodik chopping wood. Rodik was always so kind to her sister—funny, too. Even Soren laughed when he was around.

"I'm sorry, Sadira," Soren murmured, pulling her sister close. "I'm sure the future king will be very kind to you." Sadira sniffed again. "Besides, no one could ever be mean to you. I'll be there every step of the way to protect you both."

Soren slammed her palm against her forehead before smacking her head against the brick wall. The blinding pain brought her back into the cell's four walls. She was going crazy. Her mind was creating false scenarios to punish her for failing Caligh. She had no recollection of the thoughts at the forefront of her mind. Sighing, Soren pushed the tray away with her foot before curling up on the floor and resting her head on the thin blanket that had been there since she arrived.

Soren let her mind drift as she stared at the metal bars, reminding her of those in her dreams—Caligh, always before them, never letting her near. Perhaps Tajana was behind bars like these. Even though Tajana was Soren's friend, he still tortured her. *He has a reason for everything*, her mind prompted, though a different voice asked: *Are those reasons valid?* Soren ignored both voices, silencing her mind. She wanted to be alone, as she so often was.

Chapter Thirteen
Caellum

Anxiety racked Caellum's body, causing the keys in his hand to clang together as he tried to unlock the mahogany door. With a deep breath, he tried again with a click that set his teeth on edge. He turned the key and nodded to the two guards, who were to wait at the end of the hallway rather than outside the door to allow him privacy. They bowed and faced away, guarding the only entry point into the room. The door didn't budge when Caellum pressed his hand against it. He tilted his body and slammed his shoulder into the door, which gave way with a billow of dust. Covering his mouth with the crook of his arm, Caellum coughed into his tailored jacket and waved his other hand to clear his vision.

He paused on the threshold. He was always forbidden from entering his father's study. In fact, the entire hallway was off-limits to Caellum and his siblings. They would make up stories of what their father did in here. They would even pretend his unkindness was a pretence to save the realm from monsters—anything to justify the pain they endured. What would his siblings say now if they knew how close that was to the truth?

Darkness shrouded the room, with the heavy green drapes hiding the sunlight from outside. Caellum had spent the entire morning with the lords prior to venturing up to the study, though it had felt like forever. The lords all approved the rulers' plans, all except Lord Ryon, of course, who asked question after question. His presence alone made the day feel like a drag. But the day was still young as sunlight slivered from below the curtains.

Caellum strode for the drapes and dragged them back, allowing sunlight to flood the room. He paused at the walled garden below. His father's study was on the highest floor of the castle. As a child, he had never considered what it overlooked. Ivy, creeping past both sides of the glass, cast shadows across the room as Caellum turned, taking it all in.

It differed little from the rest of the castle, but something, other than its décor, made it feel darker. A deep wood coated every inch of space: the floor, walls, and ceiling. As it was so high in the castle, it lacked the vaulted height the other floors had. As with most rooms in Antor castle, all the furniture was various shades of green, an array of forest, emerald, and sage. Caellum was grateful for Sadira's arrival in Garridon. At least the castle's common areas now had other colours to brighten the space. Leather-bound books filled one wall of bookcases, while his father's successful hunting trophies hung above the fireplace. Caellum grimaced at the dead deer watching him. On the opposite wall was Wren's desk: a large mahogany beast with a deep leather top—also green, of course. Caellum wondered if his ancestors on Ithyion had always stuck religiously to decorating their spaces in the realm's colours. He began clearing the stacks of glasses from the desk, some lifting with papers still stuck to the bottom. After clearing the desk, Caellum finally walked around to the table and pulled the chair out, taking a seat. *Journal. Where would my father hide a journal?* He paused as he lowered into the chair. Staring back at him were seven small gold-framed portraits of Caellum and his siblings. He rubbed the light stubble on his chin. Were they here for show? Yet nobody ever entered his father's study, so who would he display them for? Perhaps some part of him remained inside his corrupted mind. Caellum cleared his throat and looked away from his siblings.

"I'm looking for answers," he mumbled, as though they were truly there, alongside him. He did not know what answers he expected to find but thought only of the journal Sir Cain mentioned, begging to be found and read. There was a chance his grandfather's journal was discarded long ago, but perhaps he could find some useful information to use in the future—anything that might offer insight into the mind of Caligh's victims to prevent it from happening again.

A chaotic jumble of papers, ledgers of finances, and letters to the other Lords regarding trade deals were splayed on the desk. Caellum paused while rifling through a stack between his father and Lord Ryon, who appeared to question his father as much as he did Caellum. Once the papers were stacked on one side, he examined the remaining items on the desk. A pipe sat on a silver tray to his right, beside a small trinket box. Caellum flipped the clasp and opened it up to find three pins within, each no larger than the pad of his thumb.

Caellum turned over the first pin and ran his thumb over the head of a wolf. The second held a symbol he recognised, matching the one on the Wiccan book owned by Sadira's grandmother. He squinted at the third; it was a similar shape to the Wiccan symbol but its lines curved differently, and it was too faded to discern any other differences.

The three pins felt cool on his skin as he held them flat against his palm, trying to understand their symbolism. Perhaps they once belonged to lords—symbols for those who held settlements? Caellum placed them back in the box and kept it aside, intending to take the box with him when he left the study.

His father's feather quills were lined up neatly, though dried ink marred the tips of some. Other than the trinket box, there was nothing unusual about the items on the desk. Caellum turned his attention to the cupboard door on the right-hand side of the desk and opened it to find nothing but a dagger, a blanket, and blank parchment sheets. He gave up on the cupboard and the three drawers on his left. Below it was a cupboard full of more glasses and an empty decanter. Caellum did not need to sniff it to know its contents. The middle drawer was empty, while the top contained rolled parchments. No journal. Caellum pulled the string from one parchment, which cracked as he unrolled it. He was careful laying it out. He traced his finger over the inked names and lines, pausing at a soaring hawk etched at the top. Names branched off at different points, filling the entire width and length of the scroll. The early names were faded, but as Caellum scanned the long parchment, with the top falling over the side of the desk and pooling in ribbons on the floor, a familiar name appeared. Balfour. Caellum skipped to the end, where seven names were scrawled along the bottom: Aurelia, Dalton, Kieran, Halston, Caellum, Edlen, and Eve. All Balfours. A family tree. Caellum rolled the parchment back up to the top again, squinting at each name. He tried to make out the earlier calligraphy, far more faded than that of him and his siblings, but failed. Securing the string back around the parchment, he set it by the trinket box and decided to look at them later.

Caellum sighed and sat back in the chair, resting his elbows on the carved arms. He placed his fingers together in front of his mouth and stared at the room. The family tree was interesting, and the pins raised many questions: why did his father have them? What did they mean? He had not realised the extent of the Balfour family line, though it did not matter. Neither items were the journal he came for. A gentle knock sounded on the study door, and Caellum knew at once who it was.

"Come in," he called, smiling. Golden hair peeked from around the corner, followed by a face that lit up every room.

"Am I interrupting you?"

When Caellum shook his head, Sadira entered and closed the door. Caellum offered her his hand, drifting his eyes over the pale pink fabric falling over her curves, scattered with embroidered butterflies. When she leaned down to kiss him, he gripped her waist with one hand and clasped her neck with the other, holding her in place to kiss her back with fervour.

"Hello," she murmured. She pulled back with flushed cheeks, looking down at him. Caellum smiled, tucking a strand of her hair behind her ear.

"Hi," he breathed. Sadira surveyed the desk while Caellum's hand remained on her waist, pulling her closer.

"Have you had any luck?"

Caellum shook his head and gestured at the desk.

"A long family tree and these odd pins." Sadira reached for the open trinket box. "One bears the same symbol as your Wiccan book.

"So, it does." Sadira hummed, tracing the engraving. "Remember what the two Wiccans said in Albyn. My great grandfather, Lyra's father, worked closely with the Mordane royal family. Perhaps that is why this pin is here with the symbol. Maybe it used to be hers." Caellum smiled up at her, admiring her intelligence. It was a clever deduction, but why would his father keep them?

"What do you think about the other two?" he asked, and Sadira squinted at the faded symbol and the wolf.

"We could take them with us to Albyn and ask them again? Athena at the apothecary may also know." Caellum nodded in agreement and looked around the room again. "You checked everywhere?"

He nodded, prompting Sadira to look around the room herself. She paused at the still open drawers on the left-hand side of the desk and removed herself from Caellum's side to stoop before the drawer. She inclined her head to look underneath the middle drawer.

"What are you doing?" Caellum chuckled. Sadira grinned and smacked her fist against the underside of the drawer. Something popped inside.

"False bottom." She smiled, brushing the dust off her dress. She stood back up, lifting a piece of thin wood from the drawer. Caellum leant forward as Sadira grinned, retrieving two leather-bound notebooks with frayed strings.

"How did you know?" he laughed, taking the tanned book from her hands.

"Soren and I had one in our bedroom growing up. We hid sweets from the market in them to eat at midnight." Sadira's smile wavered, and she cleared her throat, placing the other journal down for Caellum. Mentioning Soren had him recalling Sir Cain's comments about her manic state before the battle. He wrestled with whether to tell Sadira, unsure if doing so would cause her further pain when she had asked not to speak of her sister. He squeezed her hand before she let go.

"Stay. You can read one of them. I would love your company." Caellum tugged her towards him, prompting Sadira to giggle as she fell onto his lap. Accepting a journal, she rested her head against his shoulder and opened it.

"This one is Jorah's," she said, tracing the name on the front page.

"I suppose this one may be my father's then," Caellum said, unravelling the tie. The name on the front page confirmed it. He wrapped one arm around Sadira to hold her in place as they both began reading.

If anyone is reading this, then I have either lost my mind or passed away. I've started this journal out of fear for the future and the impact it may have on my family.

Caellum looked up at Sadira, who was reading the words over his shoulder. Her fearful expression matched his. *Aurelia is but five years old, Dalton is four, Kieran three, and Halston one. If the Wiccan owner of the apothecary is right, Hestia carries my next son, Caellum. I hope I get to know you; I truly do. But if I do not, then please know I would have loved you.*

I hope whoever reads this also has my father's journal, for this is where my fear begins. I have told nobody of the horrors in his mind. He is possessed, and I believe I know the man behind it. His journal talks of a carefree man, who, for all my life, was a close ally of the Mordane royal family. One day, that all changed. Yet he did only one thing before his entries descended into madness. He visited the Historian in the Neutral City to ask about three pins found in his family heirlooms. When he returned, he was changed. I never intended to be king, but here I am on a throne of lies he has passed onto me. Only after finding this journal have I started questioning who made him take this throne—what changed him.

His entries become confused, chaotic, darkened. I fear such a fate may befall me when I return from the Neutral City. I intend to document my mind for as long as I can on these pages. If I change, if I become anything like my father did, please tell my wife and children I am sorry.

Chapter Fourteen
Larelle

"Do you think the acolyte could have answers about Zarya?" Olden's question stirred Larelle from her thoughts as she stared out the carriage window at the final glimpses of the glistening ocean before the passing buildings hid it from view. Larelle wished to ride from the castle into the capital; Mera, the City of Statues, but the lords had insisted on a carriage. After a long day travelling back from Keres, she was expected to attend a meeting with the lords and the representatives of the settlements she had put in place. Larelle had been prepared to face question after question, doubt after doubt, but they were unusually quiet. While they were far from apologetic for their past opinions and treatment, there appeared to be an unspoken agreement between them that she was fit to be queen, especially since she and the other rulers prevented Caligh's darkness from overrunning Novisia. She had no doubt her representatives had aided in her absence to sway the lords. Still, they had been insistent on keeping up appearances as she journeyed to find answers on other lands, none of the Lords had any ideas as to what lands Osiris referred to.

"Vivian? Zarya seemed uncomfortable around her during our last visit, so I'm unsure if she would wish to speak with her," Larelle murmured, her eyes now fixed on the people stopping in the streets upon spotting the royal carriage arrive in the City of Statues. Their eyes flitted between Larelle's carriage and the one behind, with Zarya and Lillian inside. Her daughter had insisted on riding with Lillian to continue reading her book. Despite their extended visit to Keres, Larelle had not missed home, not when she had all the people she needed by her side wherever she went.

"Any information on the past prophecies or the Wiccan could be of some help," Olden said. Larelle waved through the window before tearing her eyes away to meet Olden's. Would it be helpful? Given both the Wiccan and prophecies related to Garridon's citizens, not Nerida's.

"Her eyes still glowed blue, like those with Nerida's power. But she appears to have some sort of foresight that lies within the Wiccan's ability."

"Neither my family line nor Riyas's mother's has any known Wiccans. I wish I could be of more help," Olden sighed, resting his head back against the velvet seat, his eyelids drooping.

"I know my family line. Riyas had the same eyes as Zarya, and the same power as mine. It's odd that Wiccan lineage exists so far back in your family's history that you're unaware of it." Larelle frowned at the suddenness of Zarya's awakened power. Many had always commented on her odd awareness and intuition, so perhaps it had now manifested fully. "It makes little sense. I do not like not knowing." The carriage grew bumpier over the stone paths as Olden leaned over to pat Larelle's hand. "And who does he think he is?" Larelle raised her voice. "Who does Osiris think he is to invade my daughter's mind?" She picked at the skin around her nails, trying to suppress her anger.

"He was sending a message he knew you would need."

Larelle gave a weary sigh. "I'm sorry to trouble you with my thoughts, Olden. You shouldn't have to listen to my frustrations." She smiled at the man she viewed as a father a soft smile which he returned.

"You know I will always listen. I may not always have a suggestion, but I will listen. Larelle, you always know what is right. Zarya's intuition, her strength, her intelligence..." Olden tapped Larelle's chest, beside her heart. "That all comes from you."

"Not from Riyas?" Larelle asked, and Olden scoffed.

"Gods no! The fool was far too carefree and aloof. You grounded him." Olden's smile slowly faded with the pain of a father who grieved his son every day. "I'm not quite awake enough to join you. If you don't mind, I may ask the carriage to return me to the castle. It's far too early for me after the journeys and events from the past few days." Larelle frowned at Olden's wince as he shifted in his seat, but she smiled when he looked at her and squeezed his hand.

"Of course."

***

Under the late morning sun, the crowds were a chorus of celebration as they filled the central square of the City of Statues. Their queen stepped from the carriage, aided by Lord Alvan's hand, who met her by the door. His cheeks were flushed from riding horseback alongside the guards. Larelle lifted her head high, where the twisted crown of waves sat atop her head and aided her in self belief as she refrained from widening her eyes at the many people awaiting her arrival. The lords had mentioned alerting the people to keep a façade of stability; she had not expected so many to be present.

Larelle did not scan the crowd for long. She sought the second royal carriage and found Zarya stood close to Lillian's side. Her curls twisted back within her tiara, revealing her face to the crowd. While she gripped Lillian's skirts with one hand, the other waved regally at the cheering crowd. Slowly, Zarya smiled, matching the grins of the people. Larelle paused to admire her daughter—the princess who had never expected such a life was adjusting quickly, despite the weighted sight she had been gifted and the dark truths it shared. But no darkness lingered in Zarya's eyes as she finally saw her mother and ran towards her. Seeming to remember herself before the people, the little girl slowed to a more regal walk until Larelle reached for her hand, angling them towards the clear pathway to the church. Royal guards held back the crowds, allowing the royal procession to approach. Stone statues, their hands cupped in welcome, greeted them.

"Mumma, there are so many people," Zarya said, waving at those lining the path. Leading the way, Larelle continued smiling and inclined her head in acknowledgement.

"They're showing their appreciation for their new princess," Larelle said. Warmth bloomed in her heart at the genuine kindness and excitement shared by the people, beholding their princess, the future queen. How different their reactions were to the whispers and silent judgement she had endured. Zarya stopped waving and moved closer to Larelle, suddenly stiff. She followed Zarya's eyeline to the end of the path, where below the stone hands stood Vivian, the acolyte they had met on their previous visit when searching for ways to contact the gods. Larelle recalled Zarya's sudden shyness the last time the acolyte had spoken with her, which was an unusual response from her daughter. Larelle squeezed Zarya's hand.

Vivian appeared unchanged since their last visit—immaculate. Not a single golden hair fell was out of place from its tight updo, which was decorated with a simple, freshly polished metal diadem resting on her forehead. The silk blue sleeves on her robe fell over her hands as she bent to lift the hem, curtseying to the queen and princess.

"Your Majesty. It is an honour to welcome you to the church again." Vivian's smile appeared genuine as she gestured towards the archway. Larelle returned it before entering.

"Thank you, sister Vivian. I am most appreciative of your kind welcome, especially given our sudden requests to visit," said Larelle. She studied the church walls, unable to ignore the beauty painted upon the bricks. The pastel murals were as beautiful and intriguing as she remembered. Sunlight shone through the glass dome, highlighting the artwork, and a shimmer captured Larelle's attention as she looked towards a depiction of a lake with two lovers on its shore. The sparkle in the water was what entranced her as she glimpsed a glittering blue tail dive within, causing a ripple effect. Larelle stepped forward to inspect it further, but Vivian's voice pulled her away.

"Do you wish to visit the archived area again?" she asked, and Larelle nodded.

"It may take us most of the day. What we are looking for is rather specific. We will likely have to filter through many books and parchments." Vivian's face appeared to stiffen before her smile returned.

"What specifically are you looking for?" she asked, strolling the dark pews towards the altar, where Larelle knew a small wooden door awaited, leading to a spiral staircase.

"Preferably maps, or any texts that mention other kingdoms or lands." Larelle was cautious to offer more detail. Vivian cleared her throat.

"And will the princess be helping with your research? If you like, I can keep her occupied. I am more than happy to." Vivian smiled down at Zarya, who tightened her grip on Larelle's hand.

"She will likely want to help us, but I will let you know if she tires," Larelle replied, sensing Zarya's discomfort. Vivian responded with a simple and polite incline of her head before opening the door. The group began the climb while Larelle's guards kept watch at the base of the stairs.

The room was as Larelle remembered, with its pale sandstone walls lit by sconces. To her right, heavy drapes shielded the old books and artefacts from the light.

"I have prepared a space for you here. The shelves in that room at the back are the oldest. The priest usually has them under lock and key, but he's taken ill, so I thought that would be a good place to start. I have not read the tomes in there myself." Vivian gestured to the large circular wooden table, where a lantern sat propped in the centre. A door, slightly ajar, was located behind it. Larelle was sceptical of the priest's illness, especially following his refusal to meet her on their last visit, disapproving of her family's inconsistent religious practice. "I will be at my desk here." Vivian moved towards the smaller table near the bookshelves.

"Are you working on much today?" Alvan asked politely, guiding Zarya to a chair at the table. Lillian took the spot beside her.

"Plenty," Vivian said. She still stood beside her desk, seeming to wait until the princess was seated and the queen had begun rifling among the shelves. "I am tasked with copying every text we have onto new parchment to be bound. Some books and parchments are so old the text is fading. Copying each will allow us to always have an accurate record of our history should the originals wear beyond use."

"I hope today's work is interesting for you," Larelle said, glancing at the names on the parchment tucked between the metal ends of the bookcases as a signal of what could be found within its depths. *Political Allegiances, Purifying Practices, Historical Lineages.*

"Very interesting, your Majesty. I do not know if it is a prophecy, a depiction of someone's life, or a completely fabricated story for reader enjoyment. However, it is rather intriguing." Zarya's eyes lit up at the mention of a story, which did not go unnoticed by the acolyte. "Perhaps if you tire of helping your mother, you could help me, princess?" Zarya offered a polite smile but glanced away quickly and leaned towards Lillian. Larelle thanked her before turning towards the unlocked door at the back wall to share a frown with Alvan. The princess was rarely shy. An uncomfortable weight rested on Larelle's chest as she stepped from the stone floor to one coated in dust. Her footprints left a trail as she pushed further in. Only a single flame on the wall lit the space. The furthest shelves appeared to hide secrets upon secrets in its depths. Only four bookcases were visible—two in front and two behind—though she was uncertain how far back the cases stretched. A shiver ran up her spine. For the first time since she was a child, Larelle feared what might lie in the dark.

The two bookcases looked like they could topple over at any minute. The lower shelves overflowed with parchments while books lined the top three, with ten on each shelf. Larelle peered around the edge of the bookcase, squinting into the darkness.

"Would—"

Larelle squeaked as a hand seized her elbow. She whirled around to face Alvan, who recoiled at Larelle's hair hitting his face. Before she could fall backward into the precariously balanced shelving, he snaked his arm around her waist to keep her upright.

"Would you like some help?" He smiled, searching her face. She blushed. Alvan removed his arm, but Larelle noted how it lingered on her lower back for a moment. "I found a book on creatures for Zarya. Lillian is helping her to read, so I'm all yours," Alvan said, scanning the worn leather books before them. Larelle glanced back through the doorway to watch her daughter, but she spoke animatedly with Lillian now, smiling.

"I can't quite reach the top shelves but these two cases appear to be about the gods, although they're written in a language I don't recognise," Larelle said. Alvan carefully pulled the books from the shelves. Garridon: *Lyve ed Daifu.*

"I'll stack those in a different language here. They might have helpful illustrations," he said, placing the books on a worn stool in the corner, the only other furniture in the room. "Have you checked the rolled parchments?" Larelle shook her head, glancing back into the darkness.

"Something tells me we may find what we need back there," she said.

"Hidden away," said Alvan, pulling the lantern from the wall. Larelle hummed her agreement and glanced around the door again to check on Zarya, whilst Alvan pulled the lantern from the wall. Her daughter was hunched over with a smile, pointing at illustrations on the pages while Lillian pointed at the words, trying to encourage the princess to read. Larelle's eyes drifted over Zarya's head to where Vivian sat. The acolyte glanced between her work and the princess, furrowing her brow. Larelle straightened. Vivian seemed interested in Zarya, but why? Could she sense something about her power?

"Shall we?" Alvan asked. Larelle turned back to him, deciding her questions for Vivian could wait. The glow of the lantern illuminated Alvan's face as he offered his hand. Their fingers easily interlocked, and she relished the blanket of warmth and security only he could provide. She led them around the two bookcases and into the darkness, where two more cases stood behind. Their shelves were bare, filled only with dust and cobwebs. Behind it, the room stretched further until she realised it was no room at all, but a widened hallway. Alvan lifted the lantern higher, but it made little difference. They could not see the end.

"There may be nothing down here," Alvan whispered.

"Then why keep it under lock and key? Even the acolyte has not been here," Larelle whispered, afraid of what might hear them in the darkness. Only the quiet footfalls of the queen and her lord echoed down the stone hallway. Alvan lifted the lantern higher at points, scanning the walls.

After nearly thirty minutes of walking, Larelle had no bearing of what direction they were headed, or where in the city they may end up; the path continued declining, suggesting they had exited the height of the church archives. Eventually, the lantern in Alvan's hands illuminated more bookcases, urging Larelle onward. She released Alvan's hand. Bookcases lined either side of the hallway, guiding whoever may look further into the darkness. They were similar to the cases in the earlier room, except they held far more books. Larelle blew the dust from the spines and reached to run her thumb over the title. Her breath caught. *Thassena.*

"Arik said this name when he took me to the cave," Larelle said, her eyes widening. Alvan hurried behind her to the next case on the opposite wall and cleared another spine with his hand, coating his fingers with dust.

"Eresydon," Alvan said, turning to her.

"Asynthos. These must be other lands. It explains why Osiris and Arik knew of them."

"Do you think they hail from one of these?" Alvan asked. Larelle moved to the next case and brushed her hand over a row of crimson leather books. Before she could brush away the dust to read its title, a crash sounded in the darkness. Alvan grabbed her hand, and the pair froze, listening. Another crash echoed down the hallway and ricocheted off the walls.

"What do you wish to do?" Alvan asked, his voice barely a whisper. Larelle glanced at the shelves, waiting for another sound. The crash had stopped, but that did not mean that something—or someone—was not hidden down the hallway, locked away from all eyes. Worry gnawed at her mind, but Larelle knew she would be doing herself and her fellow rulers a disservice by not exploring anything that might aid their plight.

"Into the darkness we go," Larelle murmured, gripping Alvan's hand.

"Together."

Chapter Fifteen
Elisara

*S*allos. *Elisara replayed the name in her mind and thought it unusual—almost as unusual as Caligh. She narrowed her eyes and suspicion rose again. What if he knew Caligh from before he was killed by the Sword of Souls?*

"What is it you want from me, Sallos?" Elisara asked. The man lifted his foot and rested it on his thigh, watching her intently with clasped hands.

"To serve you." His voice was firm and certain, his eyes unwavering as he watched Vala's queen.

"Why?"

"It is my duty," he responded as though it were obvious. Elisara frowned, sensing this man could be cryptic with his phrasing.

"We have known each other for how long? Perhaps three days? Why do you feel a sense of duty towards me?" Sallos tilted his head to watch Elisara, as if contemplating how much to reveal. "Secrets are not the best way to demonstrate your allegiance."

Sallos smiled. "Where I come from, your power is worshipped. It is a symbol of royal blood."

Elisara waved her hand. The comment meant nothing to her.

"I only have this power because Sitara shoved it inside of me when I was too young to refuse."

"It is not just the power. There was once a prophecy-"

"Enough." Elisara turned her head to the tapestry hiding where she had first read the prophecy. "I am tired of prophecies; I am tired of being told I am destined to fix everything for myself and kingdoms I have not set foot on. I am tired of gods demanding things of me-"

"You misunderstand me, your Majesty. I want nothing from you." Elisara huffed, still staring at the tapestry and refusing to meet his gaze. "I was simply stating there was once a prophecy that predicted a power such as yours would end wars and create lands. That prophecy has already been fulfilled, it is the land I once called home. Seeing your power is a reminder to my people of our creation, the beginning of our lineage. That is why it is worshipped." Elisara hesitated but finally looked at him again. She had only heard of Ithyion, though understood Caligh likely hailed from somewhere else, the place where he spent his time creating his dark creatures. The thought of other lands, where others lived with powers like hers, made her question why no one else on Novisia had the same power, or why nobody knew of these other lands or what they provided.

"What was your home like?" Elisara asked. She was intrigued by the thought of fleeing to another land to live in solitude with her heartache.

"It was beautiful once, but I have not seen it in centuries to attest to the fact that is still true." Sallos's smile faltered.

"Would you like to see it again?" Elisara spoke in a higher pitch, her tone hopeful. "You could take me there."

Sallos chuckled. "I would be revered for bringing someone of your station to my lands. Sadly, I do not know who controls it now, but I would not risk your life."

"I would," Elisara mumbled.

"You care so little for your life?" Sallos asked. The pain in her chest festered, a reminder of the broken shards inside. The very thing keeping her alive was already shattered, so what did it matter if it crumbled completely? If she simply ceased to exist?

"What do I have left to live for? The one person who I wished to live my life with is gone. Taken." Elisara slid her dagger back into her boot before bringing her legs up to her chest.

"I felt like that once," Sallos said. "And then I discovered there was an entire world to explore, to experience, to live." An entire world. More than just the four realms that formed the kingdom she called *home. She wondered how different these other lands could be; could she find one like Vala? Or Keres to remind her of Kazaar? Elisara frowned. Why had no one from these lands ever stumbled onto Novisia? What if Sallos had been trapped in the sword for so long that Caligh had already conquered these other lands before Ithyion even existed?*

"You said you would not risk my life," Elisara said.

"Not just yet." Sallos trailed off. "There is more you must learn first. Sitara would–"

"What did you just say?" The flames blazed in the fireplace, contrasting the chill in the room. Sallos glanced down as lightning skittered across the floor. "So, you do want something from me. Did she send you here?" Sallos sighed.

"She did not send me, but she is worshipped in many places in different forms. I know of her plight and what she requires. If you would just consider–"

"Get out," Elisara whispered, reaching for her dagger.

"Your Majesty—

"GET OUT!" Elisara screamed. Shadows lifted from their place of rest into spears, forming a circle around her, poised ready to strike. Sallos merely looked at them.

"I could help you learn to control and retract them as and when you wish."

"I most definitely have need of them now," Elisara hissed. "I said, get out. If you truly pledge your allegiance to me, and that was not another one of your lies, you will do as I command." Sallos assessed her for a moment longer, before bowing his head and exiting the room. Elisara willed her shadows to guard the doorway as she collapsed back onto the bed. Knowing she was already asleep, given her conversation with Sallos, felt odd, but she closed her eyes regardless and hoped to drift into nothingness again.

***

The towering trees blocked the light where Aleya crouched behind the large rock she used for defence. Pushing her red hair from her face, she glanced between the cracks, assessing if they had truly won the war. Bodies littered the castle steps and rubble crushed most of the fallen. Her eyes trailed the walls up into the treetops, where the moss-covered castle was hidden from view. Others could still be trapped in the upper levels.

"Are you calling it?" a voice whispered. She turned to meet the eye of her general, Havia.

"It seemed too easy," Aleya replied. "The castle has been under siege for three weeks, and then suddenly today the soldiers are more spread out, and the pathway to the castle is clearer." Aleya glanced through the crack again, assessing the bodies for movement. She flicked her finger forward, directing a vine to snake across the floor. She held her breath, watching and waiting to see if the sudden movement prompted any surviving soldiers to charge. Her vines reached the castle doors with ease and looped through the heavy handles. Aleya tugged.

"I want my home back as much as you do, but something feels off. I have not seen him, dead or alive."

"The man's a coward and probably fled," Havia scoffed. The image of his valiant actions in past wars came to Aleya's mind.

"He wasn't always," she murmured.

"I'll call it then. I want to get home to Athena." Havia's blood-smeared face cracked into a smile as she ran forward with her sword raised.

"Havia Balfour, get back here!" Aleya hissed.

"Are you commanding it? If that is a command then you are declaring yourself queen again, which means we have in fact WON!" Havia shouted the final word, and cheers echoed through the trees, where Aleya knew the rest of her soldiers lay in wait. Her vines sensed something by the door.

"Wait!" Aleya called. "Havia!" Aleya screamed as a darker vine, not belonging to her, whipped from the door and wrapped around

Havia's neck, tugging her back into the arms of the man Aleya had searched for.

"Come out, Aleya." His voice was just as she remembered it, his accent rough and sending tingles up her spine. Rising from behind the rock, Aleya lifted her arms in the air as she dropped her sword.

"Let her go, Evander. We both know it's me you want."

"Of course it is. Why would I not want my wife?" Evander's voice held no hatred as he stepped from the darkened doorway into the streaming light through the treetops. Aleya's heart pounded as she looked upon him. His hair was the same golden blonde, the top half braided back to reveal hundreds of different shades. He had shaved off his beard, revealing a strong jaw beneath which made his lips more prominent. Still, a golden crown sat upon his head, complementing the glow of his green eyes.

"I haven't been your wife for six years," Aleya said, stepping carefully towards the entryway and over the bodies that had fought for her. She had lost enough soldiers to understand it was a part of life, a part of war; regardless, she sent a silent prayer for them.

"Just because you were not here does not mean you weren't my wife," Evander replied.

"I was not here because of the decisions you made for our lands," Aleya spat. He had the audacity to wince, to appear hurt. Growls sounded behind the trees and Aleya took pleasure in the way Evander's eyes widened.

"They sided with your cause?"

"Of course they did," Aleya responded, whistling low to the wolves prowling the castle perimeter. Evander backed away as Aleya strolled up the stone steps towards him.

"Surrender, Evander. I will not make your life hard." Aleya's voice was soft, exactly how he liked it. Aleya locked eyes with Havia, whose hands clutched the vines around her throat. She flicked her gaze pointedly at Havia's waist, where a poisoned dagger was tucked into her belt. Havia's eyes widened as she mouthed 'are you sure?' Aleya gave the slightest nod before distracting Evander again. "You *can keep rooms in the castle under heavy guard. I will allow you access to the twins, provided I am present." Evander's eyes softened at the mention of the twins. Aleya swallowed the lump in her throat at the lie as Havia pretended to struggle, loosening one hand from the vines to reach for the dagger's hilt.*

"Do they miss me?" Evander asked, his voice cracking. Aleya swallowed, trying to keep her voice level as she spoke the truth, all the while knowing what was to come.

"Of course they miss you. You are their father. Boys need their father," Aleya whispered, just as Havia pulled the dagger free and stabbed Evander's thigh. Before he reacted, Havia spun, still trapped in vines; she launched the dagger into his chest, pushing him against the stone wall. The vines withdrew as the glow of his eyes faded. Havia embedded her dagger further into his chest before backing away, clearing the path for her queen.

Aleya's heart broke at the tears pooling in her husband's eyes and spilling over the wrinkles that had deepened since she last saw him. Evander's lip quivered. She knelt before him and cupped his cheek. The wedding ring, still on her finger, glinted in the sun, the symbol on it matching the pin on her husband's jacket. Evander reached up to Aleya's red hair, his favourite feature, and smiled.

"I still love you," he whispered. Those were his last words before his eyes went vacant, and his head lulled back.

Elisara jolted up in bed, her breathing erratic. Her heavy eyes kept fluttering open and shut. As if experiencing Aleya's pain first hand, Elisara touched her chest. She lost focus as she looked down at her arm, where scarred vines wrapped around her forearms. Was she still dreaming? The scars had not been there before she slept. The notion of killing Kazaar by stabbing a dagger in his chest was unfathomable, even if he had wronged her as it appeared Evander had Aleya. The strength and sacrifice it would take was daunting. The room blurred again, and Elisara could make out two forms of Sallos approaching from the hallway. She wondered if something had happened to Aleya after she killed her husband; perhaps she was through the hallway, too, trapped in the Sword of Souls.

"The memories will be vivid for a while," Sallos said, taking a seat on the chair beside the desk again. "Try to remember as much as possible." His voice faded as Elisara's head hit the pillow.

Chapter Sixteen
Nyzaia

"This isn't great," Jabir mumbled.

"It could be better," Rafik chimed.

"It could be worse," added Issam. The men and Nyzaia all turned to look at him.

"How could it be worse?" Farid asked, and Issam shrugged.

"We could be the ones hanging from a wall." Nyzaia sighed from where she leant against the red stone of the canyons, a corner away from the den's entrance.

"He has a point," Jabir said. Farid glanced sideways at him with narrowed eyes. "What? He does!"

Nyzaia rubbed her forehead with her hand before trailing it over her eyes, fighting the exhaustion setting in. She had gone straight from interrogating Soren to informing the lords of the rulers' plans, though it had not taken long. Lord Israar had not even shown. She had then checked in on the soldiers training the new recruits after losing so many in battle. Nyzaia was surviving on barely three hours of sleep after Jabir woke her with an urgent message from Issam and Rafik.

"When exactly were the last two sacrifices?" Nyzaia removed her hand and leaned back to focus on the sunset, her mind whirring through plans.

"They found the woman from the Blades the morning you returned to the palace after battle," Issam informed her.

"The man from the Torturers was found this morning," added Rafik. Farid's frustration rushed through Nyzaia, matching her own. Both sacrifices, the remaining two pillars of the Red Stones, occurred after Caligh fled Novisia, which meant Nyzaia's original plan of pinning the murders on him to give her more time, was officially blown.

"Do they have any suspects?" Nyzaia asked, pushing off the wall and rounding the corner. She headed straight for the hidden crack in the wall marking the entrance to her old kingdom.

"Some still suspect it is a punishment from you," Issam sighed.

"Idiots." Nyzaia rolled her eyes at the ridiculous suggestion. She had devoted years of her life to the Red Stones. Why would she punish them, even if they had changed their way of things? It was not her place anymore, not as the Queen of Keres. But, although she should be distancing from them as queen, the old position called to her still—taunting. She had failed to protect the Red Stones.

"Honestly, none of the heads have been bothered about finding the culprit. They're more focused on passing blame and prioritising themselves," Rafik sighed.

"Nothing's changed then." Nyzaia mumbled, sliding into the narrow gap in the stone. "I'm fine, Farid," she called, after he silently cursed her for entering first.

"Do you have a plan?" he yelled from behind, his tone short.

"My plan is to examine the recent scene first before the heads pester me." Her plan was cut short as she stepped into the flame-lit cavern, greeted by the very six people she intended to avoid. They stood in a line with their arms crossed, watching.

"Bow, or I'll slit your legs and force you to kneel instead," Jabir called, entering behind Nyzaia with a grin. The slim, short man at the far-right end of the line smirked and shifted his weight between his feet. He combed a hand through his long dark hair.

"Come now, Jabir. You know I'm always willing to get on my knees for you," he said. Jabir laughed at the Head of the Spies, though a spike of anger struck Nyzaia. She glanced at Farid.

"Flattered as I am, Ozan, I live in a palace now. I desire far more prestigious men." Although Jabir faced Nyzaia, it did not go unnoticed that his eyes travelled elsewhere. He glanced over her shoulder to where she sensed Farid's presence.

"I see the palace hasn't altered your wit, Jabir." A sensual voice danced towards them. Emiri, Head of the Courtesans, sauntered across the sandy floor, swaying her hips with her usual exaggerated motion; the bangles on her wrists clinked in time with each step. The woman flicked her pin straight, black locks over one shoulder, barely glancing at Nyzaia while approaching Farid. Nyzaia rolled her eyes. "And who..." She trailed a hand up his arm. "Are you?"

Farid cleared his throat and stepped closer to his queen.

"Hands off, Emiri," Jabir snapped, losing all traces of his previous humour. Nyzaia raised her eyebrows, matching the expressions of those in the cavern. Farid cleared his throat and shifted on the sand. As much as she loved teasing Jabir, Farid's awkwardness prompted her to intervene before anyone else could jest or put her captain on the spot.

"What did I do to earn such a... *gracious* welcome?" Nyzaia asked, glancing at the heads. Their faces were far from gracious. The bulky man in the middle twitched, his hand inching towards one of the many daggers strapped to his thighs. Sweat dripped off his bare chest signalling he had been in the middle of training. Nyzaia smirked at his narrowed eyes. "Perhaps you could answer, Darous?"

Instead of replying, the man grasped the handle of his dagger, while Farid grabbed the pommel of his own blade. Darous's eyes switched to the captain with a scoff. Farid would win easily; he was smarter than Darous and quicker. But no matter how entertaining that fight would be, it would get them nowhere.

"Is it not deemed respectable for the heads to welcome their *queen*?" Majida, Head of the Alchemists, asked, dragging out her vowels, amusing the man beside her. Nyzaia looked at Zahir. The Head of the Dealers was evidently in a drug-filled high, his dilated pupils a clear giveaway. Majida elbowed his side in caution, but he merely giggled and flicked her earring, one of the many piercings on her body.

"Let's cut the pretences, shall we?" Nyzaia glared at Emiri and raised her chin to gesture the courtesan back into place. For the final time, Emiri roamed her eyes over Farid before sauntering back to the rest of the committee. He shivered before resuming his usual rigid stature. "Seeing as you initially wanted to blame me for these sacrifices, let's not pretend you have any respect for my position as Queen of Keres. Hell, you barely respected me when I was Queen of the Red Stones; you only listened because our laws dictated it." Darous ground his jaw. The reminder would rile him the most. In the battle for the position of power, he had tried to intervene to kill Arjan first, which would have won him the position Nyzaia had coveted.

"It makes sense." Emiri smirked. "Scare us into submission, so we abide by anything you say, even as Queen of Keres."

Nyzaia scoffed. "Please, when has anything ever scared any of you?"

"She's not wrong," Zahir laughed. Nyzaia smelled the smoke drifting off him.

"I wouldn't be surprised if one of you was behind this, simply so you could pin it on me and solve the mystery yourself. It would be a fascinating statement that would promote one of you as the only ruler after putting an end to all these murders." Nyzaia raised her hand, examining her nails and feigning disinterest while flames danced on her fingertips. The light reflected in her eyes as she peered back at them all. "Who would be the greediest, the hungriest to take control? Who would sacrifice their own to come out on top?" Nyzaia's words trickled into the heads' ears as they exchanged worried glances. Finally, the only head yet to speak up raised her voice.

"None of us did it," said Najat, the Head of the Torturers. Her voice was still as quiet and lethal as Nyzaia remembered. She had scraped back her tightly curled hair and assessed Nyzaia with kohl-lined eyes. The woman wore the same fighting leathers as Tajana, and Nyzaia clenched her jaw to stop the fizzing emotions inside of her. Fresh blood splattered the material.

"And what makes you so confident?" Nyzaia asked, allowing her flames to fade as she stepped towards Najat. The woman glanced at the other heads.

"There is a commonality between them all, something we would not kill for." Her words prompted Emiri and Majida to share a look. They did not want Najat sharing this information.

"And why would you not kill them for this commonality?" Nyzaia stood toe-to-toe with the torturer, peering down at her, while trying to piece the puzzle together. Although she wanted to be one step ahead, she could not fathom why someone was sacrificing people.

"Because they would have been more valuable alive," Najat whispered the words as though something inside her warned she could never take them back.

"You have certainly piqued my interest," Nyzaia murmured. A single drop of gold marked Najat's dark eyes, mesmerising everyone she encountered. Najat straightened under the queen's scrutiny.

"I traced the history of them all. They were all bastards of lords or ladies across the kingdom, or at least their lineage." Nyzaia narrowed her eyes. "Every single one of them had lineage linking back to families with a long history dating back to Ithyion."

"Did they have powers?"

Najat looked at the other heads, who met her stare with narrowed eyes.

"Yes." Najat nodded. Nyzaia spun on her heel and clasped her hands behind her back. She strode towards the entrance of the Blades' quarters, glancing at Issam and Rafik as she did, who both gave a miniscule shake of their heads. They had not known such information. Nyzaia pointed one finger at the floor, signalling for Issam and Rafik to stay with the heads.

"Najat!" Nyzaia barked, pausing at the archway. "Lead the way."

***

Nyzaia had witnessed countless atrocities, much of it caused by her own blade, yet the carved open body pinned to the wall made even Nyzaia fight the urge to gag. The man was topless, and blood drenched his black leather trousers; his feet were bare, and three incisions marked the soles of each foot, still dripping blood onto the stone ground of one of the many torture chambers. Large iron nails, as thick as two fingers, pierced his palms spread wide from his sides, holding his body against the wall.

Symbols had been carved into his flesh, matching those three on the wall; the rest of his skin had been flayed off, with barely any remaining to contain the man's organs. What remained was an intricate pattern of whirls and shapes with various lines running through them, some straight or curved, and some with arrowed lines or dots up the length. Whoever had done this had taken their time, like creating art rather than inflicting pain.

The blood-etched symbols encircled him, and she checked each one, ensuring no difference existed between those on the wall and his body. Identical—all of them. Something was familiar about them, too, though she could not place what. She focused on his face again.

"His eyes?" asked Nyzaia.

"Gone," Najat murmured.

"Tongue and teeth?" Nyzaia assessed the man's face and the three slashes on his neck.

"Also gone." A part of Nyzaia was thankful she could avoid the terror in his dead eyes. Nyzaia stepped back to stand between Farid and Jabir. Farid still clutched the pommel of his sword, while Jabir crossed his arms, tilting his head at the display.

"Why sacrifice those with power and specifically members of the

Red Stones?" Jabir asked. "The army has a rank of those who can wield a flame." Nyzaia hummed, having thought the same.

"Most of those in the army are watered down, distant relatives of lords or royalty." Nyzaia looked at Najat. "Those sacrificed... were they all directly sired by a current lord or lady?"

Najat nodded. "Every single one came from current lords or their parents. Regardless, they would have all had direct claims as heirs if they had been born legitimately." Was someone eliminating threats to the throne—those who could claim her title if anything happened to her?

"I know this man, though," Jabir said, squinting at the remains of the victim's face. "He never showed any signs of power."

"Issam and Rafik didn't know either." Bitterness crept into Nyzaia's voice as she looked at the Head of the Torturers. Najat bowed her head.

"We did not want them to know yet. We wanted to investigate it ourselves. The Red Stones have always been separate to the crown." Nyzaia did not reprimand her, for she was right. Had this been a few years ago, Nyzaia would have never shared this information with her father. "As for their powers, they only started showing signs of them after you were crowned."

Nyzaia frowned, recalling Osiris's warning. *There are people waking up, memories resurfacing.* What if this was similar? What if powers were awakening because of the heirs taking their thrones? What if these sacrifices were beginning because someone—somewhere in Keres—was remembering something that had once been hidden?

"Was there anything left behind?" Nyzaia asked. "Any indication of who might have done this?"

Najat shook her head. "Nothing, the symbols were the same on every body, except the forehead." She reached for a piece of paper on the desk beside her and passed it to Nyzaia. How was it possible for the murderer to have entered the Red Stones undetected? More than one person had to be involved—maybe, perhaps a couple to keep watch or cause distractions.

"The top symbol was found on the spy and dealer, the next on the courtesan and alchemist, and then the bottom on the blade and this torturer." Nyzaia scanned the symbols again. They reminded her of something. She tapped her foot and stared at them, begging her mind to reveal the familiarity. She stopped tapping.

"I've seen these before," she murmured. They were three of the four symbols inked on Kazaar's arm. She passed the paper to Farid, who looked between them and the symbol on the man's forehead. He tapped the paper.

"I've seen a similar symbol to the one on his forehead somewhere else," Farid said. "It's on some of the pages in Princess Sadira's wiccan book." Nyzaia stared at the symbol marked on the wall. Farid was right. When Sadira was struggling, they had all attempted reading the book to help decipher the imbuement. Nyzaia had seen it too, referenced in various places throughout the book. She glanced over at the paper in Farid's hand again. *If one is a mark relating to those in Garridon, could the other two—and the other one on Kazaar's arm—symbolise the other realms?* Theories whirred through Nyzaia's mind. Why were the Red Stones involved, unless it was to get Nyzaia's attention? Farid nodded, sensing her train of thought.

"If only three symbols have been used, you need to be on alert," Nyzaia commanded before spinning to the door. "There will be another two attacks using a fourth symbol."

"But there are no more pillars," Najat called. "How do we know who the targets will be?"

Nyzaia's hand paused on the doorknob before turning over her palm to stare at the symbol marking her and Farid, a symbol that had not yet been used. It was not identical to the mark on Kazaar's arm, which she assumed symbolised Keres, but it had plenty of similarities. The lines curled into a point, speckled with dots inside. However, the main difference was the absence of a curved single line striking through it in a curve. Ignoring Najat's question,

Nyzaia opened the door and strode into the dark hallway, with Farid and Jabir flanking her on either side.

"What is our next step?" Jabir asked. Nyzaia blinked and set the wall sconces alight. She clenched her fists, internally preparing for who she must speak to next.

"There's a certain prisoner who should know more about the symbol of her people."

Chapter Seventeen
Soren

Soren did not need to open her eyes to know where she was. She could taste it—feel it—the remnants of his darkness drifting towards her skin and enveloping her in a comforting embrace. If she opened her eyes, she would have to accept that Caligh, her Lord of Darkness, was not here. If she opened her eyes, she would be reminded of all she had done for him. The fabricated memories of her sister and grandmother, haunting her every night before sleep, forced her to question the past. Had her grandmother ever instructed Soren to kill Caellum? Or simply take the throne? Had taking the throne meant placing Sadira upon it?

Soren shook her head and scrunched her eyes harder. Perhaps if she kept them closed, her mind would return to the world around her. A chill rippled through Soren but did not settle like it usually did. In fact, the air seemed oddly normal, absent of any reminders of him. But what had it been before? Could she recall her dreams as vividly as she did now when Caligh called her here? Though questions bombarded her mind, Soren had gained a sense of clarity that had been absent in the waking world as of late.

She flinched when something wet grazed her hand, but it only took a second for her to recognise the comforting touch. Releasing a deep breath, she opened her eyes, glanced down at her hand, and smiled. A small sob escaped her lips. She collapsed onto her knees and buried her face in Seiko's deep grey fur, who whined, stopping the tears from falling. When she eventually pulled back, her green eyes met Seiko's heterochromatic gaze: blue and milky white. She stroked his head as he licked her cheek.

"I've missed you," Soren murmured. "Are the others okay? Is someone taking care of you?" Seiko brushed her arm with his paw, signalling to continue with the scratches behind his ear. She did not know what Nyzaia had done with her remaining wolves in the waking world and swallowed back the lump in her throat at the thought of Baelyn. She hoped to remember this when she awoke, so she could ask. It was only when her knees felt damp that Soren tore her focus from Seiko to look below her at the grass. Over Seiko's head were luscious green fields, coated in a layer of glistening morning dew. The towering oak tree she knew all too well stood not far in the distance. If she walked over, she wondered if the space that held the talisman remained, along with the bloodstains of her fallen family. For a moment, Soren felt the blood of her grandmother drench her hands as she slit her throat, and a chill ran up her spine.

The field had not been like this when she had last dreamt of it with Caligh. The grass was crisp, long since dead, and the tree branches were bare of leaves. Everything was overtaken by darkness. Soren hesitated. When she turned this time, no dead plants crunched beneath her feet; the only sound was Seiko's light panting as he neared her side under the sunlight. Soren did not know what to make of the sight before her or what it meant. The crumbled castle of her mind remained, with its half walls and collapsing bricks. One wall was completely missing, allowing her to see the small courtyard where she so often stood. Still, ivy clung to the walls and the spiderwebs lingered, but they seemed far less haunting as they glistened beneath the sun. Licks of shadow painted the walls, twisting around the ivy and bricks as if trying to find purchase, hoping to stay there for an eternity. The same shadows coated the floor. As a whole, the castle was as she remembered it: the same dark shadow, the same state of decay, but when she looked at the iron cell bars he was always intent on keeping her from, her mouth parted. Deep within the cell, flower-coated vines writhed along the floor and up the walls, reaching for the sunlight. The vibrant green vines moved slowly, as if afraid sudden movements would alert the shadows. Soren raised her eyebrows. She had never seen such colour here before. Inhaling the luscious, floral scent from the hundreds of delicate white flowers beginning to bloom, she savoured the moment of beauty in a place so haunted.

Soren's steps were slow as she inched towards the cell, desperate to see what Caligh had hidden from her for all this time. She had always assumed it was where he entered her mind; perhaps reaching it would offer her a way to find him on her own terms. Or perhaps that was where his true form hid when he appeared before her disguised.

Soren paused, glancing at the shadows in her periphery before continuing her approach. She waited a moment until the shadows twisted again before taking a final step into the blanket of flowers. Moving carefully, she reached for the bars, making sure not to crush the delicate white flowers beneath her feet. She recognised them. Something tugged in her mind. There was something familiar about them. The petals were like velvet as Soren grazed a finger over one of the flowering buds wrapping around the bars; they felt like an extension of herself. Soren's breathing hitched when they did not wilt at her touch. She could not recall the last time she had held a flower for so long. Soren thought back to the memory of Sadira stuck in the tree, still unsure if it was real. Was that one of the last times she had used her power to wield such life? For far too long, Soren's power had been dark vines and decay; she no longer remembered how it felt to wield something with such beauty.

A clink of chains sounded from behind the bar, making Soren jump. Seiko did not growl beside her, though, nor did his hackles raise. He simply sniffed the air. The sound of a chain dragging against the floor sent shivers up Soren's spine, but she remained rooted in place, peering into the darkness between the flower-clad bars. A gasp escaped her when a pair of bright green eyes glinted in the darkness before a small, pale face peered through the cell, reaching to stroke the flowers.

"Hello Soren," murmured the girl in a voice Soren knew all too well. "I've been waiting for you to find me." Soren stumbled at the girl's golden braids dangling through the bars, brightening the glow in her eyes. Her forehead was smooth, with no frown lines yet sinking in or scars marring her skin. "Is it odd looking at your younger self and wondering what went wrong?" The girl murmured. Her eyes glowed as they widened with surprise, assessing Soren, who shook her head.

"My mind is not right. Something is wrong with my mind," Soren mumbled to herself. "You're right. Something is wrong with it, but it is not me—*we* are not the problem." Soren's younger self squeezed her face further between the bars. "You were curious, weren't you? About why the Lord of Darkness was so adamant to keep you from these bars?" Soren could not meet her younger self's eyes as guilt crept over her skin. Though she could not place why, Soren had an inherent feeling this was her fault.

"What are you, exactly?" Soren finally asked, her voice wavering. The girl smiled: a face of pure innocence.

"I am you on the day he took us. I am your mind, your sanity, your true self." The girl's eyes watered, and she averted her gaze, staring at the floor. "I am you before you sacrificed yourself for..."

"For what?" Soren snapped. "For Caligh? Is that what you were going to say? Were you going to condemn me?" The girl did not look up at Soren's harsh tone, causing guilt to skate over her again.

"I've been here all along, Soren, but the longer he was here, the weaker I became, until I was simply a distant memory in the back of your mind, suffocated by his darkness and control."

"Caligh did not control me," Soren snapped, and her younger self tilted her head.

"Were your actions entirely your own? Everything you did was by your own volition?" she asked. Soren opened her mouth but closed it. She had always felt compelled to act, to do as he requested. She never had a reason to question the consequences when her actions felt so natural. "I would not have been hidden behind these bars if everything was your choice." Soren frowned, and her eyes clocked the remaining shadows. They changed direction, creeping towards the florals.

"Someone wake her up," a voice echoed throughout the castle, a voice Soren imagined she would be accustomed to soon, while her torture continued. The girl behind the bars giggled.

"I like her," she said.

"Who?"

The girl grinned; a joyfulness lit her eyes. "Nyzaia," she strung out her name, like it was the title of a poem.

"How do you know about the Queen of Keres?" Soren asked, keeping her tone low and cautious. The girl sighed.

"You are not understanding. I am always here, watching behind the bars while you act, led by the lord's commands. I see and hear everything; I spend my days wondering what could be if you were whole again." The girl reached a hand out through the bars, "If we were reunited." The girl squeaked, jumping back as shadows lashed out towards the bars. Soren watched the darkness twist around the slowly wilting flowers.

"Wait! Let her through!" Soren screamed, wishing to speak more with the girl, desperate to understand.

"Try harder." Nyzaia's voice echoed through Soren's dream-scape.

"You should trust her," murmured the girl, cradling her arm behind the bars. A dark wound bloomed across her wrist where the shadow caught her skin. "No one ever sees me," the girl sobbed. "But I think she would understand what I have been through."

Chapter Eighteen
Caellum

The Diary of Wren Balfour, Entry Two

I was right to be suspicious, and I expect my end is inevitable. While I still feel like myself, he is there, a presence in my mind. I find myself doing and saying things without realising. It has only been a day since I returned from the Neutral City. I entered the castle estate and shoved a servant when they stumbled into me—why would I do that? I try to resist, but the darkness coils tighter around my mind, twisting until I submit. I do not know how long I have until I become like my father: devoid of emotions, actions unexplained. Until I reach that state, I will continue to write. Perhaps one day one of my children will find this, and should the same fate befall whoever rules in my place, it may help them uncover ways to help.

It was him. The Historian. Except he wears a different face and bears a name he would not tell me. I approached him in the small office within the temple, hidden down the single staircase accessed through a door only I and the other rulers know about. It was clear I should not have been there; he was not expecting me. In the brief glimpse I caught of the room, I saw all manner of unusual artefacts: statues I did not recognise, iron contraptions, maps of places I had never heard of. I could take in no more before he pushed me from the room with a force a man of such an age should not have managed.

"I've been waiting for a moment to have you alone," he sneered in my ear, his voice far younger and sinister than I had ever heard it. "It is time you follow in your father's footsteps." The next thing I knew,

darkness overcame the hallway. Mysterious shadows slammed the temple door shut, and when I looked back at the Historian, he was changed. No longer frail, old, or wise. A man with a presence that ebbed around me, and a chill that threatened my end. His hands reached for my temples. I had no chance to challenge him and ask of the three pins or my father. I had no chance to beg him not to take my mind or hurt my children. For when his nails dug into my skin, shadows invaded me. I recall my eyes rolling back, and within my mind, a place that should only belong to me, his face appeared. I stood in a nursery; a mural forest painted on the wall beside an expertly engraved mahogany crib. I knew the room instantly. It was Caellum's. The Historian peered down at my most recent son with a s neer.

"My torment will end with this generation one day. My trusted servant sees things, and I will not invade this one's mind." The Historian reached into the crib and trailed a finger along my son's cheek. "I will simply have him as vengeance against your god for far more than you know." I stepped towards him, but Caellum vanished into smoke in my mind. I stared again at the old man's face; we were back in the temple. He simply commanded I leave, and I did without question. I walked from the temple and did not turn back to say all I wished to. I simply mounted my horse and returned to the realm that could be ended at my hand one day.

Caellum turned the page with a trembling hand and read through the next few weeks of entries. The sunlight shifted around the room. Still, Sadira leaned against his shoulder, a small comfort. Neither had moved since they had first sat down to read; he imagined Sir Cain would eventually begin searching for them when they missed dinner. The entries continued in a similar manner, depicting his days. Occasionally, he acted out of character and referenced the Historian—Caligh's presence in his mind. His actions worsened the more he slept and dreamed of him.

The Diary of Wren Balfour, Entry Twenty-Eight

The nursery no longer looks the same. Where a forest mural once lived is now a wall of shadows twisting together and creeping along the wooden floor. Ivy coats the windowpanes, and the room's light is fading more rapidly now, like my mind. I hit my son today. I hit Dalton. I hit my four-year-old son. He was running through the gardens after morning rainfall and fell into the puddle by my feet, splashing mud onto my trousers. While a part of me wished to pick him up to check for injuries, shadows crept into my mind and tugged at the muscles in my arm. So, instead of reaching for him, I struck his face. I heard Aurelia's cries from where she sat on the wall, watching. I hear them still. The tall, red-headed man—Cain, I think his name is—hurried Dalton away. I could not decipher the look in his eye. Did this man know me well once? I believe he is simply my commander, though I do not know.

A chill descended on the nursery in my mind, and the Historian appeared in his true form, with his straightened posture and darkened hair.

"You're doing well, Wren. Your mind is becoming so flexible and easier to manipulate. Slowly, the Balfour line will die until they are replaced with those I can mould."

"Is there a way to expel you from my mind?" I asked boldly, widening my eyes at my confidence. He simply chuckled.

"Only when I choose to release my hold. But Wren, that fate—the insanity that comes from being stripped of a presence in your mind after so long—might just be worse than death."

I don't recall what else was said. When I awoke, sweating in the bed I share with my wife, I reached for this diary to record as much as possible. I stayed up the entire night, walking through each of my children's rooms, tears rolling down my cheeks.

Caellum cleared his throat and closed the diary briefly. He glanced at Sadira, glimpsing the tears in her eyes. He cradled her face, and she sniffed. Caellum sensed from her reaction that Jorah's journal offered similar insights.

"He didn't want to do it, Caellum. Jorah and Errard were best friends, practically brothers. Your grandfather remembered all of it, even pushing the knife into my grandfather's stomach. He cried while he did yet felt no emotion. He did not want to; he did not want the throne, nor to take the life of a family he served and loved." Caellum wiped the tears from Sadira's cheeks as she closed the journal. "But a part of him stopped himself." Caellum furrowed his brow. "Lyra, my grandmother. She did not just escape, Caellum. Jorah let her go. He watched her flee to the stables, where she would then ride to Albyn and cross to Doltas. His mind tried to make him follow to kill her, too, but he fought back for just a moment, long enough to slam a door on his hand and break it. The pain jolted his mind and allowed him to refocus, allowing Lyra more time to escape." Frowning, Sadira placed the journal on the desk with trembling hands. Tears welled in her eyes. "Is this what happened to Soren?" Sadira murmured. Caellum recalled Sir Cain's thoughts and the similarities he had witnessed in Soren. The pieces were falling into place. "Was he controlling her mind all along? Slowly changing her until she passed the point of no return?"

The regret in Sadira's eyes stopped Caellum from revealing what he had learned, that stripping Caligh's presence from her mind was a fate worse than death, though he suspected Sir Cain's insight and Sadira's deductions were correct. "I cannot read anymore; I need to clear my head." Sadira reached for the trinket box containing the three pins. "I could take these to Athena at the apothecary to see if she knows anything?" Caellum nodded and kissed her gently before she climbed from his lap and headed for the door.

"Sadira!" he called. She paused in the doorway, dabbing at the tears on her cheeks. "We will try to find a way to help her." Sadira's regret for her sister's treatment remained unspoken between them, knowing she might have endured the same as Jorah and Wren. Even Caellum felt it, the guilt in the pit of his stomach. Soren had no choice. And yet, he still doubted her. She had wanted his throne and was willing to kill him for it. Whether it was her choice or not, she was still a risk while her mind was unstable. Sadira nodded and smiled before closing the door.

Caellum continued reading late into the day. The diary entries became far less frequent as his father began losing his own thoughts and recollections, until eventually, the account of his actions held no remorse at all. Years passed, with only one or two entries.

The Diary of Wren Balfour, Entry Ninety-Three

Why do people bother having children? They are insufferable. They get in your way and do not know how to behave before lords and visitors. They are all inadequate, unworthy of the Balfour name. I must express my doubt about them, so, one day, when my crown passes, someone stronger can take the throne, just as my father did to the Mordanes.

Why would I –

Perhaps I should kill them all and be done with it. No; he said at least one would need to survive. Which one? Their names come and go.

The Diary of Wren Balfour, Entry

I hate them. I hate them all. I—

The Diary of Wren Balfour

He said he does not need me anymore because the time has come. I do not know what he means.

The Diary of Wren Bal-

I see flashes of memories that I think are tricks of the brain. Flashes of me laughing and holding my children. I saw a boy laughing in his crib long ago. What madness is befalling me? I have not seen him; he has not visited my dreams. He does not need me.

The Diary of Wren -
There is a prophecy. I am to die. Vala's queen is looking for ways to prevent it and stop it from happening. They said my children would die and I must pick one to live. My head hurt through the entire meeting until suddenly it felt light, like I was someone else. I pushed back—I don't know why; I do not like my children when I think about it now. One image appeared. The night he told me my son would be killed. Caellum. I said his name; I do not know why. I don't remember much.

Diary -
Vala's queen has failed. We meet next month. We die.

Diary -
*Scribbles*

Caellum turned the diary's final pages covered with splattered ink, spreading across the parchment with his father's tears. He wiped his face with the back of his sleeve. Caellum recalled his father being coherent in the final days before the explosion. But these pages depicted the war in his mind, the brief moments of remembering before darkness flooded him once more. If Caellum had spent less time hiding from fear, would he have seen the signs? Would he have watched his father lose his mind and perhaps sought answers to help and do more? _He remembered my name._ Caellum's siblings' portraits stared back at him, and he knew then. They remained there because some small part of his father, a tiny crack in the shadows, loved his children through it all.

Caellum lifted one of his father's quills, straightened in the desk chair, and wrote a letter to the Queen of Keres. In the chair where two kings, decayed by darkness, had sat, the new king took their place in an attempt to make things right. A king who, perhaps, if his father saw him now, would be proud of.

Chapter Nineteen

Nyzaia

"Try harder." Nyzaia sighed, leaning against the damp cell wall, her leathers deterring any moisture from seeping in. "She's a bloody deep sleeper," Jabir murmured. He shook Soren again, who lay curled up in a ball on the threadbare blanket on the ground. Nyzaia analysed the fallen queen's face, searching for any muscle movement or sign she was faking slumber to avoid another torture session. The only movement was the rapid flutter of her eyelids, leaving Nyzaia to wonder what she dreamed about so intensely. Her face was calmer, the deep-set frown having fallen with sleep. Sleeping, she appeared incapable of all she had done.

With another hard shove, Jabir knocked Soren onto her back. Her head lolled to the side, thudding the back wall of the cell. Jabir stood with an exasperated sigh while Nyzaia strode forward and crouched. Soren was completely unrecognisable from the stubborn and furious queen who battled with words and swords. Her clothing was crisp from dried blood and sand, and her face smeared with the stains of battle. Underneath it all, she looked younger lying there. Nyzaia nudged her with the handle of her dagger, but Soren did not stir. The queen rolled her eyes.

"Very well, the most effective way it is then." She drew back her hand and struck Soren across the cheek. Farid inhaled sharply behind them as the sound echoed across the cell. Soren reacted slowly. Her eyes fluttered open until a bright green glow stared back at Nyzaia, a glow so bright she didn't think she had seen it before. Gradually, Soren peered around, seeming to remember where she was. She huffed.

"Do you torture people while they sleep now too?" she asked. The Keres queen did not answer.

"Sit up," Nyzaia commanded. Soren did not resist but was slow in pushing herself off the ground. She sat propped against the wall and rested her bony forearms on her knees, glaring at Nyzaia, Farid, and Jabir. She blinked rapidly until the glow of her usually deep green eyes faded. Nyzaia clenched her jaw at the green in Soren's gaze, a reminder of the only woman she had ever loved. She recalled the lightness in Tajana's eyes and how fear filled them when Caligh fled with her chains in hand. Soren had contributed to so much pain in Nyzaia's life. "Don't think about trying to use your power to escape. There are guards stationed at every possible exit, some of whom can wield minor flames."

Soren scoffed and tilted her head. "Have you ever seen me use my powers?" Nyzaia did not respond. "Exactly. My power is a curse. It takes from life and wilts Sadira's beautiful creations, leaving death in its wake. At best, I create dying vines barely strong enough to hold a person for a few seconds." Soren furrowed her brow, as if recalling a memory. "Besides, steel is a more enjoyable way to end a life." Soren tore her eyes from Nyzaia and her guards, focusing on the damp floor instead. Nyzaia raised an eyebrow at Soren's damnation of her power, as though she wished it was different.

"Was it always like that?" Nyzaia asked. The genuine question felt obscure as it passed Nyzaia's lips, tinged with sincere curiosity. She was grateful when Soren did not reply or acknowledge her words. Instead, Nyzaia added, "I need you to look at something" and withdrew a piece of paper from her pocket as she stepped forward. Soren's flinch made Nyzaia pause and her brows raise a fraction in surprise. Soren had never appeared afraid of Nyzaia—or anyone for that matter. Was Nyzaia's torture having such an impact? Or had something else altered Soren's personality?

"Perhaps give her some space," Farid murmured, but Nyzaia ignored him and crouched.

"When you were sat on that chair beneath my blade, I told you to watch me and see the fury in my eyes." Nyzaia's voice was deadly quiet as she donned the face of the Red Stones Queen. Soren vacantly stared at the stone floor as Nyzaia retrieved a dagger from her side and pressed it against the scar on her cheek, turning her head until their eyes met. "The same applies here." Soren held Nyzaia's stare, but when she spoke again, her tone was sickly-sweet.

"My deepest apologies, your *Majesty*. Please, I beg you. Tell me how I can be of service today."

Seeing the fight return to Soren's eyes, Nyzaia smirked and handed Soren the folded papers. The chains clinked around Soren's wrists as she raised her hands. Red rings swelled on Soren's skin as the iron slipped past her wrists.

"Do you recognise it?" Nyzaia asked. Soren held the paper in different directions, focusing on Nyzaia's drawing from different angles. She traced her finger over the lines of the Wiccan symbol and hummed before repeating the motion several times. With an exasperated sigh, Nyzaia hung her head, trying to keep a leash on her temper until she had enough information. "Well? Do you?" Nyzaia probed. Soren stopped tracing the symbol and flicked her eyes up to Nyzaia's face, a cunning glance through her top lashes as her eyes bored into Nyzaia's.

"What's in it for me?" she purred. Nyzaia tilted her head at Soren's calculating, fierce, and ruthless nature, traits Nyzaia would normally admire in a woman had they not led to her brother's demise. Despite the anger boiling in Nyzaia's blood, she could not deny the sudden intrigue at Soren's change of tone, enticing her to join the game. "What is my information worth?" Soren crumpled the paper in her hand and tossed it aside, keeping her eyes on Nyzaia knelt over her who lifted her dagger and trailed the blade down Soren's cheek before resting it under her chin. Soren's eyes flickered to the blade and then Nyzaia.

"You seem to be under the impression you're in a position to negotiate," Nyzaia murmured. "Maybe we need to have some more fun in the other room." Nyzaia pressed the dagger harder into

Soren's throat.

"Cut me all you want, Nyzaia. I'll only bleed regret," Soren said in a soft, almost delicate voice. She jerked her head back, almost as baffled by her own words as Nyzaia. Soren had never used Nyzaia's name before. It was a trick; it had to be—feigning regret for her actions to leverage information. Nyzaia narrowed her eyes.

"There is plenty more for us to discuss. I'll grant you one ask, but when will you use it? Now, or when you think this information will be most important to me? Perhaps you will risk waiting until I want more from you, so you can bargain for something more important?"

"My wolves," Soren said without hesitation. "I want to see my wolves. In exchange, I will tell you what I know about the symbol."

Nyzaia smirked. "One wolf."

"Since I only have five now, it seems only fair I should be able to check on more than one." Soren averted her eyes. Nyzaia could not recall the dead wolf's name.

"*One* wolf."

"Seiko, the deep grey one."

"The blind one?" Nyzaia mocked. Soren snatched the blade with unnatural speed and shoved it from her neck. Blood trickled down her palm.

"Do not underestimate those who seem weak," Soren spat. Farid and Jabir stepped forward, but Nyzaia raised a hand, rising from her crouch and watching Soren closely. At her request, Garridon soldiers had rounded up the wolves and kept them in cages on a covered terrace under guard. Nyzaia ensured they were fed and kept cool, although several guards had lost their hands from doing so. She kept them there as bargaining chips.

"You may see Seiko once."

Soren scanned Nyzaia's face, seeming to search for a lie.

"As far as I know, the symbol represents Garridon. I have seen it in various books my grandmother owned and in other texts on Doltas. I was taught the symbols are an old language from Ithyion that Wiccans are fluent in."

Nyzaia smirked. "You should have held onto your ask; you merely confirmed what I suspected."

Soren tilted her head. "Does it look like I care? I wanted to see my wolf. I either did that now, only to suffer torture for information later, or suffer now and wait to reunite with my wolf." Nyzaia smirked. She had been right to keep the wolves as leverage.

"Well then, either answer my next questions freely, or we will move to the other room." Nyzaia spun her dagger between her fingers, earning a sigh from Soren. It was no fun enacting revenge if the captive refused to fight back. Nyzaia handed Soren one of the other papers, containing a copy of all the symbols found on the sacrificed bodies and the surrounding walls. Soren's frown intensified as she squinted and turned the paper.

"Can you read these?" Nyzaia asked. Soren paused, and Nyzaia expected—or hoped—for a retort, any reason to cut her open again and watch her bleed blood as red as Kazaar's. Instead, Soren mouthed silently to herself, assessing the paper. Nyzaia tapped her foot while Soren continued turning the paper to trace the marks.

"One is the symbol used interchangeably for drinking, fluids, and holy wines," Soren murmured, squinting. "Another is the symbol used for markets, stores, or establishments." The cogs began to turn in Nyzaia's mind.

"A tavern? Could it be a tavern?" Nyzaia asked. Soren nodded, rubbing the red mark on her wrist as she continued assessing the other symbols.

"I do not know all of these. I only learned from the texts we had remaining from Ithyion. My grandmother's Wiccan book may have more, but we could never read it as children." Soren withdrew her finger from the paper to hand it back, but then her eyes paused, squinting at one symbol. "This one at the bottom isn't Wiccan; the outside lines are, but the inside is not." Soren placed the paper down before her and leaned against the wall. Nyzaia picked it up, examining the symbol. Soren was right. The outside circular lines matched some of the other detailing, but short rough lines marked the centre, creating crescent-moon-shaped lines flowing from the top, almost like a palm tree.

"The Palm Tavern," Nyzaia murmured, glancing at Jabir and Farid. Jabir retreated from the cell.

"I'll scout it out," he said.

"Three hours. Meet at our usual spot at sundown," Nyzaia commanded. Jabir nodded and left. "Get her up," Nyzaia said to Farid, who wasted no time hauling Soren to her feet. She dug her heels in when Farid tried to move her, frantically moving back and forth between them.

"I answered your questions. Where are you taking me?" Soren spoke quickly.

"You're the only one who understands the symbols, so you're coming with us." Nyzaia exited the cell and stalked down the dark corridor, ready for answers.

"But you said three hours! Come back for me," Soren begged. Nyzaia did not know why she wished to be left in the cell as she dug her heels into the ground again.

"You need to wash and change. You'll draw attention otherwise." Nyzaia nodded pointedly at the dried blood on Soren's clothes before her feet splashed in the puddles as she climbed the steps from the dungeons and headed towards her rooms.

"Just leave me. You don't need me! I can read any symbols if you bring them back here," Soren stuttered. Nyzaia made a note to understand her fears, wondering why she would choose to rot in a cell than leave its confines.

"Do you want to see your wolf or not? Because now is your chance," Nyzaia snapped. Soren fell silent at that as Nyzaia and Farid led her to the Queen of Keres's chambers.

***

"I don't like this," Farid whispered as they watched Soren standing at the end of the large outdoor bath of Nyzaia's chambers. She decided against taking her to the communal baths to avoid rumours about a prisoner being permitted out of their cell. Soren tilted her face up to the sky and began pacing before changing directions as the birds chirped.

"She will remain in chains even while bathing. She is no threat to me," Nyzaia murmured. Farid furrowed his brow and glanced between Soren at the edge of the baths and Nyzaia, leaning on one of the many archways. "Catch up to Jabir and make sure he is okay, and then you can come back for Soren and me. She's fine here, but I don't trust she won't run the second we're outside the palace walls."

"She seemed rather set on being left in the cells. Why do you think that is?"

Nyzaia shrugged and turned her focus from Soren to Farid.

"Did you hear her mention regrets?" He nodded. "I'm not buying it, but there's no denying there's something wrong with her," Nyzaia said, tapping the side of her head.

"Workers repeated phrases when they had heat stroke at the forge." Farid frowned. "Is it possible it results from her saying Caligh's name? Expelling his control?" Nyzaia looked back at Soren.

"I don't know if she was under his control like Osiris or his army. She doesn't owe a debt, does she? With her, everything seemed intentional."

"Regardless of the debt, Caligh also controlled the soldiers actions. She could easily have been controlled, too, and his absence might be having this effect on her," Farid contemplated.

"Poor girl," Nyzaia scoffed. Farid opened his mouth but closed it, tightening his jaw while glancing again at Soren. Nyzaia straightened, moving from the pillar. She looked at Farid, who kept his eyes averted. "You pity her," Nyzaia gasped, sensing his emotions. "How could you? She is the reason Kazaar is dead. She was on Caligh's side the entire time, Farid!"

"I know, but—"

"How can there be a but?"

"You and I both know what it's like to have a man steering our path, manipulating our choices. I was forced to hide myself and slave away at the forge. Only when my father was killed did I choose to join the guards." Nyzaia looked away from Farid's face at the reminder of his early experiences, though she was pleased to have ended some of his torment by killing Arjan. "And had your father not forced you to join the Red Stones at sixteen, what might your life have looked like then?" Nyzaia remained silent at the truth in his words. "I'm not saying she shouldn't suffer for her crimes or be forgiven. But it would harm no one to try to understand why she made those decisions, and how he used her like a pawn in his game. You do not know her history, Nyzaia. Many have judged your past the way you judge her now."

"Enough," Nyzaia snapped. "You forget your place, captain. I will not stand and listen to you pity her after she took Kazaar from me. Follow Jabir. We have nothing left to discuss."

Farid bowed his head and turned on his heel. She winced at the pain piercing through her heart. He was her friend, yet she implied he was not entitled to share his thoughts. Nyzaia opened her mouth to call for him, but he had already welcomed in Soren's wolf and left. Nyzaia was alone with her regret and confusion, no longer able to determine her feelings as the fallen queen grinned at the sight of her wolf bounding towards her. Soren collapsed to her knees and buried her face in his fur. Was Farid right?

Chapter Twenty

Soren

"He will need to sit aside while you bathe," Nyzaia called, drifting from the shadows of the archway towards the large pool. Her leathers were stark against the colourful mosaic tiles. Soren kept her eyes on where they sat directly before Nyzaia as she approached the steps down into the bathing pool.

"He doesn't like water. He'll stay away." Soren rested her forehead against his and felt her muscles relax while gazing into Seiko's different eyes: one icy blue, one milky, a stark contrast to Baelyn's eyes of the deepest chestnut. "I'm sorry I lost him," Soren murmured. "Are the others okay?" She ignored Nyzaia's scoff, as she sat on a stone bench off to the side. No matter how delusional Soren may look talking to her wolves, she knew they understood. Seiko licked her face as a sign the wolves were okay before whining and lifting his paw to her shoulder. Soren pulled back. They missed her. "I miss you too," she said, feeling more sentimental than usual.

"We have little time," Nyzaia said, her words clipped. Soren sighed and stroked Seiko's head. The wolf seemed to understand Nyzaia too as he settled at the edge of the bathing pool with his head on his paws, watching the Queen of Keres. Nyzaia looked him up and down.

Soren had never been embarrassed about her body. She stripped off her trousers, wincing at her weak, aching muscles. Her hands paused on the tunic, and she tugged it in different directions, struggling with the chains around her wrists. Soren huffed, wincing at the metal digging into her skin. Nyzaia stalked across the mosaic tiles with a sigh and stood toe to toe with Soren, pursing her lips. Seiko gave a low warning growl. Soren met Nyzaia's eyes and held her breath when she pulled a dagger from her thigh. It was all a trap. Nyzaia lured her here for torture. She jumped when Nyzaia's hand caught the bottom of her tunic, pulling it taut. In one swift move, the Keres queen sliced the tunic's front, ripping the fabric until it hung on the chains. Soren winced as the back of Nyzaia's hand grazed her abdomen before stepping back. Soren was quick to turn and enter the pool, hiding her body. Perhaps she got embarrassed after all.

She glanced sideways at Nyzaia. Soren wanted to hate her, for that was what Caligh wanted. He wanted Soren to hate them all for none were worthy of his attention. They wanted him dead. But since Soren awoke from her last dream, the only words ringing in her head were that of her younger self, locked behind bars—*I like Nyzaia*—and the queen's screams when she unleashed her anger on Soren during the battle. *You deserved it*, a small, delicate voice whispered in her mind.

"Can you say something for me?" Nyzaia asked. Soren turned to face her, confused by the need for conversation while bathing. She reached for the soap in a copper bowl beside Seiko and washed what she could reach of her arms. "Say his name: Caligh Servusian." Wincing, Soren tore her gaze from Nyzaia. "Say it, Soren."

Soren swallowed, struggling to ignore the small voice in her head urging her to do as Nyzaia asked, the voice which revelled in the way Nyzaia spoke her name so calmly. Soren took a breath, wishing she could forget him.

"Caligh Servusian," Soren whispered. Her skin squirmed, and ringing erupted in her mind, but she stayed quiet, continuing to wash herself while watching Nyzaia. Something flickered in her eyes—a flame. Soren had done something wrong, but she did not know what.

"When did you meet him?" Nyzaia asked, crossing her arms. Soren watched the surrounding water darken with dirt and blood, trying to recall the exact moment, but it was unclear—a blur of bodies and places, a mumble of indecipherable words. "When?" Nyzaia raised her voice, and Soren dropped the soap, unable to think. She focused her mind, but the shadows lingering there quietly reached the corners, shrinking the ivy and flowers that tried to grow in its place.

"I-I don't know," Soren realised, mumbling her answer. Nyzaia gave a humourless laugh.

"Do not lie to me," Nyzaia hissed. "Speaking his name did nothing, not like it did with Osiris. You were never under his control. You willingly chose this path." Nyzaia paced towards the edge of the bathing pool as Soren tried to reach for the soap with her feet. But then, the pool began to warm. Wading away from Nyzaia, she heard Seiko's warning growl, seeming to realise Nyzaia was heating the pool. Soren silenced him with a look, not wishing for him to end up like Baelyn.

"When did you decide you had to try to take the throne?" Nyzaia demanded. Soren's mind dragged her back to the day she sacrificed her family, her grandmother's voice ringing in her ears. *I have seen who will lead you and Garridon into the darkness to come, and who will ensure its end. Yet for that to happen, your queen and princess's power must match that of the heirs.* Soren sifted through her memories, seeking proof that her grandmother, not Caligh, demanded Caellum's murder—evidence that her decisions were a culmination of many factors. Yet her grandmother said nothing of the throne or killing Caellum. She spoke of the darkness to come. Caligh. One memory captured her attention in particular: her grandmother informing Sadira she would marry Caellum, and their child would bring peace. Soren was to stand by their side to protect them. When was Soren instructed to kill him and take the throne for herself? Only Caligh's face appeared. It was his plan—only his.

"I-I don't know. I don't know when," Soren stuttered, telling the truth. She could not recall the moment she met Caligh, or when he advised killing Caellum, or twisted the thought so deeply in Soren's mind she believed it was her family's scheme. Soren remembered nothing. The temperature in the bath rose and steam floated across her vision. The heat was making her faint.

"You're lying," Nyzaia sneered, flames licking at her palms. Soren gasped as the water began to burn, reddening her skin. The water's edge closest to Nyzaia bubbled. Seiko whined, evidently distressed and unable to intervene, unable to disobey Soren's earlier order.

"I don't remember," Soren said, tears welling in her eyes. "I remember nothing. Why don't I remember anything?" Nyzaia's face faltered. "Why, why, why?" Soren tried to walk towards the edge of the pool as the steam faded; a misty morning appeared in her mind as she reached for the side. Seiko continued whining as Nyzaia moved until her black boots came into view. Caligh had worn black boots when he met Soren in the open clearing on Doltas Island. His face appeared, and Soren panicked at his calculating smile while Sadira cried beside her. "Get out," Soren murmured. "Get out. Leave her alone!" Her eyes grew panicked as she stared at the black of Nyzaia's boots, her breath quickening. She needed to get him out before he took her again. Soren smacked her head with her fist. "Get out!" she cried, hitting her forehead with the iron cuff. "Get out!" Hit. "Get out!" Hit. "*Get out!*"

"Soren! Stop!" Nyzaia commanded, but she was no longer listening. Caligh continued to approach while she smacked the cuffs against her head, sensing the warm blood trickle down her face. "Shit," Nyzaia mumbled. Warm hands reached for her shoulders, spinning her around. Suddenly, there were legs on either side of her in the water and arms wrapping around Soren's chest from behind, holding her tight and restricting her arms. Thrashing at the stranger's touch, Soren reached back to dig her fingers into leather-clad thighs. A woman gasped.

Soren felt the presence then of Nyzaia's mind, fluttering against the edges of hers. Together, they watched Caligh stalk towards the two young girls, no older than thirteen. One wore a beautiful pink gown with blonde bouncing curls flowing over her shoulder. The other's hair was braided, and she wore a muddied brown tunic, with a wooden sword at her hip.

"You will be a powerful queen one day, Sadira," Caligh hummed, his shadows gliding across the grass towards the young sisters. "As will your children. Think of how much safer they would be with my protection." Soren pushed Sadira behind her. Something about this man made her spine tingle and mind sharpen. There was something terrifying about him. Caligh watched Soren, intrigued. "Come, Sadira." He offered his hand to the princess, who cowered behind her older sister. "You could play a vital part in my revenge against a god. Together, you can become the Queen on the Garridon throne." His grin made Soren uncomfortable as she recalled her grandmother's words: Sadira would marry the King of Garridon one day, with Soren as her protector. This man wanted to use Sadira for something else. Soren had promised to protect her, and she would.

"Don't take Sadira, take me." Soren raised her chin, and Caligh's eyes narrowed.

"And what would you offer me? It is not you my servant has seen upon a throne; it is not you who will marry a king and slaughter him while he sleeps." When Caligh stepped forward, Soren raised an arm in front of Sadira, who squeaked in fear.

"Sadira is too kind, too sweet. She would never do such a thing."

Caligh laughed, peering up at the small birds Sadira had saved, safe in their nest.

"She would not have much choice. I would make her." He grinned.

"Then make me. Sadira will still be queen, but do not make her do something like this. I am her sister; I am a princess. I can remain close by her side and the king's." Caligh rubbed his jaw, contemplating her words. Soren felt another presence, a fiery warmth watching over the scene playing in her mind.

"Don't take Sadira, take me." Soren focused on Caligh; she was determined to do whatever this man required if it meant protecting Sadira. As Caligh watched, the chirping babies in the nest above flew free. One collided with Caligh, a shadow ripping free from him and breaking its neck.

"Very well, little bird." Caligh extended his hand to Soren. "Neither of you will remember this." When Soren placed her trembling hand in Caligh's, shadows enveloped her. She turned to face Sadira, who gazed peacefully at their surroundings, seemingly unable to recall why she was there. Soren bit her lip to keep from crying. Sadira could not see her. *What will life be like now?* she wondered as Sadira passed them both. A pit formed in Soren's stomach. Perhaps no one would ever see the real her again.

No one ever sees me, whispered the delicate voice in her mind as the memory faded. Soren gasped in sync with Nyzaia, her chest rising and falling with rapid breaths. Slowly, the water settled. She loosened her hand on Nyzaia, hoping their minds were now unlinked. Unable to process what link to her Wiccan blood had caused such a link, Soren focused on slowing her breathing, calmed by the weight of Nyzaia's arms around her chest, calming the frantic beating of her heart no longer tried to rip free of its cage.

"No one ever sees me," Soren mumbled. Nyzaia stilled. "No one understands. I don't understand. I don't know where I begin, or he ends." Tears slid down her face, and she desperately wanted to wipe them away. She did not want Nyzaia to see her cry or show weakness. The Queen of Keres had seen so much now, enough to create new torture tactics. But Nyzaia surprised Soren as she slowly removed her arms, splashing the water against the ledge as she lifted herself up. Still, Soren felt her legs remaining either side of her. Soren did not dare move. Seiko no longer growled or whined as Nyzaia dragged the copper bowl brimming with blocks of soap, to the pool's edge. Seiko faced his keeper, the one good eye flickering just behind Soren to watch Nyzaia.

"If you back up towards the wall, there is a ledge below the surface you can sit on," Nyzaia muttered, yet her voice still carried authority. Soren did as she was told and sat, the water rising to her collarbones. Nyzaia positioned herself until her knees were either side of Soren's temples. Soren crossed her arms and shivered, trying to focus. She hoped the shadows lingering in her mind would not emerge. For once, she felt like herself, though she no longer knew what that meant. A clarity had returned, a clarity she felt during her dreams when gazing at her younger self. Soren shivered again. Those bars had been erected in her mind ever since meeting Caligh, locking her true self away. A light steam drifted off the water's surface to ease Soren's shivers, less intense compared to Nyzaia's earlier fury.

Soren jumped as hands reached for her braids and stilled, waiting for Soren to calm. Gradually, she lowered her shoulders as the quiet voice in her head offered assurances. They liked and trusted Nyzaia. Nyzaia poured warm water over Soren's head with one hand, while the other shielded it from falling down her face. A moment later, Soren breathed in the scent of oranges as Nyzaia brushed the soap over each braid in turn. Soren gulped and wondered if there was some memory buried deep within of her mother doing the same. When was the last time someone had touched her like this? With care?

"Why did you start braiding your hair?" Nyzaia asked, and Soren frowned. "Focusing on one small memory, like a less traumatic moment, can help you to slowly recall more things."

"Making it easier to get information from me, then?" Soren whispered. Nyzaia's hands stilled briefly but then continued washing Soren's braids.

"So you might differentiate between yourself and his influence," Nyzaia said, her voice quiet but commanding.

"You said I did everything willingly," Soren continued. "But in my mind, I am locked behind bars. Now he is gone, I'm trying to escape, but before... before my mind was only him. Is it possible he can control people in different ways?"

Nyzaia hummed. "It would seem so."

"I was willing at first. I agreed to be in his servitude."

Nyzaia's hands froze, and suds trickled over Soren's shoulders.

"To protect Sadira?" she asked. Soren nodded.

"Always to protect Sadira. That was my job." Soren's breathing quickened, and she shifted in her seat. "I failed." She tugged at the cuffs around her wrists. "I failed. She was at risk by attending that battle. I—did I help lead him here? I don't think I did; I just did as I was told, but—" Soren gasped for breath, her chest rising quickly again. Nyzaia did not move except to pour more water over Soren's head to free her chest of suds. She rested her hand on Soren's shoulder, the touch oddly comforting.

"Why did you start braiding your hair?" Nyzaia asked again, picking up the soap again. Soren forced her eyes shut and focused on the motions of Nyzaia's hands, moving slowly around her head and alternating between brushing her braids and soaking them with water. *Why did I start braiding my hair?* Soren inhaled, holding her breath for a moment before releasing it. An image of two identical blondes running through the square in Doltas appeared, donning matching green dresses and curls.

"We looked identical when we were younger," Soren whispered.

"You and Sadira?"

"Nobody could tell us apart, and when I learned to fight, my hair got in the way. Braids helped differentiate us."

"Good. Well done." Nyzaia murmured. Soren's skin tingled before she shivered under the water running over her braids.

"Why are you being kind to me?" she whispered, prompting Nyzaia to sigh. Soren tilted her head back, looking up at the Queen of Keres. Flecks of gold still blazed in her eyes, although the pool remained at a steady temperature. Soren did not know what to think as Nyzaia paused to scan her face. She lowered Soren's head and continued washing the braids.

"The other rulers never judged me for who I was before I became queen, though a part of me still is that person. I have tortured, drugged, and killed others. I've stolen secrets, used my body for leverage, yet nobody has questioned me on it." Nyzaia squeezed the remaining suds and water from Soren's braids. "Farid reminded me that my father chose that life for me. It sounds as though your life was never yours, either." Slowly, Soren nodded. Finally, someone understood what it was like, but she did not deserve this kindness.

"But I am the reason Kazaar is dead," Soren whispered. Nyzaia released Soren's braids and hesitated before pushing herself up from the edge and away from the fallen queen. Boots padded across the tiles as she strode into her chambers.

"There are clothes on my bed. Change and meet me at the door in ten minutes," Nyzaia called, her voice having adopted its usual sharpness. Finally turning her head, Soren met Seiko's eyes from where he watched her at the side of the bathing pool. Soren pulled her legs up until her feet rested on the ledge below the water and wrapped her hand arms around them. She was alone again.

Chapter Twenty-One

Elisara

"*A re you certain?*" *Olirah murmured, cupping Jessemiah's face in time to catch a falling tear with her thumb. Jessmiah nodded and rested her forehead against Olirah's, her dark hair tumbling forward.*

"It is the only way," she responded, pulling Olirah into an embrace. Olirah winced at the cries outside the tower. Over Jessemiah's shoulder, she saw the feathered wings of her comrades as they fell to their deaths. A screech sounded again, and the room darkened.

"He is coming for us," Olirah murmured, pulling back.

"This is the only way to save the state." Jessemiah smiled, reaching for a dagger resting on the bed beside them. Olirah mimicked her action, picking up a matching dagger with a jewel-encrusted hilt.

"I love you," Olirah's voice cracked.

"From my first breath to my last, I was always destined to be yours," Jessamiah replied, angling her dagger into Olirah's abdomen, where the matching mark to her own lay beneath her clothing. Olirah did the same and kissed Jessamiah. The women clung to each other in a tearful kiss as they pierced their daggers to the sounds of the dying outside.

Elisara woke up, teary-eyed. Was this now her fate—reliving the pain of others' deaths? But their pain was nothing compared to losing Kazaar.

Aches settled into Elisara's bones as she fixed her eyes on the canopy above the bed. For at least two hours, she lay there, replaying the dreams as a distraction. So far, all three focused on the death of loved ones, a punishment from the universe for her failure to avenge Kazaar. She narrowed her eyes on the canopy. Sitara had lost someone too. What if she was planting these dreams somehow as a constant reminder to locate Sonos—to reunite at least one love story?

A shadow moved now and then before the fireplace, but it was not her own shadows, a sign she was truly awake. Sallos had returned to his shadowed form. Elisara sighed, blinking back the dryness in her eyes. She did not know how long she had slept. Who guided the lords or Vala's people in her absence? How was the state of the wider kingdom since she fled? Truthfully, she did not care. Responsibility was an expectation she no longer wished to bear. Did that make her selfish? Perhaps. Or it simply made her human.

Elisara dragged her hands down her face before clasping them together, her arms brushing something rough against her chest. She ran her hand along it, feeling raised scars in swirling patterns, like the ship in the crook of her elbow and the vines wrapped around her forearm. Only a symbol of the fire realm was left to mark her skin. Elisara pulled her hand away, and still, dirt layered her palm. It struck her all at once—how many days she had worn the same clothes and marks of war.

Pushing herself up onto the bed, Elisara spared a quick glance at Sallos, who was perched on the edge of the desk. Only darkness met her gaze, yet she sensed his head was tilted, resting on his palm, while his elbow rested on his wide-planted knees. Elisara stumbled over the stone, ignoring him, then through the narrow hallway and the waterfall, into the throne room. The water was no longer black; in fact, the water appeared welcoming, reflecting the setting sun in the opening above. *I have slept at least a day or two then*, she realised.

The ascending stairway to the lake outside was empty; she debated venturing to bathe in the waters yet felt safer in the cave's darkness. With a single command, the soldiers in the throne room turned to face the walls to offer privacy. She tilted her head at the resistance in her mind somewhere, and realised the room was filled with far less shadowed soldiers than before. She sighed, pleased by their absence. Perhaps they wandered outside by the lake, through the woods, or on the sparkling black beach. Turning, Elisara saw Sallos in the entrance to the hallway, the waterfall parting on either side of him from where she had previously wielded the water to step through. He did not turn. She felt his intrigue reach her, but what was he intrigued about? The fact she had finally risen from bed? The notion she cared enough to bathe? Or maybe he was simply intrigued to see her body?

Elisara glared and directed her own threads of shadow to drift across the floor and form a wall before him. While the dark power twisting out of her was light, acting graceful with its movements, it weighed heavily on her skin. She wished to retract the darkness, but that was the one command they ignored.

Elisara felt nothing, not even the piercing cold of the water as she stripped off her clothes and carefully placed them at the edge of the small pool created by the waterfall. She glanced at the shadow wall behind it, blocking Sallos, and waited, ensuring he would not attempt to push through. When he did not, she submerged herself beneath the water's shower, drowning her feelings beneath the weight of it, and focusing on the way it bruised her skin. As the water washed the blood and dirt of war away, she realised Kazaar's touch went with it. Salty teardrops tumbled down her cheeks, mingling with the water cascading down her back and shoulders. A sob wracked her chest as she tilted her head to soak her hair. Pushing from the water's temporary relief, Elisara fell forward and glanced at the clothing outside the pool. She should wash them too but could not bring herself to remove his scent from the fabrics. Rising from the water, she summoned her shadows from Sallos to wrap around her body until it appeared as though she was wearing a gown of unending nightfall.

Water dripped from her hair onto the checkerboard floor. She strode back into the dark hallway, ignoring and pushing past Sallos, whose cold shadows brushed her skin. Elisara halted as she entered her room. Someone had moved the mirror from the room of statues and propped it beside the fireplace. She immediately tore her gaze from her reflection, refusing to face who she had become at the hand of Sitara's meddling and Kazaar's death.

"*Move it,*" Elisara commanded silently. Why had Sallos brought it here in the first place? She sensed his hesitation as he raised his arm but stopped. "Move it!" she commanded, sliding beneath the blanket on the bed while the shadows drifted from her body. She swallowed a sigh of relief as the weight of them fell onto the bed while Sallos moved the mirror into the hallway toward the throne room. Elisara was wasting her days away by sleeping, but sleep erased all thoughts and pain about Kazaar. But now, she feared sleep, dreading Sallos awaited in her dreams, seeking something from her. Tugging the blanket further up and over herself, she ignored Sallos's reemerging presence and closed her eyes, hoping for silence.

Hamzah Fasaar had lived a humble and quiet life as a simple foot guard along the city walls. That was until he met the Princess of Carvyre. Now, he stood atop that same towering five-hundred-foot wall dividing the city from the border and prepared to jump, to take his own life, and end this all. The echo of steel on steel clashed behind him in the city, where the war raged on. Yet his eyeline focused on the calmness of sand dunes and a burning sky. If he squinted, he could spot the green forests in the distance. Perhaps someone stood atop a tree in the same place miles away, watching this very wall. Hamzah took a deep breath in and rested his brown forearms atop the stone, turning over the engagement ring in his hand. Flames licked his hands as he considered melting it.

The wall had long been breached by the Princess's army; no soldiers would be patrolling the wall now, which meant he could live his final moments in peace. Would he have done it all differently had he known the outcome would be war, loss, heartache? Perhaps he never should have volunteered to escort the new King of Q'Ohar to Carvyre. Had he not, he never would have met the princess, the king's newly betrothed. Hamzah would not have caught her eye and become her guard in the city or been the one to comfort her during moments of pain at the king's hand. If Hamzah had never joined that trip, he would not have fallen in love with a princess or been caught with her, and thus started a war. The king would not have threatened to kill Hamzah, and the princess would not have retaliated by calling her army to aid the day before the wedding.

If Hamzah had stayed but a simple foot guard, he never would have helped the princess to awaken old power in her veins to win a war, the same power appearing to manifest within his own blood. Hamzah clenched his fists, sensing something recoil in his arm, yearning to be released—he did not know what. But Hamzah was no longer a simple foot guard. He had caused a war and was the reason his love had lost herself to power, intent on taking the entirety of Q'Ohar down with her. The solution? Severing the tie between them, weakening her in the process. Glancing down, he saw nothing but the distant speck of guards below. If the princess was powerless, she may still win Q'Ohar's capital, but she would not destroy the rest of its land. Though, even that might not be enough to save the people Hamzah loved in the city. There was only one other option, one he knew deep down would be the outcome.

A door from the turret stairs opened, and Hamzah knew it was her, forewarned by whatever tied them together.

"We are going to win, Hamzah," she said gleefully. Hamzah no longer recognised the woman before him. Whatever light had once existed in her soul had been snuffed out until she was a shell of her former self. Her once luminous silver hair was limp and dull. Darkness had overcome the glistening specks of white in her purple eyes, matching the shadows within his veins. With a trembling hand, she tucked a strand of her hair behind a pointed ear laden in jewels. Her body did that often—shaking without warning, as if something within her yearned to break free.

"You might, Varlena, but I will not be here to see it," Hamzah said, throwing the engagement ring in her direction. Her face faltered

with a glimpse of sorrow, a glimpse of the true Varlena before fury w on.

"You believe you can abandon a princess, soon to be the queen of not one but two great lands?" she sneered and strode towards him in black leathers, showing the speed and strength of her legs. The purple gauze over each shoulder fluttered with her steps, secured by a silver jewel-encrusted belt that matched the ones on her crown. Hamzah expected her every move as he climbed atop the wall, and Varlena followed. She would never let him leave.

"This was never the plan, Varlena," Hazmah murmured, reaching for her cheek. Her features softened.

"It was, Hamzah. It was never meant to be the king; it was always meant to be you." She placed a hand on his still beating heart as he leant forward to plant a kiss on her forehead. She thought she had won him over with such simple words when she flashed a winning smile, one that almost had him believe she was the same girl he had first met years ago. He had been counting on her unwavering belief in their love, and he had been right to, for Varlena did not expect the dagger Hamzah slid from his waistband to stab the love of his life in the abdomen.

Varlena gasped and tried to pull back, but Hamzah clutched the back of her neck, forcing himself to look at the light that would soon fade in her eyes before they fell from the wall together. Taking her down with him was the only way to truly save the state. Panic widened her glistening purple irises as she clutched the dagger, blood gushing from it.

"The baby," she murmured. A chill ran up Hamzah's spine. She was with child. His children were in her womb. In a flash decision, Hamzah altered the course of history. Rather than dragging them both to their deaths to guarantee the end of a great power, he shoved Varlena back towards the turret before flinging himself backward towards the sands below.

As Hamzah fell, Varlena's scream shattered the sky.

Chapter Twenty-Two
Nyzaia

The fall of Nyzaia's boots as she strode from the bathing pool was the only sound amid the silence. She quickened her pace towards the chamber door. No voice called for Nyzaia to wait, no water splashed within the pool, no wolf howled or chains clinked. With a deep breath, Nyzaia refrained from turning to check Soren did as she had asked: exit the bath, dress, and prepare to leave. Soren—the woman who killed Kazaar. Why did a pang of emotion pain Nyzaia's chest when she sensed Soren's disappointment as she withdrew from her side?

When Nyzaia dropped the cleaned braids from her hands, it was like something jolted her awake, reminding her of the person sitting before her. Oh, how easy it would have been to take a braid, wrap it around the fallen queen's neck, and pull. A quick justice for her brother's death. Rubbing her forehead, Nyzaia did not turn around and instead made the final few steps to the curved hallway door. *Perhaps your inner conflict is what Soren suffers with daily.* The Queen of Keres tried not to dwell on the image of a terrified, thirteen-year-old Soren, unknowingly sacrificing her life and sanity for her sister. Did Sadira realise the extent of Soren's state of mind and manipulation? The future Queen of Garridon had a right to know, but would such information prompt Sadira to request her sister's return? Nyzaia would lose her prisoner and her chance to avenge Kazaar.

Nyzaia paused, her hand hovering over the brass doorknob. Still, no sound came from the bath. She hesitated for only a moment before opening the door, rushing through, and slamming it shut.

Nyzaia huffed at her mind's consideration of Soren's feelings. The sound of the door clattering in its frame was loud enough to hide any other sound, including the soft footsteps on Nyzaia's right as she turned left.

With a decade of training behind her, Nyzaia seized her dagger in her right hand while flames blazed in her left. She stared down at the dead guard slumped against the wall. Nyzaia did not even know his name, just one guard left at the door whilst Farid left to check on Jabir. Their celestial tie lessened the need for other guards; they easily sensed when one another was in danger. Nyzaia focused on that feeling now and tried to sense Farid, though he was likely far across the city. The queen had only stared at the body for a matter of seconds, analysing the slash across his neck and the symbol of a circle and cross carved into his forehead—it was a second too long. Air shifted behind Nyzaia as a hand clamped her mouth and another reached for the dagger.

Someone shoved a scented rag against her face, and the acidic smell was overwhelming. The edge caught fire in an instant as she engulfed herself in flames. With a grunt, the attacker held the burning rag for a second too long before shoving Nyzaia away. She rolled as she fell, a move usually enabling her to turn quickly onto her knees and crouch, pulling another dagger from her thigh. Instead, she coughed and stumbled, struggling to keep upright. The mosaic tiles beneath her hands felt far colder than usual, the spectrum of colours blurring together. She blinked repeatedly. Drugged. Burning the cloth had been a quick way to remove the liquid-drenched rag from her face, but it was not quick enough. The scent was one she knew well, having used it to drug and transport prisoners of the Red Stones. She knew what came next.

Heaviness overcame Nyzaia's head and body as she dragged herself forward. Brown hands frantically beat at the flames igniting beige robes before darkness came, and her head collided with the floor.

***

Smoke. The acrid stench of burning entered Nyzaia's senses. She opened her eyes immediately, a glaring fiery amber against the ashy darkness. As usual, her limbs felt light and nimble, and her head and vision were clear; her focus was as sharp as ever—not a usual reaction after being drugged. Nyzaia moved into a crouch and looked at where the tiles had been to see nothing but swirling smoke. It was the exact same smoke swirling all around her now, littered with glowing embers and ash. The queen was not in her chambers. Slowly, Nyzaia breathed in, assessing the fog to discern what was burning. The smell shifted, replacing the bitter sharpness with only a light smoke, concealing the scent of palm trees trying to break through. Nyzaia reached forward to stroke the surrounding smoke. When she reached for an ember to ignite it further, no power reached her fingertips.

"You cannot use your power while unconscious," a haunted voice echoed through the haze. Its movements were hurried as it twisted from Nyzaia, pulling further and further until it formed a cocoon before her that tightened. Her last dagger was a welcome reassurance in her hand, though. If she truly was unconscious, it would prove useless. The smoke twisted and thinned until forming the shape of a body. Finally, the smoke dissipated, shifting away on an imaginary breeze. A woman stood there, surrounded by a burning orange plain.

"It would appear as though you used power of your own," Nyzaia said, raising her chin. "So, forgive me if I do not believe you." The woman's indifference matched Nyzaia's as they assessed one another. Her skin was ash-toned, like the swirling smoke had been. Nyzaia imagined the woman's complexion was once warm toned like her own before greying with age. Her hollow cheeks and eyes made the woman's features sharp and unwelcoming. Prominent black brows sat above grey eyes, offering nothing but criticism and scepticism; her matching black hair was pulled taut to further accentuate her gaze. The woman might have been beautiful once, but something haunted her soul until only suffering remained.

"It is wise not to trust people." The woman lifted her chin in the same manner as Nyzaia. "But you are welcome to reach for your power to test my truth." The woman's darkly painted lips twitched at the corners, knowing Nyzaia already had. She was telling the truth. "You are the queen." Nyzaia was unsure if it was a question or statement, but gestured towards her with a flick of her hand.

"And you are?"

The woman seemed to debate her answer as smoke shifted from her arms before clinging to her form again. "Exandria," she said, her voice assuming more power as she announced her presence. The woman waited and watched Nyzaia, frowning at her lack of reaction. "You do not know who I am?" The black sash across her body, secured by a bronze pin at her waist, fluttered as she stepped forward. She donned a white shirt beneath, with fitted blood-red trousers.

"Should I?" Nyzaia asked, crossing her arms. Only when Exandria approached did Nyzaia realise just how tall she was, commanding attention from the very air itself. A heaviness pressed against Nyzaia, then, as if something urged her to back away and submit, a feeling she was unaccustomed to.

"Memories have awakened. I thought you would know more by now," she said. A closer look revealed the grey in her eyes was not colour, but swirling smoke forming patterns throughout her irises. A flash of burning ember blinked within them every so often. Nyzaia thought back to Osiris's words. Could this woman be from lands similar to his?

"You are welcome to tell me all you know." Nyzaia plastered on a fake smile. "It would make my life so much easier." Exandria scoffed and turned, raising her hands as she walked. Smoke and ash rose from her skin, wiping away the burning red plains of their surroundings. Nyzaia blinked against the blazing sun.

"Life is not easy, child," Exandria murmured, stepping to the edge of the red stone Nyzaia was all too familiar with. Swords clashed and shouts sounded across Nefere Valley below. Nyzaia strode forward, her feet feeling distant from her body. She wondered about the danger her true body was in while she floated on this unconscious plain of existence. At the valley's edge, Nyzaia's eyes widened. She stood side by side with Exandria, her head only reaching the woman's chest. Down below, steam rose from the valley, remnants of evaporating water that revealed a sea of scattered bodies below. At the valley's edge, where Nyzaia knew the oasis had once been, a scorched black mark resided, with blackened streaks stemming from it like lightning. A woman collapsed before it in glinting red armour, like she were on fire beneath the sun. A scream shattered the valley as the woman dug her nails into the sand. Her flowing black hair whipped in the wind before dissolving into smoke. Nyzaia looked up at Exandria.

There was no mistaking the look in her eyes, for Nyzaia had seen it in Elisara's—the look mirrored the devastation she felt in her heart when Caligh took Kazaar. Heartbreak. Exandria had lost someone. Nyzaia wanted to ask who and show some empathy, but questions whirred through her mind about the valley, at what the land she called home had been before her ancestors made it their own.

"Why show me this?" Nyzaia asked. Clearing her throat, Exandria shot out her arm and pulled back the smoke to blur the scene before them.

"For you to understand there are two sides to every story," Exandria said mournfully, leaving Nyzaia to question just who the woman that had once been stood on the scorched earth below was.

"But what help—" Exandria raised a hand to Nyzaia's mouth and blew smoke into her face.

***

Nyzaia's body ached. It took her a second to realise the pain was not from the hard tile floor but the after-effects of the drugs in her system. She kept her eyes closed, not wishing to alert her attacker. Movement shifted roughly six paces from her feet; blades clinked, thudding on a table, which meant the door was on her left, and the archways to the baths on her right. Her bed was further away behind her head. Taking a quiet, shallow breath, Nyzaia focused on where she had been while asleep. Was it a dream or reality? She had no time to dwell as footsteps approached. Only one pair. One attacker.

Robes brushed her ankles, where iron chains bit into her skin. Opening her eyelids a fraction, Nyzaia peeked towards her feet. The attacker wore the beige, now burned robes, with a hood concealing their features. A simple blink could set the robes alight, but she wanted to understand who they were and their intentions first. Through the archway, water sloshed against the wall of the bath. The attacker's hands stilled. Soren. They did not know Soren was here.

Their movements were slow as they dropped the chain by Nyzaia's ankle and reached for their wrist. *A man's hand*, Nyzaia realised, as he pulled a dagger from beneath his sleeve. A large gold signet ring glinted on his middle finger, graved with the letter M. The man hailed from the lord's house in Myara. Nyzaia had stared too long and did not close her eyes quick enough as the man turned and widened his eyes, clearly confused as to how she was awake so soon. Nyzaia shifted her hand, ready to set his robes alight, when a growl rumbled across the tiles and a flash of fur lunged for the man.

Nyzaia scrambled back as razor teeth clamped around the man's neck, followed by a resounding crunch throughout the chamber. The wolf's jowls clamped around the man's neck and shook with fervour. When his head thudded to the ground, the chamber doors slammed open as Farid barged in with blazing wings, his sword raised. The moment his eyes met Nyzaia's, his shoulders relaxed.

He tilted his head at the wolf as it tore off the man's arms.

"Seiko," Soren commanded. The wolf raised its head, an arm still in its mouth. "Enough." Seiko whined before dropping the arm and padding through the archway to his keeper. Nyzaia leaned back against the bed frame and watched Seiko collapse at the edge of the tile, resting his large head on soaked red paws. His milky eye stared at Nyzaia as if to say, 'You're welcome.' With a trembling hand, Soren patted his head. Her body was still submerged beneath the water, with only her eyes and forehead visible over the bath's edge.

"Are you okay?" Farid asked, kneeling before his queen and retracting his wings. He moved quickly, ripping the chains off her ankle. Nyzaia watched Soren and Seiko before finally nodding. The wolf had saved her, but why? It could have provided a distraction for Soren to escape. The queen's eyes roamed her captive's expression, yet Soren kept her eyes downcast, avoiding any attention.

"The table is littered with sharpened blades and the same nails used in the sacrifices," Farid explained. Nyzaia felt the intensity of his stare and the worry rushing between them. Tearing her gaze from Soren, she squeezed Farid's hand gently, reassuring him she was okay. He nodded and squeezed back before reassuming his usual rigid position. "Jabir reported robed men entering the Palm Tavern." Farid kicked the dead body on the floor. "I assume they are all linked."

Nyzaia cracked her neck and pushed herself to stand. Her legs trembled for a moment as she reached for the clothes she had laid out for Soren. A jar of ash sat on the table, a reminder of the smoke and ash that seemed to form Exandria's entire being in her unconscious state. She frowned before slowly approaching Seiko and Soren with a wary level of respect for the wolf. She dropped the clothes in front of Soren, whose green eyes peered up at Nyzaia through her lashes.

"Time to get some answers."

Chapter Twenty-Three

Sadira

Something about the dull brass bell ringing above Sadira's head felt comforting. Since arriving on Garridon, she had learnt more hidden knowledge of the Wiccan people and her own ancestry than she had on Doltas Island. While she was raised learning the Wiccan ways, like an attachment to plants, reading ancient symbols—something Soren had always excelled more at—she felt like Athena and the Wiccan from Albyn could teach her far more. The male, in particular, had appeared old enough to have hailed from Ithyion and likely had hidden memories that might have now unravelled.

"We're closing," said Athena's quiet voice behind the raised counter. She did not look up but continued tying strings around dried herbs. The apothecary was darker compared to her last visit, a consequence of the night sky developing outside. She had struggled to leave the castle initially, overwhelmed with empathy for Jorah's experiences and the realisation Soren might have experienced the same. She tried to recall a specific moment when a shift occurred in Soren, changing her into a more driven and power-hungry person, focusing solely on plans for Garridon. Nothing came to mind. One moment, they were happy children—perhaps even friends—and the next, they were distant. Strangers. When Sadira had left the castle before sunset, she looked up at the tallest turret, noticing a glow emanating through the window. Caellum was still reading, having lit the candles in his father's study.

"I was hoping you would make an exception," Sadira responded, balancing the silver trinket box under her arm as she removed her velvet gloves. Crinkling paper filled the silence before Athena answered.

"War has aged you," she said, focusing on her herbs. Despite the tremor of old age in her hands, she swiftly tied the strings before wrapping bundles in brown paper. Sadira noted two of her fingers were frozen crooked.

"It has?" Sadira asked, glancing around the room. It had not changed since she was last here: wax dripped on piles of books, and the scent of herbs drifted from the mortar and pestles nestled in corners.

"There is an air about you—authority, certainty." Athena finally looked up with wide hazel eyes, blowing a tuft of grey hair from her vision. "Like a queen." Her lip quirked as she brushed her hands on her splattered apron, knocking fragments of dried sage onto the floor.

"We are not yet married. I am still a princess." Sadira smiled and approached the counter, placing the silver trinket box before Athena. The old Wiccan did not immediately look at the box but watched Sadira with a tilted head.

"The marriage is merely a formality. You are and always have been destined to be a queen. And remember, queen or not, you still owe me a secret." Sadira recalled the woman's last words from her previous visit, a secret owed in exchange for knowing Athena's secret: she was Wiccan, and a skilled one at that. Though it was information that did not need to remain a secret. Not when neither Caellum nor Sadira would condemn the race as Wren and Jorah had before them. The old woman pulled the box towards her and flicked open the lids. Her hands stilled. She glanced at Sadira through her lashes. "Where did you find these?" she whispered, wide-eyed. Athena knew something.

"The king found them in his father's belongings."

A phantom of a smile traced Athena's lips as she whispered, seemingly to herself. "That would make sense."

"Why?"

She did not reply. Instead, Athena reached for the candle at the edge of the countertop, bringing it into her eye line and squinting. She hovered the pin with the wolf's head by the flame to better see the engravings. Patiently, Sadira waited as Athena switched between the pins, pausing longer on the one Sadira could also not discern, the symbol similar to the Wiccan one but harsher in its lines.

"This one." Athena held up one. It was the symbol of the Brodie Clan, her family lineage from the non-royal side, which she had learned from the Wiccans in Albyn. It matched the one on her book.

"It is the symbol of the Wiccan," Athena said, and Sadira frowned.

"Not a specific clan?" Athena raised an eyebrow, moving the wrinkles on her forehead.

"Once, yes, but they were the first clan, thus it became the symbol for *all* Wiccans." Sadira nodded slowly in understanding. Her family line from her great-grandfather's side, Lyra's father, had been the very first Wiccan clan. Perhaps even the first ever Wiccan.

"Who would wear such a pin?" Sadira asked, and Athena shrugged.

"It could simply be an old pin worn by Wiccans to identify themselves to others of their kind."

"Then why would it be in the Balfour family's possessions?" asked Sadira. Caellum's family had no connection to the Wiccan lineage. Jorah himself had outlawed them on Garridon. Athena frowned, swaying where she sat on her stool, the pins slipping from her fingers and clinking against the table. When the old woman clutched her head, Sadira rushed around the counter to join her, steadying Athena on her stool. Sadira glanced at the window, wondering whether to summon her personal guard, Taryn.

"I am fine," Athena mumbled, waving Sadira off. "I have had odd visions recently."

"Of the future?" Sadira asked, recalling Athena had once foreseen the creatures' attack. Athena shook her head.

"I cannot tell."

"Memories," Sadira murmured. Athena glanced at her, pouring a liquid into a glass. She glugged it before wiping her mouth with the back of her hand and focusing on the pins again. "There is a man from different lands." At that, Athena finally met Sadira's gaze. "He said there was a power withholding the memories of those on Novisia; he said when the prophecy was triggered, people would begin remembering things." Athena glanced at a painting on the back wall, hidden by trailing plants. Sadira could barely discern its contents, though it appeared to be a castle hidden amongst towering tree trunks, with a slumped body on the castle wall, and a red-headed woman lifting a sword. What had prompted Athena to look at it?

"A painting from a story?" Sadira asked, but Athena simply frowned and turned her attention back to the pins.

"Who is this man?"

"Osiris," Sadira said.

"Last name?" Sadira opened her mouth to answer but realised she did not know.

"Can you trust the information of a man who has not revealed everything he possibly could?" Athena stared at the pin with the unreadable symbol, gripping the counter's edge and squinting.

"Please, let me get help," Sadira begged. Athena shook her head before shooting up to meet Sadira's stare. She dropped the pin in a pot of ink. When her voice emerged from her throat, it echoed throughout the room and sent shivers along Sadira's arms.

"What once was hidden can again be found,
Listen to the land and understand you are bound.
A reverse, a reflection, a sister, a mirror,
Find the truth beneath you and all will be clearer.
Healing and prophecies, curses and spells,
One abides, one rebels.

For the cost of a curse, there must be a price,
Find your reflection in the ancient and say goodbye."

Athena gasped for air as Sadira poured another glass from the woman's canter, unsure of its contents. Blinking rapidly, Athena accepted the glass from Sadira, who scribbled the words onto parchment littered across the countertop.

"A prophecy," Sadira said while Athena glugged. "But I have heard the first part from Osiris, and given his age, I assume it stems from another land, someplace old." Athena hit her chest as she spluttered. Finally, she calmed and glanced between Sadira and the inkpot now soaking the pin. With hurried hands, she pulled a piece of cloth free from under a stack of parchment.

"Prophecies are often triggered by the energy held within items," Athena murmured, dipping her finger into the inkpot to pull the pin free. "My words are somehow linked to this pin." Athena wiped the cloth over the pin before lifting it to the light. The faded engraving was now filled with black ink and made the symbol easier to see. While Sadira could now see the symbol more clearly—the sharp criss-crossing lines and scattered dots—she knew nothing of its meaning.

"Do you know what it means?" asked Sadira. Athena lifted the other pin with the Wiccan symbol, holding them side by side.

"No, but it is a variation of the old language. It shares similarities to the symbols we use, but it's different enough." *One abides, one rebels.* "Whatever the man told you, whatever you must find or discover, is linked to the owners or history of these two pins." Athena dropped the two trinkets back into the box, along with the wolf head pin. Before Sadira could ask more, Taryn stormed into the apothecary, wide-eyed, followed by the other three guards. His mouth hung open, panting. Reaching for the fabric hanging above the window, he tugged the rope, allowing it to fall, cursing when it only covered the upper half of the window. The other guards leant against the doors, their hands on the pommels of their swords.

"What is the meaning of—" Athena stopped when a phantom breeze drifted through the room, snuffing out half of the candles in the process. A chill drifted around Sadira, who wrapped her cloak tighter around herself as she approached Taryn. The guard pushed his blonde hair back and held a finger to his lips, quelling her many questions. Sadira did as instructed. Silence fell across the room as they all waited, though Sadira did not know what for.

"Let me pass," Athena hissed, trying to shove the guards aside.

"Athena, if they say not to go outside, don't—"

Three dark figures slowly hovered past the window and paused right before the door. Sadira watched, waiting to see if they pulled for a weapon, but only as she stared at the faint glow of the remaining candles did she see the dark wisps. They were not men; they were Elisara's soldiers.

"It is fine. They will not harm us." Sadira smiled at Athena, who shook her head. Sadira's smile faltered.

"If you wish to keep your fears and emotions in check, you will let me get to the door," Athena hissed at the guards. The men looked at Taryn and then Sadira, who nodded, permitting them to step aside. Athena withdrew a blade from under her apron and sliced her wrist before shoving the handle into the guard's chest in a bid to take it. Outside, the shadows shifted, like they could smell the blood. Athena was swift as she traced her finger over the crimson liquid and painted a Wiccan symbol on the door: an encircled cross with a swirl at its centre, like a lock in chains. Locked, null, pause. Athena was stopping the dark soldiers from crossing into the apothecary, though her actions had earned wary glances from the guards.

They waited silently as the soldiers passed the window and reached the door. Sadira jumped when it rattled. As the guards drew their blades, the silence was broken only by the echo of steel. They halted as the door stopped moving. Taryn edged towards the window and stooped to peer through the glass. Sadira held her breath.

"Gone," Taryn whispered. "For now." Sadira gave a sigh of relief.

"Stay here until sunrise," Athena murmured, reaching for a basket of blankets under a table.

"They protected us in Keres. Why would they be different now?"

Athena shook the blankets free of dust as she looked at Sadira.

"It would appear I am not the only one remembering things."

Chapter Twenty-Four

Nyzaia

Nyzaia fidgeted more than usual, refusing to meet Soren's eye as she stood captive in Jabir's clutches in the dark, dusty alleyway. The Palm Tavern was quiet from outside, with no drunk revellers or thunderous music echoing from within. Even the rule-breakers appeared to abide by the curfew that had been enforced ever since the battle. The journey to the tavern had been tense; Farid was on high alert after the attack in Nyzaia's chambers, and Soren jumped at every shout near the alleyways.

"Jabir said the owner is still inside. He saw at least four men in hooded apparel enter through this back entrance," Farid relayed to his queen, keeping his voice hushed. Nyzaia nodded, unsurprised. It sounded like they resembled the man who had attacked her. Farid glanced over his shoulder at Soren, but the fallen queen stared only at her boots. With the dirt and blood washed from her skin, Soren looked small, with her hunched shoulders and golden braids catching the light. Her dark brown tunic and trousers she had been provided washed her out; she was a shadow of the fierce warrior she displayed in battle. She looked lost.

"You feel sorry for her," Farid said.

"No!" Nyzaia snapped, prompting Farid to raise his eyebrow. Nyzaia looked away, her blood simmering again. The memory of Caligh and Soren on the Ashun Desert flashed through her mind. Nothing had happened when she spoke his name in the bathing pool, confirming the way Caligh had controlled her mind, was different to the control the debt had over Osiris. "I can't forgive her, Farid. Regardless of her broken state, she is the reason my brother is dead, and why Elisara is the way she is. She has caused too much damage."

"You do not need to forgive to understand or help someone."

"She doesn't deserve help."

"Even after she saved you today?"

"Her *wolf* did. Besides, I was moments away from handling the situation." Nyzaia clenched her jaw.

"She could have told him not to but didn't." Farid pushed, but Nyzaia did not respond. "What now? Should she rot for crimes she committed not of her free will, even after allowing you to be saved? I sense your feelings, Nyzaia. I know you checked. While she was not controlled the same as Osiris, I felt your shock. You discovered something about his hold over her." Nyzaia replayed the scene in her mind—the memory of Soren, Sadira, and Caligh. It felt so real, as if she had been there as it happened, watching the events unfold. She could not explain what had connected her mind with Soren's.

"Why are you so damn reasonable?" Nyzaia muttered, pressing her ear to the tavern's back entrance. The corner of Farid's lips twitched.

"Seeing someone broken reminds me what it was like to find someone who helped me piece myself back together." Farid's appreciation flooded through Nyzaia as he glanced at Jabir. Nyzaia smiled and decided to apologise.

"About earlier, I'm s—"

"I know."

"If you two have finished with whatever emotional heart to heart you're having, could we maybe, I don't know, prevent more human sacrifices?" Jabir half-whispered, half-shouted. Nyzaia sighed and nodded at Farid. They were ready. When he returned the nod, Nyzaia knocked on the battered wooden door, but no response came. No voice shouted they were closed. They heard only the creak of the door from the other end of the hallway before heavy footsteps approached. Nyzaia palmed two daggers in her hands as the door opened and swiftly pressed the dagger against the owner's throat as Farid held the man's shoulder against the wall, securing him in place.

Before Nyzaia could have her fun with threats, the man spoke in his usual gruff voice. "They're waiting for you," he said, gesturing to where a trapdoor lay open on the floor. "Well, go on then. I have tables to clean." Nyzaia pressed her dagger deeper into his throat before signalling for Jabir to step forward.

"Unfortunately, the table cleaning will have to wait," Nyzaia hummed. "Jabir here will make sure you stay put while we head inside." The man conceded with a sigh as Jabir traded Soren for the landlord, passing her to Farid. They followed Nyzaia down the hallway.

"Did you know this door was always here?" Farid whispered.

"No," Nyzaia murmured, staring down. "I hate surprises." A rickety ladder was propped in the hole in the floor. Her chest tightened, but it was not her own. Nyzaia flicked her eyes to Farid, and she watched as he swallowed, staring at the small, cramped hole below. A sliver of orange light glowed beneath what she thought was the door, while darkness bathed the red stone walls. It reminded Nyzaia of the caverns at the Abyss Forge, where Farid had been forced into a space similar to this and was starved by his father.

"I'll go first," Nyzaia said, stepping onto the ladder.

"No," Farid said. "It's fine, I'll go. We can't risk your life." Farid guided Soren towards Nyzaia, who reached for Soren's slender fingers before thinking better of it and gripping the chains instead. Soren remained silent, watching the darkness below as Farid descended.

"You are next," Nyzaia said, pushing Soren towards the ladder. As Soren descended, Farid knocked on the door below until light flooded the space, brightening Soren's hair and face. She peered up at Nyzaia with an unknown emotion in her eyes. Farid caught her arm when she reached the last step, tugging her into the room. With a crack of her neck, Nyzaia jumped and landed in a crouch at the bottom. Light bathed her dark leathers, an entrance worthy of an assassin queen. Myara's symbol on her attacker's ring flashed in her mind; she knew who she would face.

"Hello, your Majesty," said a slick, oily voice. Nyzaia raised her head and flipped her braid over one shoulder, meeting the eyes of a man that disgusted her.

"What a lovely welcome, Lord Israar." Nyzaia smirked, assessing the lord. "Had you visited with your friend earlier, we could have avoided such a delay." Lord Israar's mouth twitched. He wore his usual blood-red sherwani, littered with flecks of golden thread that glinted in the light from the staggered flames in the room's centre. Instead of sconces, the light shone from the wooden stakes plunged into the sandy floor, forming a circle. Twelve faces, illuminated by the flames, formed a larger circle around the blaze. Nyzaia did not recognise the people gathered, but noted their wrinkles beneath the woven fabric of their hoods and robes, drowning their figures. They were all old—far older than her attacker's hands, perhaps as old as the Historian had appeared.

"It's nice to see you in your *natural* attire for once." Lord Israar smirked, perched on the edge of a table littered with leather books and papers. Nyzaia narrowed her eyes. "Come now. Did you think I knew of Tajana's identity, but not your own?" He chuckled, entertained by Nyzaia's naivety. She merely grinned, tugging her daggers back into her thighs.

"I simply did not care, Israar. I am Queen of Keres. Your opinion matters little when I control this realm." Nyzaia scanned the room—it was bare, mostly. Twelve wooden chairs lined one wall, matching the number of people standing in a circle, their eyes downcast. She could not determine the purpose. Patterned rugs lay scattered on the ground; perhaps it was their usual dining spot. No weapons peeked out from clasped hands, no markings were on the walls, or blood on the floor. From what she could tell, no sacrifices had occurred here. Soren's chains clinked as she wriggled in Farid's grip, staring at the floor in the centre of the circle while avoiding the eyes in the room.

"You really should care, your Majesty." Israar pushed off from the table and turned to look at his books; he feigned reading the pages. "I imagine you have questions and are here to accuse me of unnecessary murder." Nyzaia glanced between the lord and those in the circle. No one moved; they kept their wrinkled eyes averted. She could not imagine such elderly people committing murder. Perhaps the attacker Seiko had butchered was the main assassin, maybe a son of one of the elders.

"So, you did not break into the Red Stones den and sacrifice six of my men and women?" Nyzaia asked. "And then have someone attempt the same on me?" Israar did not turn around, though he stroked his oily beard.

"Your men and women? Last I heard, the Red Stones are now a democracy."

"They are residents of Keres. That makes them my people."

"Do you feel remorse knowing your people grieve for those who died at your own hands, assassin?"

Nyzaia did not flinch. "Enough, Israar," she snapped. "You and I both know our thoughts on one another. The simple matter of the fact is, I am *queen*, and you are sacrificing people for gods know what reason."

"Ah!" Israar spun to look at her again, holding three objects. "For gods, that's just it. All of this is to speak with them."

Nyzaia frowned. "You want to speak with Keres and the others? Why?"

"Who said they were the only gods?" Israar smirked and strode towards the circle; the flames licked to warm him as he stepped onto the carpets and positioned three objects in a triangle: a rusting dagger, a red feather as long as her forearm, dipped in gold, and a single jar of what appeared to be ash. Nyzaia kept her face neutral. A jar of ash had been present on the table when Farid found her. She thought of Exandria, how she shifted with smoke as ash filtered through her very being. Something told Nyzaia the odd encounter was more than a drug-hazed dream.

"If there are more gods, I'd like to know where the hell they've been while we've faced war," Nyzaia scoffed.

"Why would they serve those who worship the celestial four, tyrants who believe themselves to be the only worthy gods?" While Israar's expression remained neutral, the robed men and woman sneered at his description. The mark on Nyzaia's palm burned—a *celestial* tie. Why did Israar differentiate Novisia's gods from these supposed others?

"Don't the other gods also consider themselves more worthy?" Nyzaia scoffed.

"Ah, but they would be correct." Israar smiled. "I'll do you a kindness, a final piece of information before I take your life." In the circle, Israar spun until he faced her again. Nyzaia snorted at the absurd notion he was capable of taking her life. "You have only been queen for a short while; I have been a lord for far longer, providing answers when people asked and money where needed." Israar looked at each face around the circle. "You may see me as greedy or self-motivated, but in offering my services, I became the most sought-after person when citizens of this realm needed secrecy and assistance, trusting the word of a lord over the Red Stones. Thus, when an old man appeared at my door and spoke of old awakened memories, and different gods and lands—a place where I could be king, if only I helped with one thing—who was I to refuse?"

Israar's tale seemed as farfetched as the idea of Caligh's once did, except the notion of other lands was becoming more and more plausible following Osiris's claims, and now this. What if the gods Israar believed existed originated from other lands? On Nyzaia's left, Soren continued fidgeting, as if trying to reach the circle; her eyes fixed on the ground. "Tobias here"—Israar gestured to an old man—"originally hailed from Keres, but married into a Garridon family soon after arriving on Novisia. Imagine his surprise when one morning he awoke to recall memories that had long been hidden." Nyzaia clenched her fists. Her assumptions about Osiris's warning and the link to the sacrifices were correct.

"Oh, do tell us more about these fascinating very *real* memories." Nyzaia feigned disbelief, prompting Israar to narrow his eyes, offended by her mockery.

"Tobias hailed from a religious family, a religion no one on Novisia can recall; it worships undocumented gods and great warriors who once ruled desert lands. We questioned where Tobias had come from and if he was really from Ithyion." When Israar reached for a dagger in his jacket pocket, Farid and Nyzaia shared a look. "And then news of the battle spread. People spoke of a man who could turn men into beasts and back again. That must confirm the existence of other lands, races, and even other gods, must it not?"

"Is that what the sacrifices are for? You want to speak to some made up gods Tobias claims his family once worshipped? To discover if he is really from Ithyion or other lands you foolishly believe you could rule?" As Nyzaia approached the circle, Soren fought against Farid more loudly, grunting as she tried to pull free from his grip. Israar chuckled. He only had eyes for the queen.

"I want to know who stole the memories of those on Novisia and *why* before I determine if it is safe for me to leave in search of these lands. "Israar's dark eyes glinted. "We have one more sacrifice to make, a sacrifice representing Novisia and Ithyion's last god, Keres."

"Why are sacrifices required in the names of the celestial gods?" Nyzaia's toes were at the circle's edge.

"Because there is no one else the deities hate more." Israar smirked and flung the dagger at Nyzaia's face.

"Nyzaia, don't!" Soren shouted. Fury overcame Nyzaia, who dodged the dagger and stepped into the circle. Heat rushed through her, like she was burning from the inside out, knocking her to her knees. "Farid!" Soren screamed as the captain dived towards Nyzaia, reaching for her shoulders. He lifted her up before he, too, grunted in pain. Nyzaia trained her eyes on the carpet, where a drawn symbol in the sand peeked out from the edge: a circle surrounding a cross, with a small swirl in its centre. Nyzaia turned to Soren, who stared at the mark on the floor. She tried to warn her.

"How does it feel, your Majesty?" Israar asked. Nyzaia grunted at the burning pain within and rose beside Farid, gripping his arm for purchase as he fought against a similar feeling. Israar looked towards him as Nyzaia reached for her dagger, yet her fingers were numb and motionless, unable to find purchase. This was worse—far worse than the attempt on her life at the chambers. They must have known the attacker was dead when he did not return. Now, they knew to try harder to successfully restrain a queen with Keres's fire in her veins. Israar narrowed his eyes at Farid. "Interesting. I did not know you had any power the old language would null." He knelt and folded back a piece of the rug, revealing the repeated symbol drawn in the sand, which wielded a power to stop her. *Nulling.* The flame within Nyzaia flickered then, and the pain subsided as darkness took over. She blinked, hoping to conjure a flame, but nothing appeared. Her body numbed, as did Farid's, and they collapsed to the floor as the sparks within them extinguished.

Chapter Twenty Five

Soren

Soren had not panicked for anyone but herself for as long as she could remember, not since the day Caligh wanted to take Sadira. Yet all she felt was panic as two robed men rushed forward, seizing her hands, preventing her from running to Farid and Nyzaia. Though what they expected her to do while bound in chains, Soren did not know. While Israar reeled Nyzaia in with his petty words and foolish claims, Soren did what was now normal for her—staring at the smooth, sand-carpeted floor, avoiding all attention. Doing so had notified Soren of the anomaly at the carpet's edge: a rough mark reaching out from beneath the rug, like someone had traced their finger through it. She had stared at the symbol, willing herself to remember its meaning.

Focus on something small, Nyzaia had said when helping Soren to recall a memory. So, she did just that. She thought of the room where she and Sadira had their lessons, picturing the old leather books and hastily bound pages, where symbols had once been recorded from memory. The symbol then appeared, an interchangeable meaning for locked, null, and pause. At first, Soren was unsure of Israar's intention with the circle, but knew Nyzaia should not step inside.

Soren had failed again. The robed followers dragged Nyzaia's limp body into the centre of the circle beside Farid and pierced large iron nails in each of her palms. Nyzaia could not scream; instead, she stared motionlessly at Farid as they did the same to him. Something was different about Farid, though. When they pierced the iron through his palm, a gut-wrenching scream roared from his lips. A robed man closed the door to the room, preventing Jabir or anyone else from inspecting the sound. Yet when Jabir's scream echoed nearby, Soren knew he was already on the other side, banging against the door to break it down. Farid and Nyzaia's bodies were locked up, their powers nulled. They had no way of escaping. Yet Farid still spoke and cursed at the lord standing over them, who had an intrigued and inquisitive look in his eye, like Caligh had in the memory Soren shared with Nyzaia. Soren's heart quickened, and she grunted when the two men tightened their hold on her wrists, digging the iron chains deeper into her skin.

"Soren!" Farid called. His head was still lulled to the side, watching his queen, but Nyzaia's unwavering gaze was on Soren, a silent command to do whatever Farid instructed. A man approached him with a rag. "Soren! You are not broken!" Tears welled in Soren's eyes. Farid *saw* her. No one ever saw her. "Look within yourself, Soren. You. Are. Not. *Broken*." Farid grunted the final words, his voice snuffed by the rag shoved in his mouth and secured behind his head. When the robed figures pulled Soren's arms taut, she whipped her head to the side, sneering at one man, who looked on with a passive expression. Shadows crept back into her mind after laying so long in wait. *No.*

"Does it look like I'm going anywhere?" she snapped, the usual venom returning to her voice. "I'm in chains! Why would I care about the fate of my captors?"

Soren glared at Nyzaia, and the queen's expression faltered—*no.* Darkness stroked the edges of Soren's mind, taunting her to come out and play, return to her old ways, reigniting the old feelings embedded in her soul after so many years under Caligh's words and control. Soren stared at Nyzaia as a robed woman stooped with a knife to slice through her leathers, revealing the thin fabric concealing her chest. Nyzaia's eyes fluttered when the woman began carving into her skin. Despite the rag in Farid's mouth, agony tore through his throat as another woman knelt to carve the same mark on him. Sweat broke out along Soren's back with Farid's screams in her ears. The panic in Nyzaia's eyes taunted her. *You are not broken.* Soren closed her eyes. Focus on one thing; focus on those words. *You are not broken.* The shadows in her mind remained, clawing for control, but a drop of power bloomed in Soren's stomach. *You are not broken.* As the men held out her arms, she furrowed her brow and clenched her hands into fists, focusing on the delicate white petals and vibrant green vines in her mind, fighting to break free. *You are not broken.* She thought of when she saved Sadira. *You are not broken.* As the feeling took root in her stomach, Soren finally opened her eyes to meet Nyzaia's. Although she did not move as blood trickled down her chest, Soren swore she saw a smile in her brown eyes as Soren's glowed green. A small voice broke free then: *I like Nyzaia.* Listening to that voice, Soren unclenched her fists and splayed her fingers. Roots shot up from the sand—a hungry, dormant power—reaching for the bodies in the room. Others reached for her chains and tore them in two, knocking aside the men on either side of her. Soren screamed, "Jabir!" hoping he would hear as her roots and vines tossed the body blocking the door aside. The power was overwhelming; Soren could not focus on everyone at once. Watching Nyzaia and Farid, she willed her vines to trap the arms of the two robed women and drag them to the floor.

Jabir finally burst through the door when Soren's powers reached Israar. The two men from before scrambled forward to push Soren towards the circle and null her abilities, yet blood sprayed from them as Jabir sliced the back of their knees with his dagger. He threw the blade to Soren and ran for the circle.

"Don't step inside it yet!" Soren shouted. Jabir halted at the circle's edge as the vines ensnared the last of the followers and swept them across the floor, pushing the carpet aside and removing any traces of the symbol. Sweat trickled down Soren's face as she held thirteen bodies in her grip. She found Nyzaia's eyes while Jabir tugged off his leathers and wrapped them around Nyzaia's torn attire. The queen trembled, although she watched the fallen queen with an emotion akin to awe. Soren groaned at the shadows reaching for the brightness in her soul, intent on extinguishing it.

"I can't hold this for long!" Soren cried. Jabir rested his forehead against Farid's and mumbled to him. Something snapped in Farid then, as when Jabir sat back, raging blue fire shone in Farid's eyes. Slowly, he rose to face Israar. The lord stopped thrashing against the vines the moment their eyes met. Warmth bathed Soren as flamed wings shot from Farid's back, blinding the room. Blue flames licked his arms, contrasting the orange glow of his wings.

"Nefere," said the robed followers in unison. They collapsed to their knees in the vines that held them and bowed their heads. The reaction made Soren pause, confused. She had only heard that name in relation to the valley in Keres. Taking advantage of the sudden silence, Soren strode around the room, slicing her vines at the root and drawing her remaining power back in. She left the followers kneeling on the floor, wrapped in the remaining vines.

"What are they saying?" Farid growled at Israar, whose eyes widened with a mixture of fear and awe. Israar had not been on the battlefield to witness Farid's wings, she realised, and even Soren had not witnessed the blue flames before.

Israar bowed his head. "They are worshipping you, oh great one. Nefere, God of the Xyra, protector of Q'Ohar." Farid looked at Nyzaia with raised eyebrows as Israar continued mumbling. "But we did not complete the sacrifice. How are you here in this body?"

"I'm not a god," Farid sneered, and then he sliced a dagger across Lord Israar's throat. "I'm Captain of the Queen's Guard."

Unfazed by Farid's violence in defence of his queen, Soren continued around the room, slicing at the vines. Her hands trembled, her body weakened at the rare use of power. When she had sacrificed her family, she had inherited their powers, along with Sadira. But Caligh's manipulation warped her gift to destroy Garridon's creations. Soren faced the final three robed men. They no longer watched with passive indifference. Instead, fear widened their eyes as she stalked towards them. Darkness was returning. The shadows she had extinguished with her powers had returned with a vengeance, hungry and punishing. Soren shook her head and approached the final bound men when she saw it: the darkening vines, the crumbling leaves. Her usual power was returning. The men snapped out of the decayed vines in seconds and bolted up the ladder.

Soren growled, intent on only one thing—darkness. Death. She clenched tightly to her dagger and sprinted after them before halting in the darkened alleyway. The shadows were no longer only in her mind. The three men stood face to face with shadowed soldiers—Elisara's soldiers, she realised, although Vala's queen was nowhere to be seen. The dark soldiers seemed to speak to that darkness in her mind, beckoning her forward. Steps sounded in the hallway from behind, and she lunged before anyone could stop her. In a blur of movement, Soren swiped a man's legs out from under him before slitting his throat, leaving him gurgling on the ground. *Wonderful. Beautiful. Keep going,* the soldiers encouraged, forming a barricade to keep the other men from escaping. They fell to their knees in tears. Soren wasted no time slicing their throats too. With wide eyes, they gripped their necks as blood spilled from their mouths. Soren tilted her head. Fear—is that what her family had felt? The horrifying memory of her family's deaths at her own hand overwhelmed Soren as she knelt over one man and screamed in his face, plunging her knife repeatedly into his chest, splattering blood onto her face. *He would want this for you,* the soldiers said. Caligh wanted her to do this, to become merciless. Soren moved to the next body and plunged her knife into his neck—in and out—until his head began to fall, hanging on by a tendon. Soren screamed, drenched in blood.

"Soren!" a voice commanded, though she did not recognise it. Darkness consumed her mind, suffocating a tiny white flower in its centre, struggling for breath. "Soren!" the voice yelled. A hand seized her wrist, stopping her dagger mid-air. Soren screamed at the woman, who shouted, "Drop the dagger!" The woman's eyes burned with fire, matching the flames in her other hand. Something pulled at Soren's mind then. The shadows halted as the flower began to blossom, trying to break free. Soren stared back at the woman, panting, as blood dripped down her head and into her mouth. The woman did not look at Soren or the blood with disgust. Instead, her burning eyes seemed to peer deep into Soren's soul.

"I see you." Those three simple words prompted Soren to drop the dagger, blinking. A man with flaming wings appeared behind the woman, prompting the shadowed soldiers to flee. "I see you, Soren," she repeated. *I like Nyzaia,* whispered a small voice in her mind. Soren slumped into Nyzaia's arms with a strangled cry. "I see you."

Chapter Twenty-Six
Larelle

If someone predicted a year ago that Larelle would be walking down an unending tunnel within the city's church, hand in hand with a man she had known briefly as a child, she would have thought them delusional. Routine and a quiet life had been the staples of Larelle's life for the five years after her banishment. But something lay beneath her rapidly beating chest, sweating hands, and anxious breathing—excitement about the unknown. She wanted to hurry forward. Such experiences, like her brush with death at the engagement ball, the war, and even now in the looming tunnel, made her feel *alive*, converting her from a comfortable mother at home to a risk-taking queen. As she glanced at the man whose hand she held, she did not believe it was entirely because of the new life thrust upon her.

The crash did not sound again, but as Alvan and Larelle quickened their pace along the hallway, they heard other indistinguishable noises crawling toward them.

"There," Larelle murmured, pointing at a slither of light in the darkness.

"The bottom of a doorway?" Alvan suggested, and Larelle was inclined to agree. Their feet slowed as the noises soon became murmurs; someone was talking—occasionally shouting—to themselves, but neither could discern his words.

Sea-salt tinged the air. Even within the walls, Larelle knew they had ventured closer to the edge of the city towards the sea. Alvan tugged Larelle's hand, stopping them. Still several feet from the slither of light, Alvan lifted the lantern, illuminating what appeared to be the front of a house in a soft glow. Larelle frowned, puzzled by a tunnel connecting a house to the church. It was definitely a house; she could see its dark wooden door, and a square she assumed was a window, covered by a thin piece of hanging fabric to shield the light. The house appeared like any other on the outskirts of Mera, meaning the house was likely built first and was then connected to the church shortly after. Larelle wondered why anyone in Mera would hide a tunnel between two locations. She recalled the last row of homes before the city met the beach, the end ones built directly in front of the cliffy rock that eventually met The Bay. If this home was in front of the cliffs, it seemed plausible that an underground tunnel had been created through it to reach the church.

Alvan placed the lantern at their feet before they carefully approached the door, avoiding bringing the light too close to the hidden window to avoid getting caught. Larelle jumped when a voice shouted from inside, their words incoherent.

"Are you certain about this?" whispered Alvan, reaching the door and covered window. Larelle nodded and touched the brown woven cloth, like the sacks used to collect olives in Amoro. Stepping aside, she pressed her face against the stone, the dampness seeping into her skin. Ignoring the small tremble in her hand, Larelle moved the fabric aside—just an inch—and peered through. Alvan mirrored Larelle on the other side: two faces peering into the unknown.

The light seemed to drift from a single window on the opposite wall, yet there was nothing but an alleyway through it. For some reason, the house was completely penned in. That small glimpse of the outside world allowed a view of a small home, a dirty home at that, as though the resident, whose back was turned, had no regard for daily chores. A single bed was shoved into one corner, draped in once white sheets, now crumpled and yellowing. The long table beside it filled the length of the wall and parchments scattered the surface, held down by old, dripping candles, collecting wax on the pages in lumps. Trickles of black smoke from the candles stained the wall behind, having been left to burn too close. A yellow tinge tarnished the remaining bricks; the only difference in colour was a white patch beneath the window, where a piece of furniture must have sat for some time. A billow of smoke drifted around the mumbling man, holding a pipe.

Larelle inched her fingers to where the window was partially cracked open and trained her eyes on the man. He had little hair, except for a few white strands barely covering his scalp, indicating where it had either fallen or been pulled out over time. His wrinkled hands trembled as he removed the pipe from his mouth and lifted it again, appearing discontented at the lack of substance. Larelle pulled the window slightly, so she might better hear what he was saying. When the window creaked, his hand stilled and his mumbling stopped. Alvan grabbed Larelle's free arm and tugged her away from the window, flattening them both against the wall. The pair listened with bated breath as the window creaked again. The drape twitched, and Larelle knew the man peered outside into the tunnel. The lantern, an arm's reach away, was the only sign someone was outside of his home. Larelle jumped when he rattled the door handle from inside, but it did not open.

"Locked in," he mumbled. His voice was clearer now as he opened the window further, peering out. "Locked in. She locked me in. Still locked in. Locked in." Waiting until his voice drifted back to the centre of the room, Larelle pulled away from Alvan.

"One abides, one rebels," muttered the man as Larelle inched towards the widened gap in the drapes and crouched, looking inside. Alvan rested a hand on her shoulder to peer in, too. "Listen, listen, listen to the land—LISTEN!" he shouted, beginning to pace. Only when he reached the other end of the room did Larelle recognise him from her occasional church visit as a child—Father Zoro, the priest of the very church they were visiting. Upon their first visit, Vivian said he had not wished to see Larelle, given her family's loose connection to the church. Today, the acolyte said the priest was sick. Larelle was inclined to agree, though his sickness appeared to be of the mind. "A reverse, a reflection, beneath—beneath you all." Father Zoro screamed before hurling his pipe at the mirror leaning against the wall beside the window, cracking the glass. Staggering over, he smacked his forehead repeatedly with his fist and then rested his hand along the fracture. He stilled, staring closely at the shards before pressing his other hand on the other side to peer closer at the crack. "A reverse, a reflection, a sister, a mirror. A MIRROR!" Father Zoro laughed hysterically, his eyes moving to where Larelle's reflection could be seen behind him, peering through the window. The old man spun and ran, his movements spider-like, as he bridged the distance and pushed his hand against the window, where Larelle jumped back with Alvan. The window did not budge; a locking mechanism appeared to stop it from creating a gap large enough for him to crawl out of. The man's eyes bulged in their hollowed-out sockets as he shoved his face through the gap, revealing rotting teeth. He stared at the pair.

"A queeeeen," the man sang. "A queen has come to see me?" His voice lilted, like he silently questioned if she was truly present or a figment of the mind. Alvan gripped Larelle's hand and shook his head, telling her not to answer. Larelle's gaze drifted to a glint of gold around the man's neck, a long chain dangling from beneath his shirt. Larelle squinted but she was too far away to see the detail. "Tell her to let me out! Get that sorceress bitch to let me OUT!"

"He doesn't sound particularly religious," Alvan murmured.

"Who, sir?" Larelle asked, though she suspected she knew the answer. The man trained his eyes on Larelle.

"I'm meant to keep the balance, the balance, the balance between three." Father Zoro shook his head, hitting the window as he did.

"What balance, Father Zoro?" asked Alvan, earning a grunt from the old man who ignored him, watching only Larelle with manic eyes.

"Useless, useless. There is a price, a price for the curse." Larelle stepped forward. *Curse. Osiris's lands were cursed.*

"What curse?" she asked.

"The ancient one. There is always a price, always a way to undo and keep the balance—I must keep the balance." Larelle stepped closer to the priest, prompting Alvan to hesitantly release his queen's hand.

"How do you break the curse?" she asked. The man's face saddened, softening his manic features until tears pooled in his eyes.

"Now? Or later?"

Larelle frowned. "Is there a difference?"

"Two curses, two sides of a coin. Linked."

"The first curse," Larelle demanded, though her frustration rose at the possibility there was more than one.

"Find the beneath," Father Zoro breathed. "A reverse, a reflection, a sister, a mirror." Larelle did not ask what he meant. By the look in his eye, he would give no sane response.

"The second curse?"

"Sacrifice."

"Sacrifice who?" Larelle asked.

"Sacrifice and fulfil the prophecy; sacrifice and reunite the lands." The priest bowed his head, and his sudden laughter morphed into a coughing fit. The chain around his neck dangled over the window ledge, and something inside Larelle urged her to take it. Never one to doubt her intuition, she reached for the gold circle in one swift move and tugged, snapping the chain. The priest's head snapped up, yet he was oblivious to her theft, too lost in his delusions.

"I am still the balance, still the balance," the priest murmured, stumbling back from the window and into his room. Larelle's chest twinged as Alvan approached her again, holding the lantern.

"We should help him," she whispered, gripping the talisman-like object in her hand. Alvan stroked her back.

"Unfortunately, I think he is beyond help," Alvan said as Father Zoro paced around his small home, clutching his hair. Slowly,

Larelle nodded, pained by the sight of one of Nerida's people in such a state. "Let's get back." Alvan kissed the top of Larelle's head. Together, they strode through the darkness towards the bookshelves.

It was a half-hour walk at least, and Larelle hoped Zarya was not worrying about her whereabouts. They paused upon finally reaching the bookshelves. Larelle unfurled her fingers from the pendant and furrowed her brow, tracing the engravings of a wolf and two symbols, one of which she recognised from Sadira's Wiccan book. Larelle turned it over and found the Garridon Sigil with the hawk on it raised.

"Was he from Garridon?" Alvan asked.

"I have no idea. As far as I knew, he has always been a priest in Nerida. Though, perhaps it is possible his mother or father hailed from a Garridon family when our ancestors were still on Ithyion." Larelle frowned at the three marks on the back.

"Odd that he is a Neridian priest, given his obvious devotion to Garridon," Alvan said, pulling books from the shelves.

"He knew about a curse," Larelle said. "Osiris said many on Novisia would begin to remember and reveal more to us. What if Father Zoro hailed from Garridon, but when his family fled from Ithyion, they hid something in his memories, leading him to a different realm instead?"

"It seems plausible, but without knowing the full extent of why memories were hidden, and why Osiris's lands were cursed, we will not know for certain." Alvan grunted, placing a tenth book atop the stack in his arms.

"What are you doing?" Larelle asked. Alvan jerked his head to the lantern, and she reached for it.

"I don't particularly want to stay in here. I will carry the books to the front of the room, so we can read them near Zarya and Lillian. It will only take a couple of trips." Larelle nodded and reached for four copies of the navy covers titled *Thassena*, balancing them under one arm. They walked back along the dark hallway until reaching the two cases hiding the darkness. She was keen to return and discuss the priest with Vivian.

"Mumma, is that you?" Zarya's voice sang from the other side of the door from where she still sat at the table. Placing the books on the stool, Larelle peeked around the door to smile at her daughter.

"What is all this?" Larelle asked in an excited voice, noting her daughter's grin, and the many large parchments spread across the table.

Zarya clapped her hands. "Maps!"

"Sorry, Larelle," said Lillian. "She burst in after you both, insisting she knew what to look for. She came back with all these scrolls."

"Do not apologise," Larelle murmured, recalling what Osiris had told Zarya. "We should trust her intuition."

"How many maps did you find, Zarya?" Alvan asked, peering over Zarya's shoulder.

"One, two, three, four, five, six, seven, eight!" Zarya counted, pointing at each in turn. She had laid them out, using books to hold down the many corners. "This one is Novisia," Zarya said, pointing to the nearest. "And this one is Novisia too, but without any of the places or names on it. It's empty, except for this circle in the middle." Larelle stood beside Alvan, inspecting the map. Zarya was right. But why would anyone create a duplicated yet empty map of Novisia? Vivian closed her book and strode over from her desk, watching the princess. Larelle moved closer to Zarya. The acolyte may be keeping the priest locked away for his own safety, or she may know more about his jumbled thoughts. Larelle's uncertainty on the acolyte's intentions made her wary.

"Perhaps it's a map from when our ancestors first arrived on Novisia, before they divided it into realms and began building," suggested Alvan.

"These three don't have names, only marks for places on the land, but these three do," Zarya continued, pointing at the three maps above Novisia, with a scrawled font etched in the corners of each. Lillian read them out for Zarya, who struggled to pronounce them. "Xyliar, Carvyre, and Thassena." Larelle's eyes immediately tugged to the map titled Thassena. Though she had not heard of the other two names before, Osiris had mentioned the third, and she had since found it on the map and spines of books.

"They're all huge," Alvan murmured. He was right. The lands on all six maps were far bigger than Novisia—in fact, they were triple the size, perhaps more. Larelle circled the table, intent on examining the map of Thassena, but her eyes paused on Vivian, who returned to her desk and scribbled a note in her book, stealing another glance at Zarya.

"Could you help Alvan organise all these books, Zarya?" Larelle asked Alvan. She strode over to the acolyte, who promptly closed her book when noticing Larelle's approach. "You appear to be fascinated with my daughter," Larelle said sharply, driven by a fierce protectiveness. The acolyte widened her eyes and stepped back, clasping her hands.

"She will one day be our ruler. It is natural to document her history," Vivian said, though there was a tremble to her voice.

"What did you write?" Larelle asked, reaching for the book. Vivian snapped it up. "Are you refusing your queen, sister Vivian?" Larelle's eyes glowed, and the glass of water on the desk shook.

"I—"

"Is that why you have Father Zoro locked away, too? So you may study him and document his history?" Larelle urged. The acolyte's expression changed, and the fear faded to a stony-like appearance.

"Father Zoro is a danger to himself," she said, her words clipped. Larelle opened her mouth to counter, the gold pendant burning in her clenched fist, but a crash from behind the curtain, below in the pews, stopped her. The guards that had been stationed below barrelled into the archives, blocking the door behind them. Larelle rushed forward with Vivian as Alvan ushered Zarya back in her chair before joining his queen. Taking a deep breath, Larelle pulled back the curtain, a replay of the day's earlier events.

"Darkness." Vivian shook. "Darkness has come to claim us." Under the glass dome, shadowed soldiers stalked between the pews. Larelle relaxed when she realised the shadows fought for Elisara, but something about their movements, slow and prowling, raised the hairs on Larelle's arms. One lone soldier had pushed over the altar and swiped items off the tables. Elisara had no reason to send her soldiers to Nerida—or anywhere, for that matter—especially not to behave like this.

"They're not listening to her," Zarya called. Larelle faced her daughter, who seemed bored of the maps now. She drew on a blank piece of paper instead.

"What do you mean Zarya?" asked Larelle, moving towards the princess. Alvan kept watch of the shadows below.

"Some of them don't want to listen. She's sleeping, so she doesn't know the bad people are ignoring her," Zarya said, adding the finishing touches to her drawing. "Do you like it?" She held up the picture to her mother, who pursed her lips as the reality of Zarya's intuition settled in. Larelle gazed at a drawing of a place Zarya had never seen: a towering mountain in the middle of a lake, where a dark-winged creature roamed the sky. Although Larelle had never visited herself, it matched Elisara and Kazaar's descriptions. Larelle knew where the Queen of Vala was taking refuge. *The Unsanctioned Isle.* Behind her, despite the panic of the darkness, Vivian scribbled in a book again. Larelle intended to have Alvan steal it amongst their other books when they left.

"Vivian, do you have an Avery attached to the church?" Larelle asked, holding Zarya's drawing. The acolyte jolted, but then nodded in agreement. "I need to send three letters." The acolyte gathered parchment and a quill for the queen. She would write a letter for the Queen of Keres, King of Garridon, and Vala's new commander, Vlad, summoning them to the Unsanctioned Isle. Though it pained Larelle to force Elisara to confront reality so soon after her loss, it was time for the rulers of Novisia to get answers and protect their kingdom.

Chapter Twenty-Seven

Caellum

"Where is she?" Caellum shouted; his voice filled with trepidation as he stormed down the grand staircase into the entrance hall of the castle. Sir Cain approached and raised his hands, his face devoid of warmth. He intended to stop Caellum, which meant he knew where she was. Something was wrong. "She is not in our rooms. It is three o'clock in the morning, and my *queen* is not in our rooms." Caellum brushed Sir Cain aside and stalked towards the doors. The guards moved into position to block him, moving their hands to the pommel of their swords. He could take six men, especially if it meant finding Sadira.

"Caellum, she is fine." Sir Cain tried to reassure him. *I shouldn't have stayed up so late.* He had read late into the early morning, having moved on from his father's diary to his grandfather's. He assumed Sadira had returned to their rooms after her trip into the city, yet when he had finally stumbled into their chambers, bleary-eyed, he saw the empty fourposter bed in the light of the fireplace embers and low burning candles, and instantly knew something was wrong.

"Sadira's guards accompanied her." Sir Cain grabbed Caellum's arm, forcing him to face the commander. "She is fine."

Caellum scanned Sir Cain's eyes before shoving him off with a growl. "Then why can I not leave the castle?" Sir Cain pursed his lips in answer. Caellum hurried to the towering windows overlooking the dusty path from the city into the treeline toward the castle. It was dark—unusually dark. Clouds masked the moon and stars, while the sconces along the garden walls that usually burned through the night were vacant. A chill rushed through the castle.

"Tell me what is happening. Now!" Caellum planted his feet shoulder-width apart and crossed his arms. Sadira was hidden somewhere in the darkness outside. Sir Cain's voice was hushed as he told Caellum everything he knew.

"Her guards escorted her to the apothecary when the sun was setting. They estimated to be gone from the castle for around two hours." Sir Cain stood shoulder to shoulder with his king, gazing out at the city residing in darkness. "Only an hour passed when the guards at the entrance to the estate rushed to find me, reporting of soldiers whom moved like shadows shifting through the trees and approaching the city." Caellum finally tore his gaze from the darkness to meet Sir Cain's eyes. His mind instantly returned to the battle, and the horror and pain inflicted by Caligh's shadows.

"Caligh's? Or Elisara's?" Caellum asked. He doubted they had to worry about Elisara's army, but while Caligh controlled no men in shadowed form, it was not unreasonable to assume he could.

"Until someone from the city can give us a full report, we won't know for certain. Based on their description, I would suspect they are the shadows of Vala's queen."

"Why have we not sent anyone? A rank from the military?" Caellum's voice rose again.

"They cannot see anything. I sent an extra twenty soldiers to guard the estate entrance, but every time they lit the sconces, the flames blinked out of existence. The entirety of Antor is bathed in darkness, not just the night sky but as though the shadows have come alive." Caellum squinted through the glass but saw no moving figures or twisting shadows. Sir Cain was right. This was no typical cloudy night.

"So there is nothing I can do?" Caellum twisted the ring around his finger.

"You are the king. The realm cannot risk losing both of you, not without a successor." Caellum considered his commander's words. He was right. They had no succession plan, meaning the throne would likely fall to a lord. But it was the lords' idea he marry Sadira, so the citizens could trust their marriage more than the Balfour's usurped claim to the throne. Not only would losing Sadira break Caellum completely, but it could also shatter the calmness that had settled across the realm ever since she became his betrothed. While cheers had greeted them upon his return from battle, Caellum was no fool. Their cheers were not for him. They were for his queen.

"She *is* the rightful heir to the Garridon throne, and I will not place my life above hers." Caellum whirled on his heel for the castle doors. "Sir Cain, bring your most trusted soldiers to the stables." He shot the guards by the door with a look that promised severe repercussions if they disobeyed their king. Their armour clinked as they stepped aside, and with a shove fuelled by the strength of his blood, the king slammed the castle doors open, intent on finding his queen.

***

The darkness did not feel like Elisara's. Caellum had watched the shadows respond to her on the desert. Even in her most erratic state, the darkness had not felt evil. But as he slowed to a gallop across the fields bordering Antor, danger danced across his skin. It was like the shadowed soldiers had thickened the air, making it difficult to breathe. Shivers trickled up his spine as Sir Cain and four soldiers dismounted alongside him. A further sixty soldiers approached the city from the north, south, and western edges. The city was devoid of light. Even the odd glow within homes, offered by the twitching drapes, did little to guide Caellum and his companions through the city.

Caellum tapped his sword two times on the path. Two to move forward. One to halt. He had not wanted to use sound as a means of communication, but it was too dark to point. He hoped that would change the closer it came to dawn, but he had an hour to wait until the sky was tinged in a dark shade of blue before the sun painted its canvas. Sir Cain scratched a piece of stone against a wall to ignite a spark for the lantern. It dwindled the second the flame erupted, confirming what the guards at the castle had said about their lanterns.

Slowly, Caellum moved along the first street on the city's outskirt, his feet steady and his sword firm. The group paced forward until he paused outside the first door. His priority was finding Sadira, but he would fail his people if he did not ensure their safety too. Caellum had instructed the soldiers at the other ends of the city to do the same. As they moved inward, they knocked and checked each building. Athena's apothecary was located on the next street over; it would not take long to reach. But with every door knock, Caellum's heart rate spiked with worry and anticipation.

The echo of fists on wood was gentle as Caellum raised his hand again. Sir Cain was at the next door on his left; two other soldiers took the right-hand side of the street, while one stood behind Caellum. He counted to ten, waiting for anyone within to approach the window. A curtain twitched, and the inhabitant must have realised who was at their door because a moment later, a lock clicked as the door opened. A wrinkled face peered out.

"Is everyone within safe?" Caellum asked as quietly as possible. The old lady nodded, wide-eyed. "Have you or anyone else inside seen anything?" The lady glanced behind her and nodded. Footsteps sounded across the wooden floor until a man, similar in age, approached, resting a hand on her shoulder and holding a lantern in the other.

"There were murmurings at the tavern. Lord Ryon's men were there," the old man whispered. Caellum frowned. "There were mumblings that Ryon would make you regret keeping the throne from the true heirs, your Majesty."

"Did they say how?"

The old man shook his head. "I took no notice, but when night fell, these—these dark shadowed men appeared and began taunting people outside the tavern." The two seemed unconnected, but if Ryon was in the city, and the man's words were true, then Ryon had likely been spreading doubt about his claim in other ways.

"Was anyone hurt?"

"Not that I know of. I got home as quickly as I could." He raised the lamp higher, offering a clearer view of the fear in his eyes as he clutched the woman Caellum assumed was his wife. He opened his mouth to thank and reassure them but was stopped as the flame in the man's lantern blinked out. The glow from within the home, lit by the fireplace, continued, surrounded by mountains of candles. Perhaps whatever controlled the darkness could not dampen all light. Caellum peered down the street to where Sir Cain and two soldiers moved into formation, striding further along the cobbled road. Caellum swallowed, detecting a flurry of shadowed movement outside Athena's apothecary.

"Lock your doors and stay inside until sunrise," Caellum murmured. He nodded to the elderly couple before taking off down the street. He did not worry about the noise of his footsteps; he thought only of Sadira as Sir Cain raised his sword. A moment later, the drapes inside the apothecary flew open, bathing the street in light—enough for Caellum to see Sir Cain sword to sword with a shadowed soldier as two others stalked towards his men. Something was wrong about the shadows, but he trusted Elisara would not have caused this. She would never harm Novisia's people.

Although the swords clashed silently against the shadowed weapons, they held as any other weapon would. Sir Cain and his soldiers pushed the shadows back, further from the apothecary. Caellum recalled when Caligh had pierced a sword through Elisara's shadowed protector. It had been enough to send it back to the Sword of Souls until Elisara willed the shadows through again. Caellum angled his sword, hoping for the same outcome.

"Cain, low!" Caellum threw his sword with unnatural force,

watching it soar through the air. Sir Cain ducked low, just as it met its mark in the soldier's chest. The shadows dissipated and did not reform. Caellum charged forward at the remaining shadows drifting down the street with speed, likely noting they were outnumbered. The air felt lighter as Caellum rushed forward and pressed his hand against the glass panes of the apothecary. At least half of the candles burned brightly inside, illuminating his queen's golden hair. Sadira stumbled forward, resting her palm against his on the glass. Caellum was about to command a solider to open the door before shouts rang out in the distance, sounding near the city square. His eyes widened as he turned back to Sadira, but he knew what to do before she opened her mouth.

"Go!" Though her shout was muffled, her words were clear. Caellum pulled his hand away and kissed his fingertips before touching the glass again.

"Stay with her," Caellum commanded the soldiers. Only Sir Cain travelled with him, grabbing his sword from the ground and rushing through the streets.

Neither the king nor his commander were quiet as they sprinted down the cobbles, illuminated occasionally by the movement of drapes within homes as citizens searched for the noise. The shouting grew louder, and Caellum recognized a voice he knew. Lord Ryon.

"See what has befallen your city under the care of the usurper!" he shouted as Caellum turned from the last street into the square. The sky was lightening to a deep blue, making the square more visible. One by one, drapes twitched, illuminating the fountain in the centre where Lord Ryon stood atop the stone, surrounded by his guards, who raised their swords at the shadowed solders now circling them. Caellum counted ten.

"He has allowed darkness into our city; he has put your lives at risk!" Lord Ryon shouted. A soldier thrust his sword at a shadow, yet it merely shifted out of the way, shaking as if laughing. Far too many lights from buildings now brightened the square; it proved too much for the shadows to dampen. Lord Ryon angled his head up at the window to his right. "Come, come! Bear witness to your king's failures." The shadows' heads turned, following the lord's eyeline to where a woman peered from the window. Caellum swore internally. The fool was drawing attention to innocent people. One shadow shifted, powering towards the front door of the woman's house before drifting through it. Other shadows followed suit. Ryon appeared unconcerned at the implications of his words. The front door opened as a shadow dragged out a screaming woman by her hair.

"Your king allows your people to be tainted by darkness and have their lives threatened!" Lord Ryon shouted. Another two women cried out as two other shadows dragged them out of the same home. More and more light filled the square as people peered out, terrified and intrigued. Caellum's blood boiled as the shadowed hands roamed the women's bodies—no part of them was safe from the darkness.

"Your king allows your women to be assaulted, to be killed!"

"Enough!" Caellum roared, dragging his sword along the cobbles as he strode into the square, head high. Even the shadows paused at his authority. Caellum glanced at the women and shadows. Lord Ryon was mistaken; Caellum cared for his people. He had grown up in this city and sought comfort in its residents when his parents offered him none. While he knew little about those who supported his crown and those wishing to see him gone, it did not erase the fact he *knew* Garridon's people. The king knew the three women before him were sisters, whose parents died of a winter illness four years ago. They were the only residents in that house, and that was all Caellum needed to know as he nodded to Sir Cain approaching from the street beside it. A warning to be ready.

"Enough!" Caellum knelt on the ground and slammed his fists into the city's stone floor, a reminder he would protect this realm. Caellum repeated the motion and a jolt rippled through the street, strong enough for the shadows to stumble and release their hold of the women who ran to Sir Cain. The shadows turned towards the king and formed a line together, the perfect position for what Caellum hoped he could manage it. While the other heirs were blessed with elemental gifts from the gods, the Balfours had always possessed strength. One day, he would perhaps know where it came from. For the first time in his life, that power truly called to him, knowing the risk to his realm. A deep need to protect thrummed in his veins as he slammed his fists into the ground again, sending a sharp crack towards the building behind the shadows, to the now empty home the women were taken from. The shadows were prepared for the responding tremor and stepped toward him.

What they were not prepared for though, was that Caellum had willed that strength and power to send the crack toward the empty home. The shadows were none the wiser as the building shifted in its foundations and began to fall. Only one shadow turned back at the noise, the others were intent on reaching the king. The single shadow shifted to one side towards Lord Ryon, just as the stone building fell on the remaining nine shadows. The sky was brighter now, with the deep blue giving way to a glow rising beyond the city. In that glow, darkness seeped from beneath the building and did not reform. Caellum winced at the pain Elisara might feel as those nine bodies returned to her and the sword.

"Your king cares not for your lords!" Lord Ryon's voice trembled as Caellum faced the fountain again. Ryon's men had disbanded, leaving him in the clutches of a shadowed soldier. They were about as loyal as their lord, it seemed. Black shadowed hands held the lord's head, and a small blade of darkness was poised at his throat. "Your king does not—" Gurgling disrupted his words when the soldier dragged its blade across the lord's neck. A moment later, an arrow pierced through the shadow's skull as soldiers from the northern side filtered into the square. As Lord Ryon's body fell with a thud, Caellum felt a fleeting sense of sadness, despite his foul words. He had lost a member of Garridon, even one who would have been thrown into prison for his treacherous words. The buildings were soon bathed in pink as the sun rose and doors opened, welcoming the soldiers who filtered in to check the safety of the citizens, who were safe because of him. Their king.

Chapter Twenty-Eight

Sadira

"Good morning," Sadira whispered into Caellum's ear as he set her down. He said nothing as he held her cold cheeks in his palms and kissed her lips. When he finally pulled back, Sadira took a deep breath, like he had stolen all the air from her lungs. "I'm okay," she murmured. Caellum scanned her eyes and undoubtedly saw the pain within them.

"You are certain?" he asked, brushing a hand through her hair. Sadira nodded.

"There is much for us to discuss, but I am okay." Sadira reached for his hand and squeezed it tightly, taking a moment for themselves amongst the chaos. Soldiers aided Garridon's citizens while others cleared the rubble of the building Caellum had collapsed. Sunlight now streamed into the city square, highlighting the impact of the king's actions. Sadira could not be prouder; in her eyes, Caellum was a beacon of strength and resilience for Garridon and their people.

"Marry me," Caellum murmured, stroking the engagement ring on her finger. Sadira laughed, and the delicate sound danced in the surrounding air. "Marry me," he said again, more seriously now.

"We're already betrothed."

"Tomorrow," Caellum murmured, and Sadira laughed.

"I cannot arrange an entire wedding and have everyone here by tomorrow."

"We need no one else." Sadira stopped laughing at the sincerity in his tone. "We only need you and I, a witness and an officiant. Sir Cain would do it in a heartbeat."

"You're serious." Sadira's smile brightened her eyes as Caellum nodded.

"I do not want to wait. There is too much at stake, too many occasions where we could lose one another, and the realm could lose a ruler. I need only you, Sadira." Caellum kissed her gently again.

"I need to visit Albyn first. Before I left the apothecary, Athena told me to reconnect with the Wiccan we met last time to find more answers about the sword and perhaps the pins."

Caellum nodded eagerly. "We will go now. We will head to Albyn to meet with the Wiccan and marry at sunrise tomorrow morning."

"In a field of flowers?" Sadira whispered. Caellum grinned and leant in.

"I will marry you in a field of irises," he murmured against her lips. "Together, we'll experience a hundred new beginnings."

***

Albyn's flower fields called to Sadira as she dismounted her horse, ready to enter the town with her king's arm looped through hers. In the morning, she would become a wife—a queen. Sadira would promise herself to the man she never anticipated to love, the man she was told she would marry all those years ago. The endless flowers waved to her as they swayed in the light breeze. The coastal settlement, Albyn, felt like the perfect place to wed Caellum; not only was it steeped in nature she adored, but it was closest to the land where she was raised. If Sadira strode through the rows of homes and shops to the other end, she could stand at the cliff's edge and gaze out over the sea to Doltas Island in the distance.

Although Sadira was not yet queen, she still had matters to attend to in Albyn to protect her people. Only after could she enjoy a moment with her future husband. After a restless night in the apothecary, her mind had been a constant string of thoughts, especially when Caellum ran into danger. Questions had raced through her head. Why were Elisara's soldiers here, acting like the enemy? What did Athena's prophecy mean? Why did she sense the three pins now tucked inside Caellum's jacket were a clue to helping Novisia move forward to protect the lands or defeat Caligh? Was Caellum okay? Sadira suspected many of her questions would not be answered immediately, but her intentions were set with the Wiccan she hoped would seek her out again. Like last time, Athena suggested Albyn would hold some answers. But a rare anger inside Sadira threatened to bloom from her fingertips, remembering how the red-haired Wiccan and older gentleman had confidently guided her to the imbuement of the swords, potentially knowing it was not to create a weapon to kill Caligh's creatures, but instead link those they slaughtered to the Sword of Souls. Sadira clenched and unclenched her fists, yet refused to let such negative presumptions cloud her ability to speak rationally.

"Do we assume they will find us again, like last time?" Caellum asked as they strolled arm in arm along the town's small promenade. Sadira smiled at the florist and bent to sniff a bunch of pink roses.

Caellum cleared his throat and nodded at passersby as people slowed when realising their King was present. Sir Cain strolled several steps ahead, clearing a path to assess for danger. Taryn strolled close to Sadira's right, while four guards patrolled the rear.

"We could always greet Lord Gregor and wait in the tavern like last time." Sadira blushed at Caellum's smile, recalling the night they shared in the inn attached to the tavern.

"He's expecting us. I sent our belongings to his lodge with the request to stay with him this evening, but we could head there now." Caellum agreed, just as a flash of red hair blew out from beneath a deep-purple hooded cloak. Sadira tapped Caellum's arm discretely, inclining her head towards the woman weaving amongst the throngs of people, crossing towards an alleyway nestled be-

tween a blacksmiths and a confectionary store. The woman paused
to glance over her shoulder. Sadira murmured to Taryn, request-
ing he catch up with Sir Cain and alert him to the change in
direction while the remaining guards sealed the alleyway. Sadira
trailed behind Caellum towards the woman, who stilled as she
approached the alleyway and turned her head to glance at the king
and future queen, ensuring they followed. Darkness closed around
them when they entered the narrow alley, with the height of the
guards preventing more light from filtering through. Despite the
clear blue skies and sunlight bathing Albyn's fields, the closely
packed buildings, and thick, overhanging thatched roofs created
a sense of foreboding.

Three sets of footsteps were all that could be heard along the
cobbled stones as Sadira and Caellum rushed to keep up. The
redhead raised a hand when she reached a dead end, signalling for
them to wait. They did. She knocked on a door in a practiced
pattern, and a creak followed as it opened. Sadira and Caellum
exchanged a look before the woman's hand peeked from within
the doorway to beckon them inside.

"What if this is a bad idea?" Caellum murmured, and Sadira
glanced behind to where the guards sealed the alleyway. Sir Cain
and Taryn waited at the halfway point, close enough to hear the
king or Sadira should they need aid.

"We have one another," Sadira reassured him. Flourishing her
fingers, she willed vines to twist along the walls and stop before the
door, close enough for her to beckon them inside if they needed
assistance. Caellum tapped the pommel of his sword before they
approached the door together.

The room was how Sadira would have pictured Athena's home
based on the apothecary's decor. Only a single window on the
opposite wall lit the room, looking out onto another wall in a
different alleyway. The thatched roof cast shadows on the window
in place of sunlight. From the right, a fireplace warmed the room,
crafted from many different stones, likely forged from whatever

materials they could find. An iron-made fire guard, mimicking the shape of ivy, guarded the fire, though sparks still spat free, burning into a worn yellow rug that filled the entire space, speckled with soot the nearer it was to the flames. A large greyhound lifted its head lazily from the cushions piled against the side of the chimney. It seemed uninterested in the visitors, as it slowly lowered its head onto its paws and closed its eyes.

"Take a seat wherever you prefer," said the woman, removing her cloak and shaking free her waist-length red curls, which fell around the shoulders of her white blouse and ended at the leather band of her trousers. Her voice was calm—welcoming, even. She had clearly expected their arrival. Sadira stepped towards the two-seater sofa, its colour concealed by several multicoloured, woven blankets. Before she sat, a ginger tabby cat leapt into the spot, stretching across most of the sofa. "Sorry. She is rather particular about things belonging to her." The woman pulled china cups from a long wooden shelf filled with misshaped crockery, while Caellum inched away from the cat, stealing glances at it. Sadira suppressed a laugh.

"Aren't we all?" Sadira gave what she hoped seemed like a genuine smile as Caellum pulled a wooden chair from beneath the slanted round table behind the sofa. Sadira sat down, assessing the rest of the room, while Caellum lowered himself onto the chair beside her, shifting it close enough toward her that their knees touched. On the left-hand side of the room, opposite the window, was a small kitchen and worktop, where dried herbs hung from a long wooden shelf above the open stove. Years of condensation had peeled the sage-coloured paint on the wall, revealing blue paint beneath, likely from the previous owners. Sadira clasped her trembling hands as worry rose within her about these people and their intentions.

"Come in," the woman called, exactly three seconds before Sadira heard approaching footsteps. The owner did not knock. Sadira looked around the room then, confused as to who had let the woman in when she knocked. After scanning the room several times, Sadira finally noticed what she had initially thought was a wardrobe door swing open. Another cat skulked through, prowling towards the fireplace. She glimpsed the top of a staircase before the door closed.

"Sorry I'm late." The gruff voice belonged to the old man they had last met in Albyn. Caellum glanced at Sadira. They had expected them. Sadira shrugged. She was learning that the Wiccan on the mainland had a far greater sense of foresight, perhaps even more so than those on Doltas. She wondered why. The old man reached for the counter ledge to guide himself towards the table. His milky eyes moved to Sadira, who glanced away, a chill running up her spine, even though he could not see.

"Do you have a preference when it comes to tea?" asked the woman.

"Any is fine," Sadira replied curtly, growing impatient. The Wiccans acted like nothing had happened, as if they were oblivious to the true purpose of the incantation. Neither Sadira, Caellum, nor the old man spoke. The only sounds were the clinking spoons as the woman stirred herbs in cups, the cats' purrs, and the crackling fireplace. Finally, she sat down and placed a tray of four cups in the table's centre. Sadira reached for one, but waited with Caellum for the hosts to drink before sipping their own. A floral, honey-sweetened taste washed over Sadira's tongue. In normal circumstances, she would have asked politely for the recipe, but she did not wish to break the tension first. Athena had guided her here, but the hosts should provide insight into the reasons why.

"Arabella," the redhead finally said, crossing her legs. "My name is Arabella. Forgive me, but I won't provide my surname. While I hold no debt over you, you have since witnessed what knowing someone's name can do in the right circumstances, under the right spells, and with the way your king is glaring at me, I would not be surprised if you were to weave my name within a curse." Arabella smiled and sipped her tea.

"Darragh," the old man grunted. The ginger tabby cat jumped onto his lap and curled with a purr.

"I imagine you have a lot of questions." Arabella smiled, flicking her hair over her shoulder. Sadira and Caellum remained silent. "Frosty," she murmured. "I understand why."

"Do you?" Caellum snapped. She looked Caellum up and down.

"I told you we were sent to set you on a path. I did not reveal what that path entailed or where it would take you."

"So, you knew," Sadira said. "You knew the imbuement would not create a weapon to kill Caligh's men." Arabella flinched at his name. "Instead, you knew it would link them to the Sword of Souls."

"It still killed them, did it not? You still won the war and now have an even larger army at your disposal." Arabella pursed her lips. Sadira's vines crept under the table and climbed around her ankles. Anger threatened to consume her. Yet she was reminded of Elisara and how willing she had been to manipulate the souls for their bidding. How did that make them any better than Caligh?

"We have an out-of-control army because the queen who wields them is grieving. Did you know the commander would die? Did you foresee that?" Caellum kept his voice firm, challenging the Wiccan. Arabella glanced at her hands.

"Sometimes, the paths we are destined for are not what we always like or will survive." Sadira shook her head. How could Sadira sit across from Arabella, a woman who knowingly put Elisara in this position, knowing Kazaar would die?

"Why did my grandmother possess such an imbuement?" Sadira asked coldly.

"The book is old," Darragh finally contributed to the conversation. "She did not know what it was or what it did."

"That book is sacred, Sadira. It was a history of all that is right with the Wiccan race, all we have built and held dear. However, that one imbuement, those words and power..." Arabella cleared her throat, though her emotions were unclear. "That is the reason the divide among our people is so severe it may never be mended. The consequences of that imbuement stretch far beyond the souls and Caligh, it—"

"Too much, Bella. Too much," Darragh said. Arabella sighed and bit her lip, averting her eyes. Sadira sensed her regret, though she still distrusted the woman.

"If she wants to tell us, she should tell us," Caellum said, his voice harsh yet strong.

"We cannot alter destinies; we cannot reveal anything that could affect fate's plans," Darragh countered. Hoping to learn more, Sadira referred to something else Arabella said.

"You said there is a severe divide among our people. Can you at least explain that? Is it a divide in Garridon? Novisia? Is there something else we should know?" Sadira asked. Arabella shook her head, darting her eyes to Darragh before continuing.

"Amongst the Wiccans. But it is that divide in history that affects your paths today."

"Does it have anything to do with these?" Caellum asked, pulling the three pins from his jacket pocket, and dropping them in the table's centre. Arabella's eyes widened. Seeming to sense Arabella's shift in demeanour, Darragh leant forward to trace each pin with his thumb.

"Where did you get these?" he asked, his tone far more urgent than before.

"I found them amongst my family's belongings."

"This is what you described in your dream." Arabella clasped her grandfather's hand. "These were the three symbols."

"A dream?" Sadira asked. Darragh gripped his head in pain the same way Athena had. "Or a memory?"

Forcing his head up, Darragh trained his milky eyes on Sadira. "A memory," he murmured. "It is how Bella knows of the incantation, a history shown to her you should not yet know." Sadira remained quiet, hoping Darragh would elaborate. Arabella had mentioned their history too. They needed more information to know how to move forward. "After the explosion, I had odd dreams about myself as a child, but only flashes of objects and places. It felt so real. I saw these symbols—these pins."

"Why do you not wish for us to know this history? What are you keeping from us?" Sadira frowned. Osiris's lands were cursed, preventing him from revealing more. However, Darragh and Arabella made a purposeful choice to stay on fate's side.

"It's not his fault. She told us we cannot tell you and that knowing could detour your path. You need to find the mirror first—the reflection—and then we may be permitted to tell you more."

"Who?" Caellum asked.

"Our deity," Arabella whispered as Darragh focused on one pin, the wolf's head, and turned it over in his fingers.

"You do not worship Garridon?" Sadira asked, having assumed these Wiccans had descended from the realm. She had never questioned that perhaps, back on Ithyion, they had travelled the other realms and populated multiple places.

"Different faces have come to me in visions," Arabella began, but Darragh cut her off with a gasp.

"Shapeshifters," he whispered, tracing the wolf's head. Sadira's eyes shot to his.

"What do you mean?" Caellum asked. Darragh became flushed, then, and pushed the three pins back towards the king.

"You must leave," he said, pushing back from the table. "Night is creeping upon us, and you do not wish to be in the streets should the shadows from Antor venture to Albyn tonight." Darragh strode towards the door, concealing the staircase and whoever resided on the floor above. *Shapeshifters.* Sadira turned the word over in her mind, having never heard it before. It related to the wolf's head and Garridon.

"You cannot reveal everything you have and leave us with more questions! At least tell us what shapeshifters are or their importance in understanding our history? Or a way to defeat Caligh should he return! Is it linked to saving another land? Please, give us something!" Sadira begged.

"Go!" Darragh shouted. "Find the mirror, find the reflection, and then—then you will be on the right path to understand it all." Darragh slammed the door to the staircase behind him, leaving a stunned silence to settle around the room. Arabella cleared her throat and gestured towards the door. Caellum huffed and rose, guiding Sadira to the exit and opening it to face a cool breeze.

"Sadira," Arabella murmured, reaching for the princess's hand. "Please know we are not trying to make things difficult for you." Sadira opened her mouth to protest, but the Wiccan pressed something into her palm. "For your wedding. It's a token of our family history. The deity will inform me when I can confide in you completely, but for now, please accept this as a promise I will be by your side one day."

***

Sleeping alone, Sadira stared at the masterpiece of a painting above the bed. While her wedding to Caellum in the morning would be unconventional, they had kept to some traditions by sleeping separately the night before. Though she imagined he was likely lying awake, as she was now, turning over the jumble of information, or lack of, in his mind. They had debriefed over dinner and shared their theories, but their conclusions were always the same: they were clueless. *Shapeshifter.* That word rang through her mind most consistently as she examined the beautiful brushstrokes of the painting in Lord Gregor's home. A depiction of rolling fields, towering trees, and wolves and deer running wild through golden wheat. Sadira lifted the brooch in her hand to examine it in the light emanating from the bedside lantern. Arabella had hurriedly pressed it into her hands with a promise.

A golden hawk glinted in the flame's light. It was small, no larger than the top of her thumb. Despite its size, she could make out the grooves of its feathers on its sweeping wings. The emerald in its eye flashed. Sadira did not know what it meant or who Arabella's ancestors had once been, yet. All she knew for certain, despite everything that had transpired so far, was to trust her.

Chapter Twenty-Nine

Elisara

*E*lisara's eyes snapped open when darkness claimed Hamzah in her dream. Threads of shadows twitched at her side, recognising she was awake and staring at the wall. As they moved to comfort her, tears fell from her eyes at yet another memory of loss. Tormented, yet again. Her eyes trailed to her arm stretched across the pillow. Beneath the scarred vines wrapping around her forearm was a raised, flaming dagger. A lump rose in Elisara's throat. Now she would never know what happened before Kazaar found that scar on his skin. Elisara's mind recalled the dagger Hamzah used to take his own life and frowned. Kazaar's scars had emerged when using a new power, while Elisara's emerged after these dreams. She had no answers. The ink on Kazaar's scars had been beautiful. On Elisara, the scars made her look even more broken, mirroring her internal st ate.

"Can you recall the memories?" Sallos asked. Elisara closed her eyes and sighed. She was not yet awake.

"No," she lied, staring at the wall again. She did not want to relive the pain of someone's loss, nor did she trust Sallos.

"You are still mad at me," Sallos said. Elisara blinked, ignoring him. "I apologise, your Majesty. It was too soon to mention Sitara's plight." One moment, Elisara lay limp on the bed; the next, darkness consumed her, bringing her before Sallos. The shadows fell away, except for those shielding Elisara's naked body as she stood toe-to-toe with Sallos, looking up at him. He was at least two heads taller, and she felt far less like a queen in his presence. Sallos's throat bobbed as he glanced down at the queen before staring over her head.

"I will gut you if you so much as mention her name again," Elisara sneered. "I want nothing to do with her plight, her broken heart, or searching for her other half. It does not affect me or my people—" Sallos opened his mouth yet closed it at Elisara's glare. Having abandoned her people to be here, she doubted they were pleased with her. Perhaps she should try to send a message to Vlad, relinquishing her throne to him. Elisara turned from Sallos and strode towards the bed.

"I have some clothes for you," Sallos finally said. Elisara turned her head enough to see the fabrics on the chair by the desk. "I didn't wash the ones you were wearing; they're in the chest at the end of the bed." When Sallos clasped his hands behind his back, Elisara almost felt bad. The wrinkles in his eyes were flat, and his expression serious; his regret bled between them. Elisara winced as she walked towards the chair, threads of darkness tugging at her skin. "I can teach you," Sallos said. Elisara reached for the clothes and erected a wall of shadows between them.

"Teach me what?" she asked, unfolding the material of deep glittering bronze. Where had he managed to find this? Elisara draped the gown over her head as Sallos explained.

"I once knew people with the same power as you. I can teach you to wield the darkness and pull it back into yourself when it is unrequired." Elisara straightened the gown, untangling the pieces of fabric that flowed over her shoulder, hanging loosely over her arms like capes. The fabric glowed copper and bronze as it caught the light of the flames. It was fitted to her chest, leaving a small gap between the top of her bust and the hollow on her neck before the fabric enveloped her neck. It provided the perfect gap to display her talismans. "I know having to control it constantly is tiring you," Sallos whispered. Elisara sighed while smoothing the flowing fabric of her skirts. He was right. Every tug of the shadows exhausted her further. Willing the wall of shadows to fall, Elisara faced Sallos, who rocked back on his heels, watching her in silence. She felt uncomfortable dressed as a queen again. "You look—"

"*What would helping me look like?*" *Elisara cut him off and perched on the edge of the bed, her arms crossed.*

"*We would need some space,*" *Sallos said, gesturing towards the throne room.* "*We need to focus on what is blocking your mental space. Silent meditation would work—*"

"*No.*"

"*It is a simple exercise—*"

"*No.*" *Elisara winced at the memories of Kazaar—the moments they meditated before the war, trying to unlock any additional power. Sallos averted his eyes, and Elisara knew he felt her grief.* "*Find another way.*"

"*There are not many other ways I can think of, your Majesty. You can control the shadows perfectly fine in all other ways. I only assume the inability to withdraw them is linked to your mind, wishing them to remain present.*"

"*I cannot,*" *Elisara said quietly but firmly. Sallos ran a hand through his hair and sighed.*

"*You need to.*"

"*Why?*"

"*Because your inability to recall your own power is affecting your ability to control us,*" *Sallos said, taking a cautious step closer. Elisara assessed him and straightened.*

"*My ability to control you all is fine. I did so just before I bathed.*" *She raised her chin in defiance as Sallos crouched, meeting her eyes. Elisara tried not to recoil as she forced herself to meet his gaze like a queen. Yet when he approached in a way that spoke of comfort and kindness, she felt unworthy. She had failed.*

"*Those of us you control feel the tug of your commands and obey willingly—currently.*" *Sallos softened his voice.* "*There are others in this sword for a reason; since the battle, they can easily ignore that tug, particularly when you order us away. They will claim they obeyed yet will act against your will. When you sleep, and sometimes when you awake briefly at night, there are soldiers slipping from your control. Some have travelled to the realms and stalked not just*

Vala's people, but the others too." Elisara scanned his eyes, looking for signs he was lying. Though she would feel his betrayal if he was. Why would they venture to other realms?

"Have they hurt anyone?" she murmured. Despite its absence, the weight of the crown felt heavy on her head, though it remained alongside her other possessions in the Ashun Desert. Sallos shook his head, and his hand twitched, like he wished to reach forward and offer comfort.

"They have hurt people in Garridon, but the king intervened. You have slept so much you have missed the return of the slain soldiers." Sallos lifted the corner of his lips slightly in a soft, sad smile before asking, "What would Kazaar tell you to do?" Elisara looked down at her hands; her chest constricted upon hearing his name aloud. "Think about it." Sallos rose and backed away to his station in front of the hallway. "But you will need to try channel in your waking body." Slowly, Elisara nodded before sliding down the edge of the bed onto the floor. She pulled her knees up under her chin and waited for herself to wake.

*****

Pink skies shone through the opening at the top of the mountain. Elisara debated going outside; the fresh air and calming sky would likely help with meditating, but she was not yet ready to face the world. Instead, Elisara sat directly under that small opening of light. The laws of dreams seemed not to apply as she sat in the same deep bronze dress Sallos had given her. She wanted to wear Kazaar's shirt, but knew it was too dirty now. She resorted to placing it on her pillow at night, so it was the last thing she saw before sleeping and the first thing when she woke. She twisted her hand around the leather on her neck, where Sitara's talisman—once his—pressed against her chest. It hummed in her hand, the threads of silvery light twisting amongst the whirling shadows within. Elisara grazed the tiny chip in the back—the missing part she knew was some-where in her arm beneath the raised scars decorating her skin.

What would Kazaar tell you to do? Sallos's question rang through her mind as she stared at the deep crack in the chequered floor, where the creature had landed during their first visit. Who knew such a simple question could focus her mind? Kazaar would say she was better than this and stronger than her heartbreak. Although she would not believe him, that is what he would say. Elisara smiled, recalling the moment Kazaar had ignited a flicker of flame within her. His memory would centre her again, even for the selfish act of lightening her aches. A part of her mind warned that no matter how much she feigned indifference, she yearned to regain control over the soldiers—the one thing she could protect her people from.

Finally, Elisara raised her head and looked up at the mirror, now propped against what had once been a tomb of ice, long since melted. Depictions of the elements were etched on the gold frame, along with the sun and moon at its crown. It was difficult to focus on the reflection and not the engraved words of the prophecy on the glass. In the aftermath of everything that happened, the prophecy had always been about her. Elisara straightened, ignoring the words. She glanced briefly at Sallos, who stood to the side of the mirror that reached up to his shoulders. His shadowed form raised a hand to his chest, exaggerating the motion of inhaling. Elisara nodded and returned her focus to her reflection. Her loose curls, frizzy from sleeping on it wet, hung behind her back, while the shadows under her eyes matched the darkness twisting on the floor. Were she in better health, the deep bronze dress would have complimented her hair and skin, both of which now paled in the darkness. In some lights, it almost looked like armour, a similar tone to the copper army, but darker. Elisara clenched her jaw at the returning memory of battle and took a deep breath. She exhaled, closing her eyes. *Find the source of your power*, Kazaar had once said. But how could she, knowing it stemmed from a piece of stone in her left arm, wrapped in Sitara's essence?

When Elisara focused on her arm, the shadows approached, twisting up her elbows. She felt the darkness in her skin, the link to the sword. Perhaps she should just cut it out, hide the talisman, and end the connection to the shadowed army. Sallos flinched at her thought. The darkness continued, twisting up Elisara's arms and around her chest until the pressure was suffocating. She furrowed her brows, thinking of the dark fragment in her arm, but that flicker of Sitara's essence around it felt absent, as though it had spent so many years drifting through her it no longer had a tethered home. Elisara clenched her hands as the threads of power crawled across her skin, trying to offer comfort but achieving the opposite.

"Leave me alone," Elisara murmured, picturing Kazaar's face. His memory had ignited that flame before—she could do it again. But Elisara stilled when she thought of him. One day, she would forget the details of his face, the positioning of his stubble, and the changing shades of his eyes. A tear rolled down Elisara's cheek, and a shadow wiped it away. "Stop," she whispered, but sensing her sadness only drew them closer. Kazaar was gone because of this power, because Sitara decided Elisara was the perfect vessel to host both the essence and link to the sword. But why her? The shadows cried along with their queen, skating over her skin like a gentle caress. If Elisara had not harboured the essence, Caligh would not have come looking for them. He would not have killed Kazaar. "It's my fault," she choked. She sensed Sallos step towards her, but she pushed him back and commanded him against the wall with the others. She cried, sagging under the weight of her powers. Still, the shadows ignored her pleas and continued twisting and stroking her hair.

"STOP!" Elisara screamed. When she opened her eyes, her irises were black, consumed by anger in the mirror. She wanted them out, wanted them gone. Given the chance, she would rip the power from her body for their role in Kazaar's death. Elisara panted, watching her reflection. The shadows paused, wondering if her threat was true. Elisara screamed, and with a single, forceful thought, commanded a strip of darkness to lash the flesh along her back, cutting open her skin, and hopefully ripping the power out with it.

Chapter Thirty
Caellum

Caellum had spent most of his life in wariness and uncertainty, worried for himself, his siblings, and the mood his father might be in. But as he strode through a field of flowers, with the morning dew dampening the ends of his trousers, any uncertainties about his life drifted away on the breeze. A glow of pink tinted the field of white irises as the sun rose behind the clifftops and glinted across the ocean, a serene backdrop for their fairytale. The breathtaking haze of petals stretched as far as the eye could see until reaching the sea on one side, and the forest on the other, where a row of guards stood. Their backs were turned, watching for anyone approaching.

Caellum let loose a shaky breath as Sir Cain grinned. The man who had been a father figure to Caellum, when his own could not, clasped his forearm and embraced him with a pat on the back.

"Everything you asked for is all set up," Sir Cain said, a smile plastered on his face. He walked alongside Caellum into the clearing, where a woven archway stood, intertwined with the same vines and white flowers from the chairs at their engagement ball. Off to the side were three men playing stringed instruments, the only other people present for the marriage between a king and princess. Caellum had always expected their wedding to be a large affair to symbolise Garridon becoming whole again. Perhaps they should have waited to provide their people with such a joyous moment, but this felt right. "The blanket and all other items are by the cliff's edge." Sir Cain guided Caellum's shoulders and positioned him off-centre to the archway, turning his back from where he knew Sadira waited with her guards. He took several deep breaths, reminding himself to enjoy this one peaceful moment together before they travelled to the Unsanctioned Isle to aid Elisara, as per the request on Larelle's letter that reached him late last night. Elisara appeared to have lost control over her shadowed soldiers, who had invaded not only the settlements of Garridon, but Keres and Nerida too. Caellum and Sadira had one moment together at sunrise, but by the time the sun was signalling the beginning of afternoon, they would set sail for the Unsanctioned Isle.

"Ready?" Sir Cain asked. Caellum looked up at the sky as eight birds soared past the clouds. Eight hawks, one for each member of his family. As the birds settled behind him on the treeline, where his bride waited, Caellum smiled. The largest one seemed to watch him closely.

"Ready," Caellum breathed. Sir Cain nodded, and music wove amongst the flowers, along with the many butterflies floating into view. Caellum straightened the lapels of his forest green jacket. He wanted to reach for the crown atop his head and check that was straight too, but a breeze brushed Sadira's scent towards him and wrapped around his heart: roses and morning dew. She was near. Sir Cain squeezed his shoulder, and Caellum turned.

During the time he had known Sadira, the king had described her in many ways: beautiful, breathtaking, ethereal. Yet as Caellum's eyes watered, he could not think of a single word in existence that captured the woman who had claimed his heart forever. Sadira was the first breath of countryside air, calming his whole being, and the first glimpse of spring flowers to signal a beautiful day. Sadira was both the rise of the sun and the power of rainfall; she was his beginning, end, and his constant in the unknown. Sadira was simply everything.

Caellum did not blink back his tears as he watched his queen. She held a bouquet of irises in one hand, perfectly plucked from the surrounding field, while her other was looped with Taryn's arm as he escorted her down the makeshift aisle. Taryn faded from view, though, for Caellum only had eyes for Sadira as she glided through the flowers. Her gown appeared white from afar, but as she approached, he saw it was the palest sage. Caellum smiled. It matched the dress he had first seen her in as she had exited the carriage in Garridon for the very first time. The dress cinched at her waist, while the bodice accentuated her chest just so. White lace patterned its structure, fanning out into off-the-shoulder sleeves. The numerous, bunched folds where her skirts met her bodice cascaded into silk, embellished with white lace in the pattern of flowers. Caellum's gaze trailed Sadira until they locked eyes. She beamed. Her curls hung over her shoulders, pulled back by what he knew would be a single green ribbon that matched the green of her eyes. A few curls were left to frame her face, and the crown of Garridon rested atop her golden hair, as it rightly should. The sun finally began to crest over the clifftops, it bathed Sadira in a warm, golden light. A breeze rustled through the irises, and a flight of white butterflies fluttered around the soon-to-be Queen of Garridon, whose delicate laugh melted into the music.

Taryn bowed to the king and extended his arm for Sadira to move her hand from his to Caellum's. The pair turned to face one another in the centre of the archway. Behind them, Sir Cain stood with an open book. Caellum did not need to say she looked beautiful. He knew Sadira was aware as he watched her, mesmerised. Biting her lip, she glanced down briefly with a smile before looking up at Caellum again.

"We are gathered here today in intimate company to bless the marriage of Caellum Balfour, King of Garridon, and Sadira Mordane, soon to be Queen of Garridon. I have only wed two people before, two people who meant just as much to me as the two of you do now, not only to myself but the entire realm." Caellum smiled. "So, I will read the sacred words I once recited at your parents' wedding." Caellum tore his gaze from Sadira to look at Sir Cain. Emotion brimmed in his commander's eyes, and a slight crack broke his voice as the eight birds settled atop the archway above.

"Do you promise to nurture your marriage with the same intent the god of this realm once did in its creation?" At the same time, Sadira and Caellum said, "'I do," prompting Sir Cain to continue his questioning until all but one remained unanswered.

"When your union faces stormy weather that might threaten to uproot all you have created together, do you promise to brace through that storm, side by side? When sickness invades the mind or body of the other, do you promise to be a healer, comforter, and friend? Do you promise to love one another from this day until your dying breath?"

"I do," Sadira and Caellum said for the final time, a smile on both of their faces. A sniff sounded from behind, where Taryn stood watching his king and now queen.

"It is my... greatest honour"—Sir Cain no longer hid his emotion as tears clogged his throat—"to pronounce you husband and wife, king and queen, partners in this life and the next. Cal." Sir Cain grinned. "You may kiss your queen." Caellum wasted no time in solidifying the display of his marriage and his hands gripped Sadira's waist as he pulled her into him, prompting her to lock her hands behind his neck, bringing them closer. When their lips interlocked, he wished they could stay in this moment forever.

***

The crashing waves against the cliffs below almost drowned Sadira's laughter as strawberry juice dripped down her chin. Caellum caught the drip with his finger before it could fall and stain her chest. Sadira watched him lick the red juice from his fingertip.

"I could not eat another thing," she sighed, shifting to lie on the blanket. Caellum pushed aside the platter of Sadira's favourite foods: strawberries, honey cakes, peaches, and jam-coated pastries. Downing the remnants of the sparkling celebratory wine, he lay down beside her, and together, they stared up at the sky as it slowly lost its pink hue. It would not be long before they had to abandon their moment of blissful solitude.

"There is a tradition in the Wiccan culture on days like this," Sadira murmured, tracing circles on Caellum's hand. He hummed in silent question, watching the clouds float above them. "Each family presents a piece of fabric from their home. The pieces are woven together and tied around the couples' hand, signifying the creation of a new family." A sad lilt entered Sadira's voice at the word *family* as the realisation dawned—they only had each other. His family were gone, and Sadira had yet to untangle her many thoughts and feelings about Soren. Not wanting Sadira to feel the absence of her family, Caellum reached for his jacket and tore off the sleeve. After ripping it again to form one longer strip of green velvet, he turned on his side and dangled the fabric between them.

"Will this do?" he asked. Sadira's eyes watered, but she grinned and reached for the hem of her dress. Caellum did not laugh at her frustration. Instead, he dropped his piece of fabric and reached for her gown, easily tearing off a small strip. "Show me." Caellum wiped at Sadira's stray tear, and then lay back on his side, watching the sunrise behind her, depicting his queen as a painting he would hang in every room of their castle. Sadira gently knotted the two pieces of fabric together and pulled Caellum's hand from his side, balancing it in the air between them. She traced the lines on his palm before sliding her hand into his and wrapping the fabric around them, securing the knot under Caellum's wrist with a giggle.

"It is not as easy without an extra pair of hands." Yet she continued wrapping until it was complete. "And so, the Mordane and Balfour families are bound together. My home is your home, my heart is your heart, and my life is yours from this day until we part." Sadira leant down to Caellum to place a gentle kiss on his lips, one which quickly deepened.

"We may not have our families," Caellum murmured as Sadira pushed him onto his back and crawled on top of him. "But this celebrates us, the family we have become and will be." Caellum wove his hand into her hair, prompting a groan from Sadira as she lifted the skirts of her dress to press against him with more ease. Caellum tightened his grip on her hair before trailing it down her body to drift under her skirts, clenching the soft skin of her thighs. Sadira pulled back. Her breathing was rushed as hair fell over one shoulder, and a glow returned to her eyes. A shadow fell over them as Sadira grew a row of bushes behind the pair, shielding them from view until it was only them in the field of irises on the cliffs overlooking the ocean.

"I love you," Sadira murmured, resting a palm against his cheek. Caellum kissed her before pulling back.

"I will love you for eternity. There is no war, no threat of darkness, no death that could ever keep me from holding you in my heart forever. And when we are but seeds returned to the earth, I will find you again. Our love will bring us together in every lifetime."

Sadira deepened their kiss and brushed her hands against Caellum's as he stroked her inner thighs. She reached for the waistband of his trousers and gripped him, trailing kisses along his neck. He inhaled sharply and squeezed Sadira's hand, still bound to his. She moved back and forth over him, a tantalising depiction of what was yet to come. A delicate sigh drifted from Sadira's lips as she lowered herself onto him, causing Caellum's eyes to roll back in pleasure. And when he finally opened his eyes again, he saw Sadira's crown glinting in the rising sun as she rose and fell above him: his wife, his queen—*his*. When she opened her eyes, they softly glowed, but no sign of her power manifested. He did not question it, even when the glow matched the shimmer to her skin. Caellum simply watched his queen, savouring every moment. Gripping harder onto Sadira's hip, he let her show just how much she loved him.

Chapter Thirty-One

Larelle

Standing at the ship's bow, the ocean spray coated Larelle's hair as she gracefully swayed her hand to hurry the ships through the waters. Larelle had left at first light, along with Alvan, Zarya, Olden, and Lillian. While Zarya had slept peacefully in an armchair amongst the books at the church, Alvan had kept watch of the shadowed soldiers in the pews and insisted Larelle should sleep too. While she had occasionally dosed on and off at the table, leaning her head in her hands, her mind was still distracted as Vivian scribbled away in her book. The soldiers had not attempted the door leading to their hiding place. In fact, they did not stay long in the church at all. Though Larelle soon realised, from the distant screams throughout the night, that the shadows had encountered some of her people. Far fewer citizens graced the streets when they left Mera that morning.

Larelle looked right, noticing a blonde head of hair on the neighbouring ship. Sadira stood with her arm around Caellum, who bowed his head over the side. Clearly, he was not one for boats. The green sails of Garridon's ship billowed with the wind as Larelle urged the ocean under them. She had spotted their approach not long after leaving The Bay. Larelle hoped her letter had reached Nyzaia and she, too, was headed for the Unsanctioned Isle.

Larelle smiled when Alvan wrapped an arm around her waist and planted a kiss on her cheek. "You seem very at ease up here," he said, and Larelle sighed, leaning into him as she continued motioning with her hands.

"I rarely use my powers on a daily basis." Larelle tried to recall the last time she had done so outside of the battlefield, but her only recollection was the meeting with her lords, where she forced a man to choke on water. He appeared to have forgotten it, though, when Larelle gathered with the lords again before leaving for the church. If he—or anyone—tried to question her crown again, she would have no qualms about reminding them of her power.

"You should practise something every day," Alvan said. "While you need little practice, given the extent of your power, it might be a good habit to form, especially as you enjoy it so much." Larelle hummed in agreement as they banked the final corner of Vala's borders to where the Unsanctioned Isle appeared in the distance, appearing as a blur of red trees this far away. Larelle squinted at what appeared to be the sails of a Keres boat, but they were too far to be certain.

"I'm going to check on Olden," Larelle said, kissing Alvan gently before walking to the other end of the ship, intending to spend some time with him now they had reunited after the day at the church. His tiredness worried her. She wanted to ensure there was nothing else wrong in case they required a healer, but when Larelle reached the end of the ship, she found Olden asleep on a wooden bench with a blanket draped over his legs. The wind whipped at his grey hair, and a small smile graced his lips as he slept atop the waves. Larelle stooped and kissed his forehead before sitting beside him in silence, savouring the moment of peace before their journey continued.

***

It did not take much longer for the boats to sail closer to the shores of the Unsanctioned Isle and for Larelle to confirm the ship ahead was indeed from Keres and hurry it along. Wielding the waves, Larelle guided the three ships along the sandbank, alongside one that bore Vala's vigil. Vlad already stood on the shore, waiting for them to disembark.

"Vlad, it's good to see you," greeted Alvan, gripping the commander's arm. Vlad smiled and bowed as Larelle approached. His blonde hair had grown so much it nearly reached his shoulders; his beard was much fuller compared to their last encounter, and the circles beneath his eyes darker. Etchings of a constant frown appeared on his brow. The new commander was evidently exhausted in his queen's absence.

"How are things in Vala?" Larelle asked as Alvan gently lowered her from the ship's ladder onto the sparkling black sands, a reminder of the night sky. Vlad's smile wavered at the question.

"With Eli gone, the lords are trying to force their hands to rule. I'm trying to hold them off, but I'm outnumbered if she doesn't return soon or at least contact them."

"And the shadows?" asked Alvan. "Have you had any of her soldiers arrive on your shores?" Vlad nodded grimly, just as Sadira and Caellum reached them.

"There was one instance where they tore apart a tavern—just the same as a few drunkards might—but enough to show they didn't intend to be pleasant guests in the city." Sadira wore a worried frown as she listened, gripping Caellum's hand while holding her pink gown in the other as the strong winds threatened to uproot her skirts.

"They were worse in Tabheri," Nyzaia said, donning black leathers. She had added a few extras to her attire: a red sash secured with a gold pin and her crown. Farid and Jabir dropped from the ship and approached, with Soren sandwiched between them. Larelle widened her eyes and glanced at Sadira and Caellum. Sadira's eyes watered as she made to move forward but seemed to think better of it, clenching her jaw. Caellum's attention was fixed on Soren's movements and unchained hands. She was not being treated like a prisoner. Although Larelle would have kept a prisoner under closer guard, it was not her place to decide another ruler's actions, though she worried about what Elisara might do if she saw Soren walking so freely. "It's why Soren is here. They heightened the... *temperamental* state of her mind. I couldn't risk leaving her in Tabheri."

Soren glanced away from the group. What must have occurred for Nyzaia to have beaten the fallen queen to the brink of death to where she now walked freely, unchained, while suggesting there was something wrong with her mind? The fallen queen's clothes were loose around her figure, and Larelle easily recognised the signs of malnourishment visible in the hollows of her cheeks and eyes. There was no scowl on Soren's face. She simply glanced between everyone and the dark, sandy floor. Still, Sadira and Caellum did not speak.

"Is there anything else we should all know before we look for Elisara?" Larelle asked.

"I'll scout ahead," Vlad said, motioning for all the guards from each realm to follow. Farid and Jabir stayed on either side of Soren, who continued staring at Nyzaia.

"I found people whose memories had resurfaced since our crowning," Nyzaia said.

"So did we," said Sadira. Larelle and Alvan exchanged a look and nodded, recalling Father Zoro.

"There's a cult operating in Keres; they worship other gods and act as though they may not be from Ithyion," Nyzaia explained, holding the pommel of her sword at her waist.

"Were they all old enough to have hailed from Ithyion?" Larelle asked, and Nyzaia nodded.

"They were old enough to have travelled from Ithyion and remember it, but what if they weren't from Ithyion at all? They mentioned a deity, not our god, Keres. What if our realm comprises of people from many places, but we've just been fed some made-up story about our homeland?" The other rulers frowned. Ithyion's history seemed so certain. No logical reason seemed to exist as to why a made-up kingdom would hide those hailing from different lands. "We cannot trust anything the Historian ever told us or our families."

"But my grandmother was still alive, and she remembered Ithyion," Sadira explained.

"How are we to know her memories weren't altered too when she arrived in Novisia? Or the memories of the two Wiccans as well?" Nyzaia pushed. Larelle considered it.

"We saw a priest," said Larelle. "I can't be certain if he was remembering things, as he was far from sane, but everything he said was linked to Osiris's words. He spoke of curses and wore a clear symbol of Garridon, a realm that existed on Ithyion." Alvan pulled the priest's amulet from his pocket and handed it to Caellum and Sadira, who shared a look.

"These symbols reside on three pins in my father's belongings," Caellum said, tracing a thumb over the images on the back of the gold emblem.

"It still proves nothing about Ithyion," Nyzaia pushed. "I stand by what I said. Ithyion might have never existed. All our ancestors could have hailed from completely different lands, perhaps four *separate* lands."

"But why?" Larelle asked. "What reason would there be to lie about where we came from or why they settled here in Novisia?" Nobody had an answer. The rulers all looked at one another as the wind whipped around them.

"We should head into the trees to find shelter from the wind before making our way in land," Larelle suggested. "We can continue talking on route."

"Mumma!" shouted a small voice from Nerida's ship. "I need to come with you," Zarya called as Lillian tried to tug her back. Larelle frowned at her daughter's wild eyes and frantic jumping. "I *need* to come with you!" Zarya emphasised.

"You don't think she'd start using what Osiris said as an excuse to stay close, do you?" Alvan asked. At the mention of Osiris, all eyes fell on the pair.

"I don't think so," Larelle murmured, waving at Lillian to bring

Zarya down.

"When did Osiris speak with her?" Nyzaia asked.

"It's a long story," Larelle sighed. "I'll tell you on the way."

"Actually," Sadira interjected, "Would you mind if we spoke to you first about something, Nyzaia?" Sadira offered Larelle an apologetic smile, but the Queen of Nerida took no offence. She trusted there was a reason Nyzaia deserved to hear it first. As Farid and Jabir guided Soren ahead, she glanced back at her sister and Nyzaia. Larelle followed as soon as Zarya grabbed her and Alvan's hands, swinging in between the two of them after waving goodbye to Lillian and Olden on the boat.

When Sadira, Caellum, and Nyzaia caught up, Larelle explained everything about Osiris, and the maps and books they found in the church. With Vivian's permission, not that a queen needed it, they took the books. The acolyte had not noticed when Alvan successfully slid the notes about Zarya into their pile. Currently, the books resided on the ship, ready for reading on the way back to land. Nyzaia revealed more about the cult in Keres, how they had tried to sacrifice her and Farid before seeing Farid's wings and believing him to be the living embodiment of a different god, Nefere. Intrigued at first, Larelle's fascination soon turned to frustration as she struggled to piece it all together—memories had been hidden, but why? Other lands existed, but their whereabouts remained unknown, while the truth about their ancestors and Ithyion remained a mystery. If the priest was correct, at least two curses plagued Novisia or all lands, but the rulers decided to focus on the curse preventing Osiris from revealing more information, a curse no one knew how to reverse. The Wiccan were at play—potentially shapeshifters, too, whatever that meant—and a third faction related to Garridon, all of which were linked to the prophecy they had now heard from Osiris, Athena, and Father Zoro. To add to it all, they still had no idea about Caligh's whereabouts, despite his huge risk to Novisia and other lands. It was exhausting for Larelle to think about, especially while grappling to understand her daughter's power. Eventually, Zarya grew tired, and Alvan carried the princess on his back, allowing Sadira to fall into step beside Larelle.

"I'm sorry. I spoke with Nyzaia first as it was directly related to Soren," Sadira murmured, using her powers to clear their path of tree branches, scattering red leaves on the ground.

"Do not apologise," Larelle said. "Is everything okay?"

Sadira shrugged. "I do not know. We found Caellum's father and grandfather's journals, which details the moments Caligh entered their minds and seized control." Sadira stared at Soren's back, who seemed to turn her head before thinking better of it and slumping her shoulders. "It shows them slowly losing their minds as a result." Larelle nodded.

"Did that align with Nyzaia's depiction of how Soren has been in Keres?" Larelle asked, and Sadira nodded. "How does that make you feel?"

Chewing on her bottom lip, Sadira twisted a curl around her fingertip as if coming to terms with her thoughts. "I do not know. I hate her for what she did by betraying us all and assisting in Kazaar's murder. But now, knowing it was not entirely her free will, and that his control had been taking root for who knows how long..."

"Did Nyzaia give a reason as to why she believed this?" Larelle asked, surprised that Nyzaia, out of everyone, had been so lenient with Soren, having always been the most on edge in her presence.

"She saw into a memory of Soren's, though that in itself remains a mystery; perhaps it's some dormant part of Soren's Wiccan bloodline." Sadira sighed. "But Nyzaia was reluctant to give me any details and said it should come from Soren." Walking alongside Soren and her two guards, Nyzaia's behaviour was much changed from before. Every so often, Nyzaia leaned towards Soren and murmured something, though Larelle could not discern their words or if Soren replied.

"Will you speak with her?" Larelle asked. Sadira frowned, contemplating it.

"I will think about it."

"For now, that's all you can do."

Nyzaia dropped back, and the three queens continued to share everything they had learned. By the time they reached the lake in the centre of the isle, they had told each other everything—everything except for the gold wedding band on Sadira's finger beneath her engagement ring, and the matching one on the king's. Larelle smiled and kept it to herself. They would announce it when they were ready, when good news could finally be celebrated.

"Wow! It looks like my drawings!" Zarya exclaimed, surveying the glistening turquoise lake. Larelle thought the same. The lake sparkled beautifully under the rising sun, peeking above the trees and shining a light on the mountain in the centre, carved by nature. Larelle waved a hand, and the lake separated into two towering walls of water, forming a path to what Larelle knew lay within. Zarya's mouth fell open in awe as she squealed and clapped her hands. It did not take the group long to cross, and the water crashed behind them once they were inside. Larelle glanced back for a moment, surprised by the water's unexpected roughness, seemingly defying her gentle guidance. A scream from within the cave stopped her contemplation, making her stiffen. The group exchanged a glance before Vlad ran into the darkness.

"Eli!" he shouted, and Nyzaia followed. Larelle turned to ask Alvan to watch Zarya, but he assured her before she could speak.

"Go! She is fine."

Jabir held Soren, who stepped forward briefly, watching Nyzaia and Farid. Her green eyes glowed for a second, and her bottom lip trembled as they ran ahead.

"The guards will stay with you," Larelle called back, running forward with Sadira and Caellum. A pained scream echoed again as they ran through the darkness. Farid spanned his wings to light the way as they dodged a hole in the floor before reaching the top of a staircase. As she looked down below at Vlad and Nyzaia, trying to push through the army of shadows, Larelle's hand flew to her mouth. There in the centre of the room, Elisara knelt in a pool of her own blood, with lines down her back as threads of shadow whipped her skin.

Chapter Thirty-Two
Elisara

Physical pain felt like a worthy punishment, and perhaps Elisara would succumb to it until she was reunited with Kazaar. Then, she would no longer have to live with reminders of him or endure each day, numb, knowing the power inside her was the reason he was dead. There would be no weight on her shoulders to lead a realm, fight a war, break a curse, or win back lands for others. The growing list of expectations was as long as the whip formed from her shadows. Each time the whip struck with force, she felt the icy-cold wind along with it, though its bite was nothing compared to her tearing skin. She relished in it—finally *feeling* something, something worthy of what Kazaar endured, and what they all had because of Caligh. Because Caligh wanted Elisara. Elisara did not know how long she had knelt, shredding her skin at her shadows' hands. Eventually, her skirts dampened, and when she briefly leaned back from her hunched over position, blood coated her hands. *Red*. Another reminder she was no longer tied to Kazaar. He was gone.

Elisara sensed Sallos pleading as she glanced briefly through her lashes. His shadows pulled taut, trying to push towards Elisara to stop her. Other than the relief of punishment, only one other positive came from Elisara's submission to pain. The shadowed army were finally listening. She recalled Sallos words whilst she was sleeping, some of the soldiers were simply choosing to ignore the tug of her commands. She knew Sallos's inability to force his way to her now, meant her control over them all was holding strong.

"Change it," Elisara begged. "Change the prophecy! I want no part in this," she sobbed, hoping Sitara was watching and listening to her cries. There was nothing but silence as she looked at the words inscribed on the mirror and the blood pooling at her feet. Finally, Elisara stared at her reflection. Her skin was far paler than normal, perhaps even paler than Osiris's, highlighting the dark shadows beneath her eyes and the blue veins protruding under her skin from where her muscles had deteriorated. She paused on the scar on her collarbone, the moon still visible despite its absent glow. An internal roar reached her as Sallos tried to move again. "Please," she whispered. Another lash struck her back, and she screamed. The force was not as strong as the previous lashes. She was struggling to break more skin, though whether that was because of the lack of force—or lack of skin—she did not know. Elisara looked back at the mirror again, but her vision grew hazy. For a split second, she could have sworn, in the reflection of the ancient mirror, someone ran down the stairs behind her. Then she heard it, a faint cry over the ringing in her ears.

"Eli!" screamed the voice. Elisara swayed where she knelt, steadying her hands on the floor and coating them with blood. Few people ever called her that. She scrunched her eyes shut, struggling to focus on the sound of the voice. "Eli!" the voice cried again. Leaning back, a flash of golden blonde hair appeared on her left, trying to break through her army. Her command held firm. Shoulder to shoulder, the dark soldiers formed a protective ring around her, and she had no strength left to disband them. The woven strands of shifting darkness moved again, and the whip came down with a subconscious thought. Elisara's screams had stopped. She hunched over, limp, trying to focus on the surrounding voices. Was she dying? Were these the voices of the other dead?

"I can't get through!" a male shouted, a deep voice, one she recognised, though it held more authority than it once had. Three women appeared behind her in the mirror, trying to shove past her army. Elisara looked at Sallos, her mouth half open, as if a part of her wanted to tell him to let them in, even though, in her blood-drained haze, she couldn't recall who they were. Sallos knelt now, just as he had when he bowed to her on the sands, but his former honour and pride were tainted by fear and pity.

"Farid!" one woman shouted. "They've never liked your wings. Try to push through." The man with flamed wings appeared on her left, standing opposite the rows of shadows. Despite her command, the soldiers pushed back as the man strode through, with the three women following close behind. They broke the ranks of soldiers. Fear rippled through Elisara at the flaming wings rushing forward. Losing control, her panicked shadows wrapped around her body, afraid of the man with wings like the sun.

"I can't get through her power," the man grunted. Elisara was conscious of a blue light creeping into the cocoon of darkness she had formed around herself. Alone with her pain and the mirror's prophecy, she sobbed.

"When she was here with Kazaar, it was the first time their powers had tried to merge," A different female voice spoke, strong and powerful, despite the softness in her tone. *Kazaar.* Her lip wobbled again as she stared at her reflection. She recognised this voice; this voice carried the same pain of grief and had done so the last time she heard it. Elisara remembered the moment they found and stood before the mirror, with Kazaar's breath tickling her neck from behind. For a moment, she thought she saw the scene play out on the glass, hallucinating snippets of him. "Perhaps if we try merging our own power, we can break through," the female voice urged. Elisara lost all strength as she slumped onto the cold ground, coating her cheek and hair with blood. She stared at her body in the mirror. Time melted into nothing while she lay there, numb and blinking. She calmed her breathing, waiting for death.

Her shadows loosened, stretching into threads, allowing the bright light outside it to seep in. Her eyes flickered down, a quick glance at who had tried to save her in her final moments before death. Through the fading darkness, she saw a woman with beautiful brown skin and hair the same shade as Kazaar's. The leathers were the same too, save for the red sash across her body. The woman glowed; a white light emanated from her hands, stretching outward. Elisara flicked her eyes back to the mirror. Behind her was a woman with curly dark hair in a flowing navy gown; a silver crown of waves sat atop her head. The same light flowed from her hands, connecting her to the woman that looked like Kazaar. The third woman had hair that formed a halo, surrounded in white light. Threads of brightness tied the three together, repelling Elisara's shadows. Her eyes fell on the man standing behind the blonde; he rested his hand on her shoulder, a ring glinting on his finger. The sight tugged at a distant memory as darkness crept into her vision. Elisara looked at the owner's face: a powerful jaw, hair falling just above his eyeline, and tears rolling down a small scar on his cheek. Pain marred his brown eyes. He didn't want her to die. Elisara frowned.

"Star, please," he said, standing on the sidelines, his face crumpling. The shadows stretched further, pulling at her skin, and distancing themselves as whatever power connecting the women tried to dissipate.

"Caellum," Elisara murmured, remembering them as children, when he fell and gained the small scar on his cheek.

"He would not want this, Star!" Caellum shouted. "Kazaar would not want this!"

Elisara frowned. *He does not know Kazaar like I do. Kazaar would want to see me again.* Returning to look at the mirror, she pictured them standing in his rooms after their powers had merged. He had stared at her reflection with a look of complete adoration and devotion, his eyes promising she was his sun, moon, and stars—his everything. Elisara watched his face and smiled at the hallucination, happy to picture him one last time before they were reunited.

"He wouldn't want it, Elisara!" said the woman with golden brown skin. *Nyzaia. She knew him.* Her eyes flickered to the image of Kazaar in the mirror again. *Fight*, she imagined him saying, pounding his fists against the glass. *You are stronger than this.*

"I'm not." Elisara closed her eyes and sobbed. *Eyes on me, angel.* His voice rang through her mind. The memory of his voice was suffocating as she looked back at the hallucination. *You are a queen, my queen.* Elisara blinked, recalling the first time he called her that. She was strong, he had always known it. Elisara fought the darkness creeping into her vision as the hallucination of him faded. *He wouldn't want me to do this,* Elisara thought, focusing on his words and finding the flicker in her soul, the origin of Sitara's power. She tugged, drawing her darkness back into her with a scream of relief. With that, the weight lifted, and the light trying to pull apart her power faded. Feet thundered on the tiles, rushing forward. Before Elisara closed her eyes, she saw Sallos's shadowed boots approach as he knelt at her side.

"Eli!" Vlad cried. "Get Vigor! He's on the ship with Helena." His command echoed in Elisara's mind before everything went dark.

***

Elisara's unconscious state was at peace. She did not dream of other lives or see Sallos. Instead, there was simply darkness, and for once, it was not a burden. Despite relenting, despite knowing she had to go on, a part of her wished to stay in that darkness until a murmured conversation prompted her eyes to open.

"Hey," said a soft voice. Someone stroked Elisara's hair as her eyes slowly opened. She blinked several times until her vision finally focused on white hair and blue eyes. Her friend's hand was cool against her forehead, using her power to calm her clammy skin.

"Helena," Elisara croaked. Helena reached for the cup of water at the side of the bed and brought it to Elisara's mouth. The queen tried to sit up and drink but winced when she tried to roll back.

"Stay on your side for at least thirty minutes," said Vigor, coming into focus beside his wife. "I used healing water from the stalactites to mend what I could and stitched the rest together. The water should take effect in an hour and mend the stitches quick enough for you to stand and walk around. I won't be able to prevent scarring, though." Slowly, Elisara nodded as Helena withdrew the cup from her lips. As Elisara glanced between the two of them, she felt a prominent absence; someone else was missing.

"Talia—" Elisara intended to explain the complicated nature of their former friend's death.

"I know," Helena interrupted, a sadness entering her eyes. "I miss her, even after what she did. But we must move on from our losses and fight for our future." She squeezed Elisara's hands, the meaning of her words extending beyond Talia.

"Is she awake?" Vlad called from where he likely stood watch in the hallway. Elisara angled her head to look at Vlad, who stalked past the shadow with a glare, his posture stiff and rigid. He kept his eyes locked on the protector until he reached Elisara and knelt, grasping her hands. Red rimmed his eyes, and exhaustion marred his features.

"I'm sorry," Elisara's voice cracked. Hushing, Helena stroked her hair while Vigor held his wife's shoulder.

"You do not need to apologise for grieving, Eli," Vlad murmured, squeezing her hand.

"Apologise for the fact we haven't played cards since you became queen." He smiled at Elisara's laughter, which quickly dissolved into sobs.

"Once this is all over," Elisara murmured eventually, squeezing Vlad's hand and looking up at her friends. "Cards in the tavern, like old times." Helena and Vigor nodded, teary-eyed. "Is everything okay? In Vala?"

Vlad rolled his eyes. "Other than the lords insisting on taking the throne, you mean? I've kept them at bay for now. We will send word once you have rested." Footsteps sounded down the hallway. Elisara recognised the footfall immediately.

"Oh, sorry. I can come back," Caellum said, retreating through the doorway.

Helena bowed her head. "It's okay."

"We need to get some more healing supplies from the ship, anyway. Vlad and Jabir said they would escort us now it's getting dark." Elisara glanced at Sallos as the three left and Caellum walked in. If it was darkening, the soldiers who had ignored her might start wandering. Sallos shook his head, a silent confirmation they were now listening, and she had full control.

"How are you feeling?" Caellum asked. He knelt on the floor beside the bed, ignoring the stool. He rested his hands awkwardly on the blanket. Elisara reached for his right, brushing the ring she had given him for his birthday. "Sorry, I know no one ever knows how to answer that question." He brushed a hand through his hair. The gold glinting on his ring finger was unmistakeable.

"You're married," she breathed. Caellum glanced away, unsure of what to say, but there was no hiding his smile. Elisara released his hand before reaching to cup his cheek, brushing the scar she had given them as children. Caellum looked back at her with eyes she had known since she was five years old. "I'm happy for you." Her smile made Caellum's lip wobble as he cleared his throat.

"You are?"

Elisara nodded and clasped his hand, smiling sadly.

"One of us deserves to be happy."

"I thought—" Caellum choked. "I thought you were going to die." Elisara felt the tears well at the genuine pain and fear etched in his face. "I thought you were going to die thinking I never truly wanted to be with you—never loved you." Elisara frowned through her tears, unsure of what he meant. "I was never unfaithful, star, except for that one kiss. I never looked or thought of another woman; I never wanted to be with anyone but you." Elisara opened her mouth to stop him. None of it mattered now, but he continued. "Everything I said was a lie. I had been with only you. I did not resent you for Keres or the way it changed you. You are not selfish or controlling; you are not draining to be with, and I certainly was not being forced to marry you." Caellum wiped a tear from his face with the back of his jacket.

"I don't understand," Elisara murmured.

"It was all a lie. The lords told me I had to marry someone from Garridon for the sake of the realm. But I knew—I knew if a part of you still wanted me, I would have caved and betrayed my future wife, and that's not who I am. It makes me sick even thinking about that kiss." Caellum did not meet her eye while looking down at their intertwined hands. She swallowed, processing his words. It mattered little whether he kissed the lady in the gardens for they could never have wed. And, if she was truly honest with herself, there had already been something there—a small spark with Kazaar when they visited the Unsanctioned Isle. Kazaar had always been the one destined for her, and Sadira for Caellum.

"I understand, Cal," Elisara murmured. He finally looked back at her. "I knew things would not work out, not after we took our thrones. I was returning from my mission with Kazaar and knew deep down I would need to end things for the sake of our realms. While you could have gone about it a better way..." Elisara smiled and squeezed his hand. "I understand. If the tie I once had is anything to go by, there is a destiny we are each bound for. Kazaar was mine, and I think"—Elisara nodded at the gold band on his finger—"Sadira is yours."

Caellum sniffed, nodding. "I truly did love you," he said.

"I loved you too."

Chapter Thirty-Three

Nyzaia

"Are you okay?" Soren asked. Nyzaia hunched over, resting her hands on her thighs as she took deep breaths, mirroring Sadira and Larelle's exhaustion. They slumped against the large rectangular rock holding up the mirror, identical to the replica in her father's office. Nyzaia nodded, pushing the loose strands of hair sticking to the sweat on her forehead as she stood up, wobbling. Soren shot out her hands to steady her waist. Flinching, Nyzaia cleared her throat. They had spoken little since Soren had saved her and Farid in the tavern, other than hushed instructions and ensuring her mind was stable. Nyzaia didn't particularly have the energy to talk now. She knew Kazaar and Elisara had merged powers, but did not realise it was possible for others. A jolt of shock ran through her when she unleashed flames from her hands, colliding with Larelle's water, and the other with a twisting vine so similar to Soren's creations in the tavern. Moments later, the points of connection flared with bright light that crawled back along the lines of power until Nyzaia, Larelle, and Sadira were encompassed in a glow.

Fighting Elisara's shadows had felt wrong. Nyzaia recognised they were a part of her now but they appeared to be self-aware, trying to protect her. The three queens had not even succeeded. No matter the energy they put into the essence of their merging powers, it had only pulled the shadows apart, but not enough to banish them permanently. Something in Elisara's mind brought back her focus and control. Nyzaia looked up at the hole in the mountain, where the dusky sky turned deep blue, and prayed

Kazaar was watching over her and his queen. He would be heartbroken to see Elisara now, yet proud of her strength.

"You do not look okay," Soren said, scanning Nyzaia's body.

"I am fine, Soren," Nyzaia snapped. Kazaar was still at the forefront of her mind. The fallen queen did not respond. She tilted her head, watching Nyzaia with a moment of clarity. Nyzaia was beginning to learn when she was present and when her mind wandered, allowing the dark remnants to scratch and pull at her memories, toying and pushing her in the wrong directions. Her eyes gave it away—vacant, angry, or fearful. Now, brightness replaced them. Sadira and Caellum had relayed everything they had found in the deceased Kings of Garridon's journals, and it immediately resonated with what Nyzaia had witnessed in Soren's behaviour since Caligh's departure. Nyzaia had told them as much yet struggled to interpret Sadira's emotions. Had she blinked back tears of relief or frustration, as though she was unsure how to move forward? Soren looked away from Nyzaia to scan the shadowed soldiers standing to attention around the room. Some filtered in and out to survey the isle, moving like humans, unlike Caligh's shadows. With a closer look, she noticed a silvery tinge to them, perhaps reflecting their souls flowing throughout. Soren lowered her brow, the brightness dimming in her eyes.

"Hey!" Nyzaia snapped, clicking her fingers in Soren's face. She should have realised the darkness could trigger those in her mind. Soren spun her head and sneered. "Cut it out," Nyzaia said in a low, threatening tone.

"Or what?" she spat.

Nyzaia smirked and prowled closer. "Do you want a second round with our fists?" Soren stepped forward until the two women stood toe-to-toe.

"You've seen what I can do with a knife. Maybe that would be more fun," Soren whispered, staring Nyzaia down before peering over the Queen of Keres's shoulder to where Sadira rose from her slumped position beside Larelle.

"Do you want to talk to her?" Nyzaia asked. "To tell her the truth about the past?" Soren's eyes met Nyzaia's.

"Who?"

"Sadira," said Nyzaia. Soren's brow furrowed, and the light in her eyes returned, glazed with fear.

"Sadira," Soren murmured. Her face seemed to relax before she clenched her jaw. "I don't want to hurt Sadira. Sadira, I—don't take Sadira." Nyzaia swore and tugged Soren closer.

"I see you," Nyzaia said, hoping it pulled her focus back the way it had before. Soren narrowed her eyes on Nyzaia but continued to fidget, rocking on the balls of her feet and tapping her thighs. "Farid, put the chains back on, just in case."

Soren frantically looked around the room and stumbled towards the staircase, away from the soldiers before Farid clicked the cuffs around her wrists.

"Do you think it will make much difference? We've seen she can use her power just fine," said Farid, descending the staircase with Alvan and Zarya. Wide-eyed, the young princess struggled to focus, flitting between the shadowed soldiers, Farid's flamed wings, and the magnificence of the throne room.

"I believe she can only control it properly when her mind is more present—when she is herself," Nyzaia said. "When the darkness takes over, it seems to alter her ability, hence the dying plants whenever she wields. It's like she is poisoned." Soren winced at Nyzaia's words. Perhaps poisoned wasn't the right term, even if it was true.

"Do you want us to come with you?" Still, Farid kept his wings out as a deterrent. Like Nyzaia, he did not trust the shadowed soldiers. Given how easily he incited fear in them, Nyzaia wondered if Farid was a descendant of a god after all.

"No, I don't want to overwhelm Elisara. You and Jabir stay out here."

Jabir grinned at Farid.

"Fantastic," Farid mumbled.

"Don't worry. I offered to escort Helena and Vigor to the ship with Vlad, so you won't have to suffer through my jokes." Jabir grinned. They had all been resting for a few hours, allowing Elisara time to heal from Vigor's work. Nyzaia had kept Soren as far from everyone as possible, hoping to avoid discussions of her past allegiance with Caligh. Given Elisara's quick departure from Keres, she was clueless about Soren's part in separating her and Kazaar during the battle.

Larelle parted the waterfall Elisara's protector had shown them, and Nyzaia followed the Queen of Nerida through the narrow walkway, igniting a flame to light their path. Sadira followed closely behind.

A soft glow from the fireplace met the three queens, who were forced to graze against one another as they walked through the room, filled by furniture and the presence of Elisara's self-appointed protector. It would have felt claustrophobic if not for the fireplace, although the shadowed soldier leaning on the desk did pull down the warmth of the room.

"Look who's awake," Nyzaia chirped, entering the room. Elisara was propped against a mountain of pillows on the four-poster bed while Caellum poured her a fresh glass of water. Nyzaia moved towards the stool and sat down, propping her forearms on her knees as she leaned towards her friend. "Don't you ever scare me like that again, do you understand?" Nyzaia said, the smile gone from her face. Her eyes were serious yet glassy as she surveyed the frail queen.

Elisara nodded and gave a small smile. Addressing the shadow, she said, "Sallos, can you leave us?"

"He has a name?" Larelle asked, moving as far from the man as possible to perch on the bed at Elisara's other side. Nyzaia studied the shadowed man. His rigid posture seemed practiced, like he was used to standing to attention in a room of royals.

"That's all I know about him," Elisara said. "And he's stubborn," she emphasised as the soldier hesitated at the door before conceding.

"He moves like someone well accustomed to fighting and war," Sadira said, sitting at the end of the bed. Four queens, reunited.

"He doesn't look like one," Elisara said.

"You mean you can see past the shadows?" Caellum asked from his seat at the desk. Elisara shook her head.

"Only when I sleep. When I am sleeping, he appears without the shadows. Apparently, they all do, though I have only seen him. He looks rather... normal."

"Don't let him hear you say that," Nyzaia scoffed. "Most men would be offended by such a remark." Nyzaia noted Elisara's arms, furrowing her brow at the raised scars on her skin, images she had seen before.

"They match Kazaar's," Elisara murmured, stroking a thumb over the raised vines on her forearm. "Do you know how he inked his?" Nyzaia nodded with an understanding smile.

"Would you like me to ink yours?"

Elisara smiled. "I think it would be nice to have a permanent reminder of him, even if he is always here," she replied, resting a hand on her heart.

"Caellum," Nyzaia called, feeling odd at the civility in her tone. "Could you see if Vigor left any needles in his healing bag?" Caellum nodded and left the four queens together as Nyzaia rose to retrieve a pot of ink from the desk.

Sadira frowned. "Should you be leaning on your back like that?"

"Vigor wrapped it and said I should be okay for now, as long as I rest." Elisara smiled at the princess's hands. Sadira shifted, clasping one hand over the other.

"We have a lot to discuss." Larelle leaned beside Elisara and hummed, keeping her eyes on Sadira. "You noticed as well, then?"

"Noticed what?" Nyzaia asked, sitting back on the stool.

"I saw it on Caellum's finger." Elisara smiled at Sadira. "Congratulations."

Nyzaia glanced between the women. "Am I missing something?" As Sadira blushed and tucked a strand of hair behind her ear, the glinting gold band captured Nyzaia's attention. "Wow, I'm losing my touch!"

Larelle chuckled. "Does that mean we would make better assassins than you?"

"Absolutely not," Nyzaia scoffed. "You and Sadira could perhaps be Alchemists as you're both smart enough—or Courtesans. Plenty of men and women would hand information over to you." Nyzaia smirked when the two women blushed. "Elisara would perhaps make it in the Blades."

"You know damn well I would," Elisara exclaimed, though her smile faltered.

"Where was the wedding?" Larelle asked. Sadira glanced at Elisara, but her face was welcoming.

"We married on a field of irises at the edge of Albyn. It was just us, Sir Cain, and Taryn."

"Did Sir Cain cry? I always thought he was rather a sentimental man," said Elisara, earning a laugh from Sadira.

"He did. Taryn and Caellum did too. Come to think of it, I was the only one who didn't."

Larelle laughed.

"What was your dress like?" asked Elisara.

"Oh gods! Are we really going to sit and talk about dresses?" groaned Nyzaia. Elisara elbowed her friend.

"Just because you don't favour them doesn't mean you cannot appreciate them."

"I would rather sit and listen to how good the sex was afterward than talk about dresses."

"Nyzaia!" Larelle chastised.

"What! Does that not make my feelings on dresses clear enough?" Nyzaia rolled her eyes, and Sadira stifled a laugh, forcing Nyzaia to smile. She looked at each of the three women in turn: a tired Elisara in a fresh white shirt, Larelle in her regal navy gown, her head held high even when relaxed, and Sadira in pink florals, highlighting the kindness in her face. And there Nyzaia sat in her leathers. Four queens, acting as though they were just friends at a tavern.

"Do you remember when we were getting ready for the welcome ball at my palace?" Nyzaia asked.

"That seems like an age ago now." Elisara glanced at the cup of water in her hands, her smile gone.

"We were talking and laughing while getting ready." Nyzaia smiled and squeezed Elisara's hand, knowing she thought of that night with Kazaar. "We wondered if we would ever get to sit together like that again."

"I remember," Larelle nodded. "I said we would. I knew we would have a day in the future where we would sit like this, laughing or crying. We would be together." Larelle reached for Sadira and Elisara's hands and squeezed them both. The three queens stared at Nyzaia, who rolled her eyes before joining hands with them, a calm energy flowing between them all. Nyzaia looked at the three queens, her heart warming. Despite her worries and Tajana's absence, she felt safe with these women and realised then that they were her friends, not her fellow rulers.

"And there will be another day, another moment like this." Nyzaia smiled, hope filling her veins. "In the future."

Chapter Thirty-Four

Larelle

Nyzaia's hand was steady and methodical as she dipped the needle in ink and dotted it across the scars on Elisara's arms, her tongue poking out in concentration. Larelle had a newfound appreciation for the ones on Alvan's scalp, nearly hidden beneath his hair now. She did not know how he endured it and doubted she would ever ink anything on herself. Despite Larelle's aversion to the idea, a small smile graced Elisara's lips as Nyzaia finished the sails in the crook of her elbow. From her exterior, Elisara appeared content while watching Nyzaia work, but her smile had faltered on many occasions before she put on a brave face for the sake of everyone else. Larelle had done the same for Olden after losing Riyas. Though she had good and bad days, all that mattered was she never descended to the state they found Elisara in. Entrenched in her grief, Larelle thought they might have lost her completely. The smell of Elisara's blood still lingered; the memory of finding her hunched over, with open wounds streaked across her back, was one she would never forget.

Caellum moved his chair closer to Sadira at the end of the bed; they both watched Elisara with saddened eyes. The room was rife with pity and pain, making Larelle wonder if Elisara sensed it too. Despite the sadness of such emotions, it showed just how many people cared.

"I imagine I have missed a lot," Elisara said, watching Nyzaia's steady hands.

"We could say the same," Caellum said, pausing to glance at the other queens. "We still do not know exactly what happened to you before the second half of the battle." Caellum seemed to choose his words carefully and spoke slowly to prevent triggering Elisara's pain.

"Let me go first. I can summarise the important parts of what you missed," Larelle said. Elisara finally tore her gaze from Nyzaia to nod at Larelle. "After you left, Osiris gave us as much information as he could. It would seem the lands he is from are somehow cursed, preventing him from giving us much information. But it would suggest his own lands have also fallen victim to Caligh's destruction, just like Novisia and Ithyion before it. He implied we are but one part of a much bigger problem and that other lands exist out there. Finding and freeing these lands will hopefully aid us in defeating Caligh together."

"He spoke words that resembled a prophecy of sorts," Sadira said, and Elisara groaned. "A Wiccan I know fell into a trance and relayed the rest; her words aligned with bits and pieces Larelle heard from a priest, who potentially descended from Garridon rather than Nerida." Sadira handed Elisara a piece of paper with the words on it, who furrowed her brow while reading.

"Have you uncovered what it means?" Elisara asked. The three queens and the king shook their heads.

"Caellum and I think part of it is linked to the people of Garridon. Healing and prophecies, curses and spells—all of these gifts are linked heavily to the Wiccan of Garridon, and thus 'one abides, one rebels' seems to reference two parallels. We were told something has divided the Wiccans. Perhaps one half represents those who rebelled, aligned to curses and spells," Sadira said.

Caellum pulled the pins from his pocket and passed them to Elisara. "One symbol represents shapeshifters, though we do not fully understand what they are. The other two symbols are similar, but different. One is Wiccan, but we don't know the other. They might be the opposites that are mentioned, or perhaps something to do with whatever power hid people's memories."

Elisara looked up from examining the paper. "Sitara said something about memories.

She said that this world is crumbling because Caligh took Sonos, and minds would soon awaken and memories return." What type of chaos could befall their kingdom to compare it to the world crumbling away.

"So, Sitara knows something about the curse," Larelle surmised. "What if the gods are involved? Someone had to be strong enough to overpower another god."

"I don't think they are. Something was stopping Sitara from telling me everything," Elisara said. "Is the memories part true then?" Sadira nodded, shifting further onto the bed. "We met someone with memories awakening in Garridon. We think the priest in Nerida was suffering with it, too."

"But why would Caligh need to hide people's memories?" Elisara asked. "We're assuming it's Caligh, aren't we?"

"That is what we can't quite work out," murmured Nyzaia, dipping her needle back into the inkpot. "In Tabheri, there's a cult devoted to different gods. We thought Novisia might be made up of people from many lands, and that Ithyion never existed. Those who first settled here had the memories of their lands erased."

"It would align with Osiris being from a different land," Larelle said. "We just do not know why our ancestors would arrive on Novisia only to be hidden away. What purpose would that serve Caligh?"

"If what we're saying about different lands is true—and that all lands are potentially under threat from Caligh—then what Sitara asked of me makes some sense," Elisara murmured. Larelle waited for Elisara to divulge more, seemingly sorting through her memories. Elisara winced. "Sitara said the world was crumbling, but it was because Caligh took Sonos. This new prophecy speaks of the cost of a curse. What if the price of taking Sonos is an imbalance in the world?"

Larelle thought through the implication. Sitara and Sonos represented dusk and dawn. It made sense that the absence of one would cause an imbalance, but was Caligh truly powerful enough to take down a god and hide the other away?

"It's definitely an option, but Osiris's lands are physically cursed; they're not crumbling because of some imbalance," Larelle countered.

"Perhaps they are linked. Sonos's capture must have created an imbalance," Elisara said. "In taking Sonos, curses arose on the lands with different consequences, including not being able to share the curses with us. Perhaps that's why we are separated? We are cursed by our lack of knowledge and memories." Larelle rubbed her brow. The endless information and theories were becoming too much, even for her. She tried to simplify it.

"We had three tasks. One, confirm if memories were returning," Larelle said.

"Which we have done," agreed Nyzaia.

"Two, learn more about the Wiccans' power and their link to the land," Larelle continued.

"We know some Wiccan know of the Sword of Souls; they implied it divided their people, which could explain the differing symbols on the pins and the pendant Larelle took from the priest. The notion of there being a divide or 'two,' the healing, prophecies, curses, and spells—all of that suggests that the divided Wiccan are tied to the words Osiris recited and perhaps are linked to the curse on his lands. The Wiccan could have been used in whatever curse hid the memories," said Sadira.

"We had to confirm there were more lands and how to save them to gather more people to fight Caligh. I found maps of other places, but no indication of where they resided, and still, we don't know how to break the curse." Larelle sighed. They had barely made any progress.

"And Sitara wants us to find Sonos," Elisara added.

"Oh fantastic," Nyzaia mumbled. "Let's just add finding the God of Dawn to our world-saving to-do list."

"Must we prioritise breaking the curse on somebody else's

land?" Caellum asked.

"If it helps us gain allies before Caligh's return, then yes," Larelle said—unless their land suffered from a curse far worse than missing memories, which appeared to be broken when the rulers took the thrones. Perhaps they could find answers in the books taken from the church. They had not yet read through them or analysed the maps, instead prioritising the trip to the Unsanctioned Isle. Now seemed like an ideal time to read them, with multiple sets of eyes to help.

"Zarya!" a stern voice shouted from outside the hallway. Alvan was not quick enough to stop the little girl from bounding into the room, her curls flying about her face.

"Oh," Zarya paused as all the rulers turned to look. She blushed as Alvan strode in and placed a hand on her shoulder.

"I apologise all. She insisted on telling her mother something and said it could not wait." Alvan gave Larelle an exasperated look, as if to say he had done everything he could to stop her.

"Zarya, sweetie, if Alvan tells you to wait, you need to wait, okay?" Larelle rose from the bed and crouched before her daughter. "Now you are here, quickly tell me what it is." Larelle smoothed down her daughter's curls while Zarya glanced over Larelle's shoulder at the other rulers.

"You know what Ossie said about my intu–"

"Your intuition?" Larelle prompted.

"I'm sorry, Ossie?" Nyzaia barked a laugh, and Zarya grinned at the Queen of Keres.

"Yes! That! Well, I need to show you something." Zarya grabbed her mother's hand and tugged her into the hallway. "All of you!"

"Gods, she's bossy—I love it," Nyzaia chuckled, helping Elisara up from the bed. Larelle had taken off her shoes to be comfortable, and the onyx and marble floor beneath her feet was cold. The waterfall parted, and Sallos, the name of Elisara's protector, paced back and forth in the centre of the throne room.

"He agrees with me!" Zarya said, pointing at the shadowed soldier. He waved an arm, as though hurrying them along.

"You can sense him?" Elisara asked, shuffling into the room. She rested her hand on Nyzaia's shoulder to steady herself.

"Uh huh," Zarya sang, dragging her mother to the mirror in the room's centre. "There!" Zarya pointed at the glass, and Larelle frowned, reading the words of the original prophecy.

"Zarya, sweetie, we have already read this," said Larelle, crouching again. The other rulers came to stand behind her, squeezing into the reflection.

"You can't see it?" Zarya asked, her smile fading. She frowned at the mirror, then at her mother and the others, before asking them the same question. Sallos pointed and approached the mirror. Larelle looked at Elisara for elaboration, who frowned.

"I can't hear him, but there's a sense of urgency about the mirror."

"Well, what can you see, princess?" Nyzaia asked from behind, a curious lilt in her tone.

"It looks like that dream place," Zarya said.

"The one you saw Osiris in?" Larelle asked, and Zarya nodded.

"Look, I'll show you!" Zarya giggled and rushed towards the mirror, placing her hand against it—only, it didn't stop there. Her hand sank through the glass, wrapping tightly around her wrist. Larelle's instincts kicked in as she grabbed the back of Zarya's dress, tugging her back before she walked through.

"Well, I saw *that*," Nyzaia said, drawing closer to the glass.

"Find your reflection in the ancient and say goodbye." Elisara murmured the final words from the paper. "The mirror could definitely be ancient. The words also tell of mirrors, reflections, reveres, opposites."

"The priest was transfixed on the mirror in his room, as though he was piecing something together," Larelle murmured. They all looked at the glass, which appeared completely normal without Zarya's hand inside it.

"I'm going to be honest. I don't love the sound of saying goodbye," Nyzaia said. "What if we don't come back if we go through?"

"I suppose it's a risk we must take." Sadira shared a look with her husband.

"Well... shall we then?" Elisara asked. The rulers exchanged a look with each other and their friends behind them. Larelle rose from her crouch and before she could tell Zarya to stay with Olden and Lillian on the ship, her daughter tugged her hand and pulled her through the mirror.

Chapter Thirty-Five
Soren

S oren shielded her eyes against the stark light, a shock from the dimly lit throne room from moments ago. Her heart quickened, and her palms clammed with sweat. Was she hallucinating? While the rulers discussed the mirror, she did exactly as Farid had asked—standing silently at his side without moving a muscle. Yet as she blinked now, Soren was not in the throne room, and Farid and Nyzaia were nowhere to be seen. Birds chirped overhead, and she looked into the tree, where a nest was buried amongst the branches. Yet the shade of green seemed wrong; it was not luscious or full of life. Had Caligh learned to infiltrate her mind in new ways? She frantically scanned the trees, where above, the bluebirds had an unusual brown tinge to them. Soren lowered her gaze to where she brushed the rough bark of the tree trunk, where the brown was faded. This was Garridon, she realised, while beginning to navigate the roots and fallen branches. Antor Castle could be spotted through the last trees, towards the end of the sandy path. It was the route she had travelled with Sadira when arriving, except there was a wrongness to it.

As Soren broke through the final row of trees, she took in the landscape. It was like someone had taken a paintbrush and coated the land in pale sepia, tinging her entire vision a warm brown. Soren took a deep breath. The air felt stale and lacked Garridon's usual freshness and scents, devoid of sap from the trees and pollen from the flowers. As she approached the castle wall, laughter sounded from within. Children's laughter. Soren halted to listen, reminded of when she and Sadira were young. The fallen queen blinked, realising how clearly she recalled memories and the absence of the dark shadows. The sound of howling wolves had Soren spinning in the opposite direction and quickening into a jog to the city's entrance. Something was freeing about this place, even though she had no idea how she ended up here. All worry left her, the weight lifting from her chest and shoulders. Still, she felt the darkness, dormant in the corners of her mind. It seemed afraid to come out and taunt her.

Soren slowed, panting from the exercise. She had not trained since the end of battle and was weak because of it. She wished Nyzaia could see her like this. Normal. They had exchanged only a few words since that night at the tavern when Soren had let the darkness creep in. Yet she couldn't control when it reared its ugly head and demanded a return to her old ways of pleasing Caligh. But now, wherever she was, her mind was quiet. She wanted to apologise to the queen while she was of sound mind. Maybe Soren would never leave this place and would learn to live in peace with her mind.

Her footsteps slowed as voices drifted through Antor's streets. Soren stilled when rounding the corner, staring wide-eyed at the city square. It was filled with people, though she recognised none of them, and their clothes seemed older than the styles worn in Garridon now. Two little girls ran past, giggling, like Soren and Sadira so often had; their hands grazed Soren. Cold. As cold as death. Mumbling began as the people looked at her, forming a crowd. Soren peered down at her clothing; she donned the same brown trousers, green shirt, and boots—the colours a stark contrast to the sepia world. Soren backed up and hit a wall as the figures drifted towards her, still talking. With her head pounding, she was unable to focus on their words. Instead, she forced her eyes shut as darkness crept into the corners of her mind, slowly waking and stepping into the light. Before she could worry, a rough voice called across the square.

"Soren Mordane." She opened her eyes at the parting crowd and immediately knelt, bowing her head. He wore a deep green jacket, crisp trousers, and freshly polished shoes. He clasped his hands behind his back and turned from the crowd, heading down a street that led to the edge of Hybrooke Forest. "Walk with me," the God of Earth, Garridon, called in a rough accent. Soren wasted no time in rising and hurrying past the crowd behind her god.

He was taller than she remembered, his stance wider and presence more demanding. Soren recalled their last meeting, the way he sensed Caligh's presence in her mind and stopped her killing Caellum. In a clearer state of mind, she realised how grateful she was for his interference. She could not bear to think about the look on Sadira's face had she followed through with it. It was not what Soren wanted. Caellum protected her sister and made her happy when Soren could not.

"You seem in calmer spirits," Garridon said, slowing his pace for Soren to catch up as they exited the city and strode for the forest.

"There is something about this place that repels the darkness in my mind," Soren said, stealing a look at her god.

"That does not surprise me. Caligh may hate me, but power has a trace, Soren. It remembers things, and his darkness in you remembers the past. Being here, the darkness is both curious and scared." As Garridon walked, the trees shifted for him, clearing a path as a hawk landed on his shoulder, watching. Soren tilted her head and smiled. Before Caligh, she always had a natural calling to animals.

"My guardian. Pay him no attention," Garridon said, stopping in a small clearing in the woods. Moss coated the floor and ivy climbed up the tree stump in the centre where Garridon perched on the edge and crossed his legs.

"If I may, how did you know Caligh?" Soren asked, bowing her head. Garridon smiled and glanced down, tapping his thigh.

"Caligh was a friend once. Well, he was more than that at another point in time." Soren raised her eyebrows at the thought of being romantically involved with someone so evil. Garridon patted the spot on the stump beside him, and she hesitated. It seemed so informal to sit next to the god she had been raised to respect. Yet when Garridon paused his story, she sat. "We have a long and sordid history—I will spare you many of the details. But I discovered Caligh was using my people in ways I did not condone. It divided us and my lands. The Wiccan people, once a great race, have since halved and are now embroiled in war."

"War? Where?" Soren asked, oblivious to any discontent between the Wiccan she had known. Wolves howled in the distance, and Soren straightened, searching for Seiko or Varna.

"They are not your wolves," Garridon said, ignoring her question. "They are my first wolves, the oldest." Garridon tapped his fingers again. "Where was I? Ah! Yes. When I found out he was using my people, I banished him from my lands and cut off his access to the *things* he had created. He never forgave me; he has a bitter heart." Garridon turned to face his descendent, tucking a stray piece of hair behind her ear. "It is sadly why he targeted my realm for his corruption and why he targeted you. I am sorry for that, Soren." Emotion overcame Soren, who swallowed her tears at his sincerity, surprised he would care for one small person in the blip of his existence.

"Is that why you stopped me in the temple from killing the king?" Soren asked. "You knew it was not truly my action or will." The god nodded and extended his arm for the hawk. "Thank you," she whispered. "I don't know if I would have ever come back from that."

"Eventually you would have, especially if you ended up here. But your relationship with Sadira would not have survived." Garridon whistled, and the hawk took off. A lump rose in Soren's throat at the idea of never making amends with her sister.

"Why do you care about me?" Soren asked, and the god chuckled. She hoped she had not offended him.

"Besides feeling a sense of duty to you after Caligh's revenge, I am also the creator of life," he said, letting a flower blossom in his palm. "It is natural I should care about my creations. It is why I tethered past souls here." Soren frowned, recalling the bodies drifting through the city.

"There are no souls from the other realms?"

"Not a single one. It took a great deal to get away with this, but there are some people who are not ready to move on, people I allow to stay until they are ready to leave." Soren peered down at her hands; anxiety sat in her stomach as she tried to voice her next question. Garridon patiently waited and tucked a flower behind her hair.

"Are my parents here? My grandmother?"

He smiled. "Perhaps. If you journey further through the forest, you might find them."

"I do not know if I can face them after all I have done," she murmured. Garridon squeezed her knee.

"I can take it away, if you wish." Soren stilled, watching him. "I can remove the remnants of his power lingering in your mind, the power that resurfaces and strangles your spirit. I can take it away, but heed my warning, it will worsen before it gets better. It is the consequence of disturbing such power."

"Do it," Soren said without a single doubt in her mind. She wanted it gone, no matter the pain or hallucinations she might experience in the meantime—none of it mattered if it meant ridding his power completely.

"Very well."

Chapter Thirty-Six

Nyzaia

The air rushed out of Nyzaia's lungs as someone yanked her back with force, gripping tightly to the red sash wrapped over her chest. She only had a second to comprehend what had happened before opening her eyes, peering down into the depths of Nefere Valley—a treacherous drop of jagged rocks which levelled out into the dry cracked earth with nothing to cushion her fall. Rock crumbled at her toes and were it not for the hand pulling Nyzaia back, a second later she would have tipped forward and plunged to her death. She spun as the hand released her, finding Farid surveying their surroundings, confusion underlying his stoic assessment of any threat.

"Perhaps our shared destiny means I'll always be here to save you from plummeting to your death." Farid kept his face neutral and his hand on the pommel of his sword as he stepped back towards the edge. Nyzaia stood by his side, more cautious this time, firmly keeping the toes of her boots a step behind Farid's as they stared out across the realm. Despite the odd brown tinge to the sky and sun, the heat of the realm beat down on their necks with its usual ferocity.

"If the celestial tie would just grant me access to your power and the ability to have wings, I wouldn't have a problem," Nyzaia grumbled, crossing her arms and peering over the drop. The corner of Farid's lips quirked, watching her from the corner of his eye. Nyzaia was reminded of Lord Israar's reaction to his wings. *Nefere.* He had called Farid the same name as the valley they now stood before, a valley Nyzaia had been shown in a different form during her drug-induced dream. The many references left her wondering if there was something greater about Farid, something key to helping them understand the different people and lands, especially as his wings were so unique in Novisia.

"This is... different," he said. Nyzaia frowned at the valley before glancing up at the sky. "Keres isn't exactly a vibrant place, particularly across the sands and canyons, but *this* feels drained," Farid continued, and Nyzaia nodded. The path through Nefere Valley, the surrounding canyon rock, and the sands of the deserts, had always been varying shades of brown-tinged orange. Yet here, the sky matched it, and the trees in the distant oasis were tinged the same shade. Something was wrong.

"Where exactly are we?"

"It appears to be laid out like Novisia, but something's off." Farid turned and spun slowly to look in every direction. "Everything is flipped. From where we stand, Tabheri should be on our left, the Neutral City on our right, and Vala behind us. But from here, I can see the mountains."

"It's like a mirror," Nyzaia murmured, squinting at the snow-capped mountains in the distance. Had Elisara emerged there, alone?

"A reverse, a reflection, a sister, a mirror," Farid murmured, the lines Osiris had recited.

"Find the truth beneath you and all will be clearer," Nyzaia continued. "So, has this been here all along? This... I don't even know what to call it."

"Bound," Farid said, perplexed. "Listen to the land and understand you are bound."

"So, this place is somehow bound to Novisia?" Nyzaia contemplated, her eyes turning to the oasis and recalling how only a week ago she sat by the water's edge to remember Kazaar's life. The realm around her felt as dead as him.

"Or are we bound to this existence?" Farid murmured. Nyzaia tried to understand the implications of where they were and what they should do when movement stirred in the distance. She focused her eyes to track the movement. Someone with dark hair and deep-red clothing walked from around the palm trees and sat by the water's edge. The man moved his hands back and forth, but from here, she could not identify him.

"Why don't we ask him?" Nyzaia suggested, tilting her head in his direction. Farid followed her eyeline and nodded before turning. The valley's high rock walls meant they had to backtrack, climb down, and circle around to the oasis. Usually, during missions through the canyons or the valley, dust from the dry paths would blow up in her face, but Nyzaia quickly noticed the lack of wind and stagnant air as the dust lined her boots rather than her leathers. Farid and Nyzaia walked in comfortable silence until Farid finally broke it.

"I like the sash addition," he said, eyeing the red gauze pinned to her upper half. "Why did you decide to add it?"

Nyzaia shrugged, yet the reminder of her near-death flashed before her eyes—the pain she felt while powerless. "I don't know... After what happened in the tavern with Israar, I realised if I hadn't survived that night, the realm would have no queen—no one to lead them, no symbol of Keres. I've never really cared about being queen before, but in the face of death, it made me question if I should start taking my duty more seriously."

"So, it's a symbol?" Farid asked.

"I suppose so. It's like this uncomfortable crown. I think I just realised..." Nyzaia kicked the sand at her feet. "Maybe I do care about being queen and protecting the people. I can't keep ignoring the fact I am."

"So, wearing the red and the crown is a sign of your acceptance—daily acknowledgement?" Farid asked with a small smile. Nyzaia nodded. "What happens if you do die?"

"Gods, Farid! Talk about depressing conversation," Nyzaia joked, but Farid remained silent, waiting. "You can have the crown." She grinned and pushed aside the real possibility of death, and the lack of a plan in place if that occurred. She thought of Lord Israar. At least he could not try to take her throne if she was dead. For all she cared, the other lords could fight for it.

"Absolutely not." Farid scoffed before falling silent again. A sheen of sweat beaded his forehead as they quickened their pace. "What if I die when you die? Could the tie do that?"

"I don't think so; Elisara didn't..." Nyzaia trailed off, not wishing to speak of Kazaar.

"I assumed that was because they had fulfilled their shared destiny. They were destined to draw out Caligh and go to war to fulfil the prophecy. Kazaar was destined to..." Farid paused, as though searching for the right words. "He was destined to benefit Caligh."

"Perhaps whoever is at the oasis could answer that question. I sense this is not a place of normal existence," Nyzaia said as they reached the final bend in the rocks and finally saw the oasis. The man sat at its edge, his hair reaching past his shoulders. "Couldn't you have flown us down and saved us from doubling round?"

"It was the first thing I tried. I can't draw my wings out here," Farid said, a sad lilt entering his voice. Nyzaia hoped his gloom was because he finally recognised his wings as a beautiful part of himself, a part he could naturally call upon rather than hide away. Extending her hand, Nyzaia focused on channelling her power, but found she could not. Yet she still sensed her power flickering within her soul, unlike when she was drugged or weakened within the circle. Its presence provided some comfort, though, despite its disobedience. The conversations of death and 'what ifs' made Nyzaia's mind spiral. Craving a distraction, she glanced at Farid and studied his face.

"I think you and Jabir would make fine kings." Nyzaia waited for his reaction or a tell in his expression that confirmed her suspicions. His face remained neutral.

"Remember, I can sense your intentions. I can practically feel your laughter running through me," Farid murmured.

"You didn't answer the question."

"You didn't ask a question."

"Come on, Farid, you know what I meant." Nyzaia elbowed his side, but he remained rigid until finally glancing sideways at her. When Nyzaia grinned, Farid relented. Light burned in his pale blue eyes.

"We just talk is all," Farid said, his mouth twitching.

"I have quite literally never heard you say more than a few sentences to him."

"If that's so, why are you making assumptions?"

"You may have only said a few sentences, but I felt the tension in them," Nyzaia laughed. "Why am I not privy to these conversations?"

"They are while you're sleeping. We take shifts guarding your chambers at night. When we crossover, we talk for a bit."

"What constitutes 'a bit'?" Nyzaia was intrigued by Farid's honesty, especially as her question about Jabir had coaxed it from him. Farid's as his smile stretched into a wide, almost complete smile, for once.

"It started as brief comments and small talk when we changed over. Then, on one occasion, he bought me some food and ate with me while we were on guard. I don't really know when it changed, but small talk slowly became an hour, and then two. Then we were nearly always outside your chambers and so would alternate our sleeping patterns during the day instead." Farid appeared to realise how personal his remarks were and cleared his throat, refocusing on the approaching oasis.

"You mean to tell me there has been a love story unfolding outside my chamber doors at night and I *missed* it?" Nyzaia exclaimed.

"Please, you do not care about love stories," Farid scoffed. He was right; Nyzaia was not one for fantasies or romantic tales. She had only cared about her love—her only love. Nyzaia lost her smile as her mind replayed all the recent deaths and destruction. What was happening to Tajana at this very moment? Nyzaia sighed, bumping Farid's arm.

"I care about your love story," she whispered. Farid looked down at her with softened eyes.

"Thank you," he murmured. "Do you think he is safe?"

"If he is not with us, I'm sure he is still back on the isle. He wasn't as close to the mirror as you were when I walked through," she said. Farid gave a small nod and smiled. Nyzaia tilted her head at him, mesmerised by the emotions she rarely saw. They made him appear younger and lifted the weight of his traumatic upbringing. She wondered how different he might have been growing up without his father and the wings on his back.

"Can I officiate your wedding?" Nyzaia beamed, distracting him from any worry.

"I'll push you in the water. With all the fire you wield, I assume you're like a cat who hates getting wet."

"Did you just compare me to a cat?" Nyzaia asked. Her smile slipped when she saw the man by the water's edge rise and turn to face them. He held a sword in one hand and a cloth in the other, using it to polish his golden blade. His red robes grazed the sand, revealing his bare feet beneath. His grey beard was manicured into a sharp point while his dark and greying hair hung loose, framing his face. Mischief twinkled in his flaming amber eyes as he approached.

"I see I made an entertaining choice in tying your destinies together," Keres chuckled.

Chapter Thirty-Seven

Sadira

Soft petals grazed Sadira's fingers as she opened her eyes, finding herself cross-legged in a patch of petunias. Plucking one gently from the ground, she brought the flower to her eyeline, turning it in different directions to determine what colour it had been. It was definitely a pale colour, but it was tinged with a sad brown, like the rest of the field. Only now, noting the contrast of her pale pink dress amongst the sepia-shaded fields, Sadira realised how much she valued colour. She raised her head, realising it was not just the flowers drained of vibrancy; the small town opposite appeared the same way. Seley was a melding of stone and thatched houses. While she had only visited once during her travel back from her first ball in Nerida, she easily remembered the strange blend of the two realms, with its bright white walls and pale sandstone.

Sadira turned her head to scan the fields behind her and the Hybrooke Forest on the other side, but she could not see her husband. Her hand flew to her mouth as she turned in the flowers, her pulse quickening. A pale figure mirrored her position. Sadira would have jumped were it not for the deep smile lines and wrinkles around her once bright green eyes. Sadira blinked back tears.

"Hello child," said her grandmother, reaching towards her.

"Am I..." Sadira began to panic, but her grandmother shook her head and offered reassurance.

"You're not dead," Lyra reassured. Sadira had so many questions but was too overwhelmed by the opportunity to see her family.

"I miss you," Sadira breathed, a tear rolling down her cheek. Lyra tilted her head as her own eyes watered, assessing her granddaughter.

"You're thriving, Sadira," Lyra said, glancing at the golden band on her finger with a gentle smile. "Does he make you happy? I see glimpses of the two of you—a perk of being here—but I wish to know what is in your heart." Lyra rested her hand on Sadira's chest.

"Very. I am very happy," Sadira choked.

"In my lifetime, I have been gifted and cursed with many prophecies and fortunes. When I saw you with him and watched your wedding, you were *so* young. It didn't happen exactly as I had foreseen as prophecies and visions are open to interpretation, but it was the happiest I have ever been at a vision," Lyra said, her voice cracking. In this version of Novisia, Sadira's grandmother seemed peaceful. Sadira had always felt loved by her family, but a tainted aura marred her grandmother on Doltas—sadness after losing so much. Yet here, her grandmother seemed truly happy and at peace; only one person would make her feel that way.

"Is Errard here?" Sadira asked.

"He was." Although Lyra smiled, Sadira saddened at the past tense, knowing their time was yet again cut short, leaving her here. "We're fortunate our god has such measures in place to allow those of us with unfinished business to reside here. The only thing your grandfather was waiting for was me." Sadira's heart clenched, thinking about her parents. "Your parents knew they had fulfilled everything required of them. As much as they loved you, they were at peace with their decisions and what was asked of them." Lyra squeezed Sadira's hands. "Errard passed on recently. Time moves differently here, and so I have no concept of how long ago that was, but we had the time we needed. I was only waiting here for you." A tear fell down Lyra's cheek while gazing at her granddaughter. "And then it will be my time to part." Sadira was overwhelmed by emotions as she waited for her grandmother to continue. She was both grateful for their time together, but also disappointed. Why had her parents not wished to wait to see her? It prompted Sadira to question whether she would pass on or linger in this place with unfinished business.

"You need to learn forgiveness, Sadira," Lyra said. Sadira frowned; she considered herself a forgiving person, always prioritising the feelings of others before her own. "Your sister." Sadira looked away, unwilling to confront her conflicting feelings about Soren. "She did not choose this path."

"She may not have chosen it, but she did not fight it, either. She did everything he asked." Sadira picked at the flower petals, knowing deep down that was untrue. Having read Jorah's journals, she understood what Caligh had done, latching his dark claws into Soren's mind to command her. Yet even they had broken through his control at points.

"Did you know Jorah allowed you to escape?" Sadira asked, and Lyra nodded.

"I did. He was waiting here too. It was part of his unfinished business to set things right with Errard and I." Slowly, Sadira nodded and clenched her hands.

"Wren remembered Caellum's name to ensure he was the one who survived," Sadira continued, and her grandmother sighed, as though sensing the direction of Sadira's thoughts. "Soren did not remember or break through once. Maybe she does not care about me as much as the others Caligh poisoned." Lyra moved her hand over Sadira's, stopping her from plucking the flower petals. She obliged and met her grandmother's eyes.

"Child, everything Soren ever did was for you." Lyra gave a pained yet honest smile. "Knowing what you have endured, I understand it's difficult to process your thoughts and emotions, but Soren is experiencing far worse." Sadira slumped at her grandmother's words.

"Nyzaia told me how unstable she has been," she said. "There were moments when she was her usual stubborn and hateful self, focusing only on her history with Caligh, but—" Sadira hesitated. "She said Soren seemed like a different person at other moments. I know *that* person is likely the Soren I once knew." Sadira sniffed. "But I lost her to him so long ago. How am I ever to believe she can truly be free of whatever plagues her mind? How can I allow her around my husband or my future children, knowing there is a part lingering inside of her that wishes Caellum dead?" Sadira wiped her tears with the back of her hand. "I cannot risk that; I cannot risk my husband, my king." Sadira tried to calm her breathing. The idea of losing Caellum and being utterly alone fuelled a rising panic in her chest.

"Your feelings are valid, Sadira," Lyra said, straightening. Sadira followed suit, standing a head taller than Lyra. "But you can take precautions while still helping Soren to recover. She is your sister, and she needs you." Lyra rested a hand on Sadira's cheek. "It is my time," Lyra whispered, peering at something over Sadira's shoulder. The Queen of Garridon turned to look at a head of blonde braids stumbling out of Hybrooke Forest.

"I—" Sadira turned back to find Lyra had vanished. She let out a sad and frustrated sigh. She had so much to ask about the Wiccan, the pins, Athena, and their friendship. Now, her chance was gone. Her grandmother was gone.

The sun in the tinged sky shone down on Sadira as she turned to face her sister, stumbling through the field in her direction. Sadira was uncertain whether she had seen her yet. With a deep breath, Sadira yelled, "Soren!"

Her sister stilled in the field and straightened at Sadira's voice. The pair walked towards one another. From afar, they appeared as two sides of a coin striding toward one another. On one side was a queen in pink, the embodiment of beauty and life, and on the other was a broken woman, her green shirt stark against the sepia-painted backdrop. Her hand rested on the empty sheath where her sword once was, twitching—a soldier, once destined to be a protector.

Sadira carefully watched Soren, searching for a tell she was not in the right mind. Only bright green eyes stared back at her, glistening with tears.

"Sadira, I-" Soren stopped as they met one another, with Sadira maintaining a distance between them. Sadira waited as Soren bowed her head, silent. Sadira said nothing. She refused to break the silence while uncertain of Soren's state of mind. "I'm sorry" was all Soren said, but when she raised her head, her features had changed. She clenched her jaw and blinked rapidly before beginning to pace, groaning and shaking her hands. She cracked her neck and kept walking, looking at the sky. "No, I don't," Soren said to no one. "I don't want to!"

While Soren's attention was elsewhere, Sadira stepped back to widen the distance. She wanted to reassure her it would be okay and keep her focused, but she was frightened of getting too close. She feared her own sister. *Perhaps I am a coward.*

Sadira frowned. She wanted to ask Soren if she was okay but did not dare risk being too close.

"Can I do anything?" Sadira finally asked, softening her tone. Soren spun and narrowed her eyes.

"You've done enough," she spat. Sadira clenched her jaw and squeezed her hands before her stomach, trying to summon her power. It ignored her. "If you had just let me do what was asked of me—if you had let me *kill* him—then I wouldn't be here! I would be far away with Caligh," Soren complained, pacing through the field. Sadira tried to control her anger, not responding to her sister's betrayal. Soren scoffed.

"I need to walk to the Neutral City; it is the most likely place the others will think to find one another," Sadira said, though she did not turn to walk towards the city. She realised then—everything here was reversed.

"Others," sneered Soren. "What others could you possibly need?"

"I need to find Caellum. I need to speak with Elisara, Larelle, and Nyzaia." At that, Soren paused and tilted her head, focusing on something unknown to Sadira. She slumped and unclenched her hands, which hung loosely at her sides. When she turned to face Sadira again, she appeared exhausted, her eyes drooping and lips down-turned. A pang of sympathy struck Sadira then, although Soren's hateful words overshadowed any feelings of forgiveness. She did not want to be alone with her.

"I will escort you," Soren whispered.

"In silence," Sadira said. "I have nothing to say to you."

Chapter Thirty-Eight

Larelle

Before Larelle opened her eyes, she heard the rush of water brushing pebbles before soaking her bare feet. At least she was near water. Her stomach had flipped when they passed through the mirror, but nothing else felt unusual about their journey; it was simply like walking through a door. Larelle's pulse spiked as she squeezed her hand yet found Zarya's absent. She breathed a sigh of relief at the sound of laughter and splashing nearby. Turning her head, she found Alvan holding Zarya's hands while she splashed in the water lapping at the stoney shore and giggled as the droplets scattered on Alvan's trousers. While the lord was doing an admirable job of occupying the princess, Larelle noted his tight jaw and roaming eyes. She rose from where she sat to take in the faded surroundings. The water, usually a vibrant blue, was dark, and the pebbles were a faded shade of brown. Even the trees on the island in the centre had lost their vibrant greenery. Larelle blinked, registering the layout of the icy water and yellow-tinted snow in the distance. They were at the Vellius Sea.

"This must be why there were two maps," said Zarya. Alvan dropped her hands as she crouched to gather pebbles and toss them across the lake. The Vellius Sea. Larelle frowned. Perhaps she was right. One map for the waking Novisia, and one for whatever this sleepy, silent land was. On the other map, there were no monuments or place names—just a plain, simple Novisia. Larelle rose, mourning the loss of water as she took uneven steps over the pebbles towards her daughter.

"Is this what it was like in your dream, Zarya?" Larelle asked, recalling how Zarya had described The Bay as colourless. The princess nodded and picked up another handful of pebbles, the water lapping at her feet. She stood ankle deep in the lake. Was Osiris here somewhere? Had he somehow pulled them all through?

"She saw this place," Alvan murmured beside Larelle. "Like a vision?"

"Or maybe a hint that we needed to be here," Larelle whispered.

"A hint from who?" Alvan asked. "Who actually gifts her with this 'intuition'?"

"It was Osiris she met in the dream. Perhaps he ensured she saw this place," Larelle murmured. Alvan was tense and cautious of the man supposedly trying to help them.

"Do you remember what Vivian said when we first visited the church? She told Zarya that dreams were a gift from the Goddess Nerida. Perhaps this is *her* way of helping us." Larelle's gaze shifted from her daughter to a figure slumped on the rocks in the distance.

"Olden," Larelle breathed. "Olden!" she shouted, pushing past Alvan to where the old man sat atop a rock, his eyes closed. How did he get here? He was on the boat with Lillian. Larelle knelt before him, wincing at the pebbles digging into her shins. "Olden," she repeated, gripping his wrinkled hands. He opened his eyes and blinked, awaking from sleep. He looked around him with eyes that mirrored Riyas's, except for the colour. Olden frowned at the tainted appearance of the realm.

"Am I dead?" he croaked.

"No, no. Of course not! Otherwise, we would be too," Larelle reassured him. "What happened before you opened your eyes?"

"Grandpa!" Zarya called. Larelle shot out her hand, signalling for Alvan to occupy the princess. Olden's eyes lit up at his grand-daughter.

"My legs were feeling wobbly on the boat, so I told Lillian I was going to wait on the sands." He stifled a yawn. "She was happy to stay on the boat and watch over me. I remember sitting down against a fallen tree, happily listening to the ocean." Olden smiled at Larelle. "You know what I'm like. The sound is just so soothing I must have fallen asleep, and when I opened my eyes, here I was." Larelle scanned his body, searching for any signs of injury, but he appeared normal—frail and tired, but normal. Larelle gave a sigh of relief.

"And Lillian was still on the boat?" she clarified. Olden nodded.

"And Jabir, he'd come to check on us while Vlad escorted Helena and Vigor to their ship." Larelle turned over the options in her mind. As Olden was on land when they walked through the mirror, it must have brought him too. When she reunited with the others, she would check if the same had happened to the likes of Soren or Vlad, Helena, and Vigor. Were the guards that had accompanied them to the Unsanctioned Isle here too?

"Do you feel okay?" Larelle asked. Olden coughed into his hand.

"Same as I have been." Olden's words did not reassure Larelle, who knew he had been tired as of late, with his age catching up to him.

"Please, stay here while we figure out what's going on. I don't want you exerting more energy than required," Larelle said, though she knew what they would need to do. Given none of the other rulers were present, Larelle assumed they had arrived in their own realms, which meant the Neutral City was the only logical meeting place. Yet now, with Olden here, she was unsure how feasible it would be for them to journey to the city, even though they were near to Nerida's gate.

"Larelle," Olden whispered; his voice trembled as he pointed behind her. It dawned on Larelle then that the giggling had stopped, and no pebbles skimmed the lake. Only Alvan's hurried half whispers reached her ears. Larelle whirled. Zarya was still knee-deep in the lake, yet a short wall of water had formed behind, blocking Alvan's attempts to pull her back to shore. Larelle waved her hand, but nothing happened. No water fell. Someone or *something* was maintaining the barrier. Larelle moved, numb to the sharp stones digging at her feet as she focused on the scales rippling through the water. Nausea rose in Larelle's stomach as she sprinted across the pebbles.

"Zarya!" Larelle screamed, hoping to alert and scare the creature swimming intently towards the princess beneath the surface. Zarya did not turn but simply tilted her head, watching the iridescent blue scales drift through the lake, its colour as vibrant as Larelle's attire. *Is it not from here?* Larelle recalled the creature Elisara had described in the Vellius Sea, the colour matching this one. Somehow, it could drift between Novisia and wherever they were now, this alternate existence. Larelle tried to climb the wall of water, but it grew to block her attempts. It fell to waist height when she took a step back. As the beast neared the shallows, Zarya took two steps towards the scales that were becoming clearer as the beast reached the shallows.

"Zarya, step out of the water," Larelle said, feigning calm, though the tremor in her voice betrayed her fear. Larelle held her breath as the beast approached, its long neck gliding through the water while its ridged back breached the surface.

"It's okay, mumma," said Zarya. "I'm meant to be here." It took everything in Larelle not to scream as the water rose again when she tried to climb it. *Trust her. Trust that her gift is from Nerida. This is meant to be; she is safe.* Larelle held her breath as the beast finally emerged from the water. As it lifted its head, water trickled down its scaled, scarred face—larger than Zarya's entire body. Most of the creature's body was hidden beneath the water, meaning a few more steps would send Zarya falling into the lake's depths. Alvan shifted closer to his queen. A glimpse of the creature's back and tail was visible beneath the water. Larelle could see the tops of its shoulders as well as its neck and head, suggesting its feet met the ground. The rest of the lake was far deeper, burying the rest of its body.

Alvan's nails dug into Larelle's hand as they helplessly watched Zarya. Though terrifying, Larelle could not deny the beauty of the creature as it blinked with purple irises surrounded by glowing silver rings. Endless shades of blue mosaic glistened on its scales. Larelle frowned at the large chains binding its middle and cutting into the skin on its back. If this creature was held captive, it was likely dangerous. Larelle tried to reach for her powers again, but still, it ignored her.

"He's sad, mumma." Zarya's voice wobbled as she extended her tiny hand and placed it on the creature's nose. When it huffed through its nostrils, Larelle was inclined to agree. The beast sounded miserable. Zarya turned to face her mother, her hand still on the creature. Larelle swallowed at the glow in Zarya's midnight blue eyes. Whatever power lived within her was awake. "I'm supposed to help him," she said. Larelle opened her mouth, unsure of what to say. There was nothing they could do; the chains were far too thick for them to break without tools. Zarya appeared to know this as a tear slid down her cheek. She sniffed. With a warbled cry, the creature rolled over in the water, highlighting its magnificent turquoise wings, bound in chains. The creature revealed its belly, showing Zarya the scars and darkened blood there, inflicted by the cutting metal. Larelle found herself wishing to cry for the creature, too. Elisara's relaying of events had made the beast sound terrifying, but as Larelle watched it with Zarya, she wondered if it was simply looking for attention—a desperate plea for help.

"I don't know how to help you," Zarya sobbed, and the creature rolled back over, facing her again. Placing both palms on its face, she leant her forehead on its scaly head and rested between its eyes. Larelle could have sworn the creature cried as its purple irises glistened. "But I know I will help you one day," Zarya murmured. Slowly, the creature gave a warbled cry and sunk into the water before the barrier between Larelle and her daughter fell.

Chapter Thirty-Nine
Caellum

Only the sound of Caellum's footfall broke the silence in Antor Castle while he roamed the halls. He was hit with confusion the moment he stepped through the glass and into the castle, appearing at the end of a corridor without Sadira's hand in his. He tried calling for her and the others, but no one answered; he heard only his voice echoing back. At the end of the hallway was a statue of a horse, watching him. Caellum sighed, recalling far happier memories of running down this hallway after Edlen and Eve, the horse being one of their most common hiding spots. Twisting the gold wedding band on his finger, Caellum gazed out of the glass, overlooking the walled garden where he watched Sadira on her first day here. This castle held so many memories, and finally, happier ones were beginning to fill it. The gardens were still beautiful, even with the colour missing. He could still make out the varying tones of brown flowers. He smiled. Sadira would be missing their colour wherever she was in Garridon. With a final sigh, he glanced past the entrance to the garden where the path led out of the castle estate towards the Neutral City. He would hopefully find Sadira on his journey.

Caellum stilled, pressing against the glass overlooking the gardens. For a moment, he could have sworn he saw someone—or something—walk through the archway, but he blinked and saw nothing. With a shake of his head, he turned to continue down the hallway and right to the staircase, but a sound stopped him. A shiver ran up his spine and he straightened. He could have sworn he heard–

A giggled sounded from behind the statue, and the surrounding temperature dropped. Caellum's breathing halted, and his muscles stiffened as he forced himself to walk ahead. Every step felt like lead as he moved, brushing his sweating palms against his jacket and swallowing the disappointment he would probably feel when he stepped around the statues. Another giggle sounded, further down the hallway. Distracted from the statue, Caellum looked away, his breath stolen from him.

"Eve," he breathed. His sister's head whipped around the corner, watching him. Caellum blinked, but he barely had time to register anything when another giggle drifted from the statue, only a few steps away. A cry fell from his lips as Edlen ran down the hallway, chasing after her sister. "Edlen!" Caellum called, choking as emotions pummelled his insides. He took off running after the girls, with delicate white roses pinned in their dusty blonde waves. Caellum followed the giggles down the hallway, taking a right and then left until he stood at the top of the staircase, watching his sisters run hand in hand out of the towering arched doors towards the walled garden. "Wait!" Caellum cried, hurrying down the stone steps towards the door. He ran without a single thought, his mind empty. Was this real or a hallucination? As he rounded the wall through the wisteria-coated archway, he expected to be hit by disappointment. Instead, he leant his hands on his thighs, bowed his head, and allowed the tears to fall.

His brothers, Dalton, Kieren, and Halston, stood below the willow tree in the distance, swords in hand, practising their techniques as Sir Cain had shown them once. Knees bent, they raised their arms and circled one another with wide-set grins. Edlen and Eve whispered in their mother's ear, who sat on a blanket by the fountain. For the first time since he could recall, his mother grinned, threading a needle through cloth. Then, there was his father, perched on the side of a walled flower bed, with Aurelia cross-legged on the grass below while he braided her hair, smiling and listening to her ramble. His fingers gently moved down her hair, and his eyes were soft as he listened.

Caellum lifted his head and steadied a hand against the archway. When Edlen and Eve stopped whispering, his mother's cry filled the air. She rushed to her feet, covering her mouth with her hand.

"You're too young! You can't be dead!" she cried, weaving amongst the flower beds to reach him.

"I—" Caellum choked, trying to reassure her he wasn't. He was fine, but she cut off his words as she reached him.

"Cal," murmured a deep voice. His father's hands stopped, sending Aurelia's hair tumbling down her back. She raised her hand to her mouth and shifted to rise. His brothers dropped their swords in the distance and began running. "Cal," his father said again, his voice cracking. He rose, and in only a few long, quick strides, Wren pulled Caellum into him, holding the back of his head and repeating his name. He had never called him Cal before.

"Father…" Caellum tried to speak, his eyes watering as he watched Edlen and Eve's matching grins while they held onto Aurelia's skirts. When his father finally pulled away, tears streamed down his face, glistening in a way Caellum had never seen. One hand still grasped the back of his neck, while the other squeezed his arm. Wren cleared his throat and stepped back, allowing Caellum's mother to embrace her son. He smiled at the comfort of her hug yet continued watching his father, who twisted his wedding band around his finger.

"Are you any better at sword fighting these days?" Dalton asked, clapping his brother on the back. Kieran and Halston beamed.

"I'd say so," Caellum sniffed.

"Hello you," Aurelia said, kissing his cheek while their parents embraced. Caellum threaded his fingers in hers and squeezed her hand. He looked down at their intertwined fingers, feeling the warmth of her skin despite her paled appearance. Aurelia followed his eyeline but was fixated on his left hand. "The wedding was beautiful," Aurelia said, releasing one hand to wipe her tears.

"You were there?" Caellum asked, allowing Aurelia to pull him towards the wall where his mother and father were, his mother's eyes glistening. Kieren and Halston encouraged Edlen and Eve to sit with them on the grass.

"Eight hawks," Dalton said with pride. Caellum recalled the birds swooping overhead moments before the wedding began.

"She's far too beautiful for you." Halston grinned.

"Please, tell her she can have any of my dresses," Aurelia said, still holding one of his hands as they perched on the wall opposite their parents. His entire family was squeezed into a gap between the flower beds.

"And my jewels," said his mother. "Though she shines without them."

"Your babies can have our toys," Edlen said.

"I don't think we're quite there yet." Caellum laughed, and Aurelia and his mother shared a look, as if eager to see him find happiness with a family of his own.

"You'll be a magnificent father, just as you are a wonderful king," his father said. Caellum sensed the silent *'unlike me,'* the regret lingering in his words. Yet when Caellum looked at his father, he did not see the years of abuse or torment, not after reading his journals and understanding his mind. Wren had tried to fight it. When Caellum looked at his father, he saw the man he would have been: the loving father, devoting husband, and respectful king. The only hatred he felt while looking at his father was towards Caligh, for taking his family from him. Caellum would devote his life to ensure Caligh never took another family as he had his.

"What's it like being here?" Caellum asked.

"It was... difficult, at first," said Hestia, squeezing Wren's hand. "But when your father looked at me the way he had on our wedding day... I knew it was him."

"You knew that Caligh—the Historian—had taken over his mind?" Caellum asked, remembering how absent his mother had been, rarely stepping in to protect them.

"He is the love of my life; I knew it was not him," said Hestia.

Wren cleared his throat and raised his head, peering up at the sky. "I knew the first time he hit me, and when he locked me away, preventing me from attending to you all. I knew if I tried to intervene, it would only worsen."

"Please," Wren whispered; his knuckles whitened where he clutched the wall with one hand. Dalton reached up to squeeze his father's knee.

"All that matters is we are here now. We have had time together to properly get to know one another," said Dalton, the brother who should have one day been the King of Garridon. For a moment, Caellum was envious; in death, they had the chance to be together. He had missed out on knowing his mother and father, and watching his siblings grow up with happy childhoods. But he had Sadira, and that thought eased his envy.

"Will you play hide and seek with us?" Edlen asked, rising from the grass and tucking a fallen white flower back into her curls.

"Please, Cal! One last time!" Eve chimed in. Caellum tried to hide his tears as he coughed into his arm and wiped his eyes.

"I'm not sure I have time. I must find my wife."

"You have time," said Hestia, picking up his hand and cupping it in her smaller palms. She smiled gently at her son. "She has her own journey here. As long as you reach the Garridon gate at nightfall, you have time."

"It will take me a while to walk that distance."

"Time is different here. Take a moment, act like you have all the time in the world, and I will tell you when you need to go." Hestia smiled when Edlen and Eve took off running.

"Very well," Caellum stood and covered his eyes before counting. "One... two... three..."

Despite the lack of colour as Caellum ran after his sisters in the walled garden of their home, he did not think there was a day, other than his wedding, as vibrant as this one. Edlen and Eve no longer tired so easily, and only when Aurelia tempted them away with daisy chains did Caellum have time to duel his brothers. They cursed and laughed every time Caellum bested them, as he always had. The willow tree swayed, hiding them beneath its strands: just four brothers, marvelling at Caellum's tales of the battle in the Ashun Desert and suggesting different techniques to relay to Sir Cain should they face another fight. When Caellum insisted on spending time with Aurelia, they begged him to stay and insisted she would only ask about his wife. Caellum laughed. He could talk about his wife all day. They were right, of course. Aurelia wanted to know everything about Sadira, the sister she would have loved as her own. So, Caellum spoke of her kindness and strength, how mesmerising it was to watch her work with plants and healing. The birds chirped around them as they spoke, as if happy to hear about their true queen, the Queen of Garridon.

When it was time to leave, his mother looked at him with a small smile and nodded.

"What will happen to you all?" he asked.

"One day, we will still be here for you. We deserve longer together as a family, and we would not fail you a second time as parents and allow you to pass alone," Hestia said, embracing her son one more time. So, Caellum did not say farewell to his siblings, for he knew he would see them again. Instead, he smiled at them in turn before walking through the archway of the walled garden with his father.

"I want you to know I'm sorry—"

"You don't need to apologise," Caellum interjected. They both twisted their wedding bands in silence while heading down the path from the castle to the city, enjoying simply *being*—no arguments, no insults, no fear. Just a father and his son, as it always should have been. The sun was setting when they reached the end of the estate. Wren turned to face Caellum.

"I have thought about this moment for a long time, wondering what I might say to you. But I don't think there are words to express how proud I am," Wren said, pulling Caellum in close and holding him tightly. Caellum closed his eyes and inhaled, committing this moment to memory: the comfort of his father's arms wrapped around his heart, welcoming him home.

"Thank you, father," Caellum said. For the only time in his life, that word—father—felt sincere and loving from his lips rather than laced with fear.

"You will be a great King, Cal," Wren said, pulling back to rest a hand on his son's shoulder. "Our family has always been protectors, and I see that in your relationships." Wren cleared his throat. "Would you do me a favour?"

"Anything."

"Would you tell Sir Cain I said thank you for raising you when I could not?" Wren's smile wobbled, and Caellum nodded. "Go. Find your wife. Go and be happy."

Caellum walked into the trees leading to Stedon's open fields, the path to the Neutral City. He turned for one final glance of his family, and a choke escaped him, part sob, part laughter. His family, all eight of them, stood with their arms around one another, watching him go.

***

The concept of time was indeed far different as he continued walking. It was almost like no time had passed at all as the moon rose in the sky. Upon reaching the Garridon gate to the Neutral City, he found Sadira pacing before it. She ran when she saw him. Caellum grinned as her hair flew behind her, golden even under the moonlight. He caught Sadira and was enveloped by her scent.

"I was getting worried," she sighed, holding him tight. "Soren has gone into the city; I did not wish to stay alone with her."

"Are you okay? Did she do anything?" Caellum asked, frowning and pulling back. Sadira shook her head and stayed close beside him, interlocking her hands behind his neck.

"I saw my grandmother." Sadira smiled.

"I saw my family," Caellum whispered, and tears glistened in Sadira's eyes as she clutched his hands tighter. "There was no darkness in my father's mind; my parents were happy, my siblings were..." He trailed off, thrown by his emotions.

"I'm so happy for you." Sadira smiled, a tear rolling down her cheek. "I wish I could have met them."

"They love you," Caellum whispered, resting his forehead against hers. "They have been watching over us and will continue to do so." Sadira sighed at his words and pressed her lips to his. Caellum made sure to savour every moment from now on, only recognising now what it was like to have missed time with those he loved.

"Ready?" Sadira asked, clasping his hand. Together, the King and Queen of Garridon walked through the gate to the city, ready to face their fate and that of the kingdom.

Chapter Forty

Larelle

To be so young and bear the weight of such strong emotions and intellect was hard, Larelle could see that as Zarya's small shoulders rose and fell where she knelt in the water. The urge to run and check she was okay, while scolding her for straying into unknown places, dampened when observing her daughter's tears. She sensed her daughter's emotions in the droop of her shoulders; she needed comforting, not reprimanding. Larelle was quiet as she pushed through the water, kneeling beside Zarya and wrapping an arm around her. The frigid water lapped at her knees, rising to Zarya's waist. Zarya tried to shrug her off.

"We didn't save him," she mumbled.

"I know," Larelle whispered into her hair before kissing the top of her head. No ripples of movement disturbed the Vellius Sea or flashes of iridescent blue. Elisara had said it was like the creature had simply disappeared in a whirl of light. A heavy sense of certainty weighed on Larelle's mind. The creature had vanished. Larelle was still as Zarya cried into her shoulder, dampening the silk with tears, like the water at her knees. Larelle would have brushed away the responsibility of finding the other rulers if it meant staying with Zarya, but then the water rippled, and bubbles approached again. Larelle braced herself for the creature to breach the surface, though it was not blue scales greeting the Queen and Princess of Nerida, but the blue eyes of their goddess. Larelle bowed her head while Zarya's mouth fell open in awe.

Treading water, Nerida watched her descendants. The water only reached her shoulders, but the Larelle saw thin braided straps holding up her gown, despite being submerged. Her dark skin glistened with water droplets, and her hair appeared longer while wet. Seeing Nerida in the flesh, rather than an apparition, meant Larelle could truly look at her. A spatter of freckles dotted her nose and cheeks, just like Zarya's. Her lashes were so long they curled when she blinked, tickling under her brow bone.

"You are sad, princess," Nerida said in the same silky voice as their last encounter.

"He wanted me to save him," Zarya mumbled, her eyes no longer glowing.

"The river drake?" The goddess tilted her head, and Zarya nodded. "Interesting." A twinkle glinted in her eye, and the corner of her mouth twitched. She knew something. Larelle opened her mouth to ask for clarity.

"Why is he called a river drake if he is not in a river?" asked Zarya.

"He was in a river once." Nerida averted her eyes, her expression forlorn. "He has travelled through many waters and endured much pain." Zarya tilted her head, and the two were silent, as though having a conversation in their minds. Nerida swam forward until the ground met her knees and she rose, standing above them. The cerulean blue gown clung to her body, accentuating her curves and muscles. Larelle was about to rise when Nerida strode past them both in her water-soaked dress. She nodded at Alvan, whose head was bowed, before striding to Olden. His mouth hung open and his eyes glistened as he looked at the goddess. Water splashed as Zarya ran towards Alvan, who crouched to catch her in a hug when they collided.

A chuckle sounded from Olden, still on his rock. He smiled at the goddess. Larelle could not hear their discussion, although she strained to listen. Nerida's hands were slow as she reached out, gently placing them on either side of Olden's head. The man who Larelle knew as a father closed his eyes with a sigh as they stayed like that for a few moments, with Nerida's hands on his head, and Olden's eyes closed, his posture relaxed. A few more minutes passed when Olden opened his eyes again. Larelle could just about glimpse the sheen in his eyes when his trembling hand reached for Nerida's. They shared a familial smile before Nerida stepped back. Larelle looked at Alvan, neither of them understanding what had transpired.

Nerida's hips swayed when she approached Larelle.

"I wish to speak with you alone." Nerida beckoned Larelle with her finger and entered the water again, making smooth forward strokes towards the island in the middle of the Vellius Sea.

"Looks like you're going swimming," Alvan murmured, holding Zarya. Larelle frowned while her daughter watched Olden with a furrowed brow. "She'll be okay with me. Go." Alvan lifted his chin in Nerida's direction, and Larelle hesitated for a second longer before following Nerida into the lake. It was much colder the higher it reached her body, perhaps from the ice on Vala's side of the invisible border. Larelle tried to ignore the thought of the creature swimming somewhere within as she caught up to Nerida.

"He's gone, do not worry," Nerida called, slowing her pace towards the edge of the island, still firmly on Nerida's border. When Larelle reached her, the goddess did not rise onto the land. Instead, she smiled and sunk below the surface. Larelle peered for her below but could no longer see the goddess. The water was too deep and dark to see clearly. *I guess I'm going down.* Larelle took a breath and exhaled, sinking into the lake's depths. Larelle had not been in the water since Alvan had found her after Caligh's visit when he was still the Historian to her. As her hands glided through it, she realised how much the water felt like a piece of her slotting into place. Her eyes took a moment to adjust before she found Nerida swimming below across the sandy bed. The Vellius Sea was far deeper than Larelle realised. Kicking her feet, Larelle swam down, and water rushed into her lungs when she took a breath.

She followed Nerida until her stomach was close to the lakebed and they swam through an opening carved into the bottom of the island. With no idea where it led, Larelle followed her goddess through what Larelle realised was a long tunnel. Further and further, the two swam. A swirl of invisible power circled Larelle, propelling the pair faster, much faster than if they had swum without it. The water lightened and its height lowered. Squinting, Larelle saw Nerida bathed in light, no longer swimming but walking along the sandy bottom at the tunnel's end. Mirroring Nerida, Larelle pushed her hair back, noting the ache in her arms, despite having had help to reach their location. Peering around her, Larelle stepped out of the tunnel onto the wet sand, the sea crashing against the rocks on her left. Larelle raised her hand to her brow to shield the sun as she looked up at the land behind. Even with the colour leeched from this plain of existence, Larelle saw where the realms merged above, where the snowy cliffs became sandy grass dunes. She had only seen the border appear between Nerida and Vala from inland, not the edge of the kingdom. There appeared to be no other way to reach the small, half-mooned beach—unless one was willing to scale the cliff edges or sail by boat. It created a serene and private cove, a space for silent reflection. Ignoring the peace and quiet, Larelle wasted no time in trying to gather information from Nerida.

"What can you tell me about Caligh?" Larelle asked, but Nerida simply looked at her. "Will he return? Is he the one who hid away memories on Novisia?" Nerida winced, but Larelle continued, rushing her words. "How do we break the curse on other lands? How do we find them?"

Nerida sighed and said firmly, "That's not why I'm here to talk with you."

The waves behind Larelle crashed, outraged.

"It is why *I* am here, though," Larelle insisted. "I care about ensuring no more harm comes to my people—to our people."

Nerida tilted her head. "Is that so you can avoid your own feelings, wants, and desires? Prioritising others instead?" Larelle pursed her lips, not appreciating the psychoanalysis. "Sit with me." Nerida leaned against the cliff-side and crossed her ankles, watching the rising and falling tide. Larelle clenched her fists but did as she asked, having always respected the goddess, despite doubting her motives now. Larelle breathed in the salty sea air and sat silently beside Nerida. Together, the two women could pass as mother and daughter; Larelle knew which mother she would have preferred. "There are many paths we can wander down in life, Larelle. And I fear you are perhaps at a crossroads," Nerida said. Larelle frowned, uncertain what the goddess referenced. "You have been holding back from the lord," she said plainly but politely. Larelle pulled back, confused by the goddess's assumptions. Larelle did not believe she was acting distant. "You may wonder why I care about such matters, but as one of my descendants, I can sense your needs and offer guidance. It is why I felt drawn to find you before you reached the Neutral City. It is likely why all of you will have encountered your gods before you reunite."

"I am happy with Alvan," Larelle said. "He makes me feel safe and desired. He is a wonderful father figure to Zarya, but—"

"He is not her father," Nerida concluded. Larelle avoided Nerida's stare, refusing to confront the truth. The guilt of not acknowledging the truth while also thinking of Riyas was overwhelming. "Do you love him?" Nerida asked, and Larelle's smile answered the question. "Then what is wrong?"

"I am happy with Alvan, but in the rare moments we're not together, I find myself thinking of all the different ways my life might have turned out had Riyas not died, if I had never become close with Alvan because Riyas was there to help me navigate becoming queen." Larelle took a breath, trying not to cry. Gently, Nerida held Larelle's chin, turning her head to face her.

"May I show you something?" she asked. When Larelle nodded, Nerida moved her palms to the side of Larelle's head. She sobbed.

Riyas roared with laughter and slammed his drink on the table, the ale spilling over the edge and coating the cards on the table. Even though the man beside him scolded his raucousness, the others continued laughing with Riyas as he scraped a pile of coins towards his growing collection. His muscles were more defined, and his hair was longer; he moved with the assurance of a man who was respected, far different from the sailor working his way up the ranks.

"I told you I'd beat you with ease," he chuckled, his midnight blue eyes twinkling under the dim light of the tavern. The man who scolded him scowled, focusing on the pile of gold coins being scraped into a sack. "Right, boys, I'll see you by the docks at sunrise." Riyas grinned, clapping the men on the shoulders as they all complained and yelled for him to stay. The white stone streets were painted in the glow of sunset as he left the establishment and took a right towards the alleyway. Stumbling, he dropped his bag of coins and swore, bending to scoop them up. A swift kick met his stomach, knocking his dark hair loose from its band as he toppled over, smacking his head against the smooth white streets. He looked up at the disgruntled man from the card table, his eyes glazed. Riyas waved a hand, as if to summon some power, but the man stamped hard onto his fingers with a resounding crunch before plunging a knife into his stomach. He did not get up but lay in the white alleyway, his eyes drifting open and shut in a pool of his own blood while the man scooped up the coins and left him for dead.

"What are you doing?" Larelle cried, trying to snatch Nerida's hand from her head, but the goddess lifted the other and held her temple tight.

Riyas winked at the brunette, handing him a glass of amber liquid. Her lavender gown was far more modest than the other women in the establishment, which only had the other men fantasising about her more.

"Can't sleep?" she asked. Riyas's eyes darkened. "Alright, alright, I won't ask." She curled a finger in the direction of the two women, beckoning them over.

"You promised you'd stop asking," Riyas said, barely glancing at the ladies as the redhead took his hand while the blonde led him towards the curtained wall.

"And you promised you'd help me get answers, but here we are."

The brunette offered a sarcastic smile as she waved him away. Riyas ducked into one of many carved away alcoves, where the flaming sconces dimmed, casting a tantalising glow over the two women undressing before him.

"Stop!" Larelle screamed, shoving Nerida away as tears spilled down her cheeks. She regretted it immediately, having laid her hands on a goddess, but only pity resided in Nerida's eyes. "What was that?" Larelle pulled her legs up under her chin.

"Other paths and possibilities that could have been," Nerida sighed. "There are plenty of what ifs in this world, Larelle. Those were two what ifs. Even if he was here, it does not mean he would be with you. Perhaps Alvan was always your destiny."

***

Larelle was silent, allowing Nerida's power to push them through the waters and return them to the Vellius Sea. A numbness settled in Larelle's bones after what she had been forced to witness. Nerida silently followed her to shore and waited at the water's edge. With a wave of her hand, she pulled the water from Larelle's hair and clothing as she looked for Alvan and Zarya, expecting to find them at the water's edge, playing. But Alvan sat on the floor beneath Olden, holding Zarya in his arms. Her body trembled as she cried.

"What's wrong?" Larelle asked, approaching. Alvan shook his head as Zarya remained buried in his arms, crying.

"I'm sorry," Alvan said. Larelle looked up at the rock Olden slept on upright. His chest did not rise and fall. His mouth hung slightly open, and his shoulders were slumped.

"No," Larelle sobbed, rushing forward and reaching for his hand. He had been fine, smiling and speaking with Nerida only recently. But as Larelle held his hand, it felt cold. Her fingers trembled as she shifted them to his wrist, searching for a pulse. The man who had been her father for the last five years was gone. "What did you do?" She whirled towards Nerida. "He was fine, but then you touched him and now he's dead!" Larelle yelled. Power rumbled in her core, aching to break free at the goddess, but she could not pull it forward. Something was holding her power down.

"He was not fine," Nerida said, her tone firm. "He has wanted to go for some time but was holding on for you and Zarya."

"What did you show him?" Larelle snapped, recalling how she held Olden's temple like she had held hers. Her goddess must have realised the pain she had caused as it manifested in the tears streaming down Larelle's cheeks.

"I showed him something he needed to know to be at peace." Those were Nerida's final words as she dived back into the water. Larelle spun back to Olden, reaching for his hand again. She would not be able to take him with her or cast him into the ocean as he deserved. But above all, what pained Larelle the most was not being able to say goodbye for the second time in her life.

Chapter Forty-One
Elisara

Elisara had stared up at the colourless sky for hours, relishing the peace and quiet. She was in a variation of Vala, it seemed. After entering the mirror, she had opened her eyes to gaze across the mountains, where one of the few rivers in Vala flowed below. At her right was Tisova in the distance. If she turned and trekked through the snowy mountains, she would eventually reach the Neutral City. That was likely where the other rulers would head, yet as Elisara was not far, she chose to relish the time alone, surrounded by nothing but silence. She lay in the snow and stared at the sky. The biting cold snow soothed her aching back, relieving the pain that was resurfacing as the effects of Vigor's stalactite water faded.

Hours had passed while lying there. Even though the colour was drained from this world, she could still differentiate when the sun became the moon and the stars began to appear. She supposed this was her natural habitat now as Sitara's essence, staring at the darkness of the sky, surrounded by night. While Sitara had not formed Elisara from her essence, she planted some of the goddess inside her. Did that mean Elisara was a goddess of dusk too? Or goddess of darkness? Elisara scoffed. She did not feel like a goddess, even if a piece of one lay inside her arm. With a sigh, she contemplated finally standing and walking to the city, but there was something so peaceful about the moon. While she owed her life to the rulers, her friends, and was grateful for their company, she preferred the peace and quiet of being alone. It was the only time she could think about Kazaar; even dreaming did not summon him when her mind was preoccupied with people she did not know and conversations with Sallos.

Was Sallos here somewhere? Or had his shadowed form prevented him from crossing through? She could not feel her shadows, darkness, or the elements. She knew they were there but could not draw on them. For a minute, she felt relieved in its absence. After all, it had summoned Caligh and started a war.

"I didn't know," a clipped voice said from Elisara's right. Elisara turned her head, unsure of whom to expect, though Vala was the last person she expected to see—the goddess of her realm. Peering down at Elisara, Vala's long white hair burned bright beneath the moonlight. Elisara did not know what she referenced, nor did she care what the goddess had to say after her treatment of Elisara and Kazaar in the temple. Lifting her head, Elisara watched the stars and hoped if she stared long enough, Vala would get the message and disappear. *You are his star.* Some of her mother's last words rang through her mind, words she now knew were first spoken by Sitara. Though Elisara was no star. How could she to be the light in someone's darkness when her own had been snuffed out?

The snow shifted beside her as Vala lay down and glanced briefly at her descendent. Her grey gown was far more ornate than their last encounter. A woven pattern of feathers and swirls in silver thread coated the skirts, and a white fur cloak hung over her shoulders. Had the snow not been tinged yellow, the two would have blended well. The goddess rested her hands on her stomach and looked up at the stars with Elisara.

"I used to love the night," Vala said. Elisara refrained from sighing at the interrupted peace and quiet. "I took after my mother in that way and many others—stubborn, strong, obsessive when I care, torn between being pragmatic and being free, as light as a feather. But from my father..." Vala's voice changed, the pride in her voice fading to sadness. Elisara realised it was not just Sitara who had lost her loved one; her children had lost their father. Elisara swallowed at the all-too-familiar loss. "From him, I get my humour." Elisara scoffed, sparing a glance at Vala, who smiled. "See, that was funny." Elisara pursed her lips and turned back to the stars. "Truthfully, I get my father's sense of protection, ensuring what is mine remains safe." Vala paused. "I have failed you there."

"I'm not really yours though, am I? So, it does not really matter," Elisara said, referencing the unspoken knowledge of Sitara's essence.

"You were my lineage before she put you on this path," Vala murmured. "I did not know." Elisara finally relented, turning her head to look at the goddess with a raised eyebrow, the only acknowledgement she was listening. "I did not know she put that *thing* inside you or her essence—that speck of dark stone encased in her power. I suspected Kazaar's potential heritage, though there are a few options. I also assumed the darkness I sensed around the pair of you came from that. I assumed he was related to Caligh and had tainted you after you merged your powers." Vala paused, allowing Elisara a moment to reflect. She wanted to ask about Kazaar's heritage—his parents, grandparents, if he had found peace with his passing, and if she would meet him again one day, somewhere else. "When I saw the mark of the celestial tie on your collarbone, I knew it was my mother's doing, though I had assumed wrong and knew far less than I thought."

"Can you not ask her?" Elisara finally asked. Vala shook her head in the snow.

"My mother has been wandering the skies for centuries, trying to right the wrongs of Caligh and the others. I have not seen her in some time."

"Others?" Elisara asked, and Vala gave a pitiful smile.

"There are many things you do not know, matters I cannot tell you, even here."

"You are under the same curse, preventing Sitara and Osiris from telling me everything?"

"No. I was locked away here before that curse was put in place. I simply know the paths you may take. Telling you too much would alter them. That and my *siblings* insist we decide on everything collectively." Vala rolled her eyes.

"You do not get along?"

"After spending an eternity with people, through war and peace, destruction and creation, chaos and order, you find that relationships become *strained*." Vala raised a hand, as if wishing to reach for Elisara before thinking better of it. "It is why I was so angry when I thought you were tainted by a dark power. It is not the first time someone has taken my descendants and moulded them into something new. The Queen of Keres's captain is a perfect example." Elisara raised her eyebrows.

"Farid was once your descendent?"

"No, but one of his many ancestors from centuries ago was. But Keres used Caligh's knowledge to twist them into something new." Elisara frowned. Wings of flaming feathers seemed a far reach from the descendent of someone who simply controlled air.

"Caligh is truly that old, then?" Elisara asked. Vala's eyes darkened.

"Older than you think," she murmured. The two women lay in silence, staring at the stars. Elisara thought of all the questions she could ask the goddess, like how could they defeat Caligh? What did he truly want from Elisara? What were the rulers' roles in saving other lands? She imagined Vala would respond with the same answer, which was no answer at all.

"How can you speak to me so freely here?"

With a look around them, Vala asked, "Do you know where we are?" Elisara shook her head. "We are on the Isle of Gods." Elisara had never heard the term before but could quickly deduce it belonged to Vala and her siblings.

"This is your home?"

"This is my prison," Vala said, her eyes glistening as she stood. The goddess reached for the queen, who hesitantly accepted her hand, the rough and worn texture etched with thousands of stories. Elisara straightened and winced at the pain in her back. Muttering sounded from behind, but before she could turn to see who it was, Vala placed a hand on her shoulder and brushed the moon scar with her thumb. "I let the loss of a love almost destroy me once," she said, the glistening more prominent in her eyes as they grew vacant, as though recalling a memory. "You are far more than your heartbreak, Elisara." Vala smiled and stepped back, dragging her cloak in the snow as she walked. "Oh," she said, glancing back again. "Sorry for calling you a whore." Elisara smiled and kicked the snow with her boot.

"I could be, for all you know," Elisara said, and the goddess laughed.

"See, you have my humour too."

"Eli!" Vlad called. Elisara whirled to find Vlad, Helena, and Vigor trekking the Zivoi mountain. Before answering, Elisara turned back to ask Vala how she survived it—the loss—but she was gone.

"What are you doing here?" Elisara asked, navigating the snow to reach them.

"Great question. We have no idea." Vigor wrapped an arm around Elisara's shoulder as she shivered in the night air. They still wore the same clothes as they did on the Unsanctioned Isle.

"We were about to board the ship, and then the next thing we know, the trees are no longer red but snow-capped," Vlad said, assessing his queen to ensure she was okay. Elisara nodded to reassure him.

"How did you find me?" she asked.

"We were trying to get as high as we could to see as far across the realm as possible, hoping to find you." Vlad put an arm around her shoulder, and Elisara tried not to flinch at the touch as he steered her towards Vigor and Helena. "Once we reached halfway, we saw Larelle in the distance. She's heading towards the Neutral City."

"I suppose that should be our next stop, then."

Chapty Forty-Two

Nyzaia

"Come. The others are already at the Neutral City," said Keres with a wave of his hand, padding along the sand barefoot. Nyzaia and Farid shared a look.

"How? We have not been here long," said Farid. Keres glanced over his shoulder to look Farid up and down. He straightened under the scrutiny.

"Time works differently on the Isle of Gods. You've been here much longer than you think." Keres picked up his sword from where he left it by the water of the oasis and propped it against his shoulder as he walked. Flames, expertly crafted of gold, blazed from the handle and climbed up the first quarter of the blade—a symbol of his power. "Now, tell me what you need from me." Nyzaia caught up to him and walked by his side, with Farid on her other.

"Why do you think we need something from you?" she asked.

"The mirror led you to me, so you must need something. The same way it sent the others to wherever their souls required answers to the thoughts in the back of their minds."

"You're rather straightforward compared to the bullshit-coded lines you gave us last time." Nyzaia crossed her arms.

"Nyzaia," Farid scolded. She should have known he would be traditional and respectful towards a god. Keres laughed.

"I suppose I passed on the same trait to you then." Keres did not look at either of them as they walked. "I couldn't speak freely on your lands because I am tied to this land—the true land. Pushing through to your existence takes a lot of effort, and we are not permitted to reveal anything that might alter fate. Broken speech seemed the most effective way to stay for as long as possible and give you as much as we could—Nerida's idea, obviously. She's always been the most intelligent, or so she thinks." Clearly, Keres seemed inclined to disagree. Nyzaia scoffed. Larelle seemed to inherit the same intelligence and natural leadership as her goddess. Nyzaia processed his admission; at least they weren't infuriating for the sake of it, some fun for eternal beings.

"So, you gave us this?" Nyzaia asked, raising her palm. He did not look.

"I already told you that. Ask what you really want to know," Keres sighed, clearly impatient.

"What is our shared destiny?" Farid asked.

"If I told you that, you could try to alter or change it."

"So, what was the point of asking?" Nyzaia exclaimed, and Keres shrugged.

"It is expected of me to ask, but maybe that's not why you were sent here," Keres said, angling his sword before him to inspect it beneath the sunlight.

"I can't say I have anything else to ask you," Nyzaia said, rolling her eyes. "Maybe there's another reason you're here." Keres finally looked at Farid, whose surprise was evident. His eyes widened as he looked at his queen. "Did you know Nefere Valley once had a river running through it?" Keres hummed. Nyzaia recalled overlooking the valley beside Exandria in her drug-induced dream; steam had risen from the valley, as if a great body of water had evaporated.

"What happened to it?" Nyzaia asked, her interest piqued.

"What is this, story time with my children?" Keres scoffed, and Nyzaia clenched her fists, wishing she could punch him. "What happened was the others tried to lock us away. They succeeded, the ungrateful bastards, though I'll never know if it was because of Caligh's input or their own greed."

"Others?" Nyzaia asked, earning a glare from Keres.

"Do you want your story or not?" Nyzaia pursed her lips but

allowed him to continue. "When they tried to lock us away here, a great battle began, drawing followers from all over. Imagine ignoring me to listen to those claiming to be better and more benevolent. Does that sound like a wise decision?" Nyzaia thought of Exandria and the peculiar way she controlled smoke and embers to shift her form. Could she have been one of those claiming to be better? A different god? One in league with Nefere?

"I don't know. You're the one apparently locked away here," Nyzaia mumbled, and Farid elbowed her side.

"Nerida used the water in the valley's river to drown Nefere's followers, twisting the water like ropes around them, suffocating and drowning them from within—she liked to alternate. Nefere thought himself more powerful and refused to watch anyone else die for his cause. He knelt, right there." Keres pointed his sword back toward the oasis. "With his burning wings out for all to see. He dug his hands into the earth and scorched the land with blue flames, allowing his power and wings to consume him, embedding his flame into the ground and burning all the water in the process. Exerting his power killed Nefere, leaving nothing but a scorched mark on the ground." Nyzaia's eyes widened. It made sense why the cult worshipped Nefere; perhaps they descended from the people Nefere had sacrificed himself for. Not to mention, his wings definitely made him appear god-like. Farid was quiet, with his hidden wings, blue eyes, and flames betraying him as one of Nefere's descendants.

"I somehow doubt the goddess of water could not pull water or create it from other things." Nyzaia scoffed.

"Exactly," Keres scoffed too. "Idiots. She admires sacrifice, though. She says it shows loyalty and dedication. Therefore, as a nod to Nefere's life, she planted the water for that oasis." Keres gestured over his shoulder at the oasis where they had met him. *There are two sides to every story*, Exandria had said.

"But something else happened. I assume the battle happened here before you were locked away."

"Observant one, aren't you?" Keres said. "Nefere was just a distraction that allowed the others to stab us in the back and finish the tasks that would bind us here. I suppose it is my punishment," Keres sighed, pausing as they reached the gate into the Neutral City. Nyzaia tucked away the information. He seemed unaware of her conversation with someone who was potentially one of the 'others' he referred to. She recalled the look of loss in Exandria's eyes. Nefere had meant something to her. There was far more to Keres's story—another side and reason they wanted to lock the gods away. Keres looked at Farid. "Your people are my greatest success and my biggest failure." Before Farid or Nyzaia could ask anymore, Keres turned and walked through the gate. "Hurry up, we're late," he said, and Nyzaia realised the sun was already beginning to set.

***

The temple was not as she remembered. Alongside her fellow rulers and their friends, Nyzaia stared up at the structure, which stood as it once had. It didn't even resemble the temple before it was blown into pieces. The spires appeared more intricate, and the windows more welcoming. Perhaps her view was tainted by the boredom she experienced as a child. Coloured glass shone in the setting sun, and she imagined the mosaic rainbow cast within. The chiselled stone wove around its frames, twisting higher in whirling directions until forming the spires and the crown atop the building. Nyzaia and Farid were the last to arrive. The others stood in a row, looking up at the temple. Keres did not acknowledge them as he strode inside.

"Has anyone figured out exactly what the Isle of Gods is?" Nyzaia asked. "How does it relate to the prophecy? Why did we need to be sent here?"

"It appears to be a reflection of Novisia, but which was here first?" asked Larelle.

"They were here first. Keres spoke of what it used to look like, though it's different from Novisia. He says it is a prison," Nyzaia said, and Elisara nodded, though the others had clearly not been told such words. The clink of chains sounded beside Nyzaia, who glanced at Soren, slowly shuffling over, away from Sadira and Caellum. Elisara and the others simply glared at the fallen queen. Nyzaia's stomach twisted. Still, she had not told Elisara about Soren's part in Kazaar's death. After witnessing Elisara's pain, harming herself with the darkness, Nyzaia could not bear to further burden her mind.

Soren's skin reddened around her wrists, and as Nyzaia no longer felt her power thrumming through her veins, she imagined Soren was the same. So, as the rulers continued speaking, Nyzaia used a dagger from her thigh to unpick the lock.

"Thank you," Soren murmured, her head twitching. Her eyes flicked back and forth between the rulers, and Nyzaia's hands stilled.

"Do I need to put them back on?" she asked. When Soren met her eye, Nyzaia relaxed at the bright green within them. "Farid will watch you." Nyzaia muttered before returning her attention to the others. Farid stepped closer to Soren.

"Are you coming in or not?" Keres bellowed from the doorway.

"Is anyone else's god an impatient ass?" Nyzaia mumbled, striding first into the temple. No one knew what awaited them within, or if they would ever be leaving.

The temple was far brighter than the decimated equivalent Nyzaia was last in. Looking up, she saw four panes of glass forming a point at the top and frowned. The sun suddenly rose above them, despite it nearly setting when they had stepped in. Nyzaia edged around the room, unsure whether to sit at the table or stand in front of the large coffins lining the room's perimeter.

"Please, sit," Nerida said, choosing to begin the discussion. Nyzaia pulled out one of the four chairs directly under the Keres banner, which boasted the sigil of three flames dancing across two swords. Soren and Farid stood behind. Elisara sat on Nyzaia's right, with Larelle opposite, and Sadira on her left. Caellum stood behind his wife and held her shoulders. Each stood in their rightful places beneath their banners, their eyes fixed on the six, pale, stone caskets wrapped in dark onyx chains. Each god perched upon one, with Vala and Nerida on one side, and Garridon and Keres on the other. Between the pairs, two more coffins lay. One was closed, but absent of a chain, while the other lay open and empty.

"Our bodies," Nerida said, gesturing to the coffin beneath her. She watched them with intense blue eyes, as though seeing into their souls. "And our mother," she concluded, placing her hand on the closed coffin beside her.

"So, it really is a prison?" Elisara asked, her eyes moving from the heavy chains to Vala, the white-haired goddess. She nodded. "And Sonos is truly missing—taken?"

Nyzaia looked at the empty coffin as Nerida lowered her eyes, her shoulders drooping momentarily.

"What of Sitara?" Larelle wrapped her arms around her body, her eyes red-rimmed as she glanced back at the temple entrance, where Zarya had been left with Alvan, Helena, and Vigor. Only Soren, Farid, and Vlad had come in with them—Farid for his power, Vlad for his status as commander, and Soren because, well, Nyzaia did not think Larelle would trust her outside with her child. Added guards would have helped, but it seemed whatever power had pulled the rulers and their confidants through had left the guards on the Unsanctioned Isle. Nyzaia wondered if that was intentional as she watched the gods.

"She is limited in her power and existence while she wanders the skies, but she is not bound to this land like we are." Nerida held the chain on her coffin to signify the difference in what had bound them.

"Who did this?" Larelle asked.

"Who do you think?" Keres scoffed, assessing his sword.

"Caligh," Nyzaia said, glaring at her god. "And some 'others' you don't want us to know about."

"What others?" Caellum asked, but the gods shared a look, unwilling to answer.

"But why?" Sadira asked beside him. Soren shifted behind Nyzaia, prompting her to look up. She watched Garridon.

"Caligh's history is a long and complicated one," said Garridon. "All you need to know is he bound us here to stop us intervening after he took our father which placed an imbalance on the world, cursing anyone from speaking of what could aid in retrieving the God of Dusk."

"*All* we need to know?" Nyzaia asked. "We need to know far more if you want our help. I assume that is why we are here—to find your father and free you so you can save the world?" Nyzaia's hate for these gods grew with every passing second. "But how?"

"That's partly what Sitara told me," Elisara whispered, the exhaustion evident in her eyes, despite the absence of her shadows.

"And Osiris is a person from one of the lands cursed not to speak of it," Larelle added. "Is this so Caligh can continue conquering more lands?"

"It is so he can have complete and utter control over everyone," Keres said, not meeting the eyes of those in the room. "And if he has you, he can create far worse creatures than those he has already; he can build even more of an army, ensuring everyone lives in fear and chaos." The other three gods exchanged a look, though what it was for, she did not know.

"Your land exists only because it is bound to ours. Destroy that link, and it will free all memories and offer complete clarity. It will crumble the sea border that hides you away, allowing for the next threads of fate to unravel," said Vala.

Finally, they had shared something concrete. Severing the link would resolve most of their issues and allow them to refocus on Caligh and Sonos, provided the rulers agreed to find him.

"Will it break the curse on other lands and allow them to speak freely?" asked Elisara.

"Yes, assuming the Prince of Xyliar follows his path correctly," said Keres.

"Xyliar?" Larelle asked. "I saw that name on one map hidden in the church. Who is the prince?"

Vala ignored the question. "This destiny was laid out for you all long ago. Do not question it, but trust you are all here for a reason. You must sever the link between the Isle of Gods and Novisia."

"What will happen when it is severed?" Nyzaia asked. Keres glanced behind her at Farid.

"You must leave immediately and return to Novisia," Keres said. Nyzaia opened her mouth to probe further, but Caellum cut her off.

"How?" he asked. Keres finally lifted his gaze from his sword to where the other three gods stared at Elisara.

"With you," Vala said, her eyes dull as she looked upon her descendant, whose own light had long since faded.

Chapter Forty-Three
Soren

Pain thundered through Soren's mind, battling between the flailing darkness in her skull and her soul's hands hammering against the metal bars, keeping her at bay. Screaming rang in her ears. Whenever Soren blinked, flashes of her younger self appeared, battling to push through the bars while darkness ate away at the vines twisting around the ruined castle in her head. Every time the darkness incinerated a vine, her head twitched; every time a flower grew in its place, her breathing calmed. Every time a young Soren screamed, her heart cracked.

It had taken Garridon only a moment. With his hands on either side of her head, he said a jumble of unrecognisable words and the darkness recoiled, as though it were ablaze. When she opened her eyes, he was gone, and she was left stumbling through the woods, trying to reach an open field to escape the suffocation she felt within the trees. Shadows from the treetops tricked her mind into thinking Garridon had failed. Branches scraping her arms felt like hands trying to claw her back. Things Caligh had said—memories of things he had Soren do—swam through her mind as she stumbled into the sun. It had all faded when she saw Sadira. *Don't take Sadira, take me.* Seeing her sister triggered the memory to the forefront of her mind and calmed Soren, though only for a moment.

Now, the shadows were back, and she hated Sadira—hated her sister for picking the man Soren must kill. Soren did not recall her words to Sadira, but then she heard a name from her lips. Nyzaia. *I see you.* Having tethered herself to that memory, she repeated those three words in her mind during the entire walk to the Neutral City to stay focused.

Soren stared at the back of Nyzaia's head now; still, her head twitched, and she clenched and unclenched her fists, listening to those around her. *I see you.*

"Why me?" asked Elisara.

"Your power, while different, stems from the same place as Caligh's, which—"

Nyzaia interrupted Vala's explanation. "Caligh's power stems from Sitara?" A chill ran through the room when Vala ignored her, and Soren flinched at the mention of his name.

"—*which* means you offer a balance to the curse. There must always be a balance, and thus a curse must always have a solution." Vala trained her eyes on her descendant. "What better solution than that which is the same but different, challenging even Caligh's power?"

"I don't..."

Weak, they're all weak. Soren twitched again yet bit her tongue, struggling to hold herself together. Farid sent her a warning look.

"All you need to do is channel your power into the ground; it should recognise your similarities," Vala said.

"You don't have to," Vlad murmured from behind his queen. "We can find another way."

"There is no other way," said Keres bluntly.

"I—" Elisara's hands trembled as she stood. *Separate Elisara and Kazaar.* Soren clenched her eyes shut but forced them open again, unable to face the image of herself screaming, wrapping vines around the iron bars, desperately trying to pull them free. Soren felt Farid's stare, but she looked only at Garridon. She could have sworn a smirk marked his lips.

"Before Elisara attempts this," Caellum began. Soren whipped her head in his direction and found him behind her sister. "We need to know more. How do we find Sonos, and if we reunite him with Sitara, can they end Caligh?"

"Finding Sonos will bring balance again, which will help you end Caligh," said Garridon, watching Caellum, the man who wore a crown he did not deserve. *My crown.*

"You keep speaking about balance, but other than lost memories and the silence of other lands, I see no imbalance," said Larelle.

"How can you know of other imbalances while trapped here?" Nerida asked, and Larelle narrowed her eyes.

"So, the imbalances are on the other lands then, like Thassena, Xyliar, Carvyre?"

Soren wanted to reach up and grasp her head at all this talking. "I assume Eresydon, Asynthos, and Q'Ohar are other kingdoms, too, all suffering from some imbalance?" Larelle continued, her words clipped. Nyzaia cocked her head, as though remembering something.

"If you leave this land, you will learn more and can search for Sonos," said Keres.

"This is getting really repetitive," said Nyzaia.

"Then shut up and do as you're asked!" Keres snapped. Farid's hands twitched near the pommel of his sword. "Do you think our lives have been easy? We have also been used and sacrificed for the greater good. I have lived for thousands of years. Yet one simple request to find one god is a '*repetitive*' ask? Perhaps we keep asking because it is the one thing that will save us, restore the balance, and allow us to finally rest. Then you're all welcome to live your insignificant lives." Keres stood, his eyes burning.

"Keres," Garridon murmured, placing a hand on his brother's shoulder. "They do not know the weight of it all."

"Don't patronise us," Nyzaia snapped. "We did not ask for this."

"No, you did not," Vala said, peering down at Elisara with saddened eyes as she wrapped both arms around herself and kept her eyes on the floor.

"I'll do it," Elisara whispered. No one dared object as the gods rose. Vala waved a hand to lift the stone table to the corner of the room, clearing the space. When she blinked, the rulers slid back in their chairs. Soren looked down at Nyzaia. She now sat directly beside her rather than in front.

"We would have just moved," Nyzaia mumbled. *I like Nyzaia,* sang the voice in her mind, a young, light, and playful voice—a happy voice before Caligh had entered her mind and tainted it.

"Just take it slow, Eli," said Caellum. Soren's focus slipped from Nyzaia to the King of Garridon. He stood next to her sister. *Kill the king. That is all I ask of you, Soren.* The light in the room darkened as Elisara crossed to the room's centre. Soren shook her head, hoping to rid the darkness. A knee nudged Soren's, and she looked down at Nyzaia, who met her eyes with a furrowed brow and inclined her head in question. The image of her burning eyes outside the tavern entered Soren's mind, allowing her to focus. *I see you.* Soren nodded.

Elisara trembled as she stood in the middle of the room and turned her palms outward.

"I haven't used it since I called it back in," she whispered. The gods shared a look before Vala reached her descendant and clasped her hands in hers. Elisara hesitated, meeting Vala's gaze.

"When you called it back in, what were you thinking of?" Vala asked. Elisara's eyes watered, and she blinked back tears.

"Kazaar," she breathed. Nyzaia shifted. Soren knew if she looked down, pain would mar Nyzaia's expression. *Separate Elisara and Kazaar.* Vala's hand moved to rest over the moon on Elisara's collarbone.

"It is because he is still a part of you. Kazaar may be gone, but you shared a tie. When he left, a piece of him remained here." Vala's hand lowered to Elisara's heart. "He is your tether. He helps you, even in death." Elisara sniffed and nodded before rolling back her shoulders. Vala bowed her head and returned to stand by her siblings, a note of pride in her eyes. As Nyzaia turned to look up at Farid, sudden envy surged within Soren at their tie. She clenched her jaw and looked ahead at Elisara.

Slowly, the Queen of Vala breathed in and out for several minutes, keeping her eyes closed as though searching for something within herself. Soren stopped fidgeting as wisps of shadows radiated from Elisara's body. Dark strands flowed from her and twisted, slow and steady, under their queen's command. Soren tilted her head. A silver string appeared to drift through them beneath the light, but when Soren blinked, she saw only darkness. In her mind, the shadows stirred, hissing at the recognition of those before them. Her eyes snapped shut. She was on the cell floor, reaching through the vine-coated bars, which had been spread wide enough for a thirteen-year-old girl to escape through, if not for the remaining darkness forming a wall to stop her. Soren tensed as she opened her eyes again. Darkness swelled around Elisara. She flourished her hands as strands of shadow spiralled around her, forming a rapidly spinning cocoon around her body as its pace quickened. The wall of darkness grew so thick Elisara was barely visible. The dark walls Caligh had conjured on the battlefield sprung to Soren's mind, matching the one keeping her sanity at bay. *Do not fail me, Soren,* he had warned on so many occasions. Soren frowned. What was his request? *Separate Elisara and Kazaar.* Kazaar was gone, but Vala said a piece of him remained in Elisara's heart. Should she kill the Queen of Vala? Soren reached for the sword at her side but grasped air. The shadows moved so fast a wind picked up in the room. Soren glanced at the dagger strapped to Nyzaia's thigh. *No,* whispered the delicate voice in her mind—cracked but present, pushing the darkness. Soren shook her head as the screaming started. Her soul tried to break free, rising onto her knees to grasp the bars.

"Now what?" Elisara shouted over the wind. Soren gripped her head as the wind whipped at her braids.

"Release it!" Garridon grinned, his eyes on Soren. Elisara's hands shot out, and the sphere of darkness shot up in a plume towards the temple's glass point. The darkness in Soren's mind watched, awe-struck, trying to reach Elisara's power while moving further away from the girl in the cell. The remnants of Caligh's power laughed with glee, ricocheting around Soren's head.

When Elisara yanked her hands down, the tower of dark magic crumbled—falling, falling, falling, until colliding with the stone ground. A crack resounded throughout the room, and the darkness in Soren's mind screamed as Elisara's power sunk deep into the Isle of Gods. *Kill the king,* said Caligh. With his original and most stern command echoing around Soren's mind, she swiped the dagger from Nyzaia's thigh and spun in one fluid motion. As Elisara's darkness sank deep into the Isle of Gods and the ground began to shake, Soren plunged a dagger into Caellum's chest. He stumbled, wide-eyed, reaching for Sadira. The wind seemed to slow as Sadira turned to look at her husband. No signs of worry, pain, or heartbreak marred her sister's eyes as she looked at Soren, and then Caellum, who held her shoulder. Her brow furrowed when she noticed his trembling hand before her eyes travelled to the handle in Soren's grip. And when the ground trembled, Soren's soul pushed through the shadows and tore apart the remaining shreds of darkness.

But it was too late.

As Sadira screamed, Soren let go of the dagger in the king's chest and stumbled back.

"I told you it would get worse before it got better," Garridon said from behind.

Chapter Forty-Four
Sadira

A part of Sadira was rotting away, dying. She felt it in her chest, the constricting of her heart as Caellum fell into her arms, knocking her from the chair. She froze the moment she fell onto her knees and watched the blood pool beneath Caellum as Nyzaia and Farid dragged Soren out of her sight. Caellum reached for the handle of the dagger protruding from his chest, and when his eyes finally met Sadira's, she screamed. She crawled through her husband's blood, as it soaked into the cracks of the floor, stretching from the hole Elisara's power had created in the table's centre. Her hand slipped when she reached for him. Sadira fell into his chest. She lay there for a moment, listening to the sound of his heartbeat as his hand rose to twist into her hair. She heard the faint thud, the deep beat of his heart belonging to her; she heard it every morning when she awoke in this exact position.

"Sadira," he mumbled, but she could not bring herself to rise or look at him, to see the agony twisting his features. "Take..." he tried to speak. "Take it out. Please." She shook her head and pounded her fist against his chest.

"No!" she screamed. Sadira had learned enough about healing and helping the injured at her engagement ball; she knew it would kill him the second she took it out. He would lose too much blood. Someone called for Vigor, as if Caellum could ever survive a stab to the heart. A hand gripped Sadira's shoulder.

"He needs to see you, Sadira," Elisara choked. "Don't let him go like this. Please." Sadira felt Caellum's chest slow. Slowly, she lifted her head, her tears streaming in rivulets through his blood on her face. Caellum lifted a hand to her cheek, and Sadira crumpled the moment his wedding ring caught the light.

"I can't do this without you," Sadira cried. "I won't do it without you. Please, someone find a way—someone help him!" Sadira looked up at Elisara standing behind, with Vigor beside her. He shook his head as Vlad wrapped an arm around Vala's queen. There was nothing he could do. Larelle bowed her head, as though already accepting the fate of Garridon's king. Nyzaia was nowhere to be seen, having dragged Caellum's murderer from the crime scene. The gods simply watched the death of yet another mortal. Garridon lacked the decency to even look saddened at the sight of his descendent sobbing over the body of her husband, her king, her love.

"It'll be okay," Caellum whispered, though his breathing was laboured. Sadira closed her eyes as more tears fell until she finally looked at her husband and brought her hand to his cheek. "It'll be okay." He started coughing.

"Please don't leave me," Sadira cried.

"I am grateful," Caellum choked. "For the fairytale you gave me." Sadira gripped the hand that bore the mark of their marriage. They deserved more time—*needed* more time.

"I will never forget you," Sadira cried. Her body shook as his blood bled into her skirts.

"I'll wait for you," Caellum wheezed. Coughs racked his body and blood filled his mouth. The damage was too much—his body was unable to cope. "I'll be okay. I'll be with my family," he said. "I need you to do something for me."

"Anything," Sadira replied.

"Can you tell Sir Cain my father said thank you for raising me when he could not." Sadira nodded but refused to believe he could not relay the message himself.

"Please don't leave me," she begged again, clinging to Caellum's body. The ground continued to shake, and rubble fell from the temple.

"Find another fairytale, Sadira." And those were his last words, spoken to the woman who had entered his life when he least expected and changed him for the better. Sadira threw her head back and screamed as the world collapsed around her. She sensed a body kneeling beside her as a shaky hand reached forward to close Caellum's eyes and wrap an arm around Sadira. In the Vala's queen embrace, the Queen of Garridon sobbed, her heart split in two.

Chapter Forty-Five
Elisara

Elisara's oldest friend, her first love, and the King of Garridon was dead. Caellum was dead. Tears filled her eyes as she held Sadira. She could have sworn she saw his final smile, the one reserved for his wife, a now widowed queen. Elisara held onto Sadira to keep her upright, not just from the grief racking her body but the trembling ground beneath their feet.

Elisara had done as the gods asked—funnelling her power into a dark tower that crashed down upon the stones. Caellum's blood now trickled into the cracks, joined with Elisara's tears. She had expected to feel terrified as the dark consumed her but was more terrified at the realisation it had not been her full strength. Elisara had used all her darkness' strength, yet the well of the elements remained untouched within. The damage she could do, if she wished it, was unimaginable. It was precisely why Caligh wanted her.

The ground beneath them vibrated. Larelle and Vlad turned to the gods as Elisara focused on the queen, falling to pieces in her arms.

"Sadira," Elisara said, trying to eliminate the croakiness in her throat. Slowly, she peeled Sadira off her to look the queen in the eye. Sadira stared back with a vacant expression. "We must leave. Something isn't right." The ground continued to tremble, and the taste of dust filled her mouth as stones cracked throughout the temple. "I'm going to need you to stand up so we can move his body." Sadira's face crumpled again, and she looked away, staring longingly at her husband.

"He never meant what he did to you," Sadira sniffed. "Please don't hate him in death. He never forgave himself for it. Please, take this." Sadira slid the ring from Caellum's right hand, where a tiny star was engraved on the inside—the ring Elisara gave Caellum all those years ago. Sadira placed it in her palm, forcing Elisara to swallow back her tears. It already felt cold, but this was not about her.

"I'd hate for him to be waiting for me over..." Sadira's eyes widened, and before Elisara could respond, the queen rose quickly, slipping in the blood at her feet. "He said he would wait for me! He's over there, where my grandmother was." Elisara grabbed her arm to keep her from running. The others refused to meet Sadira's eyes. "You don't understand! The people of Garridon can stay if they have unfinished business. He is over there! If I can just take his body there, maybe there is a way to bring him back." Elisara grabbed Sadira before she could rush to Caellum's body, saving her the embarrassment of dragging her husband's body across the floor. The two queens stumbled when the floor shook again.

"No! Please!" Sadira cried, struggling against Elisara's hold.

Out of instinct, Elisara waved a hand to guide away the falling rocks, but still, her elemental powers did not work here. She frowned. Could she only access Sitara's power due to its similarities with Caligh's? The power that turned this land into a prison? Or had the gods restrained their elemental gifts? The temple wobbled then, disrupting her train of thought.

"We need to leave!" Larelle shouted over the sound of crashing rocks. She clutched Zarya and Alvan closely, who rushed inside with the others, including Soren. The land shook, as though it were furious someone had severed its tie to Novisia. Elisara's shadows slithered within, begging to seize Soren. Elisara's shadows tore from her body and bound Soren, keeping her still and away from Sadira with the others. They must have squeezed a little too hard as her face paled before Elisara released her to Nyzaia, she would not take Sadira's vengeance.

"No!" Sadira shouted. "We must bring him back; there's a way to bring him back!" Elisara winced; the pain in her back made it increasingly difficult to hold Sadira still. Sensing her pain, Vlad came over to help as Elisara glared at Soren over her shoulder. Nyzaia restrained the fallen queen, who trembled, mumbling incoherently.

Larelle looked at Nerida for an answer on how to return, and Elisara did the same, pleading with Vala to do something. Vala waved her hand, prompting the ancient mirror from the isle to descend through the hole in the temple's roof. It drifted into the centre of the room, appearing no different from when they first entered.

"Watch for the dark one who will bring suffering to all," Nerida said clearly, stepping towards her coffin.

"The rise of old power, the Kingdom will fall," Keres continued. Elisara's eyes widened. Was this the culmination of the prophecy? She thought unlocking all four elements in battle had been the end, but was breaking the lands' tie with Novisia the true conclusion?

"Wait!" Elisara shouted. Vala swallowed as she looked at Elisara, who could have sworn tears glistened in the goddess' eyes as she backed towards her coffin.

"Find your reflection in the ancient and say goodbye," the goddess murmured, averting her gaze. Something was wrong. What had the gods done by making Elisara use her powers? Sadira struggled, staring at Garridon.

"Tell them!" she shouted. "Tell them I'm right—that he is there, and I can save him!" Garridon smirked and backed towards his coffin. As more rubble fell from the temple, the gods faded into nothing. Sadira sobbed into Elisara's shoulder, who stroked her hair to calm her.

"We need to go!" Larelle shouted. The exterior walls crumbled as more rocks fell, reminiscent of the temple after the explosion.

"Are you sure?" Nyzaia asked, restraining Soren's arms. Soren rocked back and forth, mumbling and thrashing against Nyzaia's grip around her chest.

"I don't think we have a choice!" Elisara yelled. Alvan picked up Zarya and gripped Larelle's hand before the three stepped through the mirror, hopefully returning to Novisia. Nyzaia shoved Soren through next and paused to look at Farid.

"Go!" I'll help the commander with Sadira!" he shouted. Nyzaia hesitated but rushed through, disappearing in a blur of light.

"Help me," Elisara mumbled to Vlad and Farid as the stitches tore in her back. Vlad took Sadira from Elisara and dragged her screaming towards the mirror.

"Bring his body! Please!" Elisara winced in pain but nodded as they disappeared through the mirror.

"Ready?" she asked Farid. He nodded, bending to pick up Caellum's arms while Elisara grabbed his feet, feeling the last stitch rip as she walked towards the mirror. Elisara gritted her teeth and felt the air shift when they passed through the glass, sensing the warm breeze of the Neutral City from behind as she dragged Caellum's body. She grunted through the pain, his body limp and heavy. When the earth shook, Elisara stumbled again and fell to her side with a cry.

"I've got you." Vigor knelt beside her, lifting the shirt up her back. "You're going to need stalactite water." Elisara nodded, grateful she had at least brought Caellum's body for Sadira. The queen's cries reached her, but she struggled to look before giving a cry of her own as the ground shook again. Vigor and Vlad helped Elisara to stand. She had expected the mountain on the Unsanctioned Isle to crumble, too, but as she peered up at the sun shining through the hole above, she was surprised to learn they had returned to the temple ruins in the Neutral City, far from the mountain. Everything in the room looked as it had the last time she saw the ruins. She stared up at Vala's banner, with its three mountains and stars on a backdrop of vibrant blue. As if on queue, Alvan and Larelle came running in from outside and confirmed what they all suspected. They were back in Novisia.

"Then why is the ground shaking?" Elisara asked. The shaking stopped abruptly then, as if the earth was listening. A figure appeared in the doorway. It was clear from the look on the man's face he had instantly spotted Caellum's body. Sir Cain bowed his head and rubbed his beard to compose himself.

"The ground has been shaking for fifteen minutes once a day for the last two months," Sir Cain said. Only Sadira's sobbing and her sister's incoherent mumblings broke the silence.

"What did you say?" Larelle whispered.

"You've been gone for two months." Sir Cain pulled out a chair from the large stone table and sat, lowering his head into his hands as he processed his king's death. He was the only person present to answer questions. "I've had guards from all four realms stationed in various locations across the kingdom in case any of you appeared. I've stayed here to monitor the shakes daily."

"Two months?" Nyzaia exclaimed. "Keres said time worked differently there—but TWO MONTHS!" Soren struggled against Nyzaia and eventually broke free, sprinting from the temple. "Shit," she murmured, rushing after Soren into the city.

"Do you have healers stationed in the square?" Vigor asked Garridon's commander. "I need supplies for Elisara." She was grateful he did not specify her injury as Sir Cain nodded, his expression empty.

"Two months," Larelle murmured, collapsing into a chair with Zarya, who stared over Elisara's shoulder to where Sadira sat. "Were we presumed dead?"

"We did a good job of feigning your whereabouts for the first month, ensuring nobody knew you were missing. But things are getting... tense," Sir Cain explained. "Forgive me, your majesties." Slowly, Sir Cain rose from his chair. "I am happy to answer all your questions about the kingdom soon, but right now—" Sir Cain's voice cracked. "I really must assist my queen."

Larelle and Elisara offered their apologies. Elisara sighed with relief when Vigor returned with a small vial of stalactite water.

"It's not much, but if I use it sparingly, it will start to knit your wounds together, so I can stitch the rest. You will need to rest much longer this time," he explained.

Elisara nodded and reached for Helena, kneeling before her. She squeezed Helena's hand as the water burned her flesh, though she was quickly distracted from the pain when shouting and cursing sounded from outside the temple.

Chapter Forty-Six

Nyzaia

"What have I done?" Soren yelled over and over, pacing in front of the temple entrance. Trembling, she stared at her blood-covered hands before running them through her hair and tugging at the braids.

"Clear the square!" Nyzaia commanded the row of Keres guards in their blood-red uniforms. They did little to hide their shock or relief as they looked at their queen, wide-eyed. "CLEAR THE SQUARE!" she bellowed again. The guards from Garridon, Nerida, and Vala didn't wait to see what Nyzaia would make of them if they instead chose to wait for a command from their own rulers and promptly scattered. Crowds filtered into the square to watch the spectacle, murmuring as the guards ushered them back.

"What have I done?" Soren shouted, her back to Nyzaia as she pressed her hands against the exterior rubble of the temple. A crack sounded as Soren punched the rubble, marking the pale stone in a mixture of Caellum's blood and her own. "She'll never forgive me." She punched the stone again.

"Soren," Nyzaia spoke clearly and calmly, resting a hand on her shoulder. She'd killed a king. The King of Garridon was dead. If Nyzaia had never released Soren from the cells, he would still be alive. Swallowing back her guilt, she focused on Soren to ensure she posed no danger to anyone else.

"No!" Soren shrugged Nyzaia off and resumed pacing, clutching her braids. "What am I going to do? I didn't mean it! I didn't want to. I—" Soren screamed. "It *made* me; his darkness made me. What am I going to do? I can't—I can't lose her—I can't be alone!

I can't–" Soren's breaths and steps quickened as she walked back and forth, beginning to hyperventilate.

"Soren, I *see* you," Nyzaia said, approaching slowly. Soren did not respond, but her breaths increased.

"I can't– I can't–" Nyzaia clutched her shoulders when she screamed again, grounding her. Soren shook her head. "What if it's still in there?" she panted, gripping her temples. "I can't! I can't–" Soren's panic was mirrored in her breathing, as she was unable to pause or focus on something, anything. She needed a distraction—something to tug her back to reality long enough for Nyzaia to understand if she still posed a threat. Would this be how Soren was now? Confronting the pain she caused others? Would she apologise for what she did to Kazaar and Caellum? Nyzaia tried to suppress the part of her that loathed Soren, the woman spiralling out of control before her eyes. Deep down, it was not her fault. "I can't! I can't. Nyzaia—" The way she had said her name rang through Nyzaia's mind. It was Soren's last word as the Queen of Keres grabbed her face and brought Soren's lips to hers.

Flames flickered on her arms as a jolt of energy sparked through her. Now it was no longer restricted on the Isle of Gods, her power was eager to play. The muttering crowd faded into a dull thudding in Nyzaia's ears while her back stayed rigid. It had never crossed her mind how Soren's lips tasted, though she shouldn't have stood there long enough to figure it out. Soren's shoulders relaxed as she moved her hands from her braids to graze Nyzaia's shoulders, and then her waist, her trembling fingers resting on the leather at her hips. Nyzaia counted in her head, listening to Soren's heartbeat where their chests met. One... two... three...

Soren kissed her back.

Nyzaia's flames burned brighter, setting Soren's arms alight, too, like kindling. Soren tasted of the stone fruits native to Keres, the ones Nyzaia had forced her to eat while sailing to the Unsanctioned Isle, but she still smelt like a child of Garridon, like cedar and moss on a rainy day, drowning under her guilt.

"I see you," Nyzaia murmured, pulling back enough to look into the clear green of Soren's eyes. The darkness was gone. Only when Nyzaia became aware of her lingering thoughts about Soren's taste and smell, did she pull back. The Queen of Keres cleared her throat and took two steps back, tucking her hands behind her back. She briefly glanced down before meeting Soren's eyes, the face of a queen returning. Still, Soren's hands lingered in mid-air, her lips slightly parted, and her breathing even. Nyzaia had beheld Soren in many lights—stubborn, furious, vengeful, powerful, scared, tearful, loyal—but had *never* seen her shy as she blushed and looked away. An invisible line of tension pulled taut between them in the silence.

"Is it gone?" Nyzaia finally asked, acting as though she had not just kissed the person who helped kill her brother—and worse, not feeling guilty for it. But now, as Nyzaia watched Soren, Kazaar's face faded to ash. Nyzaia blinked and tempered the fire within as the odd feeling of guilt about Caellum tried to rear its ugly head. Soren closed her eyes, breathing deeply. Her eyelids fluttered, as though searching.

"I think so," she finally whispered. "What is going to happen to me?" Nyzaia heard the slight crack in her voice but avoided looking at her. She glanced around the square instead, where the crowds were pushed further down the streets as the guards glanced between the pair. Her lip curved when Jabir pushed through the crowd, forging a path through the Keres guards. His face was slack, filled with relief. Two months they had been gone, and what did they have to show for it?

"You killed a king, Soren," Nyzaia sighed. "As Queen of Garridon, it is Sadira's decision. There is nothing I can do about it." Soren tilted her head, searching Nyzaia's eyes. Still, the Queen of Keres could not quite meet the bright green.

"And if it were you?" she asked. "What would you do?" Nyzaia looked back at the temple entrance for a way out of this conversation, for they both knew Soren's true meaning. Nyzaia had already made that decision when keeping Soren as a prisoner for her role in Kazaar's death, running blades through her arms during questioning as she lost her mind. Soren knew this—knew what Nyzaia would have done. Yet the unasked question was if she would do it again now, if anything had truly changed between them. Nyzaia turned and strode towards the temple.

"It is not my decision," Nyzaia repeated, falling into step beside Jabir as they briefly put an arm around one another and returned to the others. She surveyed the room. Elisara sat holding Helena's hand, wincing as Vigor worked on her back. Larelle sat on the opposite side of the stone table, where a banner of a ship with three sails fluttered in the breeze. The princess sat on her lap, burying her head into Larelle's shoulder while her mother spoke quietly to Alvan. Sadira's sobs still sounded through the room as Sir Cain knelt beside her, his head bowed, and his hand on her shoulder. They both leaned over Caellum's dead body, directly before the mirror at the edge of the room. Nyzaia scanned the room again and sensed Jabir shifting on his feet as they eagerly searched for the same person. Panic rose in her stomach as she rifled through the emotions within, hunting for the quiet presence that was always there, the tie that reassured her of his safety.

"Where is Farid?" Nyzaia asked, trying to keep the trembling from her voice. Soren quietly approached her side, her arms still trembling as she watched her sister with Caellum. Everybody looked around the room as the realisation settled in. Nyzaia turned to Elisara. "Where is Farid?"

Elisara opened and closed her mouth. "I–he was right behind me. He was carrying Caellum's arms," she said. Nyzaia turned cold as she searched for their tie within herself. Hurrying around the room, she paused at Caellum's body directly before the mirror, his hands still touching the glass. There was no space for Farid to have followed through.

"No," Nyzaia breathed. Sir Cain was quick to move Caellum's body as Nyzaia approached the ancient mirror, planting her palms against the glass, hard and cold to the touch. She slammed her hand against it over and over, but no matter what force she used, her body did not push through. "No!" Nyzaia shouted, pulling a dagger from her thigh. With a furious roar, she stabbed the tip into the glass, but instead of pushing through to the isle on the other side, the glass cracked.

Nyzaia's fractured reflection stared back, and she dropped the dagger with trembling hands. Silence filled the room. She no longer felt Farid's reassurance, but she felt no fear, either. She felt nothing. Turning her hand slowly, Nyzaia held her breath, terrified of what could be missing. She sighed quietly at the mark of their tie on her skin, but knew what the others were all thinking. Despite Kazaar's death, Elisara still bore her mark. Yet Nyzaia would not accept that as truth. Elisara *felt* Kazaar die. She would know if Farid was gone. That's what Nyzaia kept telling herself; he was still alive but trapped on the Isle of Gods. She refused to face the alternative.

Jabir said nothing before he cleared his throat and left the temple, his feet quick on the stone floor. He, too, ran from the possibility that Farid was gone forever. A light hand hesitantly paused on her shoulder.

"We'll find him," Soren murmured, and Nyzaia did not have the strength to shake her off. Bowing her head, she leant her palms against the mirror, refusing to let anyone see her tears.

"You do not have the authority to aid the Queen of Keres," Larelle called.

"Someone needs to help!" Soren snapped, yet no darkness lingered in the venom of her voice. Instead, her voice held determination—determination to repay Nyzaia and help search for Farid. The temperature in the room dropped.

"You murdered a king," Larelle said firmly. Nyzaia did not raise her head at the changing topic. Farid was not a priority for any of them. The quick dismissal of saving Farid made flames flicker in her palms.

"And it is not your judgement that befalls me either, Queen Larelle," Soren snapped. Nyzaia angled her head to watch Sadira rise. The widow rested her hand on Sir Cain's shoulder, keeping her steady as he knelt over his king.

"I will not bloody the Garridon lineage further by ordering your execution, even though it is deserved," Sadira said clearly. "Soren Mordane, you are hereby stripped of your family name and all ties to the royal line. You are banished from the realm of Garridon and its jurisdiction on Doltas Island. You may not wear the royal sigil or associate with my house. You are entitled to place no foot within my borders, and if you do, it is with the understanding you will face death upon your capture."

Soren remained still and silent. Nyzaia almost admired her determination not to beg or plead, especially as Nyzaia knew she had done everything for her sister. Was Sadira's grief clouding her empathy, her ability to understand that Soren had not committed such an act on purpose? "You can be claimed by any other realm or left to wander the kingdom. I no longer care what you do or who you are with." Sadira's respectful and commanding voice dropped to a whisper. She no longer spoke like a queen, but a betrayed widow. "You are no longer my sister." Nyzaia turned her head from Sadira to Soren, who kept her head high. Pain glinted in her glassy eyes as blood trickled from the nails digging into her palms. She remained silent, even as her sister took everything she had, including her realm, for she must have known it was the only decision that would allow Sadira to move on. Even now, Soren was determined to protect her sister. If Nyzaia requested it of her, Soren would willingly use that same determination to find Farid, too. Nyzaia locked eyes with the Queen of Garridon.

"Keres claims her."

Chapter Forty-Seven

Larelle

The tension floating in the temple's air was rife with unspoken questions and words as Larelle glanced between Nyzaia and Sadira. The Queen of Garridon's expression hardened, her eyes growing dark. Why would Nyzaia claim Soren as a citizen of her realm? Though perhaps it was better she was monitored, instead of being left to roam aimlessly around Novisia. Sadira and Caellum had explained the journals they found, and the state of his father and grandfather's minds, yet Larelle was still sceptical as she watched Soren now. Garridon said it would worsen before it got better, seemingly referencing the dark corners in her mind—but was she truly sane? Even if the remnants of Caligh's power had vanished, Soren had endless trauma to resolve.

"I accept," Sadira finally said, her words clipped. Nyzaia nodded.

"Wait outside with Jabir," Nyzaia commanded Soren. "Explain everything to him." Soren bowed to the Queen of Keres before turning and leaving the room, wiping her sleeve across her face.

"Sir Cain, are you able to explain more—" Sadira was cut off as the ground shook again, but it was far more violent, prompting screams from the people outside. Zarya cried into her mother's shoulder, who held tightly to her daughter. The four cracked pieces of the stone table began to separate, and Alvan was quick to tug Larelle's hand, pulling her away before the pieces fell as they once had when crushing the rulers' families.

"Shit," Nyzaia murmured as the stones fell inward. The ground in the temple's centre sank away into darkness.

"Out!" Sir Cain commanded, lifting Caellum's limp body over his shoulder, and guiding his queen forward. "I've got him! Go!"

Before Larelle waited to ensure everyone followed, Alvan dragged her from the temple while Zarya screamed. Like on the Isle of Gods, Larelle heard falling rubble, but she did not know when it landed or if it continued falling inward. She glanced one last time at the ancient mirror, not only trapping Farid but Olden's body too. She could not give him a proper farewell. He was gone.

Dust filled the square as they ran from the temple. In the square, the Neridian guards ran forward as the crowds fled, likely recalling the day of the explosion. Her guards stepped around Larelle to form a line as they backed up and away from the temple. Larelle's eyes counted every individual running from the temple—everyone was out. Everyone was safe. Yet as the temple ruins collapsed, Larelle wondered how long that would last. The place that had started it all now crumbled, falling into the ground. As a pit of darkness yawned open to swallow the temple, they backed away, terrified. *The kingdom will fall. Find your reflection in the ancient and say goodbye.* The gods had known. They had known using Elisara's power to break the tie between Novisia and the Isle of Gods would destroy their kingdom. *Listen to the land and understand you are bound*—and now, they were no longer connected. The Isle of Gods existed first, created for a reason they were yet to discover, but without the link, there was nothing keeping their kingdom bound with this existence. The shaking stopped as the dark chasm finished consuming everything in its path, including the entire temple and half the square. Larelle's eyes widened in realisation, and she gasped, pressing her fingertips to her mouth. Sir Cain had said the ground shook daily. Every day, the ground would shake and wreak havoc, taking more of the kingdom with it. Every day, until nothing remained of Novisia. The gods had sentenced their people to death.

"We need to evacuate the city," Larelle informed her guards as the other rulers edged around the square toward her, as if one wrong step would trigger the chasm to open further. The guards turned to relay the information to the others but paused when they saw Garridon's guards kneeling, their fists on their chests. Sir Cain shifted Caellum from his shoulder to lay him gently on the ground. Sadira bowed her head to her guards, murmuring something Larelle could not hear.

"We don't have time," Alvan told the Neridian guards, who hurried off to knock on doors.

"My guards are sending word to the military to help with the evacuation," Sadira said, her voice devoid of emotion as she bravely put aside her grief to be queen.

"What are we going to do?" Elisara asked, leaning against Vlad. "If this happens every day, we will end up restricted at the edges of the realms."

"Even in Nerida, we would not have enough boats for everyone, and where would we even go?" Larelle asked. Zarya sniffed and lifted her head off her mother's shoulder, wiping her eyes. Larelle was unsure if her tears were from exhaustion or sadness about Olden—perhaps both. Larelle brushed back her hair with her hand.

"Ossie said you would need to get a message to him," Zarya sniffed. Larelle watched her for a moment, trying to understand. How would he be able to help them?

"He's a prince," Larelle mumbled before raising her voice and looking at the others. "He is a prince! He is now free of Caligh's control. He must have plenty of ships to help sail our people off Novisia."

"Perhaps he is the Prince of Xyliar," Nyzaia suggested, crossing her arms. "The gods mentioned the Prince of Xyliar must follow his path correctly to help break the curse on other lands once the link between Novisia and the Isle of Gods was broken." Larelle frowned. Maybe the gods had not sentenced their people to death, but freedom.

"Is there a way to contact him?" Elisara asked, glancing at the Princess of Nerida.

"He said Zarya would find him when we were ready," Larelle murmured, thinking of the copper floral pin in the vanity of her chambers. Alvan wrapped an arm around them as everyone looked at the five-year-old in her arms. The Princess of Nerida was the only one who could save their people.

***

The ocean waves lapped against the walls of Mera castle. The salt breeze was one of the few things managing to calm Larelle as she gripped the terrace wall, staring up at the moon. It was different. She wondered if it had changed every night since her absence, or if there was something significant about tonight. The moon hovered over the ocean's horizon, five times larger than usual, with a red-tinged glow. The same glow lit the ocean, and suddenly, Larelle was reminded of all the blood spilled in battle and the lives that continued to be taken as the kingdom fell. Now would be the perfect time for Caligh to strike while their kingdom crumbled. Their focus now was moving people towards the coasts. A part of her was glad Olden was at peace and had not experienced this fear. She closed her eyes. Was that selfish of her? He had seemed prepared, as though Nerida had shown him what he needed to pass on.

"She's asleep," Alvan whispered. The glass doors to the terrace clicked shut as he strode up behind Larelle and wrapped his arms around her waist. "You'll catch a chill if you aren't careful," he murmured, kissing her shoulder. Her curls were still damp from bathing, and the silk of her navy robe was the only thing shielding her body. She was not exactly designed to keep someone warm. She slid her hands over his arms, pulling him tighter.

"I'm warm now," she whispered. He rested his chin on her head, staring up at the red moon with her.

"What are you thinking about?"

"That there may come a day where I do not see tomorrow," she whispered. "That Zarya may not find Osiris, and nobody will save us."

"If that happens, we will take as many people as we can and leave." It was a rational option, but one she could not follow. She would not abandon her people. A week had passed since leaving the Neutral City, which was now on the brink of extinction as the dark crater claimed more of the kingdom each day. How could she decide between those who would sail to new lands and those doomed to perish? "Whatever happens, I will be by your side, your sanctuary." Alvan moved Larelle's hair aside to kiss her shoulder. *Perhaps Alvan is your destiny,* Nerida had said. As they faced the unknown, Larelle knew she wanted no one else by her side. She wanted that sanctuary, someone who was her home after difficult days. Larelle tilted her head, displaying her neck for Alvan's lips, a silent command she wanted more—wanted him. Alvan's arms unwrapped from around her to grip her hips instead. She sighed when his lips continued along her neck, his teeth ever so gently grazing her skin.

"My queen," Alvan breathed, roaming his hand over the silk of her robe; one travelled to her chest and the other down her hip. "My goddess," he said between kisses. Larelle closed her eyes, a shiver running up her spine when his hand grazed her nipple. "My Larelle," he whispered. His fingers moved under the lace of her robe, brushing her heart. Larelle gripped the wall of the terrace and pushed back, rubbing against him, knowing he wanted her as much as she wanted him. Alvan groaned and gripped Larelle's hips, holding her still as he rested his forehead on her shoulder, as though uncertain if she wished to continue.

"Please," Larelle whispered, and Alvan's head lifted. "Be my sanctuary." Alvan's hands were quick and demanding as he spun Larelle and gripped her face, pressing his lips to hers with hunger. Larelle met him at the same pace, starving as she parted her lips and allowed him to take control. Alvan's scent of ocean-drowned trees enveloped Larelle as she pulled back to find the buttons on his shirt. When his lips claimed hers again, Larelle's fingers were hurried and certain as she worked her way through the buttons before pushing the fabric over his shoulders to run her hands over his muscles.

"You have no idea how long I've waited for you," Alvan murmured, pulling away from her lips to kiss a trail down her neck until reaching her chest. Her robe slipped off her shoulders, allowing him to graze his teeth over her nipple before slowly lowering to his knees.

"Do you remember what I told you on the steps of the Tabheri Palace?" he murmured, planting delicate kisses on her thighs. Larelle tried to gather her thoughts to focus on his question.

"That you would worship me," she whispered, sucking in a breath as his hand slid between her thighs.

"I meant every word," he whispered. His fingers began lazy circles, inching closer and closer, testing her patience. Larelle swallowed back a moan as her hands gripped his shoulders. "The people think they worship you, their queen and saviour from the destruction to come." Alvan's chest rose and fell quickly as he watched his queen's face the moment his fingers finally gave her what she wanted. "What would they say, Larelle, if they knew I was the only one *truly* worshipping you?" Larelle opened her mouth to speak, but words escaped her as Alvan rose from his knees before she found release. Eyes flashing open to meet his, she placed a finger under his chin.

"I want you," she breathed. "All of you." Larelle reached for the band of his trousers and quickly unhooked them. His breathing was sharp as he moved closer, resting his head on Larelle's shoulder, who slowly moved her hand up and down. Her silk robe fell completely from her shoulders as Alvan gripped her waist and lifted her onto the low terrace wall, baring her back to the ocean. Her chest rose and fell with rapid breaths under Alvan's gaze as he opened her legs, the silk falling on either side of them. Pulling her to the edge of the cold stone, he moved his fingers between her legs, and her head lulled back. Despite how good it felt, she gripped his hand.

"All of you," she said, splaying her palms on the stone wall to keep upright.

"Are you granting the prayers of my worship?" Alvan asked, devouring her with his eyes. Larelle smiled shyly and nodded.

Alvan did not delay. He obeyed his queen as his hands gripped her hips to hold her steady at the edge of the stone as he pushed into her. He silenced Larelle's cry with a kiss and held her still while she adjusted. Six years. Six years, and she finally felt at home again.

"My queen. My goddess. My Larelle." Alvan kissed her gently before slowly moving.

"Alvan," Larelle moaned. Her arms trembled as she held herself upright. He quickened his pace.

"Say my name again," he murmured, digging his fingers into her hips. Larelle's arms gave out, but Alvan clung to the back of Larelle's knees, repositioning her thigh to angle deeper. She arched her back further and leant into his other hand to keep from falling.

"Alvan," she groaned. Larelle relaxed back, her hair dangling over the edge of the wall. Beneath the red moon, as the waves crashed below them, salt-spray splashing their skin, Larelle melted into her sanctuary.

Chapter Forty-Eight
Sadira

The lords recommended a public funeral for Caellum, but Sadira had resisted, only wanting herself and Sir Cain to say goodbye. They had compromised. While there was no public burial, the people had an opportunity to pay their respects, though it was more of an opportunity for them to see Sadira as queen after keeping their wedding private. Despite the complicated history of his family, people seemed to mourn Caellum. Many citizens bowed their heads, with others wiping away their tears. The three women he had saved from the soldiers in Antor had stayed the longest, standing against the back wall with their heads lowered in respect.

That was Sadira's other compromise—a public coronation. But one step at a time. Therefore, much to Sadira's grief-stricken horror, she stood on the raised platform at the end of the throne room, watching people slowly trickling past Caellum's coffin before leaving through the other door. Sir Cain smiled from where he stood at the opposite end of the hall, manning the entrance. His silver armour, highly polished, almost showed her reflection. They counted the hours until sunset, where they would eventually bid farewell to Caellum. Swallowing her tears, Sadira clasped her hands and peered down at her dress rather than the many passing faces. Most pitied her, though some watched with intrigue. Many of the older citizens seemed displeased at Sadira's crown, having ascended to the throne without a large audience.

She smoothed over the deep green silk on her stomach and hips, the gown tumbling into a waterfall of fabric at her feet. From afar, it appeared black, though its true colour was clear up close. She peered down at her dress and chest, where Caellum's gold wedding band hung around her neck—cold. It sat below the talisman that had become hers in his death. Ever since she draped it over her head that morning, her power itched beneath her skin. Sadira had always been powerful, but part of her wanted to test this rise in magic—to grow a forest through the throne room and cast everyone out. Instead, she sighed. Only Sadira remained for her realm, and she would not let Caellum down. Though she would refuse to find a new fairytale—his last request was one she would ignore. One day, she would argue with him about it.

"Your majesty," whispered a quiet voice below. Sadira regained her focus and flashed a tight smile at Athena. "May I offer my condolences?" A cane trembled under her hand as she inclined her head to the right, a silent request. Sadira nodded and lifted her skirts, descending the wooden steps. Athena scanned her from head to toe as she did, far more intrigued than usual. "While I hated his family for what they did, I truly am sorry for your loss," she said. Sadira tensed and clenched her hands tighter.

"It was not their fault." Athena tilted her head curiously, and Sadira's next words were spoken with unusual bitterness. "It seems you are not blessed with as much information and foresight as you thought."

"Regardless of what I do or did not know, I cannot intervene and change paths. You know that." Athena kept her voice quiet. "And as tragic as this path is for you, you must accept it. Your people need you to." Sadira's eyes burned furiously as she assessed the old Wiccan. When Athena winced, Sadira's misplaced anger faded.

"Please sit, Athena," Sadira said. The old woman waved a gnarled hand.

"I may be fading away, but I still have my dignity. I won't sit in front of a grieving queen." Sadira admired her strength, and a genuine smile marked her lips, even if it was small and short-lived.

"I saw my grandmother," Sadira whispered. Athena, who usually showed little emotion, leaned forward, her eyes watering.

"You were on the Isle of Gods?" Athena breathed.

"You know of it?"

Athena shook her head. "More memories have returned since the kingdom began crumbling, but only snippets of names, conversation, and places. Not enough to be of assistance—yet." Athena was quiet for a moment. "Was she okay?"

"She was reunited with Errard. She was okay." Sadira smiled.

"And you will be okay again, too, your majesty. One day, you will glow from within and light the way for this realm, wherever we end up." Athena reached for the queen's hand and patted it. "Remember, you still owe me a secret." She smirked before turning to leave the queen in peace. Sadira watched the old woman hobble towards the door and hurried after her.

"Athena," she called, prompting the Wiccan woman to turn. Sadira stooped to whisper in her ear. Athena squeezed the queen's hand.

"A good secret."

***

"I appreciate this isn't traditional for a death in Garridon, the lack of celebrating life," Sir Cain said. Sadira placed a gentle hand on his trembling arm.

"It's exactly what he would have wanted," Sadira choked. Sir Cain and her personal guard, Taryn, lowered the coffin into the ground. Taryn nodded, the grief in his eyes matching the day she had returned to the castle once leaving the Unsanctioned Isle. From the look on her face, he had immediately known she returned to Garridon alone. Taryn walked through the long blades of grass towards the treeline, offering Sir Cain and Sadira a moment of peace. The sun set behind them, bathing the gravestones in a soft orange hue. Nine gravestones: a son and a brother, returned to his family. Sadira knelt before Caellum's coffin and blinked, filling the grave with soil until it formed a light mound. Unstrapping his breastplate, Sir Cain removed his armour until he donned plain clothes. He knelt beside his queen.

"I don't think you will ever know how grateful I am for what you did for him," Sir Cain said gruffly. Sadira turned to face him. His red hair had faded in the two months of their absence. "He was such an anxious lad with no confidence, except with those he trusted, like me, Elisara, and his siblings. The man who stood before his people at his coronation, and the man at his engagement ball, were two different people." Sir Cain smiled, a watery sheen in his eyes. "That was all you. He became confident because of you and his want to protect you. It was always his nature. He loved fiercely."

"He did," Sadira whispered, reaching for Sir Cain's hand. They knelt in silence as they thought of their beloved king. "He asked me to pass on a message to you when he was..." Sadira trailed off, unable to voice the words that he was gone. Sir Cain frowned. "When we were on the Isle of Gods, he saw his family. All of them were so happy—normal. Wren was the man he was when you truly knew him." Sir Cain pinched his brow and closed his eyes. Sadira sniffed. "Wren wanted to say thank you for being a father to Caellum and his children when he couldn't be." Sir Cain's shoulders rose and fell as he sobbed into his hands. Sadira rubbed his back until he grunted and lifted his head, wiping his face clean of tears.

"It was my honour," Sir Cain said. "As it will be to serve the Mordane-Balfour household." Smiling, he glanced down at Sadira with the knowledge of the secret she had only shared with him and Athena. "I will leave you with him," Sir Cain said. "Taryn can keep watch. I need some time alone." Sadira nodded as Sir Cain rested a hand on the grave before walking away.

The evening breeze floated through the grass as Sadira sat back on her heels with a sigh, struggling to find the words.

"Tell Aurelia I accepted the offer of her gowns." Sadira's laughter soon turned into sobs, trying to mask her pain beneath pretences. "The jewels were too extravagant, though, so please tell your mother I'm sorry." Sadira sniffed and rested her palms on the soil. She encouraged blades of grass to grow through it to match the rest of the long lawn surrounding the other eight gravestones. "I think I hate you a little bit," she whispered. "For leaving me to face all this alone. But I know you would be here if you could be." Sadira looked along the grassy field to where Taryn watched from behind the trees. She would have to flee Novisia soon, leaving the Balfour family here. An ache reopened in her chest every time she thought of being apart from Caellum. With a flourish of her hand, white irises and sweet peas sprouted across the grass—sweet peas for goodbye, and to recognise Elisara's support after receiving numerous letters from her over the last week, and irises for new beginnings—a new life without her love. One day, if she survived all this, she would replicate the walled garden and place nine new headstones within it. She would sit beside a lake under a willow tree and speak to her lost family every morning. She thought of Soren then, but she pushed the thought aside. She had heard nothing from Soren since Nyzaia claimed her as a citizen of Keres. She hoped it stayed that way. She felt nothing but hatred when she pictured Soren's face, even if her expression matched the innocence of when they were children. To avoid letting thoughts of Soren, no longer her sister, from ruining her time with Caellum, Sadira buried her anger and betrayal deep within her chest and locked it away.

"I don't know your favourite flowers," Sadira whispered, guiding the vines over each gravestone. "But I need there to be some colour to these stones while you live without it." Sadira thought of Caellum in Antor's walled garden, playing hide and seek with his sisters under the sepia-brushed sky. "These flowers are not meant to be on vines, but I'll make it work," Sadira whispered, allowing tiny, delicate blue flowers to bloom across the gravestones. "Forget-me-nots." Tears streamed down her cheeks as she shuffled closer to Caellum's grave. "I don't think you need to ask what these represent." She clenched her eyes shut before wiping her eyes with the back of her sleeve and resting a palm atop the stone. The flowers perfectly bordered the words engraved on it. *Here lies Caellum Balfour, protector of all he loved. A king, son, brother, husband, and father.*

Sadira rose, resting her hand on her stomach and the womb she knew had grown life since their wedding day. With a final tear, Sadira raised her head, ready to be crowned Queen of Garridon and ensure her children lived in a safe world. Turning to face the sunset and return to the castle, she sent a silent *I love you* to the sky. Had she looked up, she would have found nine hawks perched in the trees, watching over her and the last of the Balfour and Mordane line.

Chapter Forty-Nine

Elisara

"*That was a rather long absence.*" *Elisara whirled at Sallos's voice, realising it had worked. She had summoned only him. Her army of shadows had waited at the edge of the Neutral City as she left, commanded by Sallos in the two months she was absent. Her ability to manage her darkness had reinstated her control over all the soldiers, even those who had previously wreaked havoc throughout the realms. When Elisara crossed back into Vala, alongside Vlad, Vigor, and Helena, she had channelled them back into the sword after informing Sallos of her intentions. The ability to reclaim and wield her power on the Isle of Gods had renewed her confidence, along with Vala's reminder that Elisara was more than her heartbreak. She doubted the lords of Vala would appreciate her returning with an army of shadows, particularly after abandoning them for two months. She was right. Her return was not well-received. It had taken many conversations to convince the lords she was fit to rule. Eventually, she'd given up on civilities and willed her shadows to swarm her body like a dress, forming a crown of darkened wisps as she reminded them, she was their queen. Patience was not a virtue that came naturally to Elisara now—neither was being told what to do. The gods had used her to break the link between Novisia and the Isle of Gods, putting all of their citizens' lives at risk. Fury had festered in Elisara ever since. Fury at the gods, at Sitara. Fury at Caligh and her loss of Kazaar.*

"Is that your way of saying you missed me?" Elisara asked coldly, padding barefoot over the cold stone floor of her chambers. She paused at the archway of the balcony, where Sallos rested his forearms

on the snowy wall, overlooking the city beneath the stars.

"You are my queen. Is it not natural to worry when we are parted?"

Elisara glanced at him out of the corner of her eye. He wore the same clothes, with moisture seeping into his tanned jacket sleeves and his white linen shirt offering little reprieve from the realm.

"Aren't you cold?"

"I no longer feel the cold," he said. "I don't really feel anything."

"What a sad existence," Elisara scoffed, resting her hands on the wall as snow fell over Azuria's rooftops.

"Well, I am dead inside a sword. How joyful can I be?" Elisara pursed her lips. Dead. Caellum was dead. Kazaar was dead. Sighing, Elisara made a mental note to check the Avery in the morning. Ever since departing, Elisara and Sadira had exchanged daily letters, bound together in their grief. It was nice, having someone to write to who understood the front she had to put on as queen when all she wished to do was wallow in bed.

"How is the Queen of Garridon?" Sallos asked. Elisara looked at him.

"Don't do that."

"What?" he asked, shifting to lean against the wall and watch Elisara.

"Don't sense my thoughts or emotions or whatever you are doing." Only Kazaar was allowed in her mind. Sallos nodded, understanding her true meaning. "She is as one would expect when newly crowned and grieving. If we have no news from Larelle in the next day or so, I intend to aid with Vojta's evacuation before visiting her in Garridon." Elisara peered across the city to the settlements closest to the Neutral City. After another seven days of tremors, the destruction could extend past the realms' borders. Luckily, none of the settlements were close to the Neutral City's entrance, allowing time for evacuations. Vala's citizens were currently being evacuated to Azuria and Alvera, the most coastal locations away from the tremors.

"So, what happens if the Princess of Nerida does not succeed?"

"She will," said Elisara. "She has to."

"Why is everyone so certain?"

"The princess seems to have a certain... intuition," Elisara said. Larelle had explained as much. When Zarya last spoke with Osiris in her dreams, she awoke with glowing eyes, a sign of her power.

"Ahh," said Sallos. "She is a seer." Elisara whipped her head towards him, frowning. "If you'd summoned me sooner, I would have told you." He raised a hand to his chest, feigning offence.

"What exactly is a seer? The same as the Wiccan with their prophecies?" Elisara asked, both intrigued and frustrated by what else Sallos knew yet kept to himself.

"Wiccan are gifted with prophecies and occasional visions, which are still open to interpretation, analysis, and deduction. A seer, on the other hand, sees the exact future and knows of events that will definitely happen."

"So, was Zarya's dream about Osiris true? And Larelle must get a message to him?"

"Yes, that was true, but that was not her gift of being a seer. She did not foresee the event; Osiris told her." Elisara frowned, struggling to make sense of it.

"So, how exactly did Osiris speak with her?" Elisara asked. Sallos overlooked the city, as if unsure how much to divulge.

"Because Osiris is a child of two great lineages and possesses gifts from two lands." Sallos held out his palms. "On one hand, the Hypheria, and on the other, the Staxions."

"They are lands?" Elisara asked, rubbing her temples for focus.

"They are races, like the Wiccans and seers, but the people of Carvyre and Xyliar like to give everything a fancy name. The Hypheria are dreamwalkers. The Staxions, mind controllers." Sallos turned from Elisara and strode back into her chambers, collapsing into an armchair before the fire and reaching for a book on the table. Elisara clenched her fists and followed. She did not know why she was shocked to learn about different races. Wiccans were different, *after all, but they descended from Garridon. These races came from lands she had never been to or seen. Larelle had spoken of Xyliar and Carvyre on the maps she had found, and if Osiris was truly the prince of Xyliar, and hailed from the legacy of two kingdoms, surely he would have enough ships to save them? Elisara sat down in the armchair opposite Sallos, resting her hands on her knees. He failed to hide his smirk as he skimmed through the pages.*

"You're enjoying this, aren't you? Withholding information until I practically beg you for it?"

"Please, your Majesty. You don't seem the begging type."

Elisara cleared her throat and looked away, thinking of Kazaar.

"How did these lands come to be? These races and people?" she asked. Sallos held up a finger.

"Not people."

"If they are not people, what are they?"

"They are the gods' first attempt at humans, the first beings from which all others descend, as far back as your ancestors go. Yet they weren't quite as the two gods wanted; they were too powerful and cunning, with too much raw power flowing through their veins, with their ears deformed into points. We call them Fae." Elisara blinked. "Come now, you didn't believe humans originated the same across all lands? Or what Caligh told your ancestors before their memories were hidden was the truth?" Elisara narrowed her eyes, watching the glee morph Sallos's face as he held the power. They had grown up believing the four gods had created humans to populate their lands, as that was what Caligh taught them. He failed to mention they were, in fact, descendants of the first attempt at humans—fae.

"I trust nothing Caligh has ever said."

"Good, you shouldn't. Forget everything you have been told and pay attention."

"I'm beginning not to trust anything you tell me, Sallos."

"Gods, you sound so bitter when you say my name. Lighten up, your Majesty. New stories are the most fun." Sallos grinned. She saw no malice in his dark eyes, only entertainment. "It's why I aban-

doned my home and dedicated my life to sailing the seas to live a life of adventure, so I could one day sit in an armchair before a fireplace and tell all my wonderful stories." Elisara recalled Nyzaia's story of the cult worshipping Farid like he was a god and wondered if the creators of these fae were similar. She winced, remembering Farid was trapped on the Isle of Gods, perhaps even dead. It served as a reminder of all they still had to face.

"So, these gods attempted to create humans, yet expended too much power and created fae instead, who possessed gifts like dream walking and mind control?"

"She's piecing it together." Sallos clapped his hands. "Yes, on Xyliar, you have fae, who possess... special gifts, and then you have the Staxions. On Carvyre, again, there are some fae with certain abilities, as well as Hypheria, who are dreamwalkers. Each one has another race of sorts, too, but that's not significant right now. But remember, there are three races on each land." Sallos held up three fingers.

"And Osiris can access Zarya's mind because he can dream walk?" Elisara frowned. "But he can also control dreams, so how do we know he isn't controlling her?"

"He won't be. He's too prideful of his heritage. He wouldn't misuse it like his grandfather, nor is his power as strong. He can simply fabricate ideas rather than control an actual person." Elisara stilled as a shiver ran up her spine. A gust of wind blew through the chambers, recalling Osiris's admission of his relationship with the man who killed Kazaar. "His grandfather is Caligh." Slowly, Sallos nodded, waiting for her to piece it together. "Caligh is fae. His dark shadows are the special abilities you speak of, but he can control minds too. He is a Staxion of Xyliar." When Elisara finished her conclusion, Sallos smiled.

"You're quick when you want to be. His mind control allows him to hide his ears the same way he hid his entire true form—well, his body. I do not know if he kept it after Larelle spoke his name, breaking his control over Osiris and the army." Elisara flinched, sensing her

shadows crawl beneath her skin, even while asleep.

"But the gods said my power was akin to Caligh's, which is how I broke the link."

"Yes." Sallos leaned forward on his knees, clasping his hands together.

"But if our power is similar because he is fae..."

"Which gods do you think were messing around trying to create humans first?" Sallos asked, his eyes intent. Elisara looked up and met them.

"Sitara and Sonos." She collapsed back in her seat. There truly were other lands out there. Xyliar and Carvyre, home to races created by Sitara and Sonos. She could only assume the particular gifts of the fae on Carvyre were linked to Sonos's own gifts.

"Which is why my people worship the kind of power you have—the same power that started our lineage." Elisara quickly looked back at Sallos.

"Your lineage?"

Sallos snapped his fingers with a grin. Elisara pushed back into her armchair as she watched his canines sharpen and the tips of his ears develop into points.

"Sallos Abexu, disgraced Prince of Xyliar at your service." Sallos bowed in his chair and looked up at Elisara from beneath his lashes. "I believe you've met my brother."

Chapter Fifty
Larelle

The fragrance of the clematis plant from the terrace drifted through the open glass doors, where a bird chirped above it. Slowly, Larelle opened her eyes to the morning sun. A weight pressed against her waist, and she glanced down at Alvan's hand splayed across her bare stomach, holding her close.

"Good morning," he murmured, burying his head in her hair.

"Morning," Larelle whispered, so he could fall back to sleep. A grin marked her face when she thought of last night. Before she reached for the discarded silk robe on the floor beside her bed, she covered her mouth as a laugh escaped. This was how it felt to be falling in love—giddy, childlike, and floating on air. Complete surrender.

"Where are you going?" Alvan groaned as she slowly lifted his hand from her stomach and slid from the bed. He rubbed her back while she sat on the edge of the bed before pulling her into his arms.

"I have to meet with the lords to discuss the plans for the Amoro evacuation."

"I should be there," Alvan sighed, shifting behind her. Larelle turned to plant a hand on his chest, her robe lowering further as she rose to kiss his lips.

"I'm sure I can let you off. I am the queen, after all," she whispered. Alvan's hand brushed her back until he wove his fingers into her hair, holding her close and kissing her harder. He groaned at her absence as she pulled away and padded over to the mirror on her vanity. Alvan shuffled up against the headboard, rustling the sheets. He watched as she sat down at the vanity and pulled the robe over her shoulder where it had slipped. Larelle's hands paused as she stared at a mark on her chest. Frowning, she traced her fingers over the scar—a symbol she did not recognise. It was like the one on Nyzaia's palm. It held a different series of shapes, more circular than triangular. Larelle's eyes widened, and she turned to look at Alvan.

"What's wrong?" he asked. Larelle stared at his bare chest, which was absent of a scar. No sign of a celestial tie existed between them. Larelle fastened her robe.

"Nothing." She smiled. "When you're ready, would you mind checking on Zarya? She'll probably be asleep for at least another few hours. This is rather early for her." Alvan nodded and slid back into the sheets. Larelle felt sick to her stomach with the weight of the unknown. She ran a hand under her robe again, over the small mark covering her heart. It didn't make sense. The passage Nyzaia read on celestial ties detailed it was anointed when two beings finally acknowledged their connection and allowed their essences to merge. Larelle acknowledged her connection with Alvan, but he had no power, no essence for it to derive from. He had no mark, either. *What do celestial ties really signify?*

Larelle opened the drawer of her vanity to pull out hair clips. Her eyes caught on the copper floral pin Osiris gave her when he handed it over with the promise Zarya would know how to contact him. Perhaps the princess should wear it while trying. Larelle turned it over in her fingers, staring back at her reflection and the scar on her chest. She thought celestial ties were formed when two people shared a destiny. Perhaps *Alvan is your destiny,* Nerida had said. But if Larelle was not tied to Alvan, who was she tied to?

***

She is the prophesied of Th-- Larelle read the neatly inked calligraphy again. *My observations make it clear she is the child that will one day cause the return of–* Larelle slammed the book shut. Larelle had been trying to read the book Alvan had taken from Vivian for at least an hour but the combination of incredibly slanted calligraphy and the variations between Larelle's language and another made for an infuriating task. The first few pages she deciphered read like a children's story about great beasts and saviours. Larelle could not place its importance, aside from the occasional scribble of Zarya's name in the margins. How did Vivian know another language? Was she perhaps someone who hailed from another land too? It only seemed to prove Nyzaia's theory that Ithyion never existed.

"Mumma!" Zarya's call interrupted her reading. Larelle could tell by the strain in Zarya's voice that something had happened, but she relaxed at the accompanying footsteps. Alvan was with her. A moment later, Zarya bound round the corner of the open door, her eyes aglow. Osiris' copper pin on her dress caught the light. *Thank Nerida the lords had left five minutes before,* Larelle thought. She not yet explained Zarya's ability to them.

Zarya's grin told Larelle she had good news. The queen remained patient as Zarya hugged her and pulled back, bouncing on her feet.

"What is it, Zarya?" Larelle asked, holding her daughter's hands to keep her still. She buzzed with energy until the glow in her eyes slowly faded.

"Ossie is coming!" She giggled, attempting to pull her hands free to clap them. Larelle looked over her head at Alvan's wary expression; they needed more information.

"When, Zarya? I need you to tell me what happened when he spoke to you. It's important, sweetheart." Zarya stopped bouncing and twirled a curl in her hair.

"I was in a different place than last time! It was so much prettier, mumma! All the buildings were white and sparkly, and there were purple banners everywhere—you know I love purple!"

"You do! It's your *favourite* colour," Larelle exaggerated, trying to match her daughter's enthusiasm. Zarya grinned.

"I could hear the sea, so I walked down all these pretty white streets until I found sand, which was nearly as white as the buildings! But no one was there."

"Except Osiris?" Larelle asked. Zarya nodded, playing with the bracelet on her wrist.

"I was sitting on the sand collecting new shells for my bracelet when he came and sat beside me. He said he was coming to rescue us, but he needed time to secure the boats." Larelle frowned at Alvan. They did not have time.

"Did he say how much time, Zarya?"

"The next full moon." She beamed. Larelle remembered the large red moon last night. A month. They had to wait one month. "Do you think he'll like me in person?"

"Of course he will! Who wouldn't like you? Did he say anything else?"

"Mhmm, not really! Just that he was going to bring his friends and save us."

"Do you believe him?" Larelle asked. Zarya tilted her head, and her eyes glowed again when she nodded.

"Yes!" she exclaimed. "He's going to bring four hundred ships! I can't even count that high!" Larelle held her still again as she resumed her jumping.

"Did Osiris tell you that, Zarya? Or did you see it?"

"I saw it! Four hundred ships approaching Nerida." Zarya tapped a finger to the side of her head. Sighing, Larelle bowed her head. If she saw it, then it was likely true. In one month, Osiris, the Prince of Xyliar, would arrive on their shores to save their kingdom, so they could work to find and defeat Caligh together, wherever he was hiding.

"You've done so well, sweetheart," Larelle said, pulling her into a hug. She rested her chin on her daughter's head, squeezing her tight as she stroked a hand over her curls. Larelle frowned and wound her finger around a curl. A white curl, no wider than a child's thumbnail. The queen frowned, would there be consequences to her daughter's abilities?

"He also said he hopes your heart is happy," Zarya whispered. Larelle let go of her and frowned at her daughter's smile. Her heart? Zarya tapped a small finger on her mother's chest, exactly where the raised scar of a celestial tie had been.

"What is it?" Alvan asked, sensing the shift in Larelle's mood.

"Someone just wants focaccia for lunch." Larelle smiled.

"I can take her to see Lillian and have that arranged." Alvan offered Zarya his hand, but she ignored it and sprinted past him.

"You have to catch me first!" she laughed.

Alvan chuckled. "I guess this is my daily exercise. He planted a kiss on Larelle's cheek and left the room. She drifted her hand over her heart. *How does Osiris know?* Flustered, Larelle ignored Vivian's book and resumed her previous task, attempting to display the maps on the wall for a better view.

They had not yet read through any of the other books from the church; she had been too focused on planning evacuations and updating the lords and representatives upon her return. She had been determined to start today but now needed to urgently write to the other rulers, ensuring they were in Nerida in one month's time to greet Osiris. Perhaps it would be best if they started moving all the people to the coast of the realms now; a month may be cutting it fine. There might be no land left. She would allow the rulers to stay here in Mera, so they were together when Osiris arrived.

"Ouch," Larelle mumbled as she pricked her thumb with the final nail, trying to position it on the wall. It was a far more arduous task than she expected, seeing as the maps were longer and wider than her body. Mostly, the lands were central, surrounded by the ocean.

"That's much easier to see," Alvan said, re-entering. Larelle stepped back, examining the six maps on the wall. She had left the two of Novisia on the table, already understanding them to be the Isle of Gods and Novisia as she knew it. "Are you looking for anything in particular?" he asked, wrapping an arm around her waist. Larelle gulped, afraid to look him in the eye in case she gave away what she was hiding.

"No. I have no idea what to look for. Maybe having the other queens here as fresh sets of eyes will help." Larelle sighed. It felt odd knowing they were now all queens, with Novisia's only king dead.

"Is everything okay? After last night?" Alvan asked. Larelle avoided looking at him, but her feelings were clear. Alvan tilted her chin up to look at him. "If I've done something wrong..."

"No, no, you haven't," Larelle insisted, placing her hands on his chest. Alvan's frown deepened.

"Then, what is it?" he asked, scanning her eyes. Larelle met his gaze. She could not build a sanctuary with him upon lies. With trembling hands, she pushed aside the fabric of her dress to reveal the scar over her heart. Alvan traced it with his thumb. "When did you get it?" No fear or worry laced his voice; his eyes were merely curious.

"I woke up with it, and—"

"And what?"

"Osiris knew about it when he spoke with Zarya." Alvan tensed for a moment before nodding slowly in understanding.

"You could be tied to Osiris," Alvan murmured, inspecting the mark. "It simply means you share a destiny. It makes sense, doesn't it? Given he is to arrive on the shores of your realm?" Alvan asked with a reassuring smile. Larelle nodded, trying to convince herself the same, but something nagged at her within—something wrong. Alvan's embrace enveloped her with comfort as she tried to forget about it. "Remember not to keep it all to yourself," he murmured, stroking her back. Outside, the waves crashed against the wall as she took a moment to breathe.

"Two of the maps line up," Alvan said, moving away from Larelle to run a finger along the edges. Larelle read the names on the maps. *Xyliar and Carvyre.* Alvan was right. Where the map edges met, the curves showing the waves in the water matched. The lands were beside one another.

"Perhaps some others match up too?" Alvan suggested. They were quick to pull the pins from the other four maps, turning them in different directions and repositioning them on the wall. Finally, Thassena sat in the top left corner and matched with another map on its right, separated by the ocean. Alvan turned another and slotted it beneath Thassena, above Xyliar. The final map sat above Carvyre. Alvan reached for Larelle's hand as they stepped back to assess the maps filling the entire wall. Six pieces of land, yet only two connected: the two places above Carvyre. The rest were surrounded by the ocean.

"All the other kingdoms," Larelle breathed.

"Then where does Novisia fit?" Alvan asked. The map was less delicate than the others as Larelle picked up Novisia's map and placed it against the wall. It fit perfectly in the centre of all six lands, surrounded by enough water that the outer border were still miles and miles from any of the other six kingdoms. It was perfectly centred in the middle.

"How did we never know?" Alvan asked. "How?"

"The curse hid memories," Larelle breathed.

"But if this is Novisia, and there are six other kingdoms, where is Ithyion?" Alvan asked. Larelle placed a pin in the final corner of Novisia and backed away again.

"What if Ithyion never existed?" Larelle whispered. "We can't trust anything Caligh ever said to us or our ancestors."

Eyes wide, Alvan rubbed his face and took it all in. "Or what if this is Ithyion, and the entire kingdom never truly fell?"

Chapter Fifty-One

Soren

Thirty-seven days—the length of Soren's banishment from Garridon so far after being stripped of her name and title. She had not spoken to her sister for thirty-seven days, though at least they had lived under the same roof for the last twenty-five. Staring out of the chamber window all day was becoming both a blessing and a curse, having to face Garridon every time she looked outside. On clear days, she saw the trees in the distance and mourned the comfort they provided.

While Soren had slept, Nyzaia received word from Larelle about all rulers evacuating to Mera, where they would spend the next month preparing for Osiris's arrival. Nyzaia had not asked Soren to attend, nor had she told her not to after walking into Soren's room at the Tabheri Palace to find her packing. The Queen of Keres had been guarded since their moment outside the temple—the moment she kissed Soren. Nyzaia did not trust her, not fully, but Soren was loyal and wanted to assist with finding Farid. Having a goal and someone to serve kept her grounded—it was all she had ever known no matter the lack of willpower or sanity involved. However, the one thing nobody had allowed was for Soren to attend the rulers' meetings, though that mattered little. Soren lacked the focus to listen to numerous voices at once. Instead, she read or grew flowers in her palms to calm her mind. Nyzaia visited every evening, and nobody seemed to ask the Keres Queen why she did not dine with the other rulers, assuming her grief-stricken because of her unsuccessful search for Farid. When Nyzaia entered Soren's rooms unannounced on their first night in Nerida, carrying a tray of meats, breads, and fruits, Soren did not ask either. She did not ask on the second or third night, or the twenty-fifth—two nights before the kingdom fell. They ate in silence again.

Everybody in the castle was on edge. While Larelle appeared relieved Osiris was coming to save them and their people, Elisara's story of his brother, and the tale he had since relayed, made them all wary. An entirely different race of beings—Fae—existed with different factions of power, raising questions as to how powerful these new lands could be compared to Novisia's rulers. They had suggested Elisara call upon him again to ask for more detail, but she refused, not since he had revealed his true heritage. Whether or not she was afraid of him or just truly believed what she continued relaying to them, that he would not willingly offer more information. Nobody seemed intent on pushing Elisara further, not with how blunt and short-tempered she had been of late. Soren supposed she would be the same in Elisara's position. Speaking with a man—a fae, no less—who had shown his true teeth and revealed his ability to control minds did not sound appealing. Based on her experiences, Soren would have sided with Elisara, too, though nobody cared for her opinion. They steered clear of the fallen queen. Soren was sure it was because they wanted her dead for what she did to Caellum, and they couldn't trust themselves to keep her alive.

"What was the name again, the place to cross reference?" Soren asked, rubbing her forehead. Her memory was short-lived from the trauma inflicted in her mind. Nyzaia often had to remind Soren of certain words while she stuttered or stared at a page for too long, but other than assisting with the task at hand, the pair spoke little.

"Q'Ohar," Nyzaia said, not looking up from her book as she bit into a stone fruit. Soren's eyes lingered for a second too long at the juice dripping down Nyzaia's chin. The Queen of Keres lounged sideways on the armchair opposite Soren, with her legs swinging over the arm. In the evenings, she had taken to wearing fitted black trousers and a loose red shirt and wore her leathers and red sash during the day. She had only worn her lehenga once at Larelle's welcome dinner, another event Soren was not invited to. Seiko curled in front of Nyzaia's chair, nudging her hand.

"Q'Ohar," Soren repeated, frowning. Nyzaia's eyes peeked over the red-bound book, watching Soren, waiting to see if she continued. When she didn't, Nyzaia straightened.

"One of the lands on the map." Nyzaia pointed at the book's spine. "It's the place all these books are about." Soren blushed; it was such a simple thing to forget.

"Queen Larelle found them all in the church, along with others we also assume are the names of other lands," Soren said, her voice rising slightly for confirmation.

"Exactly," Nyzaia said. She dropped the fruit stone onto the table beside her and reached for the wine. Soren counted, waiting for the same nose scrunch Nyzaia always did after sipping from the glass. One... two... three... Next, she would say–"It's nowhere near as good as Tabheri's." Soren smiled, having predicted Nyzaia's words exactly. "Why are you smiling?"

Soren straightened and raised her book in front of her face before reaching to stroke Varna. The other three wolves were curled before the fire, but Tapesh had distanced herself from the pack with a sorrowful look in her eye, watching the flames.

"I'm not," Soren mumbled, tracing a finger under the words.

"I can tell you're lying." Soren lowered the book to find Nyzaia staring at her with a raised brow. The flames from the fireplace made her eyes brighten as if they, too, were alight.

"I should hope so. It was your job once," Soren quipped. Nyzaia's eyes widened a fraction. "Sorry, I–" Soren had not meant to offend.

"Don't apologise. It was getting boring without your snarky remarks," Nyzaia said, turning the page. Soren almost stayed silent, but something felt relaxed between them.

"Good to know I've been boring you, your majesty," Soren said, turning a page to examine a drawing. Although Nyzaia didn't reply, Soren glimpsed a faint smile on her face. Soren was on the eighth volume of the books. She had initially scanned for anything that might offer insight into the Isle of Gods, skipping past family trees, and accounts of battles and history. She needed only information that would offer them another way to reach the Isle of Gods and hunt for Farid. But Nyzaia had soon requested she switch her focus to Q'Ohar. Soren had not asked why, but Nyzaia had explained a brief reference to 'Nefere of Q'Ohar' in a different book. She relayed to Soren what Keres had revealed about Farid's ancestors and resorted to focusing only on the books of that land.

"I remember three images after reading the name in *Myths and Lies of Ithyion*," Nyzaia said. Slowly, Soren nodded, flicking through the pages for pictures first before continuing reading. Nyzaia had not found the book since the war began, though she claimed to doubt the accuracy now, given Caligh Servusian was the author. The book alternated between a language she knew and one she did not. Soren paused.

"Like these ones?" she asked. Nyzaia dropped her book on the table and leaned forward to reach for the one in Soren's lap, grazing her hand against Soren's. Her skin was warm from sitting close to the fire, and Soren tried to convince herself it was that very same flame that made her cheeks flush. Their eyes met briefly, making her wonder about Nyzaia's thoughts. Sometimes, she was certain she knew the Keres queen's thoughts, imagined them as clearly as if stood in her mind the same way Nyzaia had when they briefly connected in the bathing pool. The thought of the bathing pool and Nyzaia's hands in Soren's braids deepened her flush. Soren felt the spark ignite whenever they came into contact, but a look of regret always crossed Nyzaia's features afterward, so Soren withdrew her hand. Nyzaia's hand lingered a second longer before she returned her attention to the book.

"Yes!" She stood and aimlessly paced the room, staring at the pages. "When I saw them, they were all rather smudged—but these! I can see far more detail. Look." Nyzaia reached Soren in two strides and placed the book on Soren's lap, pointing at the pictures. Soren tried to focus but was far too distracted by the spiced orange scent of Nyzaia's soap. Nyzaia rested her arm on the back of her armchair, behind Soren's neck, while the left gestured at the page, her body surrounding Soren's.

"This person has two swords at their back. This one appears to have smoke around it, similar to Exandria, and this one." Nyzaia pointed at the third illustration. "Look familiar?" The question refocused Soren, who squinted at the drawing.

"Like Farid's wings," Soren confirmed, looking up at Nyzaia. It was the first time in thirty-seven days that Soren saw her truly smile, a smile so bright it highlighted the whites of her teeth. "It's something," Soren whispered. Their faces were in such close proximity she could smell the fruit juice on Nyzaia's breath. Nyzaia gulped. Soren clenched her hand around the edge of the book as Nyzaia's eyes roamed her features. A knock sounded at the door, then. Nyzaia moved away as quickly as she'd dodge a sword in battle. She tucked her arms behind her back as Taryn, Sadira's personal guard, entered. *Shame. Guilt. Regret.* Soren could practically taste Nyzaia's emotions.

"Apologies, your Majesty. Your guard, Jabir, said you were up here, but I assumed you were alone." Taryn bowed his head to the queen and backed away from the door. That was unsurprising, Jabir spoke little these days, keeping his grief to himself. Soren shifted in her seat.

"You don't need to leave," Nyzaia said. Taryn glanced at Soren.

"My queen wished to speak with you regarding some basic defence training." Taryn looked at Soren again, making the reason for Sadira's request clear. Soren rolled her eyes and turned back to the book in her lap.

"Very well, let's go," Nyzaia said.

"No, it is fine—"

"She is already outside the door. That is why he is so hesitant," Soren said. She always sensed her sister's presence. Taryn narrowed his eyes, and Nyzaia looked between them both. Soren shrugged, as if to say, 'Tell me where you want me to go.' The decision was made for them when Sadira entered, her head held high. Soren leaned forward in her chair and lowered her book. Something was different. Sadira's arms and face had thinned, like she had not been eating, yet the rest of her body appeared as it usually did. A deep green gown covered her entire body, except for her face and neck—a dress to show the queen in mourning. If Soren knew her sister, she would forever be. The fabric was close-fitting to her arms, neck, chest, and ribs, only flowing out into a chiffon waterfall once it hit her waist. A gold chain hung around her neck beneath the Garridon talisman. *Caellum's wedding ring.* His bloodied body beneath Soren's dagger flickered in her mind, and she forced herself to focus on her sister. Sadira only looked at Soren briefly before refocusing her attention on Nyzaia.

"I don't wish to disturb your intimate evening," she began. Soren wanted to roll her eyes at the dig, but kept her face neutral out of respect. "If we do indeed set sail in two days, I would like to spend some time on the ship learning some hand-to-hand defence. We may, of course, be entering unknown dangers, and I must be able to protect myself." Sadira smoothed the skirts; her hands lingered on her stomach. Soren tilted her head.

"Of course. We can start the first day we sail," Nyzaia said, her words clipped as if sensing Soren's discomfort. Sadira nodded at Taryn and turned to leave. Against Soren's better judgement, she opened her mouth.

"Sadira–"

"No!" Sadira whirled to face her sister. Vines twisted from the ground, enveloping Soren's arms and chaining her to the chair. Soren did not fight. Nyzaia took a step towards Soren, only one, but it was something. Varna lowered her head, a low rumble sounding in the back of her throat. "You do not speak to me; you do not look at me. If I could control it, I would not even have you *think* of me. I would wipe my existence from your memory." Soren had never seen Sadira sneer until now.

"Sadira—" Nyzaia tried to speak, her voice soft. Perhaps somebody might actually defend Soren.

"I did not question your choice, Nyzaia. Do not make me regret it. I can still have her executed." Sadira turned back to leave, and Nyzaia's eyes flickered with flames.

"No, you can't," she said. Sadira and Taryn froze.

"Excuse me?" Sadira whispered, facing the door, away from Soren.

"She was claimed by Keres—by me. If you were to kill a citizen of Keres, I would be forced to seek justice." Nyzaia raised her chin. Soren moved, wanting to diffuse the tension, but Nyzaia moved her hand the smallest amount in a silent request she stay put. She lowered herself back into the chair.

"Is that a threat?" Sadira asked. Seiko rose from his position and padded over to Nyzaia to sit by her side.

"It does not have to be," Nyzaia answered. Both queens looked at one another, waiting for the other to break. Eventually Sadira turned.

"Now is a poor time to make an enemy of one another, Nyzaia."

Chapter Fifty-Two
Sadira

Unclenching and clenching her hand, Sadira slowed the growth of the flower in her palm in time with her breathing. The sea breeze blew through the white iris before she hid it away again. Her body was restless, and she had given up on sleep hours ago, resorting to sitting out on the terrace of her chambers in Nerida. There were a number of reasons she was resistant to sleep; she was sick with anticipation, wondering whether Osiris would indeed land on the shores tomorrow, nauseous from the children growing in her womb, and suffocated from nature's absence replaced with brick and ocean. Backing onto the beach, the castle of Mera had no gardens and so the iris in the queen's palm would have to suffice.

Sadira looked to the left of her terrace, to where she could see her realm in the distance beneath the moonlight. Larelle had been sweet to offer her chambers in this direction, but Sadira's heart ached at the thought of her husband, left alone in a crumbling kingdom. Her hand crept to the chain around her neck to turn Caellum's wedding ring round and round. She still wore hers.

"I miss you," she whispered to the sky. A breeze brushed her skin in response at the same moment the sound of birds chirped somewhere above. Sighing, Sadira reached for the steaming cup on the nearest table. She glanced at the box beside it and lifted the cup to her lips, relishing the sweet floral taste. It reminded her of the tea Arabella had offered in her small home in Albyn. At the thought of the Wiccan, Sadira lifted the lid of the box. It was filled with sentimental items, things she could not bear to leave behind.

The family tree Caellum had found in his father's study, a small rattle from Edlen and Eve's old nursery, embroidery from Aurelia's collection, a necklace from the late queen, and a dagger from the one of the prince's belongings. The jacket Caellum wore on their wedding day sat beneath it all with the strips they had tied around their hands—it still smelt like him. She rummaged beneath it for the smaller trinket box hidden away.

Setting down her tea, Sadira unlocked the clasp. Four pins now sat within. The wolf head, the Wiccan symbol, and the other unknown were all a dull metal. The fourth stood out beside it. It was a golden pin of the Garridon sigil etched with a raised hawk. Sadira held it up to the moonlight and grazed her thumb over the ridges of its wings and the small emerald in its eye. Sadira thought of the redheaded Wiccan who forced it into her hand. *A promise that I will be by your side one day.* Suddenly, the wind picked up, knocking over the teacup and spilling the loose leaves across the table. Sadira cursed and moved her robes to keep from getting wet in the tea's puddle spilling onto the stone floor.

"I wondered when you might finally look at the pin again," a soft voice whispered. Sadira lunged for the dagger in the box and rose from her seat, spinning towards the voice in the darkness of her rooms.

"Show yourself," Sadira commanded, taking a cautious step back on the terrace.

"I mean no harm, I only answer your call," the female said, stepping through the open glass doors and onto the moonlit terrace.

"Arabella," Sadira said. The queen kept the dagger in front of her. The woman raised her hands.

"I am sworn to protect you, your Majesty. I mean you and your babes no harm." Sadira's hand wavered. Nobody knew about the babies. Nobody except Sir Cain and Athena. Sadira had not even told Elisara yet. Sadira pointed the dagger towards the bench, gesturing for Arabella to sit. She stepped towards it but stayed standing.

"It would be improper to sit while my queen remains standing," she said. Arabella lowered her hands and clasped them in front of her woollen cloak, hiding her clothing, but also any concealed weapons. "You can call for the captain of your guard, if you wish. I will not be offended if you desire his presence." Sadira lowered her hand at the offer but did not call Taryn from where he stood outside her door. "Please," Arabella said, gesturing to the chair that was a safe distance from the bench. Sadira lowered slowly, tightening her hold on the dagger. Only when Sadira was sat and facing Arabella did the woman finally sit too.

"Tell me where you entered, so I can prevent others from trying the same," Sadira said, her voice was level and commanding. The voice of a queen. Arabella watched the queen, her blue eyes sparkling as though excited.

"I did not enter by conventional means," Arabella said.

"If this is going to be a repeat of veiled information, I have no interest." Sadira glared, dimming the brightness in Arabella's eyes.

"I have been granted to speak freely, your Majesty." *Granted.* Sadira was the queen, so who above her could grant Arabella permission to talk? Sadira recalled the conversation in the small cottage. Darragh's warnings. He said she could not tell Sadira and Caellum too much as their deity prevented it.

"You have spoken with your deity," Sadira said, raising her chin. Arabella nodded. "How lucky I am, that now, after I have lost my husband on the hunt for further information, that your deity deems it acceptable to offer answers through you." Sadira glared, abandoning all attempts at maintaining the neutral and civil face of a queen.

"Your Majesty—"

"Speak," Sadira snapped. Neither woman said anything. Arabella had the decency to glance down at the frustration on Sadira's face. The queen did not apologise for her harsh tone. She merely waited.

"What do you wish to know first?" Arabella asked, despite the fact Sadira had just demanded to know how she appeared in her chambers. Arabella glanced at the open trinket box containing the three pins from Wren's possessions. Did she want the queen to ask about them?

"You will tell me everything you were prevented from telling me the day Caellum and I last visited you," Sadira commanded, determining such an ask would earn her as many answers as possible as opposed to thinking of specifics. Arabella extended her palm out and looked at the trinket box. Still clutching her dagger, Sadira slowly reached in to drop them into Arabella's palm. She smiled softly as she looked at them.

"Before I begin, please understand... I did not know everything I was fated to reveal this evening. Some, I knew from the memories my father began recalling, others I knew from my deity when she appeared in dreams. I only know the rest now she has confirmed the link to the Isle of Gods is broken. The curse preventing her and others from telling us all they know is gone." Sadira could not help the sigh of relief that escaped her lips. They had succeeded in one task. Learning all Arabella and Osiris knew would help them to understand Novisia's history and Caligh's role. They could gather armies to locate and end him. Sadira's heart stuttered. It still did not confirm where she would call home in the months to come. Arabella held up each pin in the light.

"Shapeshifters, Sorcerers and Wiccan," Arabella said. Sadira tilted her head. "Three races stemming from three deities. Three deities stemming from one god." Arabella looked up from the pins to meet Sadira's eye. "Your god, Garridon." Sadira clenched her jaw to keep from reacting.

"What is the importance of the three races?" Sadira asked.

"A reverse, a reflection, a sister, a mirror. Find the truth beneath you and all will be clearer. Healing and prophecies, curses and spells. One abides, one rebels. For the cost of a curse, there must be a price. Find your reflection in the ancient and say goodbye." Arabella recited the prophecy as clearly as Athena had. "The

Wiccan lived in harmony for so long until Caligh infiltrated our clans—until he divided two sisters. His dark magic twisted her mind from healing and prophecies to curses and spells, instead, creating the Sorcerers. While the Wiccan abide by the laws of nature, the Sorcerers rebel." Arabella sighed, as though pained at the information related to this prophecy.

"You spoke of a divide among the Wiccan people—a war. Is that what you reference?" Sadira asked.

"Yes. The War of Hearts. The pure, and the tainted. Wiccan and Sorcerers. Light and dark."

"You're bordering on convoluted again, Arabella," Sadira warned. "What does this have to do with Novisia?"

"It was a Sorcerer that aided Caligh in entrapping Sonos. It was a Sorcerer that placed the curse on all lands, including the one that altered memories, and prevented anyone from finding you or revealing the truth." Arabella was speaking quickly now, as though a weight lifted from her with every breath. "But every curse has a price. The curse to lock away the gods, linked it to Novisia. With the link broken, the gods are free. Free to..." Arabella trailed off, her eyes watering.

"Free to what?" Sadira pushed.

"Free to take revenge against those who aided Caligh and his Sorcerer in entrapping them and taking their father." Sadira released the grip on her dagger. That had been the gods' motive. They had knowingly forced Elisara to break the link to free themselves.

"Who aided Caligh, Arabella?" Sadira asked. The woman wiped a tear from her face and looked at her queen.

"The deities," she said. "All eighteen of them." Sadira placed the dagger down and rubbed her forehead.

"This is a lot to take in," Sadira sighed. Eighteen deities, and if what she said about the three stemming from Garridon were true, Sadira could only assume the others descended from the other Novisian Gods. Sadira recalled Elisara's account from Sallos. Three races on both Xyliar and Carvyre. Three races stemming from Sonos and Sitara. Larelle had shared the joined maps with them all, Thassena, Asynthos, Eresydon, Q'Ohar. Three deities for each land.

"My deity has told me little else. She said it was not your responsibility to uncover the rest."

"Whose responsibility is it, then?" Sadira asked. Arabella looked out over the ocean.

"The Prince of Xyliar will answer that question tomorrow," she said firmly, certain that Osiris would arrive in Novisia in the morning. "There is so much more I know she is not telling me, your Majesty, and more I know you will need Osiris for. She only grants me the knowledge she has because I am sworn to your family and our lineages are pure. She grants me this knowledge because war is coming, your Majesty."

"War?" Sadira's hand drifted to her stomach.

"The War of Gods is upon us," Arabella said, her voice foreboding. "To answer your earlier question, I did not enter through conventional means. I entered because you called upon me through the pin clutched in your left hand," Arabella said. Sadira did not respond, distracted by the worry of war. "Do you remember the first time we met in the tavern? I told you Wiccans were the first to learn to imbue things. We are powerful in it." Sadira gave the smallest nod and recalled a passage on magical imbuement she had read that very day in the dim light of the tavern. *Other items can be imbued with power, too: goblets with the ability to kill its drinker, clothing that allows the person to mimic their original owner, and books reciting to the reader what they wish to hear or transporting them to the places within.* "The pin you clutch was imbued long ago by the Brodie Clan with the ability to summon a protector to the Mordane ruler's side. To transport them."

"Your family was close to the Brodie Clan, to the Mordanes?" Sadira finally asked. Arabelle inclined her head.

"They were, your Majesty. We have been designated protectors of the Mordane family from the earliest days. It is my duty to serve at your side and protect you. My family were bred to oversee the three races, gifted with immense strength to aid us in our missions." Arabella rose from her bench and stepped towards the queen. Slowly, she pulled a dagger from beneath her cloak and Sadira reached for her own in defence. Arabella lowered to her knees before her queen.

"I once told you there is power in a name and I would not share mine completely." Sadira looked down at the woman, at the innocence in her face now as she raised a dagger to her hand and sliced across it, letting blood drop at her queen's feet. "I share it now as I make this oath. I, Arabella Balfour, swear allegiance to the Mordane Family from this day until the day I die, protecting your life."

Chapter Fifty-Three
Elisara

Elisara's hair blew from her face as she peered out across the ocean. Sadira stood to Elisara's left, their arms linked. Larelle stood on her right beside Nyzaia. Four queens looked towards what was either their salvation or downfall. But they had no other choice. Staying on Novisia was not an option. Over the last month, the land continued to cave in, until only a ring of land remained, holding what was left of Novisia's people. The wealthy had resorted to sailing their ships across the land, with no idea of where they headed, while some of the poor joined as stowaways.

"Are we certain about this?" Nyzaia asked.

"There is no other option," said Larelle.

"Once they are within reach of us, I'll raise the protections," Elisara said. "Allow them to think I'm fully exerting myself."

"We can trust Osiris," Larelle said, but her voice faltered after what Elisara had relayed Sallos's revelation about Osiris and what he had kept hidden. Larelle tried to argue the curse limited what he could share and said they could still trust him. Larelle was only trying to convince herself, though, especially after Zarya's numerous interactions with the prince.

"Even if she is a seer, I do not trust Sallos and the two are related," Elisara snapped.

"Being related doesn't mean you are the same," said Sadira, squeezing Elisara's arm gently to calm her. Elisara turned her head and squeezed her hand back. The two had been near inseparable since arriving in Nerida.

"That's them," Larelle murmured.

"Gods," Nyzaia breathed. Elisara's eyes widened as ships crested the horizon. One appeared first, then two, four, six, more and more until an endless fleet of black sails, signified with an amber flower, travelled to what remained of Novisia. The darkness within Elisara flickered with momentary fear, soon replaced with anger that Osiris had kept the true size of his army's secret, whether by choice or not. Novisia paled in comparison to the size of the lands which these ships hailed from.

"Now," Larelle said. Keeping one arm linked with Sadira, Elisara waved her other hand before her, exactly as she had done in the battle. It was merely a precaution in case they had mistakenly placed their trust in Osiris. A moat tunnelled across the sand, and, with a flick of her wrist, she filled it with twisting vines, littered with thorns, before setting them ablaze. The only change to her plan was the low twisting wall of shadows, which were high enough to meet a man's waist. With a blink, Elisara could raise it if needed. Soldiers of every realm lined the sand and stretched all the way to the castle on their left and The Bay on their right. The Sword of Souls weighed heavily on Elisara's back, but it was not uncomfortable. Her wounds had healed, leaving only scars. She no longer needed to wield the sword to call upon her army, shadows oozed from Elisara with a single command, pooling at the feet of the four queens. None blanched at the sight; they held their heads high in unity. A flurry of darkness swam from her back as the soldiers from the sword fell into formation behind their ruler, ready to move once they received word. Elisara felt Sallos's presence hovering behind her shoulder.

"Not now, Sallos," she murmured. She knew the queens heard her for they tensed, knowing the fae prince with one too many secrets stood behind them. "You are only here until I find a way to trade your life if Osiris tries to betray us." A wave of sadness washed over her, then, stemming from the prince, though she did not understand why.

"I can feel the front three ships dropping anchor," Larelle said;

her eyes flickered a glowing blue, responding to the ocean's power. The largest ship pushed forward with a forceful ocean wave, banking on the sand.

"Was that you?" Sadira asked cautiously. Larelle shook her head, frowning.

"They must have someone on board with a connection to Nerida or somewhere with an affinity for water." Ropes flew down the side of the wooden ship painted in ornate copper. "A powerful one."

"Some of the ships are different," Nyzaia said, with an edge of panic.

"An ambush?" asked Elisara, though it was hard to tell.

"The next row aren't black sails with the amber flower; they're white with purple stems," said Sadira, surveying the hundreds of ships filling the ocean.

"These three," Nyzaia murmured. "They're the leaders." Elisara sensed it as well as three bodies descended from the front ship. The one in the middle was the tallest, donning copper armour similar to that worn by Osiris' soldiers, the ones controlled by Caligh. The difference was the accents on their uniform: gold shoulder strips and swirls decorated the copper, a symbol this person was worthy of more. The man flanking on the right was shorter, but not by much, and broader, with muscles Elisara knew rippled beneath his gold armour that was so pale it was almost silver. He tilted his head as though watching her with intensity and Elisara's spine straightened. A man wearing the same white gold uniform stood on his left, appearing leaner than the other two. All three wore masked helmets concealing their identity.

"I don't like this," Sadira murmured. Elisara readied her hand. A moment later, the soldier on the left waved his, raising the water from the moat and tossing it aside in one large wave. The soldier on the right waved a hand, summoning a gust of wind to extinguish the burning vines. Elisara did not move, not yet. There were only three men; she could take them, even if they had powers. As they approached her wall of twisting darkness, she analysed their helmets, noting the metal wings on both sides. An intricate pattern of whirls was engraved on the front, while a slatted visor covered their eyes. Elisara gritted her teeth as the soldier in the middle parted his hand. Her darkness obeyed, and she let it, allowing them to believe the four queens were weak enough to take rather than save.

The three men walked through the opening, the darkness threading back together behind them. In the ocean, nobody else descended from the ships, which spanned the coastline, wrapping around the realm. Other than these three soldiers before them, there was no other threat. The middle soldier released his grip on the pommel of his sword and reached for his helmet. Elisara heard Larelle's sigh of relief as the helmet came off. The man shook out his long black hair from his face, his pointed ears peeking from beneath. Osiris grinned as a roar sounded across the sky in the distance above the incoming fleet.

"Well, this is an unusual way to greet the men who've come to save you."

Epilogue
The Captain

*F*our *Months ago*

The streets were cast in a pink glow, as they always were at this exact time of sunrise, when the sun fell just exactly between the end of the street and the promenade into the city from the docks. The captain tipped his hat to the sailors cleaning the side of the fleet and flicked a gold syiruna towards the homeless girl leaning against a wooden pillar. He winked, and she flashed him a smile, both knowing she was neither homeless nor poor, but simply one of Ophelia's spies. She shook her pot before her, mocking the people foolish enough to believe a girl so beautiful would live on the streets. Under the rising sun, a blend of gold, silver, and copper syiruna gleamed inside the pot. She had created a pile of zonri beside her, likely from visitors arriving through the ports and ridding themselves of a currency no longer in circulation here. The dark steel stood out like a sore thumb, crimped and ugly, like everything else from the land it hailed from—Xyliar. Of course, that meant it was only worth something to the poor.

The captain tipped his hat to her and continued walking. The metal on his boots clinked as he strode the marble streets leading into the city. He stepped over puddles of water being tossed from buckets onto the street, while brooms began their daily motions of polishing the marble. It was late for cleaning, but the city's day of rest was sacred to most—well, at least in the morning as everyone slept off their nights of revelry. By early noon, the streets would be filled with people seeking to satiate their appetites and waste their days, wandering about the stores and dining at the finest restaurants in the city, only the best for the wealthiest city in the kingdom. The captain reached the towering fountain at the opposite end of the city atop a circular marble slab. Behind the fountain, the palace shone, as though forever untouched by grime. However, the captain knew thousands more people, like those sweeping the streets, cleaned the palace for the city's custodian. The captain scoffed at his boss's excessive demands.

But on the day of rest, the captain did not work for her, which was why the note in his left breast pocket was so unusual. Etched in purple ink was the name of a prisoner, and simple instructions were scrawled below for him to find out what he knew. Vague as usual. But until noon, he was still eligible to rest. Even the custodian would not tempt the deities. The captain flicked another gold syiruna into the fountain, making the same silent wish he always did before taking a left down the city's most expensive street. A wish for answers to his past. Signature purple banners laced in gold hung on every other building, bearing the stemmed floral emblem in its centre. This was the hardest working street in the city; the streets already gleamed, dry from their morning clean, which was conducted two hours before every other street awoke. Ophelia knew how to keep up appearances. String music already spilled from each of the twenty establishments lining the street, but he headed for the largest in the centre, its ornate columns symbolising how deserving you had to be to grace its doors. He had no idea how the hell he achieved that status, but he bowed to the fae guard on duty and entered. He ducked as a glass sped towards his head and smashed against the wall.

"I told you not to come back until you paid me for the night you spent with Castella."

The captain grinned.

"How do you sound sultry even when you're mad?" He flashed Ophelia a smile he knew she wouldn't refuse.

"Don't sweet talk me. You owe me nine-hundred gold syiruna. She's my most expensive girl." Ophelia prowled towards him, draped in lavender gauze that blended with the silks hanging across the ceiling of the most prestigious brothel in the city, though he would never live to see it again if Ophelia heard him call it that aloud. "My success—twenty institutes, one thousand girls, the highest earner in the city for the last five years—wasn't achieved by letting men like you get free nights." Ophelia pointed a feathered fan at him while reeling off the same accomplishments she always did whenever he took advantage of her establishment. Waltzing around the stage towards him, she smiled at the customers that lounged in plush chairs while food and drink were brought to them on platters. She was right; her establishments were far more than brothels. They were renowned for everything from food and drink, tasteful entertainment to all round debauchery. It was the place to go for celebrations, business meetings, and even dirty dealings.

If the city actually had a queen, Ophelia would have given her a run for her money, and yet, "Aren't you technically still a slave?" he jabbed. Ophelia slapped him across the face with her fan before glancing at the gold inking on her ring finger. "Okay, I deserved that," he said, moving his jaw.

"What do you want here? You're due at the palace," Ophelia remarked, reaching for her ledger on the gold plinth by the door and the outrageously large gold feather quill. It was rumoured to be a gift from the Custodian of Q'Ohar, a gift passed down to his family for generations. The captain was sure it was a lie.

"Do I dare ask how you know that?" he gave an exasperated sigh and leant his arms on the plinth to face her.

"I know everything," she said.

"Not everything," a deep voice, rivalling Ophelia's in silkiness, called from an alcove. He recognised the accent but the owner forced a theatrical tone that prevented the captain from recognising his identity. "You didn't know I had arrived." The captain studied his friend's reaction, waiting to see if she tensed, and if the voice belonged to her master he was yet to meet. Instead, a feline smirk appeared on her face as she lowered her quill.

"Probably because I hadn't bothered to wonder if you'd ever return," she quipped as the tall pale fae ducked through the curtain of an alcove. He then knew why he recognised the accent. Although his friend looked like he could crack a neck in seconds, he grinned like a child as his eyes trailed Ophelia. Bold move. No one in the city had laid with Ophelia, and he doubted this arrogant fae would be the first.

"Hello Osiris." She kept her face neutral as he approached, towering over her.

"Hello *amalina*." He grinned, tucking a strand of hair behind her ear. *Beautiful*, Osiris had said in his native tongue of Xyliar. Ophelia smacked Osiris's hand away with the same fan she had pointed at the captain moments ago. "Still as feisty as ever," he said as Ophelia strode away from him. The captain swore she exaggerated the sway of her hips more so than usual. When Osiris reached for her shoulder, the captain flinched. *Bad move.* Though by the usual, teasing and grin on Osiris's face, the captain knew it was intentional. In a heartbeat, Ophelia swung back her leg and hooked it behind Osiris's, sending him tumbling to the marble floor. Grabbing a strapped dagger from her thigh, she straddled him and pressed it to his neck. Still, the fae smiled. "Come now. Don't tease me like that, *amalina*." He lifted his head, trying to lean towards Ophelia as blood trickled down his neck. "You know I like knives."

Although the string music in the domed room still played, the customers were preoccupied, watching the pair on the floor. The captain's boots clicked as he walked towards them and bent down.

"Good to see you again, mate," the captain grinned. "Glad to see I'm not the only one capable of defeating you with a knife." Osiris rolled his eyes briefly before training them back to Ophelia.

"Letting her win like this is so much more fun, though," Osiris purred, reaching a hand up to tuck a piece of hair behind Ophelia's ear. She pushed the dagger further into his neck, but did not hide her smirk.

"I feel like I'm intruding." The captain motioned between them. "I'll be back later this evening." The captain turned on his heel and moved the curtain to leave.

"NINE HUNDRED GOLD SYRIUNA, ZEE!" Ophelia shouted after him, the only person who gave him such a ridiculous nickname instead of his title as captain.

The walk to the palace was short, but he wasn't to go straight to the custodian's hearing chambers. He detoured around the back and gave three specific knocks on the sixth statue of a wing against the marble walls. It opened slowly, and the captain stepped inside. He was surprised the dungeons were not as pristine as the rest of the city; the custodian cared greatly about appearances. He half expected her to even care for the thoughts of prisoners when they had first met. She did, just for far different reasons, looking for ways they could benefit her.

The captain trailed his hand along the dark stone, embedded with purple crystals, dulled from lack of sunlight.

"Upstairs," grunted a voice at the end of the hallway. The captain tilted his head. That was why he had been called; he was to enter a cell only a certain power could control. The captain turned left instead of right and took the steps two at a time until reaching the cell bars at the top, forged from the only material capable of restraining power, the same material around the prisoner's wrists. Only the custodians possessed such knowledge, which meant this prisoner was important. His custodian did not reserve this cell for merely anyone.

The captain pushed his fist against the lock, the gold ink on his knuckles acting as a key. Slowly, the prisoner raised his head. The captain closed the bars behind him and leaned against the wall to survey the man. He didn't recognise the clothing, though he looked as if he hailed from Q'Ohar. If he looked closely, he shared similar features to Ophelia: the same dark hair and gold kissed, deep brown skin. His hair fell from a black band, and patterns of water from the wall on his right danced over his features. His black leathers were far less intricate than those from other armies, and he wondered exactly where they had dragged this man from. Blood still splattered his clothing, but no weapons were strapped to his body.

"Kazaar Elharar. I've heard so much about you." A lie, but the prisoner did not know that. The prisoner's face was neutral as he stared back, seemingly uninterested.

"It's impolite to not introduce yourself, especially when your captive has no idea where they are," the man, Kazaar, said.

"You're right. How rude of me," the captain smirked. His midnight blue eyes sparkled in the streams of light filtering through the watery cell. "Riyas Sevia, Captain of the Custodian's Fleet. Welcome to Carvyre." He snapped his fingers and the wall of water on Kazaar's left fell, revealing the blinding white marble rooftops of the surrounding city. "The Fifth State of Ithyion."

Spoiler Ahead

Find out where your journey continues in the blurb on the next page

The Lost Kingdom Saga Continues…

with a journey to Ithyion on November 24th

A commander far from home
A captain with lost memories
A prince seeking asylum.
A wanderer soaring through the skies.
A slave controlling her destiny.
A prisoner trapped within darkness.

Whilst the rulers of Novisia are dealing with the heartbreak and aftermath of Caligh's war, Kazaar wakes to find himself transported by old magic and held captive on a homeland long thought to be destroyed by darkness. As Riyas aids Kazaar in learning his heritage, in turn the commander helps the captain unlock the memories of his past life he has lost. Whilst Osiris seeks the help of a childhood friend, paths of fate begin to cross and an unlikely group of strays may be the key to saving the citizens on the lost Kingdom of Novisia and reuniting all of Ithyion as gods awake and war begins.

(Blurb subject to change)

Spoiler on Previous Page

I'm putting this here to prevent you from accidentally reading the blurb for book four on the previous page whilst flicking to the glossary. You're welcome.

Glossary and Pronunciation Guide

A

Aalto [Al-toe] - *Past Prince of Nerida, brother to Larelle [deceased]*

Abis Forge [ah-biss] - *Metal forge in Keres*

Adar [Ay-d-are] - *Lord of Port of Elvera*

Adrianus [Ay-dree-an-us] – *Past King of Nerida, father to Larelle [deceased]*

Albyn [Al-bin] - *Settlement in Garridon*

Aleya [Ah-lay-ah]

Alvan [Al-ven] - *Lord of Seley*

Amir [Ah- mear] - *Past Prince of Keres, brother to Nyzaia [deceased]*

Amoro [Ah -more - oh] - *Settlement in Nerida*

Antor [An - tore] - *Capital of Garridon*

Arabella [Ah-rah-bell-ah] – *Wiccan woman, daughter of Darragh*

Arik [Ah-rick]

Arion[Ah-ree-on] - *Past King of Vala, father to Elisara [deceased]*

Arnav [Are-nav] - *Lord of Khami*

Asdale [As -dale] - *Settlement in Garridon*

Ashun Desert [Ash - un] - *Desert in Keres*

Asynthos[Ah-sinth-oss]

Auralia [Or-ay-lee-ah] - *Past Princess of Garridon, sister to Caellum [deceased]*

Azuria [Ah-zure -ee -ah] - *Capital of Vala*

_B_

_C_
Caellum [Cay-lum] - *King of Garridon*
Cain [Cay -n] - *Commander of Garridon*
Caligh Seruvian [Cal-ee-gh Sir -ooh -vee -an] – *Bad Guy? Like I'm going to put more detail about him here...*
Carvyre [Car-v-eye-rh]
Cormac [Core - mac] - *Lord of Asdale*

_D_
Daeva [Day-vah] - *Past Princess of Vala, sister to Elisara [deceased]*
Dalton [Doll - ton] - *Past Prince of Garridon, brother to Caellum [deceased]*
Darous [D-are-us] – *Head of the Blade (Red Stones)*
Darragh [Dah-rah-gh] – *Wiccan man, father of Arabella*
Doltas Island [Doll -tass] - *Island within Garridon's jurisdiction*

_E_
Edlen [Ed -len] - *Past Princess of Garridon, sister to Caellum [deceased]*
Elharar [El - har - ah] - *Family name of rulers of Keres*
Elisara [El -ih - s - are - ah]- *Queen of Vala*
Ellowyn [El -oh -win] - *Past Princess of Garridon and Doltas Island, mother to Soren and Sadira[deceased]*
Emiri [Em-ih-ree] – *Head opf the Courtesans (Red Stones)*
Elvera [El -veer -ah] - *Port of Vala*
Eresydon [Eh-rahs-don]
Errard [Eh -r-are -d]- *Past King of Garridon, grandfather to Soren & Sadira [usurped] [deceased]*
Evander [Eh-van-der]
Eve [eeh -v] - *Past Princess of Garridon, sister to Caellum [de-*

ceased]
Exandria [Ex-and-ree-ah]

_F_
Farid [Far -eed] - *Member of the Queen's Guard in Keres*

_G_
Garridon [Gah -rih -don] - *Earth realm, named after the God of Earth*
Gregor Vernir [Greg-or V-ur-neer] - *High Priest of Azuria*
Gregor [Greg-or] - *Lord of Albyn*

_H_
Halston [Hol -ston] - *Past Prince of Garridon, brother to Caellum [deceased]*
Hamzah [Ham-zah]
Havia [Hahh-vee-ah]
Helena [Hell -ain -ah] - *Bakery owner and friend of Queen Elisara*
Hestia [Hest -eeh -ah] - *Past Queen of Garridon, mother to Caellum [deceased]*
Hybrooke [High-brook] - *Forest in Garridon*
Hypheria [High-fear-ee-ah]
Hystone [High- stone] - *Forest in Garridon*

_I_
Isaam [Is-am] - *Friend of Queen Nyzaia and member of the Red Stones*
Isha [Ee-sh -ah] - *Courtesan/alchemist apprentice of the Red Stones [deceased]*
Ithyion [Ih-thee-on] - *Home Kingdom that was lost to darkness*
Izaiah [Ih-zie -ah] - *Past second in command to Commander Kazaar [deceased]*
Izraar [Ih-zr-are] - *Lord of Port of Myara*

I

Jabir [Jab-eer] - *Friend of Queen Nyzaia and member of the Red Stones*

Jessemiah [Jess-eh-my-ah]

Jorah [J -or -ah] - *Caellum's grandfather [usurper] [deceased]*

K

Kalon Hakim [Kay -lon H-ah-Keem] - *Merchant [deceased]*

Kai [K-eye]

Katerina [Kat -erh-een-ah] - *Past Princess of Vala, sister to Elisara [deceased]*

Kavean [Kay-vee-an] – *Past Prince of Keres, brother to Nyzaia [deceased]*

Kazaar [Kah-z-are] - *Commander of Vala [deceased]*

Keres [K-eh-res] - *Fire realm, named after the God of Fire*

Kessem [K-eh-ss-em] - *Past Prince of Keres, brother to Nyzaia [deceased]*

Khami [Kh-am -eeh] - *Settlement in Keres*

Kieren [K-ear-en] - *Past Prince of Garridon, brother to Caellum [deceased]*

L

Larelle [L-are-elle] - *Queen of Nerida*

Levanna [Leh-van-ah]

Lillian [L-ill-ee-an] - *Friend to Queen Larelle*

Lyra [Lie-rah] - *Past Queen of Garridon, grandmother to Soren & Sadira [deceased]*

M

Majida [Mah-jeed-ah] – *Head of the Alchemists (Red Stones)*

Makaria [Mack-are-ee-ah]

Marnovo [M-arn-oh-voh] *Settlement in Vala*

Mera [M-ee-rah] - *Capital of Nerida*

Meera [M-ee-rah] - *Consort to Prince Aalto [deceased]*

N

Najat [Nah-jh-at] – *Head of the Torturers*

Nefere Valley [N -eff-ear] - *Valley/canyon named after famed warrior on Ithyion*

Nerida [Neh-rid-ah] - *Water realm, named after the Goddess of water*

Nile [N-eye-l] - *Past Prince of Nerida, nephew of Queen Larelle [deceased]*

Novisia [No-vis-ee-ah] - *Kingdom*

Nyzaia [N-zie-ah] - *Queen of Keres and Past Queen of the Red Stones*

O

Osiris [Oh-sigh-riss]

Olden [Old -en] - *Grandfather to Princess Zarya*

Olirah [Oh-lie-rah]

Ophelia [Oh-fee-lee-ah]

Oriana [Or-ee-an-ah] - *Past Queen of Nerida, mother to Larelle [deceased]*

Orlo [Or-low]- *Baker and friend to Queen Larelle*

Orphian [Or-fee-an]

Ozan [-Oh-zan] – *Head of the Spies (Red Stones)*

P

Petrov[Pet -r-oh-v] - *Lord of Vojta*

Port of Elvera [El-veer-ah] - *Settlement in Vala*

Q

Q'Ohar [Koh-are]

R

Rafik [R-ah-feek] - *Friend of Queen Nyzaia and member of the Red Stones*

Rajan [R-ah-jan] - *Alchemist in the Red Stones*

Razik [R-ah-zeek] - *Past King of Keres, father to Nyzaia [deceased]*

Red Stones - *Rulers of the Kingdom's underworld/Assassins*

Riyas [Reey-us] - *Father of Zarya and partner of Larelle [deceased]*

Rodik [Rod-ick] - *Settler on Doltas Island*

Ryon [Reey-on] - *Lord of Stedon*

S

Sadira [Sad-eer-ah] *Fallen Princess and betrothed of King Caellum, sister to Soren*

Sallos [Sal-os]

Seley [Seal-ee] - *Settlement that sits across Garridon and Nerida*

Sevia [See-vee-ah] - *Family name of rulers of Nerida*

Sitara [Sit-are-ah] - *Goddess of Dusk*

Stedon [Sted-on] - *Settlement in Garridon*

Sonos [S-on-os] - *God of Dawn*

Soren [S-oh-ren] *Fallen Queen, true heir to the Garridon throne, sister to Sadira*

Staxion [Stack-zee-on]

Sturmov [Stir-mov] - *Family name of rulers of Vala*

Sulien [S-ooh-lee-en]

Syiruna [See-roo-h-nah]

T

Tabheri [Tab-er-eye] - *Capital of Keres*

Tajana [Taj-arh-nah]- *Lover of Queen Nyzaia, Captain of the Queen's Guard, member of the Red Stones*

Talia [Tal-ee-ah]- *Friend of Queen Elisara*

Thain [Th-ain]- *Captain of the Nerida royal fleet*

Thassena [Thas-seena]

The Bay - *Location within jurisdiction of Mera*

Tisova [Tiss-oh-vah]- *Settlement in Vala*
Trosso [Tr-oh-ss-oh] - *Settlement in Nerida*

<u>U</u>

Unsanctioned Isle - *Land north of Novisia mainland, ruled by no family*

<u>V</u>

Vala [V-agh-lah] - *Air realm, named after the Goddess of Air*
Varlena [Var-leen-ah]
Vellius Sea [Vell-ee-us] -*Large lake bordering Nerida and Vala*
Vespera [Ves-peer-ah] - *Past Queen of Vala, mother to Elisara [deceased]*
Vigor [Vee-gore] - *Physician and friend of Queen Elisara*
Vivian [Viv-ee-an] – *Acolyte at the Church of Mera*
Vlad [V-lad] - *Friend of Queen Elisara, Captain of the Queen's Guard*
Vojta [V-oi–ta] - *Settlement in Vala*

<u>W</u>

Wren [Ren] - *Past King of Garridon, son of Jorah, father to Caellum [deceased]*

<u>X</u>

Xyliar [Z-eye-liar]
Xyra [Z-eye-rah]

<u>Y</u>

<u>Z</u>

Zahir [Za-hear] – *Head of the Dealers (Red Stones)*
Zarya [Zah-rie-ya] *Princess of Nerida, daughter of Larelle*
Zee
Zonri [Zon-rhee]

Playlist

Heart of Darkness by Steelfeather *(Prologue)*
Me and the Devil by Soap&Skin *(Chapter Two)*
Look What You Made Me Do by Taylor Swift *(Chapter Three)*
Through the Fire by Euphoria *(Chapter Four)*
Touch by Sleeping at Last *(Chapter Five)*
Brother by Kodaline *(Chapter Seven)*
Family Line by Conan Gray *(Chapter Eight)*
This is how you fall in love by Jeremy Zucker, Chelsea Cutler *(Chapter Nine)*
Monsters – Acoustic by Ruelle *(Chapter Eleven)*
Mad Woman by Taylor Swift *(Chapter Twelve)*
Lovely by Daisy Gray *(Chapter Seventeen)*
Bad Dreams – Stripped by Faouzia *(Chapter Twenty)*
Silhouette by Aquila *(Chapter Twenty-Five)*
The Prophecy by Taylor Swift *(Chapter Twenty-Nine)*
Daylight by Taylor Swift, Today was a Fairytale by Taylor Swift *(Chapter Thirty)*
Hang on a Little Longer by UNSECRET & Ruelle, Hold on by Chord Street *(Chapter Thirty-Two)*
Birds of a Feather by Billie Eilish *(Chapter Thirty-Six)*
Marjorie by Taylor Swift *(Chapter Thirty-Eight)*
Unsteady by X Ambassadors, The Scientist by Coldplay *(Chap-*

ter Thirty-Nine)

It'll be Okay by Rachel Grae *(Chapter Forty-Four)*

Already Gone by Sleeping At Last *(Chapter Forty-Five)*

The End (stripped) by JPOLAND, Pan do Bare, Chess Theory *(Chapter Forty-Six)*

Simply the Best by Billiane *(Chapter Forty-Seven)*

Turning Page by Sydney Rose *(Chapter Forty-Eight)*

I Look in People's Windows by Taylro Swift *(Chapter Fifty-One)*

The Winner Takes it All (acoustic) by Jae Hall *(Chapter Fifty-Two)*

Things We Lost in the Fire – Abbey Road Session by Bastille *(Chapter Fifty-Three)*

IDK You Yet by Alexander 23 *(Epilogue)*

Acknowledgements

How do people write these without beginning to sound repetitive? Three books down, and who I have to thank is largely unchanged. As always, my first and most important thanks go to my parents and family for their unwaivering support of me and my books. I know with every book I publish you'll become even prouder.

To my editor and friend, Eden, as always, your advice and guidance has made this book what it was always meant to be. Your excitement and reactions at every stage and for the future plots of the series keep me going even when I'm doubting myself. Being a writer can be lonely in the early stages of a book, but having you as my first reader, every single time, always reassures me. I can't wait to finally meet in March and work on book four and five together this year!

To Aly, who never complains with my very minor changes to covers, thank you for bringing my vision to life with each cover. I know, at the time of writing this, you're working on the next two covers and I just know they'll be as beautiful as the first three.

To my beta readers; Elisha, Hannah and Kristin, thank you for your offers of support and love for me. This has been such a journey and regardless of whether you have the time to continue on it with the next books, I'm so thankful for your help.

To my ARC Readers, FINALLY reading this!! There are so many of you that have joined this journey with me, whether before Secrets of the Dead, or as each new book has released. I hope the emotional journey of Return of the Darkness continues to live up to your expectations and only excites you further for the next book in November. Now you've read that cliffhanger and blurb, you know why I've been trying so hard to get both out in 2024! Thank you for all of you that continue to shout about this series without me ever needing to ask, it means everything to me.

To Chlo and Mel, the two closest friends that have had far too much of this series spoiled for them because of how impatient I am. Thank you for being on this journey with me from book one. Whilst you weren't there as I wrote the beginning of this story, you have been with me as it has grown page by page. Not only have you been a part of my story in words, you have been with me for every new chapter of my life in the last two years. I couldn't have asked for two better friends to be by my side through heartbreak, big changes and all the manifesting and adventures to come. Whilst there is a general dedication at the beginning of this book, please know that really, this book is for you.

A Note From the Author

Reviews on Amazon, Good Reads, StoryGraph and other sites are one of the biggest ways to help indie authors. I would be eternally grateful if you could leave a review on your preferred platform as well as Amazon. Reviews have to exceed a set amount for Amazon to begin pushing indie books – so if you can, posting here will make a big difference.

I started this journey sharing this book through my socials, and I'm sure I've met many of you there. So, if you feel obliged, please share your thoughts and feelings around this book on your own socials so I can sit and cry tears of joy at this story reaching people.

Instagram: @author_lauracarter

Tik Tok: @authorlauracarter

Youtube: @authorlauracarter

So, you've finished Return of the Darkness, and you're (hopefully) eager to get your hands on book four in the Lost Kingdom Saga, especially after that blurb. Whilst I haven't released any details on book three yet, I share all my first looks and sneak peeks to my newsletter subscribers before my socials. If you want to be kept up to date, you can sign up through the links provided on my social channels. Book four will be coming to you November 24th.

If you're a die hard fan of the Lost Kingdom Saga and want to show it off, you can find licensed merchandise for the series by the wonderful Chloe, at dumbblondeclub.co.uk

About the author

Laura grew up in rural Scotland before moving to London to study for her degree in English Literature, where she lived for ten years before moving to the countryside with her Romanian rescue dog, Rez. She grew up constantly immersed in different worlds through reading and always dreamed of becoming an author. When her love of fantasy and romance was re-ignited after three years of only ever critically analysing work, her dream of creating her own worlds returned. She now balances working full time for a cancer charity with writing her debut series, The Lost Kingdom Saga. She has a further thirteen plus books planned so you won't be getting rid of her any time soon.